PURSUIT

By Robert L. Pike

DEADLINE: 2 A.M.
BANK JOB
THE GREMLIN'S GRAMPA
REARDON
POLICE BLOTTER

THE QUARRY
MUTE WITNESS
 (MYSTERY WRITERS OF AMER-
 ICA EDGAR AWARD WINNER)

José Da Silva Novels by Robert L. Fish

TROUBLE IN PARADISE
THE GREEN HELL TREASURE
THE XAVIER AFFAIR
THE BRIDGE THAT WENT NOWHERE
ALWAYS KILL A STRANGER
BRAZILIAN SLEIGH RIDE

THE DIAMOND BUBBLE
THE SHRUNKEN HEAD
ISLE OF THE SNAKES
THE FUGITIVE
 (M.W.A. EDGAR AWARD
 WINNER)

By the Same Author

EVERY CRIME IN THE BOOK
 (M.W.A. ANTHOLOGY)
THE MEMOIRS OF
 SCHLOCK HOMES
THE WAGER
RUB-A-DUB-DUB
TRICKS OF THE TRADE
WHIRLIGIG
WITH MALICE TOWARDS ALL
 (M.W.A. ANTHOLOGY)
THE MURDER LEAGUE
THE HOCHMANN MINIATURES
MY LIFE AND THE BEAUTIFUL
 GAME (IN COLLABORATION
 WITH PELÉ)

THE INCREDIBLE SCHLOCK HOMES
THE TRIALS OF O'BRIEN
THE ASSASSINATION BUREAU
 (COMPLETION OF AN
 UNFINISHED WORK BY JACK
 LONDON)
THE HANDY DEATH
 (IN COLLABORATION WITH
 HENRY ROTHBLATT)
WEEKEND '33
 (IN COLLABORATION WITH
 BOB THOMAS)

PURSUIT

A Novel

ROBERT L. FISH

DOUBLEDAY & COMPANY, INC., GARDEN CITY, NEW YORK, 1978

Based upon an original plot idea of Jules Victor Schwerin

ISBN: 0-385-13398-7
Library of Congress Catalog Card Number 77–27700

For

MAME

PURSUIT

Prologue

Summer—1944

The Russian T-34-76 tanks clank forward in the summer heat like huge beetles, their newly equipped 80-mm cannon weaving slowly, restlessly from side to side, rigid antennae searching out the enemy. The four-man crew take turns at the hatch, relishing a breath of air. Between the rows of moving tanks spread across the barren plain the cavalry ride, the horses gaunt, the riders' faces wrapped against the clouds of powdered earth churned up by the tanks. The newly supplied American personnel carriers follow, and then the foot soldiers, unable to find room on the crowded trucks, the ear flaps of their caps buttoned back, their greatcoats almost brushing the ground, their eyes squinting against the acrid dust. In addition to his rifle, each soldier carries a bag on his back with bread or vegetables or anything else he has been able to collect from the fields or from the destroyed villages on the hurried march; the horses eat the moldy straw from the thatched roofs of razed cottages. Above, in the blue sky, the reconnaissance planes buzz like angry bees, darting ahead to scout and then swooping back in sight, radioing their findings. There is an even level of noise in the air, so steady as to appear as silence to the inured ears of the troops.

Occasionally, when his supply lines are considered sufficiently short-ened, when his reinforcements have arrived, when a supposedly advanta-geous terrain has been reached—or when the pressure from Berlin be-comes too great or too dangerous to disobey—then the enemy turns and makes a stand, often against the better judgment of the Wehrmacht. His tanks wheel about awkwardly to dig in facing the Russians; his troops throw themselves down behind whatever protection they can find, bringing up their rifles and unloosening their grenades; the sky suddenly darkens with Stukas and Messerschmitts while Russian fighter planes rise like flies to challenge them. The heavy artillery in the Russian rear opens up, the big guns blasting their steel and smoke; the bursts plow huge craters in the earth, erupting great clouds of dirt, tossing tanks aside like toys. Truck-mounted rocket launchers send swarms of Katushas flashing across the battlefield like brief chalk marks against a sky suddenly darkened by the smoke of the struggle. The mortars give their deep asthmatic cough; the soldiers of both sides run, half-crouched, under the protection of the tanks to suddenly stand erect and throw their grenades. Then the Shturmovics come in, the dreaded flying tank-killers with their 37-mm cannon, disregarding the German fighters, concentrating on the enemy armor, and tanks explode and burn and tip over like helpless bugs while attempting to escape, and men burn and blow up with their grenades, and over it all the hellish shrieking of the planes and the roar of the cannon and the screaming of wounded horses and the cries of dying men, and the shaking, shaking, shaking, shaking of the tortured earth.

And when the battle is over and the enemy has withdrawn leaving his dead and wounded on the plain together with the Russian dead, the torn bodies of the injured are given whatever first aid is possible, and sent to the rear with the prisoners. The tanks move forward once again, lumbering around their burning or dismantled or upended counterparts of both sides, past wrecked and smoldering planes, their pilots crushed into their instrument panels, picking their way through the carnage of burning men and equipment, trying to avoid having their huge treads pulverize their own dead, taking up the relentless pursuit again. And the cavalry gathers together what is left of itself and follows and the remaining personnel carriers wait until they are once again jammed with troops and then join in the advance, while the foot soldiers pause long enough to hastily search the corpses for whatever food they might be carrying, or hurriedly cut up the dead horses, sharing with each other, each man cramming as much as he can carry of the bloody carcasses into his bag before running to catch up.

Villages come and go, all leveled to the ground. There are no cattle to be seen, and most of the people they find are either hanging from gibbets or laid in trenches, newly slain. They are not soldiers, these hanging bodies, these carelessly thrown corpses; they are civilians. At Zhoblin a trench contains 2,500 cadavers, their blood not yet congealed, old men, old women, children. The troops march past, the tanks slow so that their crews can stare wordlessly at the horror, and all faces grow harder and their hatred more bitter. It is three years almost to the day since their land was invaded, an invasion many had welcomed at the time, until they learned at firsthand the nature of the enemy in the endless senseless executions, the relentless and needless destruction, the wholesale enslavement of men and women, the brutal slaughter of the innocent. Now they are on the march, regaining their own territory, averaging between eight and ten miles a day, and they are determined not to be stopped by anyone or anything until they have reached Germany itself and have exacted from every German man, woman, or child their terrible revenge.

Cities are come upon and marched through, the tanks crushing the rubble beneath their treads so the troops can pass, the personnel carriers bumping their way over the broken concrete, the horses of the cavalry whinnying at the strong smell of death. Half-standing walls confront them, mountains of debris, fumbled through by a few old women searching for God knows what. The mark of the retreating army is visible in the endless display of the dead, swinging from the well-used gallows in every town and village. The troops march past, eyes left, eyes right, their resolve made more cruel by the cruelty they see, and their hatred grows and expands with every rotting corpse in every ditch, with every devastated town, with every sight of a plowed-under crop, or a destroyed village, or a shattered tree.

The Polish border is crossed at last, and the marching soldiers look about themselves in utter amazement. It is as if they had been led by their tanks into a new world, a world that has never seen war. The cottages are newly painted in neat white, the cattle graze peacefully, trees are leafy, people stare at them from the evenly planted fields as if they were men from another planet.

And the fury grows, and the tanks and the cavalry and the troop carriers and the foot soldiers roll on, an army grinding out its daily advance, its ultimate goal never out of sight. Berlin—and blood. And whatever stands between.

BOOK I

Chapter 1

Colonel Helmut von Schraeder surveyed the lobby of the old hotel as he gently tugged his gloves free. He was remarkably young for his rank, a tall athletic figure, handsome, with clear ice-cold slate-blue eyes, and a sharp, almost classic profile. His military cap with its SS insignia was cocked just a trifle to give the wearer a look of insouciance, his uniform was neatly pressed and fitted perfectly, and his boots gleamed.

There was no sense of nostalgia in his inspection; Colonel von Schraeder was not a man who lived in the past. Usually he lived just in the present, but of late he had been living more and more in the future. But, he thought, one would think he would remember the physical appearance of the place, at least. After all, it was the last place he could remember having been happy; it was after their Rhine vacation that year of 1924—he had been seven at the time, he remembered—that things in Mecklenberg had begun to fall apart. But either his recollection was faulty or the place had been done over, for nothing looked familiar. The colonel shrugged and tucked his gloves into his pocket; nothing could have been of less importance. Instead he glanced at the clock over the reception desk, saw there was ample time for a drink before the meeting was scheduled to start, and moved in the direction of the arrow pointing to the bar. And then he heard his name called.

"Helmut!"

He swung about and smiled, his usual cold smile. "Hello, Willi."

"Heading for the bar, weren't you? I'll join you." Major Willi Gehrmann, a friend since their days as fellow students at the Technical Institute, now holding down a desk at the War Ministry. Gehrmann was a short, stocky man with thick glasses; he took von Schraeder's elbow and led the way into the bar. It was quite deserted and they selected a corner booth, isolated but commanding a view of the room. They ordered their drinks and then sat and smiled at each other with the meaningless smiles of people waiting to be served. Von Schraeder placed a cigarette in a long holder and leaned across the table to accept a light from the major. He leaned back, exhaling smoke.

"What do you know about—?"

He paused to allow the waiter to place their drinks on the table, waited until the waiter had discreetly retired, and then returned to his question.

"—this meeting?"

Gehrmann shrugged. "Quite a bit, I suppose. What about you?"

"Nothing, other than it's supposed to be top secret. I was in Berlin taking care of some personal business when I was asked to attend—very quietly—and asked to keep pretty quiet about it, too." He sipped his drink, placed the glass back on the table, and returned to his smoking, speaking about the holder, exhibiting perfect teeth. "I was also told, without details, that there would be some rather important names here today."

"There will be." Gehrmann tried to sound noncommittal, but there was a glint in the eyes swimming behind the thick lenses. "Georg von Schnitzler of I. G. Farben, for one. Krupp von Bohlen of Krupp steel, for another. Top representatives of Roehling, of Messerschmitt, from the Goering Werke in Linz, and others. Some important bankers, the leading men in the chemical and oil industries, a few like myself—very selected, I assure you—from the War and Armament ministries, as well as some of the big family names who can be trusted—like you." He smiled. "Are those people important enough for you?"

Von Schraeder returned the smile coldly. "The last one or two, at least. And what are all these important names here to talk about? So secretly?"

Willi looked him in the eye, assuming an air of importance that struck von Schraeder, who knew him, as being both theatrical and ridiculous.

"They're going to talk about the future of Germany and the future of the Party." He lowered his voice. "It is their feeling that the war is lost. It's also mine. They want to start making plans now, for the time when that fact finally sinks into the heads of—well, into other heads."

"Such as our Fuehrer, for example. Yes." Von Schraeder crushed out his cigarette, tipped it free into an ashtray without having to soil his fingers, blew through the holder to clear it, and tucked it neatly into a pocket. The action had all the ceremony of a ritual. His cold eyes came up. "What type of plans?"

The major shrugged. "We'll learn the details at the meeting."

Von Schraeder nodded, and then also dropped his voice, although they had not been speaking loudly. He did not make the mistake of leaning forward in any manner to compensate.

"And are these important names aware that certain officers in the army have their own plans?"

Despite himself the major could not help but look about to see if von Schraeder might possibly have been overheard. With an effort he tried to erase the look of alarm that had instantly crossed his face.

"Helmut! For God's sake!"

"Smile," von Schraeder said quietly, and did so himself. *Gruss Gott!* If the army plot was in the hands of men as nervous as Gehrmann, he couldn't picture it being successful! "Smile; I just told you a very funny joke. And asked you a question."

"No," Gehrmann said, and managed a weak smirk; it looked like a rictus. "No, they have no idea of our plans. They not only don't know, but they would be the last people on earth to be told. They're loyal, you know, at least in their fashion."

"I suppose so." Von Schraeder didn't sound as if he considered this a particular virtue, or the big names particularly virtuous. In fact, he honestly considered them little better than shopkeepers. Rich, certainly, and shopkeepers on a grand scale, but still not Junkers, not gentlemen. "Of course, the army maintains if their plan works there would be no need for any other plans. Incidentally, speaking of plans, when is the Valkyrie plan supposed to be put into effect?" He suddenly laughed aloud. "Get that look off your face.

We're just telling funny stories. I asked you, what is the schedule for von Stauffenberg and Valkyrie?"

Willi did his best to smile but it was a ghastly effort.

"July the twentieth, at Rastenburg. We don't speak of this. Let's drop it, for God's sake!"

"All right," von Schraeder said easily. "Now, that wasn't so hard, was it?" He raised his glass in a small gesture of a toast, drained it, and dabbed at his lips with a handkerchief taken from his sleeve. "Well, drink up and let's get to that meeting. Let's find out why such important names want such unimportant people as Major Gehrmann or Colonel von Schraeder, trusted or not, to attend their precious secret meeting."

They sat around a large rectangular table, some thirty of the most important people of Nazi Germany's industrial machine, speaking with a frankness that had been unknown in the country for many years. Beyond the circle of the chosen ones at the table were observers, of whom Gehrmann and von Schraeder were two; these sat on hard wooden chairs along the walls of the room. The meeting had been going on for several hours, the room was filled with blue smoke from thick cigars, and von Schraeder had the beginnings of a headache. At his side Major Gehrmann sat silently, leaning forward a bit, listening intently as speaker after speaker gave his views. And then, at long last, there was a brief intermission during which those at the table conferred quietly, scribbling notes. When the meeting was called back to order, the chairman came to his feet.

"Gentlemen—"

The room slowly settled back to silence, chairs scraped and were raised to be moved more quietly, someone shut a window that had been opened for ventilation during the intermission. Von Schraeder bit back a yawn and tried to find a more comfortable position on the hard chair. He sincerely hoped the statement would be short. If he wanted to reach Lublin during daylight hours the following day, he would have to leave Strasbourg soon. If he made Munich by nightfall, he would be all right; if they drove a while longer and got as far as Salzburg, all the better. The chairman cleared his throat and bent down, making reference to the paper in his hand. He straightened up.

"Gentlemen, let us try and summarize our discussions. If we have differed today it has only been in degree, not in substance. We are in substantial agreement on the following points—that Germany has lost the war and that German industry must prepare for the postwar economic campaign. Each of us here—and others in industry who will be contacted who we know are in agreement with us—must seek contacts with firms abroad without creating attention. We must be prepared to finance the Party, which will be forced to go underground for some time. We will establish appropriate committees to select the countries where money must be invested, and by whom and how much. The first step in our program, of course, is to see that no funds, deposits, blueprints of new weapons or designs of new equipment or information on new processes fall into the hands of the Allies."

He paused to sip from a glass of water. Even von Schraeder had to admire the detail that had gone into the planning for the meeting, and the detail with which the meeting planned for the future. But then von Schraeder had always admired planning. The chairman continued.

"We must also expect, from the continuing Allied threats, that there will be war-crimes trials and that some of our members will be convicted as war criminals. Therefore, preparations must be made *now* to see that as many of those members of the Nazi Party, particularly the SS, who find themselves in that position, be given means of escaping from Germany when the proper time comes, as well as the financial assistance they will require. It is why we are here. We shall call ourselves ODESSA. It stands for Organisation der SS-Angehorigen. Those members we help can be useful in our foreign enterprises; in many spheres."

His eyes left those around the table to sweep over the observers on the hard chairs along the walls. The hard stare touched on von Schraeder in passing, took in Gehrmann and the others, and then came back to the table.

"Some of the younger members present today fall into this category. They will be expected to take advantage of this offer, and to carry out any decisions of this meeting or of future meetings with the full devotion of loyal and dedicated Party members. A committee will be established to study escape routes and to arrange safehouses along those routes, as well as permanent refuge in certain selected foreign countries. Preparations are also under way, also through ODESSA, to—"

There was the harsh sound of a chair being scraped back, and two men were heard to argue in subdued tones from a place beyond the table of the chosen, somewhere along the wall. The chairman frowned impatiently in the direction of the disturbance.

"Yes? What is the problem? Is there a question?"

One of the two men threw off the arm of the other and came to his feet.

"You keep talking about the Party. I just want to know if these plans, these preparations, have the authority of the Fuehrer and the other top Party officials?"

There was a moment's silence. Then the chairman spoke quietly.

"These preparations are being made in the best interests of the Fuehrer, of Germany, of the Nazi Party—"

"That doesn't answer my question."

The chairman's heavy jaw tightened. "That's the best answer I can give you."

Von Schraeder stared through the gloom of the room at the stupid person who had asked the stupid question, as someone near the man pulled him back into his seat. Stupidity, to von Schraeder, was the unforgivable sin. Someone would undoubtedly talk to that man in depth—as well as to the person who invited him to the meeting— and if he didn't get the message he would probably end up in a ditch. Which was where stupid people belonged.

The chairman was continuing.

"As I was saying, preparations are already under way to locate and destroy the fingerprint records of members who might be—in the eyes of the Allies only, I hasten to add—in the category of war criminals, wherever these records might exist. Some of the members will have to establish completely new identities—"

Von Schraeder smiled to himself sardonically. There would be war-crimes trials unless Valkyrie was successful, and probably even then; that he was sure of. But he was equally sure that no Krupp von Bohlen nor any Georg von Schnitzler would ever dangle at the end of a rope. Nor would they have their fingerprint records destroyed, nor their identities changed one iota.

Carry out the decisions of the meeting and of future meetings? What they meant, of course, was that the dirty work, the risks, would be done and taken by the "younger" members, while the "older," "safer" members would collect whatever reward was to be garnered in these foreign endeavors. And if these "younger"

members were ever caught, he knew they could count on blessed little help from the Group. No, the Group would depend upon their silence and loyalty, even to the gallows.

And that "financial" help that had been offered, together with an
escape route? If he knew anything at all about the banking brains
seated at the table, any war criminal who made it to safety abroad
through the sponsorship of the Group would have complete records
kept of every pfennig he received, so that he could never deny having received them. And fingerprints or no fingerprints, and new identities or no new identities, those financial geniuses at the table could
trace a man through his bank account better than any security department could through his prints or the name on his identity card.

To be saved by the Group, in short, meant to become enslaved by
the Group. No, that road was not for Helmut von Schraeder.

And as for their considered opinion that the war was lost; well,
that was a conclusion he had reached a long time before, when these
shopkeepers were making fortunes and were still inept enough to
lose the war. He had known the war was lost when Stalingrad fell,
when Hamburg had been blasted into rubble by Allied bombers and
Goering's vaunted air force and Hamburg's scientifically advanced
air defenses—the model for all German air defenses—had been
meaningless. And he had started his own plans then, not waited for
an invitation to a meeting of the Strasbourg Group to save his skin
for their own ends.

The chairman had finished speaking; the meeting was breaking up.
A small group was gathered about the man who had raised the question of the meeting's legitimacy; he seemed to be arguing volubly. A
suicide, von Schraeder thought disdainfully, and joined Willi, leaving the room and walking down the broad, carpeted stairs to the
main lobby. They saw the bar was filling rapidly, and walked outside.
The two uniformed men walked to the curb and von Schraeder
raised his arm to signal his driver, but Willi quickly pulled it down.

"Let's talk a bit first," he said. "You have time, I'm sure. Let's
take a short walk and talk." He started off and von Schraeder, after a
glance over his shoulder, followed. Behind him his driver was coming
from the parking area and the colonel knew the man would keep the
car exactly five paces behind him as he walked.

Willi turned in the direction of the river; ahead of them the spires of the cathedral were outlined against a cloudless summer sky. The major turned to look up at his taller companion.

"Well? What do you think?"

"It sounded very good," von Schraeder said, his voice sounding quite sincere.

"Especially for you," Willi said. "I saw the pictures of you being decorated by Himmler not so long ago. And I've been reading about you; Eichmann seems to hold you in high regard." He tried to sound objective but there was a slight touch of envy in his voice, as if being a candidate for a war-crimes trial and almost certain execution were somehow to be desired, if only in the abstract as building reputation. He glanced at von Schraeder. "That's the sort of record I imagine it would be well to escape from, once the war is over."

"I couldn't agree more," von Schraeder said, and smiled genially.

"Of course," Willi went on, "if Klaus Stauffenberg is successful, we'll be demanding total amnesty in return for an instant surrender. The Allies certainly should be willing to forgo what really amounts to petty revenge on a few men, in return for the Allied lives that would be saved if the war should continue, don't you think?"

"It makes sense," von Schraeder said noncommittally, and thought what an optimistic idiot Willi Gehrmann was, indeed! If Valkyrie was successful, if Klaus Stauffenberg did his job, would it really make any great difference as far as he and the others in his position were concerned? Of course it would do no harm to wait and see the outcome of the Valkyrie plan, but in general he suspected it was an idle dream. If the Allies were offered a total surrender with the condition of total amnesty, and countered with an acceptance of the surrender, but still demanded their pound of flesh, would Beck, or Olbricht, or Goerdeler hesitate for one split second to accept? Would they jeopardize a peace they felt essential in order to save the lives of SS officers they themselves would have been happy to hang? It was insanity to think so for a moment.

Willi was speaking a bit more rapidly, as he felt he was losing the attention of his audience.

"In any event, there is always the plan the Group proposed today." He looked up at von Schraeder. "You know, your fingerprint file and records were among the first to be dug out and destroyed. We've gotten them all, I'm sure." His glance traveled to von Schraeder's bare hands, and he grinned. "So if you rob a bank, be sure and wear your gloves."

Von Schraeder gave the required smile. "I shall do that." He stopped and held up his hand; his car drew up instantly, his driver out of his seat in a moment, holding open the door. "I really must go, Willi. I have a long drive ahead of me both today and tomorrow."

Willi leaned in the open window as the driver climbed back into his seat. The stocky major spoke in a low voice, sure that the sergeant could not hear him through the glass partition.

"But in any event there's no need to worry, Helmut," he said quietly. "Between Valkyrie and the Group here today, we—you've—two strings to your bow." He stepped back, gave a half salute, and watched as the car pulled away.

In the rear seat of the car, von Schraeder leaned back, fitting a cigarette into his holder, smiling to himself. *One* string, he thought with satisfaction; only one string to my bow, but it is neither as frayed as the Strasbourg Group, nor as gossamer as Valkyrie. It is my own string, which, in any event, is the only string anyone can ever depend upon.

Chapter 2

Beneath the wings of the small spotter plane, the Polish landscape spread to the city of Lublin a few miles to the west. The pilot checked his map. There was the village of Dsiesiata, there the villages of Kalinowka and Abramowicz, all clearly identifiable. There was the Cholm Road, and alongside it, only a mile or so from Lublin, was an obvious suburb noted on his map as Maidanek, and —not noted on his map—a sprawling encampment of some sort. From the height of the droning plane the barracks-like buildings looked like a vast arrangement of children's blocks. Black smoke billowed from a tall square stack rising at the extreme end of the encampment, dissipating itself over the tilled fields beyond.

There was a sudden chatter of machine-gun fire from one of the watchtowers set at regular intervals about the encampment; other guns joined in instantly. The small reconnaissance plane banked almost insolently and drifted off to the east. Inside the cockpit the observer made a note of the strange buildings and its armed watchtowers, and then shrugged as he slid his pencil back into his jacket-sleeve pocket. Whatever it was, they would find out fairly soon. Their troops were less than a hundred and fifty miles from Lublin.

In the area outside the command post barrack, Colonel von Schraeder, deputy commandant of the encampment, paused to study the disappearing plane with a frown. His eyes narrowed as he considered the ease with which the small reconnaissance plane had penetrated the area. He had been back from Strasbourg a day; when he had left for Berlin ten days before, such aerial intrusion would have been unthinkable. He watched the plane disappear in the growing evening dusk, shrugged, and pushed his way into the building.

In the conference room of the command post barrack, the fifteen principal officers responsible for the day-to-day operation of the camp either sat or stood, awaiting the start of the urgent meeting that had been called. Through the open windows the endless sound of the evening roll call from Field I could be heard faintly, now that the chatter of the machine guns had finally ceased. Some of the officers stared from the windows, watching the area of the sky where the plane had disappeared, each with his own disturbing thoughts.

There was a sudden movement at the door and the pudgy red face of the camp commandant, Klaus Mittendorf, was there. He jerked one ham-like hand abruptly; those standing hurried to find seats. A second downward movement of the hand and a young lieutenant walked quickly down one wall of the room, bending over fellow officers, closing windows. In the silence that followed the commandant's voice was harsh.

"Gentlemen! The Russians are approaching the Polish border; Minsk has been recaptured. Reports are that the Army Group *Mitte* has been destroyed—"

A jeering voice broke out. "Propaganda, Commandant!"

"From Guderian?" The commandant was staring at the officer who had made the comment. His fat face was hard, his lips tight. He glared the man into defeat, then walked to his desk at the head of the conference room. He sat down abruptly and looked out over his subordinates. "All right, gentlemen. We have work to do." He took a paper from an inner pocket and placed it on the desk. "Our orders, gentlemen. We are to exterminate as many of the present prison population as possible, then evacuate the camp and destroy any evidence it ever existed, or at least destroy any evidence as to the purpose of the camp."

There was a general shifting of bodies; the officers stared at one another. Commandant Mittendorf properly interpreted the reaction to his statement.

"Destroy any evidence it ever existed," he repeated firmly. "It is an order. We have not lost a camp to the enemy yet, but it is quite possible this one must be evacuated. There must be no evidence, is that clear? None whatsoever. That is an order! So let's get on with it." He reached across the desk for a list, ran his finger down it until he found the name he wanted; those lesser officers, or those in sections or duties unable to contribute to the purpose of the meeting, were not present. Mittendorf looked up. "Captain Müeller!"

"Sir!"

"How long do you estimate it would take you to dynamite the baths and the gas chamber, as well as the crematoria—both the old and the new—and then bulldoze them level, cover them with earth, and plant grass over them?"

Müeller stared. "Plant grass, sir? Grass takes—"

"Sod, then." Mittendorf waved a thick hand. "You know what I mean. Take sod from the surrounding farms. Or even seed over the area. Who knows? The soil is rich here—" It was quite true; they all knew the soil was extremely rich. It was thoroughly mixed with human ashes and produced the finest cabbages in all Poland. Which was a fortunate circumstance, since cabbage had been the main staple of their diet for some weeks. The commandant's face hardened. "Well? How long?"

Müeller considered the question carefully; he was a careful man and was not to be rushed into statements if he were to be held responsible for their fulfillment.

"Well, sir, we could probably dynamite the buildings to rough rubble in a matter of hours; that is no problem. If we have sufficient dynamite on hand, of course. But to crush this rubble to fine particles and bulldoze them level will take some time. Covering the resultant area with dirt will be a problem, too. I assume we don't want them to look like burial mounds—"

Mittendorf glared. "I asked, how long? I didn't ask for a speech!"

"If we can arrange the necessary equipment," Müeller said carefully, aware he was treading on dangerous ground but determined to do his job properly, "and if we have sufficient dynamite, as I said, and if we can take the fine particles and spread them over the fields rather than trying to cover them—which may well kill the cabbage crop, of course—"

"The devil with the cabbages! If we leave here we won't be coming back!" Mittendorf felt the eyes upon him. "At least not for a while," he added gruffly.

"Then I should say probably three or four days, working nights as well, of course. If I can get an electrician or two to rig up lights—"

"Four days," Mittendorf said, dismissing him. "No, make that three." He made a note and passed on. Müeller fell silent, but it was evident he was unhappy at being pressured. It was also evident that Müeller's unhappiness was the least of the commandant's worries. His sausage-like finger moved down the list. "Lieutenant Burgsteller—"

"Sir?"

"Present prisoner population?"

"Let's see, sir. We have roughly ten thousand women in Field V, mostly Poles. Very few Jews left, sir, and even less Russians. And no Gypsies at all. As far as the men are concerned, in Field I—"

"How many all together, Burgsteller! We don't have all day!"

The lieutenant reddened. "I'm sorry, sir. I don't have the exact figures with me. I didn't know you were going to want—" He saw the look on Mittendorf's face and hastily added, "Forty thousand, sir, roughly, but it's very close. It's been approximately that figure for some months past, now, sir. They ship them in as fast as we—"

"Forty thousand." The fingers wrote and moved on. "Colonel Schneller."

"Sir."

"Transportation possibilities. How many prisoners can be moved by rail back to camps further west? Or back to Germany, itself? In the next two weeks, say."

Schneller had been anticipating the question. He had been going

over the transportation possibilities in his mind ever since the commandant had made his first announcement, and the results as far as
he could see were apt to bring out another burst of temper from
Mittendorf. He frowned.

"The problem, you see, sir, is boxcars. They're extremely tight.
With the situation at the front—"

"The situation at the front is the problem of the army," Mittendorf said, his voice rasping. "The evacuation of this camp is my responsibility. And according to my orders it takes top priority. How
many prisoners do you estimate we can move if we have to?"

Schneller looked unhappy.

"I just can't give you a definite answer without checking the rail
yards at Lublin, sir, but I would be greatly surprised if I could manage to get more than thirty or forty cars, at the maximum. Even at a
hundred people to a car, that would be—" He paused to calculate.

"Three thousand to four thousand. Not even ten per cent." Mittendorf shook his head almost despondently. Rail shipments, obviously, did not seem to be the answer. His finger moved down the list,
and then moved up again, near the top. "Colonel von Schraeder—"

"Yes."

If Mittendorf noted the calmness of the response, he made no
comment on it. Von Schraeder was looking at him with a sardonic
look on his patrician face. The commandant bit back a retort; it
would not be good for discipline to get into an argument with the
bastard before the other men. Von Schraeder had been an insolent
and independent shit ever since he had been assigned to Mittendorf
as his deputy. A full colonel at twenty-nine years of age! If only the
miserable son of a bitch could be left in charge of the camp to be
picked up by the Russians! What a pleasure to picture the haughty,
supercilious bastard, gloves and all, hanging from a rope in the center of one of the fields, that big mouth open to the flies, and that
glib, sarcastic tongue black with congested blood and quiet for once!
Unfortunately, the papers for von Schraeder's transfer had already
been signed by the brass in Berlin and were on the commandant's
desk at the moment. The shit certainly managed to push that Junker
family name of his, although the arrogant bastard didn't even have a
family anymore! A father a suicide, a mother dead of something long
since, probably syphilis if she was anything like that prick of a son of
hers! And the family estates long gone to pay debts. So what had the

high-nosed, patronizing shit to be so proud of? Mittendorf forced the bile from his throat, bringing his mind back to the matter at hand.

"Colonel—what is the maximum number we can handle in the gas chambers and the ovens? And don't tell me what we've been doing. I want to know the *maximum*."

"In what period of time?"

Now the commandant finally lost his temper. What difference did it really make what the men thought? Discipline would be gone in a few weeks in any event, so to hell with what the men thought! His tiny eyes, buried like little burned raisins in the doughy mass of his face, blazed briefly and then narrowed dangerously until they were almost completely out of sight.

"How the hell do I know? You tell me, von Schraeder, you're so damned smart! How far away are the Russians at this moment? How fast will they move? How much resistance will our troops be able to put up? Will the Russians stop to destroy everything in Poland once they get here? Or to screw every girl? Or hang every man?" He brought himself forcibly under control, hating himself for his burst of temper, but hating von Schraeder even more for having provoked it. "That was a Russian reconnaissance plane over us a few minutes ago, Colonel. We don't have a month to discuss the matter. So just tell me how many people our equipment can handle per day. Maximum!"

Von Schraeder's only reaction to his superior's outburst was to look faintly amused.

"The maximum we can handle is two thousand per day, exactly what we are doing at the present. No more, no less." The colonel paused to take a cigarette from a gold case; he twisted it lightly into his holder, lit the cigarette, and set the holder in his mouth at a jaunty angle. He spoke around the smoke. "We can gas many more, of course; the gas pens have a capacity of almost two thousand by themselves. The gas is effective in five minutes." He glanced at the ceiling, calculating. "If you figure an hour to get them all in, to gas them, to clear the air with the fans; then another hour, say, for the *Sonderkommandos* to get the bodies loaded into the carts for the ovens, we could probably clear out the entire prisoner population in two days." He leaned over to negligently tip the ash from his cigarette onto the polished floor. "The problem is, of course, that the oven capacity is limited to two thousand bodies per day, taking an average body of men, women, and children. That's the maximum. As I believe I've mentioned to you several times in the past."

Mittendorf chose to disregard the final remark.

"What about the old ovens? The ones that were here before we built the new ones?"

"No burners," von Schraeder said calmly. "We cannibalized the burners for the new ovens."

"And no way to improvise?"

Von Schraeder merely shrugged. He seemed to be enjoying Mittendorf's discomfiture.

"Two thousand per day . . ." Mittendorf picked up his pencil, made a rapid calculation, and then almost threw the pencil from him. "*Gott in Himmel!* It can't be done!"

"Commandant—"

It was a Sergeant Schmidt. Schmidt had been in charge of the firing squads in Krepiecki Forest, six miles from the camp, and after that he had handled all deaths by gunfire at the Maidanek camp before even the old carbon-monoxide death trucks had been available. Now he was in charge of all hangings in the squares of the six fields. Sergeant Schmidt was a busy man.

Mittendorf looked at him sourly, sure that Schmidt was somehow going to compound the problem. He usually did. "Yes?"

"You said we were supposedly to destroy all the evidence—"

"That is correct."

"What about the pits, sir?"

Mittendorf almost threw up his hands. He had been right about Schmidt; the pits were going to be an additional problem. The corpses from the firing squads had been buried in shallow pits, in layers, and then a small amount of lye and a thin layer of dirt thrown over them. The pits were easily identifiable; rats and moles had burrowed in them for food. It wouldn't take any genius Russian investigator to uncover them; their damned soldiers would fall over them if they didn't fall into them! Damn! It was easy enough for some big shot in Berlin to sit on his fat ass and issue orders, but carrying out those orders was something else. The pit in the Krepiecki Forest was almost three years old, the result of executions before the camp had been properly prepared for the job. Possibly by now the bodies would have disintegrated, rotted, disappeared somehow. Maybe animals had uncovered them and dragged them away. Well, it was something they would have to hope for, because he would have enough problems with the pits on the camp grounds proper, without sending men and equipment six miles to handle the trouble at Krepiecki.

"We'll come to the matter of the pits," he said unhappily, and ran his finger down the list again. He looked up. "Dr. Schlossberg—"

"Here, sir."

The doctor was the only person in the room not in regulation uniform; instead he wore a long laboratory jacket. He was a man in his early forties, cavernous and prematurely bald, who always looked as if he expected to be blamed for something and was ill prepared to offer an excuse for whatever it was. Mittendorf studied him without expression. He had profound contempt for the doctor, not because of any lack of professional ability—although Mittendorf himself would not have let the man treat him for a hangnail—but because of the man's apparent weakness.

"How is your assignment going at the hospital?"

"My assignment?" The doctor rubbed the bare top of his head as if, genie fashion, to raise an answer there. Before the war Schlossberg had a reputation as a brilliant surgeon, although Mittendorf found it hard to believe the doctor could have made the necessary difficult decisions.

"Your experiments, Doctor!"

"Oh, the experiments. Why, they're going along all right, sir." The doctor suddenly realized the question had been asked in conjunction with the questions others in the meeting had been called upon to answer. "Oh, you mean about evacuating the camp, sir. They can be stopped without—none of them are long-term experiments . . ." The doctor suddenly further understood the question. "Oh, the patients will be no problem, Commandant. We have various means—"

"And more corpses for the *verdamnt* ovens!" Mittendorf's thick fingers drummed restlessly on his desk while he considered all phases of the enormous problem. "All right," he said at last, making up his mind. "Sergeant Schmidt, I want you to take charge of the pits—" For raising the question, he told himself. "Forget those in Krepiecki; concentrate on those inside the camp area itself. You will have to dig them up and rebury the bodies deeper, much deeper. Put enough lye

on them this time. If you have time, try to start some sort of construction over them to hide them—"

"Commandant?" It was Schmidt again. Mittendorf's face darkened. What now? Hadn't the idiot caused enough problems already?

"Yes? What is it?"

"Why not make a latrine over the old pit? The one back of the
baths? The new pit is probably too far away to convince anyone it
was used as a latrine, but the old pit is close enough. The Russians
will never dig up a pit that is full of shit."

The officers grinned; even Mittendorf permitted himself a brief
smile. For once Sergeant Schmidt had made a constructive suggestion, although it had obviously been triggered by his own idea of
constructing something over the pits.

"Good enough. Have plans prepared for building it. Inmates of
Fields II and III can use it. Maybe you can make the old pit also
look as if it was once used as a latrine. If you have time have some
prisoners haul some shit down there and spread it around; we have
plenty of it. In any event, it's your assignment, Sergeant. Do what
you have to do."

He swung about.

"Colonel Schneller, get into Lublin and see what you can do
about arranging boxcars. As soon as you get any, load them up and
ship them west. Contact Auschwitz and have them check their companion camps, and they can check Birkenau next door. See how
many people they can take. Possibly we can get a turnaround on the
cars going to camps that aren't too far away. See what you can do.
And we'll push the ovens to capacity. In a week or so, when we see
where we are, we'll start making arrangements to destroy the ovens
and the gas pens and move the rest of the prisoners out on foot with
the balance of the guards. All right. Any questions? Any comments?"

"Sir?" It was a Lieutenant Frisch. As Mittendorf recalled, another
idiot who probably shouldn't even have been at the meeting. "We
tried pyres once—"

"Which weren't worth the petrol they burned. Any other comments? Captain Müeller?"

"Sir, if we could start clearing the fields one by one, rather than
sending men to the gas chamber a few from each field, I could get a
head start by burning those barracks once they're cleared—"

"Not a bad idea." Mittendorf made a note and then scratched

through it. It was a terrible idea. "We do not have to burn the barracks. What do barracks signify? There was an army camp here.
Don't waste your time; concentrate on the ovens and the gas pens."

"Yes, sir." Müeller sounded doubtful. "I'll still need the time and
the men and the dynamite to get the job done, and that's four days
at the very least—"

"You'll have it! If we have it, that is. Good God! All right—anything else? All right, gentlemen, let's get to work. Heil Hitler!"
There was a murmur of response as the men came to their feet. The
commandant cleared his throat. "Colonel von Schraeder, if you
please. And Dr. Schlossberg. If you two might remain a moment
after the others."

The two men settled back into their chairs while the others filed
out. The tall thin doctor looked guilty at being selected, as though—
while he had no idea of the details of his crime—he was sure he
must have committed it. Von Schraeder merely looked bored. He
ejected his cigarette from his holder and ground it out beneath his
boot heel on the conference-room floor, well aware that Mittendorf
was watching and equally aware of the commandant's pride in the
neat appearance of the command post. When the door had closed
after the final man, the commandant turned first to the doctor.

"Doctor, your work is in order?"

"Why—yes, sir."

"Good. I want you to turn everything you have in progress over to
your chief assistant. You are being transferred, together with Colonel
von Schraeder."

The doctor looked alarmed. "I beg your pardon?"

"I said you are being transferred to a different camp." Good God!
Couldn't the idiot understand simple German? "You will leave for
Buchenwald camp tomorrow morning. I have your orders here. Colonel von Schraeder's car will pick you up tomorrow morning at your
quarters at five o'clock sharp. Be ready to leave."

"Yes, sir." The doctor stroked his bald spot almost frantically.
"But, sir—I didn't ask for a transfer . . ."

"I know," Mittendorf said dryly. "And I didn't request one for
you, either. But it's evident someone did. In any event, it's really of
no great importance. You'll just be leaving a bit earlier than the rest
of us, the way the situation appears." He turned to the colonel, trying his best to sound normal, a commandant speaking with a subor-

dinate, fighting to hide the bitterness, the hatred that twisted his stomach each time he had to deal with the colonel. "I'm sure you're not surprised to be transferred, are you, Colonel?"

Von Schraeder shrugged, looking faintly amused at the commandant's attempt to be subtle.

"I try not to be surprised at anything, Commandant."

"Yes . . ." Mittendorf looked into the colonel's cold slate-blue eyes but could read nothing there. "Well, your orders are to be transferred to Buchenwald, as well. After you've gone"—he could not help but add—"we'll see if we can't improve on your vaunted efficiency. Get a bit more out of the ovens than you were able to do."

"I'm sure you'll do your best," von Schraeder said. His tone indicated that Mittendorf's best would break no records. He came to his feet and raised his hand in a half salute that was customary with him. "Possibly we'll meet again, sometime." He reached over casually, removing the papers from Mittendorf's hand, checking them as if the commandant might not be trusted to give him the right ones. He handed the proper set to the doctor. Schlossberg paused long enough to first salute, then shake hands, and finally say "Heil Hitler" before following the colonel from the room. He closed the door quietly behind him.

In the now deserted conference room, Klaus Mittendorf stared at the closed door, his loathing for von Schraeder almost making him physically ill. He had been, first, with the Brown Shirts, then with the SS since the bully-boy days of the early twenties, and had never gotten beyond the rank of sergeant major, and although rank had nothing to do with position in concentration-camp leadership—the commandant was commandant regardless of military rank, and received the respect due him—it still rankled. Mittendorf sat and gritted his teeth; he would have given a month's pay to know how von Schraeder had managed to pull strings and get both himself and Dr. Schlossberg transferred without his approval. It was done on the Berlin trip, of course; if he thought for a moment messages had gone back and forth from the camp communications center without his knowledge, someone would pay for it dearly. But he was sure it had been handled on von Schraeder's last leave of absence. Personal business! What a story! And why the transfer at this particular time? Did von Schraeder think the Maidanek camp was going to be surrendered to the Russians with all personnel attached? Although if Mittendorf could have done it, he would have loved to leave his deputy in charge when the evacuation was complete. But it would have been impossible, and von Schraeder should have known it. He was merely anticipating a transfer that would have taken place in any event in another week or two. Why? *Why?*

And why the transfer of the doctor at the same time to the same camp? It was all part of whatever von Schraeder had in mind, because no one on earth was ever going to make him believe that it was mere coincidence. Was it possible there might be something between the two men? Something sexual? Although that seemed ridiculous, considering Colonel von Schraeder's reputation as a womanizer; the endless parade of women prisoners through the deputy commandant's house, on their way either to the *soldatenheim*, the brothel, or—if they got pregnant—to the ovens, was no great secret at Maidanek.

Ah, the fucking bastard! And that story of his for never saluting properly, that he had broken his arm as a child and it had never healed properly! *Gruss Gott*, what an alibi! Well, so the colonel said that possibly they might meet again sometime, eh? It was possible; everything was possible. And at that future meeting, whenever and wherever it took place, it was also possible that army rank might mean nothing, and it was also possible that von Schraeder might not have so many fine friends in high places. Then on that lovely day we shall see, my fine-feathered young colonel. We shall see. . . .

With a curse for von Schraeder and a sigh for the work that had to be done, Mittendorf bent back to his lists, trying to correlate the impossible numbers. People, including superiors who should have known better considering their own experience, seemed to have no idea of the difficulty of killing huge numbers of prisoners and getting rid of the bodies. On paper it looked simple; a bullet in the nape of the neck or the spray of a machine gun or a whiff of gas; but that was just the beginning. You couldn't leave the dead bodies lying around like cordwood, spreading disease and stinking up the place; you had to get rid of them. Once he had been permitted to bury them, but now his orders were to destroy them completely, although nobody bothered to tell him exactly how this was to be accomplished.

It was true, he had grudgingly to admit, that when that Junker prick von Schraeder had originally been assigned to Maidanek, the intention had been to make the camp a labor source for the industrial complex that was to be built there; it was also true that when, in May of 1942, the decision had been made not to build the industrial portion but to turn the camp into a *vernichtungslager*—an extermination camp—von Schraeder had not hesitated a moment. The colonel seemed to enjoy mass killing, the cold-blooded bastard! At any rate, he certainly enjoyed resolving the technical problems involved in mass killing. It was von Schraeder who had dismantled the original crematory and built the new one at the extreme rear of the camp so that those newcomers entering were not immediately aware of the end purpose of the place. It had been von Schraeder who had insisted upon the victims entering the shower area actually getting a shower before being herded into the concrete pens in the next room to be gassed. At other camps the shower heads were false; not at Maidanek. It meant far less trouble, more docility on the part of the prisoners on their way to death.

And it was von Schraeder, to give the devil his due, who had stopped the use of carbon monoxide copied from Treblinka and substituted it with the far quicker Zyclon B, working with the chemists and technicians of Tesch & Stabinow of Hamburg, and the engineers of Degesch of Dessau, the two German firms that had acquired the patent for the crystals from I. G. Farben, in order to determine the optimum quantity needed to get the job done without undue waste. And von Schraeder had brought in the engineers of C. H. Kori and worked with them on the design of the new ovens to determine the proper temperature and best fuel to cremate the bodies more rapidly. Before that innovation they had been lucky to handle a thousand through the ovens in a day.

Still, what Berlin seemed to forget was that Colonel von Schraeder, Junker prick, had done all of his engineering marvels under the direction of his commandant, although one would never have suspected it from the praise the colonel got from Berlin, while the brass there acted as if Klaus Mittendorf didn't even exist! God! If he could only expose von Schraeder for the thousand upon thousands of Deutschemarks he had sent to his secret account in Switzerland, money taken in bribes from prisoners to keep them or someone in their family alive, only to send them to the gas chamber once the last pfennig had been extracted. Or the money from the gold in the prisoners' teeth, often taken before they were killed; or the clothing on their back—all moneys that by law should have gone to the Reich. It was a charge of that nature that had finished Koch at Buchenwald. But, unfortunately, that was one closet door better left unopened; many had gotten rich at Maidanek, von Schraeder and Mittendorf included. If he could only demonstrate the colonel's complicity without having his own divulged—no, damn it! it would be too dangerous. But someday . . .

Ah, well, dwelling on the shit von Schraeder would do nothing to resolve the problem of forty thousand men, women, and children who would have to be removed one way or another before the Russians got within striking distance of the camp, not to mention doing something about the hundreds of thousands of bodies, either shot or hung, poorly buried in the various pits. What was it Eichmann had said? Ten dead are a catastrophe; ten million are a statistic. It was easy enough for Eichmann to say; he didn't have to resolve the problem of that statistic. It wasn't numbers Mittendorf had to get rid of; it was bodies, bodies, bodies!

Back to work.

In the area outside the command post barrack, young Colonel von Schraeder carefully tucked his travel orders into an inner pocket, tugged his uniform jacket straight, and smiled at the doctor in a fashion unusually friendly for him.

"An oaf," he said, obviously referring to the commandant, "as well as being a fool. But then," he added, quite as if he were voicing a common opinion, "they are all acting like fools."

"I beg your pardon?" The doctor's mind was on something else.

"Don't you agree, my friend, that it's rather stupid to use boxcars to haul Jews and Poles and Gypsies and Russians back and forth all over Asia and Europe, when our troops need the cars for transporting ammunition and food and clothing and the million and other things an army needs to fight?" He shook his head half humorously. "I swear that future military historians simply will not believe it!"

"Yes," said Schlossberg, who hadn't heard a word. "Colonel—"

"You know," the colonel said reminiscently as if Schlossberg had not spoken, "when I joined the SS it was an elite organization. It had high standards—" He started to stroll in the direction of his villa; the doctor, not wishing to be impolite, was forced to walk with him. "It was limited to men from fine families, and there were many qualifications, physical qualifications, educational qualifications. Nowadays—well, look at Mittendorf as an example! We've let the bars down completely. A Brown Shirt bully-boy! He's short, fat, he looks like a pig and he has that animal's mentality, not to mention its manners. If he managed to get through the first form in school I should by very surprised, and God knows where he comes from. A navvy's son, by the looks of him."

"Yes, sir," said Schlossberg, who had been waiting impatiently to get a word in. "Colonel—"

"Ah, Franz! That is your name, is it not? You must call me Helmut. We are friends, *nicht wahr?* And destined to become much closer friends, I'm sure."

"Yes, sir, Colonel. I mean, Helmut." The doctor hesitated, his hand automatically coming up to pat and then rub his bald head. "Could I ask you a question, sir? Helmut?"

"Of course."

"Did you—I mean, were you responsible for my transfer? The way Commandant Mittendorf spoke—"

They were passing the barracks of the women guards at the northeast corner of Field I; there was the sound of giggling from the second floor of the building. As they walked the colonel screwed a cigarette into his holder, held his lighter to it, and inhaled deeply. In the growing dusk the cigarette end glowed and ebbed.

"Colonel—"

"Helmut," said the colonel, and smiled. "Look, Doctor. Franz. We have a very long and very tiresome drive ahead of us tomorrow if we are to make Weimar and the Buchenwald camp in one day. We'll have more than ample time to speak of anything you wish in the car. It will be diverting."

"But—" Schlossberg floundered. "I was simply wondering why—"

Von Schraeder raised an eyebrow as he looked at the thin medical officer. For the first time he seemed slightly disappointed with his new-found friend.

"Why? Why what? Have you any objections to being transferred?"

"Oh, no! No, no! I was simply wondering—"

"We'll talk of it tomorrow," von Schraeder said firmly. "It's too nice an evening to discuss Mittendorf or other unpleasant subjects. Come over to the house and have a drink."

"I really can't, Colonel."

"Helmut," von Schraeder said patiently. "Why not?"

"I really don't have the time. I've got to pack, and I have to turn all my work and notes over to Zellerbach, my assistant, and—oh, there are a hundred things to do."

Von Schraeder looked at the doctor this time in genuine surprise.

"Do you mean it? Do you honestly and truly mean it? Franz, Franz! The Russians are within days of this place, a few weeks at the most. Do you really think it makes the slightest difference if you turn your work over to whoever-he-is, or if you don't?"

"But Zellerbach will have to handle the problem of the prisoners we've been experimenting with," Schlossberg said sincerely, truly wishing the colonel—Helmut, his new-found friend—to understand. "You heard the orders; they came from Berlin, not from the commandant. Zellerbach wasn't at the meeting. He'll have to be told they want all evidence of what we've been doing here destroyed."

Von Schraeder snorted.

"So you can tell what's-his-name that in two minutes. Come along and have that drink. There is no chance that Mittendorf, our brilliant commandant, will have the time—or the ability to use it—to dynamite the gas chambers and the ovens, let alone spread them over his cabbage fields and hide them. Grass, for heaven's sake! The man's a maniac. It's a dream at best, don't you see?"

"I beg your pardon?"

"And I wish you would get over that habit of saying 'I beg your pardon' all the time," von Schraeder said testily. Despite his best intention of being charming, the doctor was beginning to grate. "It's most annoying. We'll have to talk about that in the car tomorrow, as well."

"But I mean—a dream . . . ?"

"A fantasy," von Schraeder said firmly. His tone was that of a teacher trying his best to drive a lesson through the head of an exceptionally obtuse student. He took Schlossberg by the arm, as if taking him into his confidence. "For one reason, how can we possibly hide what we have been doing here? Everyone in Lublin knows what we have been doing here; anyone with a nose has been able to smell it for years. People from the town write in to the camp asking for clothes from the victims; they want the best pick of everything before we ship it to the central warehouse in town. One woman, bless her, even wrote in asking for a baby carriage; she said she preferred a new one if we could let her have it. At least she was considerate enough not to specify color." He looked at the doctor. "It's true, you know."

"I believe you, but—"

"But what?" Von Schraeder did not wait for an answer. "Is our genius of a commandant going to cap the total destruction of the Maidanek camp by dynamiting the entire city of Lublin as well? Assuming Müeller can find the dynamite? Is he going to order the bulldozing over of a whole city? Does he intend to plant his precious grass on what is left of Lublin Castle afterward, and plant sod on the rubble of Radziwell Palace? And what about the million pairs of shoes in the central warehouse? Is he going to cover them with his grass seed and hope the Russians will think the shoelaces are plant shoots? It's ridiculous!"

"Still—" Having said that, the doctor had nothing more to say. He marched along, studying the ground beneath his feet.

"Besides," von Shraeder added, not particularly touched by the look of woe on the doctor's face, but feeling the man needed a little encouragement none the less, "when and if an exact description of what we have been doing here is given to the world, very few will believe it. Very few. Atrocity stories are old. They wouldn't believe it coming from Catholic nuns, let alone from the mouths of Russians."

Of course the very few would probably include the justices at any war-crimes trials, but von Schraeder saw no need to mention this to the doctor, at least not at this time. This was one further point for discussion in the car the next day, and had been planned, almost orchestrated, for that period. He paused to eject his cigarette stub from the holder, blew through the holder to clear it of remaining smoke, and tucked it into his pocket. Above them the floodlights suddenly blazed into light from the trapezoidal watchtowers set about the six fields, bathing the area in cold unnatural light, wiping the sight of Lublin's silhouetted skyline from the night. Von Schraeder sighed.

"But enough of these topics. Let's get that drink. Besides, you've had your eye on that girl Sarah ever since I picked her out of the last shipment and brought her home. I have a feeling you'd be willing to postpone your packing for an hour or so if you could take her to bed."

"I? My eye on her? Never!" The doctor did his best to sound shocked at the suggestion. "I don't even know her—"

"The girl you examined for venereal disease," von Schraeder said gently. "The last one, less than ten days ago. I was there when you examined her, remember? I saw the look on your face. And the bulge in your pants."

"Oh, her," Schlossberg said, his face reddening. "She's Jewish—"

"True," von Schraeder said dryly, "and the vodka we'll be drinking is Russian, and the *slivovitz* will be Polish, and that never stopped us from enjoying them, did it?" He smiled at the doctor. "If it eases your conscience, she isn't circumcised. I've looked."

They were almost by Field I by this time, approaching the baths and the gas pens. The flower beds surrounding the baths and the gas chambers gave a heady perfume to the night; water splashed from the fountain in front of the death house the prisoners had built under orders. Within the angled barbed wire of Field I prisoners stood or wandered about aimlessly. Those at the wire, staring hopelessly out, turned quickly at sight of the trim colonel and his awkward-looking companion; Colonel von Schraeder had been known to select men for the gas chamber merely because he had not cared for the way they looked at him. But tonight they were safe; the colonel's thoughts were on the girl in his villa, and particularly on the doctor's reaction to her.

Schlossberg wet his thin lips and tried to sound noncommittal, as if he were merely making male conversation.

"What's she like?"

"You obviously mean in bed." Von Schraeder gave him a lewd wink. "She's like nothing you've ever experienced! She comes to bed like a statue, resolved each time to lie there like a broomstick and not give me the slightest satisfaction. Everything about her is limp. I take her hand and put it between my legs and she makes no attempt to either resist or comply; she just lets her hand rest where I put it, neither holding me nor squeezing me, and for some reason this excites me more than if she were all over me with her hands or her mouth. She simply lies there, those marvelous breasts of hers as soft as pillows, and when I touch them and rub the nipples gently, and then run my tongue around them and find the nipples with my lips, they get hard as rocks, swelled out like grapes. I know she hates herself for not being able to control them. And when I slide my hand gently over her belly and run it down her legs, I do it very gently— not like that bull Mittendorf coupling with one of his cows down at the brothel."

He glanced across at the doctor. Schlossberg was breathing more rapidly, his eyes slightly glazed, his mouth a bit open. Von Schraeder bit back a smile and went on.

"She's quite hairy between her legs, you know, and I like that. It's not the wire you find on some women; it's soft, like thick moss. When I part the lips and start to stroke her there, I barely touch her. I just barely run the tip of my finger over her little button and she shivers and starts to breathe faster, and then she begins to cry, as silently as she can, and I know she hates herself more and more— more, I think, than she hates me. And she hates me, believe it! But she can't help herself; she gets wetter and wetter and she twitches every time my fingertip slides up and down her slit. It's like rubbing your finger in jelly. And when at last I finally get on top of her and go into her, it's like being dipped into a pot of hot honey. She does her best to lie still but she can't help responding, and before we're done she's panting like a mare in heat, using every muscle she has to suck me deeper and deeper inside of her. And when we finally explode together—because she can't help exploding any more than I can—she lies there, still pulsing inside, and bites her lips until they bleed." He looked over at the doctor. "You'll find her everything you've dreamed about, Franz, I'm sure."

Schlossberg wet his lips and tried to act as if the picture of the girl writhing sensuously beneath him in bed was not all that was on his mind at the moment.

"And what will happen to her after tomorrow, when you leave?"

Von Schraeder shrugged.

"What difference does it make? As you said, she's a Jew. Maybe Mittendorf will take her, just because he thinks it will get back at me somehow—although I have a feeling he'll be a little busy these next few days to spend much time worrying about women. Or he may send her to the ovens, just because I enjoyed her. Or, if she's lucky, she still may be alive when the Russians get here."

Chapter 3

They left Maidanek at dawn the following day, with the windows of the heavy military limousine drawn up against a rather unusual chill morning breeze, driving through Lublin when the ancient city was just beginning to show signs of life. They passed the square, avoiding the market that was beginning to be set up blocking traffic, swung past the railroad station deserted in the early hours, and drove swiftly through the empty streets past the university and out of the city. The chauffeur had chosen the Radom road through past experience and they drove through the awakening countryside at a high rate of speed, taking advantage of the untrafficked road conditions, conditions both von Schraeder and the driver knew would not last for long.

The colonel sat quietly in one corner of the large rear seat of the official military limousine, smoking a cigarette, looking out at the neat farmhouses and the grazing cattle with vast disinterest, his mind on other things. In the other corner Dr. Schlossberg sat, his eyes half closed, the faint lascivious smile on his face clearly indicating he was reliving the pleasures of the night before. The girl had been everything the colonel had promised, nor for a moment did he believe she was Jewish, since intercourse between Aryan and Jew was forbidden. But why the colonel had presented him with that extraordinary delicacy was something the doctor did not understand. In fact, the sudden friendliness of the previously cold colonel was as mysterious as the offer of the girl's services.

It was very odd. In the year since Franz Schlossberg had been transferred from repairing shattered bodies and faces at the Laukhammer Military Hospital to Maidanek camp at Lublin, Poland, he had seen the colonel various times. He had, of course, seen him at the officers' mess, evenings in the canteen, at meetings, and occasionally on the camp grounds, but his only personal contact had been when he had examined the girl Sarah for venereal disease. He recalled that examination very well, with the girl on the table, her marvelous breasts straining the hospital gown, the gown up around her waist, her feet in the stirrups, those lovely legs spread wide to open that fabulous slit to view, and that mask of dead indifference on her face that did nothing to hide her hatred for a moment. Who would ever have thought he would have a chance to delve those sweet depths with anything but a rubber-gloved finger?

The smile faded from his lips as he suddenly remembered something else. In the year since he had been at Maidanek, Colonel von Schraeder must have taken at least ten girls to bed according to canteen rumors, few of them lasting much more than a month, and each had previously been checked for disease—but this was the first time the colonel had specifically asked that Dr. Schlossberg handle the assignment. Actually, it wasn't really in his field. Very odd. As odd, for example, as this sudden transfer back to Germany—

"Colonel—"

"Helmut," von Schraeder said as if by rote, not taking his eyes from the pastoral scenery outside the speeding car.

"Helmut." The name seemed difficult for the doctor to say. "We were going to speak of my transfer."

"If you insist." Von Schraeder finally brought his attention back to the interior of the car, his thoughts from far away. He crushed out his cigarette in the ashtray, followed his usual ritual with the holder, and then leaned forward, sliding the glass partition shut between the chauffeur and themselves. He then leaned back negligently, crossing one leg over the other, one hand stroking the smooth polished leather of the boot sensuously, almost as if it were Sarah's belly or haunch. "Well? What about it?"

"I mean—did you arrange for my transfer from Maidanek? The commandant seemed to think you did."

"And for once our genius of a commandant was correct," von Schraeder said calmly.

"But—why?"

"Quite simple," von Schraeder said evenly. He had been studying exactly how to answer this question and had come to the conclusion that the truth would be as confusing to the doctor as anything. "It's possible that I may need your help."

"*My* help?" The doctor was truly surprised. Von Schraeder looked in the peak of health, although there was, of course, the stories he had heard of the colonel's poorly set arm. "Is it your arm?"

"It was never my arm, it was my shoulder," the colonel said shortly. "But that's not it."

"Then what help—"

"You might help me survive." Von Schraeder looked at the doctor across the width of the car. "It is not certain yet that I will need your help, but I don't believe in leaving things to chance."

"Survive? I don't understand—"

"What don't you understand? The meaning of survival?" Von Schraeder tented his fingers and stared at them. He looked quite professorial. "Survival, my dear Franz, is living longer—or continuing longer—than another person or thing. In my case survival is living longer than I would if I didn't take the necessary steps to stay that way. To me it's rather important." Having made that understatement, he glanced at the doctor from the corners of his eyes. "If, after our experience at Maidanek we haven't learned that, we've learned nothing."

"What has Maidanek got to do with it—?"

"My dear Franz, have you ever looked through the peephole into the gas pens when the crystals are dropped?" The doctor stared at him dumbly and shook his head. Von Schraeder shrugged. "A pity. You would know what I was talking about. You would have seen the prisoners fighting like animals, trying to get to the door, even though they know it is useless. Some of them have heard stories—there were a few escapes from Auschwitz and stories got around—but they couldn't bring themselves to believe them. And when they go into the showers and there really is water coming from the shower heads, they are relieved. But when they get into the pens and the door is locked behind them, and then the crystals start coming down like blue snowflakes, then they finally know. They *know*, do you understand?" Von Schraeder was leaning toward the doctor now, more intent than he had planned to be. "They climb all over each other, scratching, punching, pulling, screaming, begging, crying, shitting and pissing all over each other and sliding in it trying to reach that door that means nothing. Why?" He leaned back, relaxing a bit. "Trying to survive, my friend. Trying to survive."

The doctor was staring at him, his eyes wide. He had never seen the usually imperturbable colonel like this, nor had he ever imagined to see him like this. Von Schraeder went on in a calmer tone.

"If you haven't looked through the peephole, at least you must have seen the *Sonderkommandos* with their gas masks and their high boots opening the doors afterward and hosing down the corpses to wash the shit and piss and vomit off them before they lift them with their hooks into the carts and roll them off to the ovens. They hook their own wives, their own children; they shovel their relatives and their dearest friends onto the grates and turn up the fires. Why? To survive, my friend. To survive!"

The doctor seemed dazed by the conversation.

"But how can arranging for my transfer possibly help you survive?"

"It's the first step," von Schraeder said calmly. His past emotion seemed to have evaporated completely. "I had a professor once when I was in the Technical Institute, a professor in mechanical engineering; as I recall, his name was Werner. If you gave him the correct answer to a problem but omitted any step in the solution, he would fail you. 'From one step to the next!' he would scream. 'First things first, then second things second, all in order, all in order, until the answer comes! No jumps! No skips!' I thought at the time that he was crazy, a hysterical old man, but he was absolutely right. It's the secret of engineering; basically it's the secret of all science. No skips, no jumps. I have a feeling it's also the secret of survival."

He looked at the doctor with that cold smile on his lips.

"So the first step was to get out of Maidanek, since being there when the Russians come marching through the gate is certainly no way to survive. With an idiot like Mittendorf in charge, I expect that when the Russians get there they'll find, not only some of the prisoners, but some of the SS as well. Not Mittendorf himself you may be sure, the pig also has a strong sense of survival, but there will be others. Men the commandant dislikes, men he envies for qualities he lacks. And the commandant would have liked nothing better than to have Colonel von Schraeder numbered among them. It was a chance I did not choose to take."

"But, me—?"

"You? I did not want to take the chance of losing you. You could have been transferred to some other camp, out of my sight. That was also a chance I did not choose to take."

The doctor removed his military cap and rubbed his head furiously.

"But the Russians may be stopped before they reach the camp—"

Von Schraeder contemplated the doctor as he would a specimen under glass, foreign and difficult to understand. The doctor's response had truly surprised the colonel.

"Franz, my friend, if you believe that, you'll believe anything. The Russians won't be stopped before they get to Maidanek. They won't be stopped before they get to Berlin. It's all over. The war is lost, my friend."

Schlossberg was truly shocked. His eyes fled to the impassive profile of the driver outside the glass partition. "That's—that's treason!"

"He can't hear us, if that's what bothers you," von Schraeder said dryly.

"It's not a question of whether he can hear us," Schlossberg said heatedly, his Nazi background compelling him to protest. "Saying the war is lost is nothing but treason!"

Colonel von Schraeder seemed faintly disappointed, as if a favored pupil had failed an easy question on an exam.

"Franz, listen to me. To me, treason is using boxcars wastefully when the army is in desperate need of them. There was a time when we could afford the luxury of using ammunition to shoot Jews, women, children, what have you, but that time is past. Today it is treasonable to waste this ammunition. To me it has been becoming more and more treasonable to kill men who can work in factories and manufacture things we need. My God! We're like two separate countries working against each other, the country of the Wehrmacht, and the country of the Mittendorfs! We seem to have forgotten the Russians and the British and the French and the Americans! So now we have to pay. The war is lost. That is the payment."

He stared into the doctor's eyes.

"Be logical, Franz. You've had scientific training. You're a graduate of Heidelberg with honors; you received your medical training at the Berlin Institute of Surgery; you practiced under the great Dr. Feddermann before the war—" Schlossberg stared in surprise at this knowledge of his background. "Well, then," von Schraeder went on, his voice friendly, "use that scientific training, or if not, at least use common sense. What can be treasonable—or patriotic, for that matter—in stating a simple fact? You heard Mittendorf announce that our Middle Army Group in Russia had been destroyed, and he cited Guderian as his source. Well, I can tell you we lost twenty-five divisions in that fiasco, more than we lost at Stalingrad. It was a worse loss than Stalingrad, much worse, in every sense. And my source in Berlin is fully as reliable as Guderian!"

"Your source—?"

"Obviously," von Schraeder said almost wearily, "I have connections in Berlin or I should not have been able to arrange our transfers. The name von Schraeder still means something to some people."

"But even if we lost twenty-five divisions—"

"*Even* if we lost twenty-five divisions? Where are the replacements to come from?" The colonel almost sounded savage. "The war is lost! Reconcile yourself to that fact. To fight on when there is no hope of winning—that, to me, is treason. It is treason to a country and a people who have supported our efforts in every way. It is treason to the soldiers who will be killed needlessly and the civilians who will starve, if they aren't wiped out in the increased bombings. The war was lost long ago, with the Allied invasion in Normandy; and now with the present Russian advance, I should think the blindest optimist could see it!"

There were several minutes of silence as the doctor sat in stunned consideration of the colonel's words. The truth was that the war itself had never really interested him; as a good German and a good Nazi he supported it fully, but his own work was of such paramount interest that the war was only the background against which his art was played, first at the Laukhammer Hospital with war wounds, and then at Maidanek with prisoners. Now he was being told his background was to be taken away from him. He looked up, his slightly horse-like face almost pitiable, a child deprived of a favorite toy.

"Do you think we will surrender, then?"

"As long as Hitler is alive, no."

"As long as Hitler is *alive?*" Now the doctor was really shocked.

"That's right. As long as Hitler is alive, we will not surrender. We will fight to the last living thing in Germany, to the last brick in the last factory, to the last shingle on the last shed, to the last tree and the last blade of grass. We will waste everything. But," von Schraeder added grimly, "they will not waste me!"

"I see."

The doctor didn't see at all, nor did he sound as if he did. His mind was whirling. He only knew that the man who had just spoken was a far different person than the stiff colonel he had known in the camp. A chameleon, this Colonel von Schraeder! But the doctor somehow knew instinctively that regardless of the spurious logic with which von Schraeder was attempting to disguise the fact, what he spoke was arrant treason. And to even suggest that the Fuehrer's death could alleviate Germany's problems—that was total treason! What of their oaths as Germans? What of their pledges as officers of the Schutzstaffel, personally, to Adolf Hitler? And even if the war *was* lost—which was far from a demonstrable truth—anyone who would refuse to fight for the Fuehrer and the Fatherland, *especially* under those conditions, was the most despicable of traitors!

On the other hand, it could well be that the colonel was merely testing his own loyalty, waiting for him to agree to his monstrous propositions in order to denounce him to the authorities. But why would the colonel do that? Why, in that case, would he have offered his friendship? Offered? Almost forced it, first with the girl the night before, then with the transfer, which, if the Russians were really all that close, might well have been a lifesaver. And even Mittendorf had acknowledged that the enemy was closing in.

No, the colonel was quite serious in his treasonous statements.

But, then, a big question. Why would a man as sophisticated as the colonel, as smart as he was rumored to be in the camp, why would a man like that make statements that left him at the mercy of the person he was speaking to? Why would the sharp and normally taciturn Colonel Helmut von Schraeder volubly place himself at the mercy of ordinary Dr. Franz Schlossberg for possible denunciation to the authorities and almost certain death by hanging?

The colonel was watching the play of expression across the doctor's face as each succeeding thought registered, one after the other, almost as if they were being projected on a screen.

"No," he said quietly.

Schlossberg looked up, startled. "I beg your pardon?"

"I said, no. I am as safe in your hands as I was in the hands of my

nanny as a child. To begin with, I doubt if your word of this conversation would carry much weight against mine—" The doctor's face
reddened at having his thoughts read so accurately. Von Schraeder
continued easily before the doctor could even deny it. "Secondly, do
you honestly believe I would speak to you as I have if I didn't have
the assurance of your silence? My dear Franz, I have appealed to
your friendship with the girl Sarah and with this transfer, for which I
am sure you will eventually be grateful. I later intend to appeal to
your greed with offers of money, should the need for your services
arise. But at the moment, I merely intend to appeal to your own
sense of salvation—"

"*My* sense of salvation?"

"Exactly. My dear Franz, I have planned this quite carefully, I assure you. I have in my possession papers clearly indicating you are a
member of a group actively plotting against the Fuehrer's life . . ."

"*I? Me?*" The doctor's face was ashen as he listened to the monstrous fabrication. "I never! It's a lie! It's a horrible lie!"

"I believe you," von Schraeder said calmly, "but who else will?
The papers appear quite authentic, I assure you . . ."

"I—" The doctor fell silent, as recognition of his position slowly
came to him. Oddly enough, the actual realization of his terrible
state somehow seemed to calm him. He considered the colonel with
almost fatalistic detachment.

"Why?"

"I thought I had explained that. Because there is a good chance
that I will need your professional help, and when the time comes—if
it comes, which I hope it will not—then I should not like to have a
great many discussions about the matter. There very well might not
be time."

"And when the time comes, if the time comes—which you hope it
will not—exactly what service will you wish me to perform that you
don't want any discussion about at the time?"

Von Schraeder laughed.

"You know, Franz," he said amicably, "we may end up being
friends, yet. When the pressure is on, you come together nicely. I always thought you would have to, in your profession." His laughter
disappeared as quickly as it had come; he suddenly looked grim.
"You are being transferred to Ward Forty-six at Buchenwald. I am
going there as assistant deputy commandant. Isolation Ward Forty-

six at Buchenwald handles all typhus and virus research. When the time comes—if it comes which I sincerely hope it does not—what I will want from you is very simple. I expect you to help me die. Of typhus."

The doctor stared. Von Schraeder smiled faintly.

"I think we had best get some rest. It's a long way yet." And he leaned back in his corner and closed his eyes, the faint smile still on his lips.

They had passed Radom some time before. At Piotrkow-Tribunalski the chauffeur turned to intercept the highway from Lodz to Breslau at Lask, turning into it, heading south. Here, as both von Schraeder and the chauffeur had anticipated, the road was crowded with the movement and sound of war. Although the day had warmed considerably, the car windows were now kept shut against the dust. Troop carriers edged past in the opposite direction, the soldiers on them leaning forward, their rifles pressed tightly against the floor for balance, their faces a mixture of too young and too old, dulled with the boredom of their seemingly endless journey, being carried to Warsaw and the Vistula, the new front. Other troops on foot slogged wearily toward the rear, toward a rest camp, a hospital, or some restaging area. Their faces spelled their ordeal; they paid little attention to the carriers with the fresh troops, or to the chauffeur-driven limousine with the SS flag on the fender and the two officers seated in comfort as it edged past them. Tanks clanked along the road, heading to the east, diverted from other fronts, forcing vehicular and foot traffic to the shoulder. High in the sky unidentifiable planes seemed to wander about as if lost.

At Kepno they paused for lunch and von Schraeder roused himself from his nap. They pulled several hundred yards from the crowded main road along a deserted cart path, and their taciturn driver brought a hamper from the trunk, rummaged in it for his share, and went to sit under a tree to eat, apart from his superiors. Von Schraeder and Schlossberg took their meal inside the car, the doors open to catch some breeze, watching the troops on the road.

They know, von Schraeder thought; they know the war is lost. They must know, those innocent young faces, those old lined faces. A few months ago the young ones were still in school, waiting impatiently to graduate and take their place in the brave new world we were winning for them; the old men were sucking their pipes around the fireplace of the nearest tavern, off duty from spotting planes or growing victory gardens. Now they are decked out in ill-fitting uniforms after a hasty training with broomsticks. They must know the war is lost, yet they still march to their annihilation, like ants on a trail. Or, more aptly, like steers in an abattoir, to their death. And what does this do to your theory of survival? he asked himself, and satisfied himself with his answer: there will always be lemmings. But none, he added with satisfaction, named von Schraeder.

He finished his bottle of wine and tossed it negligently from the car, almost as a symbol of his nonreturn. Their driver had come to his feet and was brushing crumbs from his uniform, preparing to return to the car and the resumption of their journey. Schlossberg dumped his rubbish out of the car door and closed it, leaning back in his corner, closing his eyes, as if by doing so he could shut away the thoughts in turmoil in his head. Von Schraeder closed his door as well, leaning back, glancing at the doctor. The conversation before had gone well, he thought. He had given the doctor the stick; now perhaps a return to the carrot was in order.

The car was put in motion; they bumped their way back to the main road, waited for a break in the endless traffic, and joined the parade, speeding up a bit whenever possible, passing ambulances and troop carriers and lines of men marching single file on the shoulders of the road, lines that stretched for miles. A fog had fallen shortly after they regained the road and now it began to drizzle, although the increasing downpour seemed to make little difference to the weary men trudging dispiritedly back down the road to Breslau. Von Schraeder cleared his throat.

"Doctor—"

Schlossberg's eyes flew open. "Yes?"

"When I was in Berlin last week there was quite a bit of discussion about Allied leaflets that had been dropped from planes. Talk of war-crimes trials. They call Hitler a war criminal, of course, as well as Goering and Himmler, Goebbels, and—"

"Of course they would consider our leaders to be war criminals!" Schlossberg said bitterly. "It's to hide their own crimes and the crimes of the Jews! What about the torture of our prisoners in their prisons? What about the Russians raping women and killing children in Poland when they retreated to Stalingrad last year? Do they

think nobody knows of those things? What about the murders they
committed in bombing Hamburg, an unarmed city? What of the
fact that they bomb civilians everywhere, even their own allies, just
because there happens to be some German troops in the area? What
about those things?" He turned to look from the car window,
dismissing the discussion.

"Yes," von Schraeder said quietly, "but that was not my point.
The leaflets also speak of searching out and hanging some of the SS
men who mistreated prisoners—"

He smiled faintly at the thought, although his slate-blue eyes were
cold and grim. Mistreated prisoners? What would they do and say
when they uncovered places like Maidanek, or Auschwitz-Birkenau,
or Sibibor, or Treblinka, or Ravensbrook, or Sachenhausen, or
Dachau, or all the other hundreds of camps? Possibly the world
might think for a while that the horror stories were merely atrocity
scares, but the war-crimes justices would know better. He glanced
over at Schlossberg; the doctor seemed disinterested.

"—as well," von Schraeder continued, "as searching out and hanging a few doctors."

"Doctors?" Schlossberg swung around, his attention captured.
"Why?"

"They mention some names in particular—Professor Hirt, for example, late of Buchenwald, now at Natzweiler, I believe. Vaernet,
and Haagen. Also Mrgowski was mentioned, as I recall—and a certain Dr. Franz Schlossberg . . ."

The doctor stared; he looked as if he might begin to cry. He
wanted desperately to deny the charge, or believe the colonel was
only saying it to disturb him, but he was sure the colonel was telling
the truth. As the colonel was, indeed. Franz Schlossberg had made it
to the atrocity list.

Schlossberg was almost wailing, "But, why? *Why?*"

"Well, they mentioned experimenting on human beings without
benefit of anesthetics, for example. They speak of the removal of
healthy organs, or arms and legs. They say something about inducing
diseases, such as typhus, purposely—"

"They have no right to talk of punishing us! We were only doing
our duty!"

Von Schraeder nodded as if in complete agreement.

"Yes, but your duty to whom? Hippocrates? Humanity? The men

you wrapped in sheets so they couldn't move, last winter, when you soaked them in water and put them outside to freeze—?"

"It was a scientific experiment," Schlossberg said hotly. "We tried to revive them afterward and even saved a few. Our fliers face being forced down in the North Sea during winter—"

"And the women you sterilized by burning their ovaries with high doses of x rays? Without, I might mention, bothering to anesthetize them, even locally?"

"We were following orders! We were only doing our duty!"

"You mean, *befehl ist befehl?* An order is an order? My friend, believe me when I tell you they won't hang you one inch less high for having done your duty."

Schlossberg stared at his fingers as if seeing them for the first time, for the first time aware of the power their talent had to get him in trouble, possibly even to get him hanged.

"But I am telling the truth," he said, almost as if he were speaking to himself. "I did it for my country and for the Fuehrer, whether they laugh or sneer at that explanation or not, or whether they accept it or not. But," he added under his breath, still speaking to himself, "I hated it. I always hated it!" He looked up. "I wasn't like the others. I am a doctor, a surgeon. At Laukhammer I saved many, many lives! It's true, it's on the record! I'm not like the others! Hirt isn't even a doctor. I hate to give pain. If a patient was in pain—"

"You injected him with carbolic or evipan out of humanitarian principles, of course," von Schraeder said smoothly.

"It's true! I have done it!" Schlossberg turned on the colonel, his eyes blazing, his control slipping. Von Schraeder watched him with amusement. "It's true! I'm not like you! You've killed hundreds of thousands in your gas chambers, and you talk of me! I know all about you! Before you came to Maidanek you were at the front for a year, killing, killing, killing! You like killing!"

Von Schraeder nodded calmly.

"Do you expect me to deny it? I liked being at the front and seeing a man die under my bullet. All men like killing. If they didn't, there would be no wars. Why do men hunt? Because they enjoy killing; in fact they call it a sport, a blood sport. Really, you know, it's the opposite side of the coin of survival. How can one enjoy sweet if he has never tasted sour? Or enjoy pleasure if he has never known pain? And how can a man enjoy the feeling of being alive if he has never seen others die and imagined what it must be like? How can a man feel the power of life if he has never enjoyed the power of death?"

Dr. Schlossberg was staring at him in disbelief. Von Schraeder shook his head a bit impatiently.

"My dear Franz, do not look at me as if I were insane. I'm only being honest. If it comes to war-crimes trials, do you think the men who hang us will not enjoy it? Oh, they'll make very pious speeches about our monstrous crimes, but the truth is they would enjoy hanging their own judges just as much. It makes a man realize how very much alive he is, to walk out of a room where someone has just been hanged by the neck. He is walking out and the other is gone, dead, never to walk anywhere again. Just to be buried. Hidden."

He stared from the window and went on.

"But the gassing of people in the camp was not like this," he said, almost to himself. "That was simply an engineering problem. There was none of the pleasure of battle in it. There was no satisfaction, other than in having done a necessary job as well as it could be done. Do you understand?" He turned from the window, looking across the car at his companion. He sighed. "No—I suppose not."

The doctor might not have been listening to him, for Schlossberg said quietly, "Why are you threatening me?"

Von Schraeder looked honestly surprised.

"I'm not threatening you," he said patiently. "I'm trying to tell you how to survive. When and if the time comes."

"Which you hope will not."

"Which I hope will not—but greatly fear will. Then I will tell you where to go and whom to see to get you out of the country and save your neck."

"I see." Schlossberg nodded. "After which you will die. Of typhus."

Von Schraeder smiled, a humorless smile, and leaned back. "Now you understand."

Chapter 4

Buchenwald concentration camp lay a few miles north of the town of Weimar, laid out in uneven clearings spread across the desolate wooded slopes of the Ettersberg. The neat officers' homes with their gardens were built along Eicke Street on the more protected southern flank of the mountain, while the prisoners' barracks were in a wire-enclosed area on the more open upper slope. Beyond the narrow two-story gatehouse with its motto "Right or Wrong—My Country" lay the roll-call area, a barren yard that was a dust bowl in the dry days and a sea of mud in the rain. Then came the barracks, row upon row, fanning out from the roll-call yard, wooden buildings without windows, stretching up the slope almost to the summit. Unlike Maidanek or Auschwitz or the majority of the German concentration camps in Poland, Buchenwald was not an extermination camp but had been built in the early days of the Nazi regime as a detention camp for dissenters, and had later been expanded to furnish labor to the Gustloff Armament Works and the German Armament Works, both built on the outskirts of the camp. In addition, the camp furnished labor for any other endeavor in the area that was recommended to the SS, from the railroad to Weimar that was never used because of its poor construction to the huge riding hall that had been constructed to satisfy the whim of the wife of the ex-commandant, Frau Ilsa Koch, and which had been used only half an hour a day for her horseback exercises.

To Colonel Helmut von Schraeder, the camp was a disgrace. For one thing, for a camp dedicated to furnishing labor and not to extermination, the pair of ovens in the crematory behind the high wall in the southeast corner of the prisoners' area seldom lacked customers

—while at the same time half the machines at the Gustloff and German Works were idle for lack of proper personnel. Still, he could hardly be surprised; an organization run by a bureaucracy that would criminally misuse boxcars would certainly not be intelligent enough to properly use labor.

The camp also lacked order, lacked that discipline the colonel's engineering soul demanded. Prisoners would rip out electric wires when the night food containers arrived, and in the darkness fight savagely and even kill to get an extra ration of food, while the Kapos and barracks orderlies would mill about helplessly, unable to control their charges. And inmates too weak or too crowded in their tiered bunks to climb down and make their way to the latrines would relieve themselves into their mess gear instead, or climb to the barrack roof, removing planks and tar paper, and then defecate onto the roof itself, or foul the beams and often the prisoners below.

But it was not the fighting for a scrap of food, or the filth in which the men lived, or the pile of corpses that were deposited daily outside the barracks and had to be removed that bothered the colonel. These were, after all, animals, and nothing more could be expected of them. What bothered von Schraeder was the waste. Even the small amount of food the inmates received, even the small amount of space they occupied, should have been repaid by having some useful labor extracted from them. If Colonel von Schraeder had been running the camp, the prisoners would have been separated into two groups: those able to work and those unable to work. The first group would have been given sufficient rations to sustain them, enough room on the tiers to get proper rest, and they would have the duty to keep the Gustloff and the German Armament Works functioning. If they did not, they would instantly join the second group and go to the gas chambers, which would have been the first thing constructed.

He would sit in his office in the command barrack with little to do, leaning back and consuming cigarette after cigarette, constantly analyzing his alternate plan, should Valkyrie fail. It was at these moments that the barren camp, its stench and drabness, its filthy prisoners, and its constant outpouring of skeletal bodies for the furnaces would disappear, and in its place would come a vision of his plan. And with it would come a gentle chiding of himself for worrying about the operation of the camp. What importance could one give, at this moment in time, to the armaments Gustloff produced or did not produce, or the food the prisoners ate or killed to eat or did not eat at all, or where they chose to shit or upon whom? All this minutiae were of no concern to him; his concern was the survival of Helmut vòn Schraeder and nothing else.

At such moments he was thankful that his mother was dead and there was nobody alive to concern him. The aunt who had raised him in Hamburg after his mother's death had gone up in the fire storm that swept the city after the Allied bombings; he had been fortunate in never having any woman make a claim on him for anything beyond the moment's pleasure. As for his father—he had never been sure about his feelings toward his father. As a child he had wept uncontrollably when he learned of his father's death; the heavy man with the rough tweed clothing who smelled of tobacco and brandy and shaving lotion who would toss him in the air and catch him, and kiss him, nuzzling his thick beard against his face. And when he was older, old enough to understand, and had learned that his father's death was a suicide, he could not recall his first reaction. He knew he felt it wrong for a general in the Kaiser's army to commit suicide, regardless of the reason. There had been the loss of the estates; he remembered vaguely driving away from them, his aunt holding his hand tightly, leaning back to watch them disappear, the stable the last thing he had seen before the trees and a curve in the road blocked them from view. But he had heard that there were debts, run up and owed to Jews; and there had been the persecution, he had also heard, by the Communists who ran the Weimar Government in the twenties, before Hitler. But still, should a general have succumbed to *any* amount of pressure, to the extent of surrendering to death before death had won with its own weapons? No!

Von Schraeder would feel a rare and unwanted prickling behind his eyes when these thoughts came; he would crush out his cigarette and wave a hand to dissipate the smoke, blinking rapidly. How did he really feel about his father? He told himself repeatedly he really didn't know. When the general had been found with a gun in his hand, a bullet in his brain, and an apology to his family on his desk, Helmut had been too young. But he remembered many things. He remembered the mustiness of the study, always a forbidden place to play, with the ancestral pictures on the wall and the huge fireplace lit only on important occasions, the patterned carpets, the furniture upholstered in thick velvet, shiny with age, the heavy drapes, his father's massive desk, the endless bookshelves, and the all-pervading odor of pipe tobacco. Why? *Why?* A general should be stronger. A *von Schraeder* should be stronger! The general should have been a survivor, as his son was determined to be!

And how could a father have deserted a small boy, a small helpless imaginative son, who needed him . . . ?

Von Schraeder shook his head, clearing it of the unpleasant recollections, and glanced at his desk calender. July 16, four days until the Valkyrie plan was to go into effect. And after that, one way or the other, all this would soon be memories: the camps, the war, the barracks, the entire business. A trip to Switzerland to collect from his numbered account, held in a name no one knew but him, and then —where? He suddenly realized he hadn't considered that phase at all as yet; it had always seemed too far in the future. But the decision would have to be made; the planning would have to be gone into. Assuming that Valkyrie were to be successful and a general amnesty granted—in itself a doubtful assumption—would he care to remain in Germany? No. Even with amnesty Germany was not the place he wanted to be. The country would take years to recover and rebuild, and would demand sacrifices during that period. Sacrifices were for people without money; he would not fall into that category. The United States? Probably not. Admittedly the life was easy in America, but the Jews, even though a tiny minority, seemed to run the place. South America? Again a possibility, but the weather, he had heard, was a bit unpleasant. Remain in Switzerland once he was there? Another possibility. He leaned back in his chair, fingering his cigarette holder, feeling expansive. With money, the possibilities were endless.

He smiled as he thought back on his conversation with Franz Schlossberg in the car that day, driving from Lublin to Weimar. Undoubtedly the good doctor had managed to convince himself by now that the conversation had never taken place at all, or if it had, that he must have completely misunderstood the colonel. It would be so like Schlossberg. They saw each other occasionally in the mess hall or in the canteen in the evenings, but on those occasions the doctor would turn his head resolutely, as if fearing he might be drawn into conversation. An idiot, von Schraeder would think indulgently, a man with a God-given talent in his fingers and cotton in his head.

Ah, well—very shortly he might have to remind the good doctor of their conversation, although in all honesty, he hoped not.

Four more days to Valkyrie.

Hitler's headquarters at Rastenburg in East Prussia, the famed *Wolfschantze*, or Wolf's Lair, was set in a thickly forested area within three concentric protected rings, each thoroughly defended by pillboxes, mine fields, electrified barbed-wire fences, and heavily armed and dedicated SS troops. To enter, a special pass was required, good for just one visit, and the visitor also had to pass the personal inspection of SS Oberfuehrer Rattenhuber, Himmler's chief of security for the area.

On the morning of July 20, Colonel Klaus von Stauffenberg, accompanied by his adjutant, Lieutenant Werner von Haeften, easily passed the three checkpoints and entered the main area, their papers quite in order. In addition to their passes, Field Marshal Keitel had informed the gates of the coming presence of the colonel, so no trouble had been expected, nor was any forthcoming.

In von Stauffenberg's briefcase, in addition to the report on the new *Volkgrenadier* divisions on which he was to speak to the conference in the early afternoon, there was a time bomb, carefully wrapped in a shirt. The mechanism of the bomb was simple; it was set off by breaking a small glass vial which would release acid to eat through a thin wire, releasing the firing pin against the percussion cap. The time required to complete this cycle was determined by the thickness of the wire. Today the wire was as thin as the makers of the bomb considered safe for the deliverer of the weapon. It was estimated it would take no more than ten minutes for the wire to eat through and the bomb explode.

As the colonel and Field Marshal Keitel left the field marshal's quarters to walk to the conference, Stauffenberg suddenly paused.

"Sir—"

"Well, what?" It was Keitel's usual bark.

"My belt—my cap—" Without another word Stauffenberg turned and hurried back to the anteroom of the field marshal's quarters. There he quickly opened his briefcase and activated the bomb by breaking the glass capsule. He was in the process of closing the briefcase when Keitel's angry bullying voice could be heard.

"*Stauffenberg!*"

"Coming, sir!"

He seized his cap and belt and hurried outside. Keitel, never known for his patience with subordinates at any time, was glaring at him.

"What have you been doing in there? We're going to be late! Idiot!"

"Yes, sir."

He caught up with the field marshal and marched with him across the area to the conference room. As they entered, he looked around and then took his seat, leaning down to place the briefcase on the floor between General Korten, Air Force Chief of Staff, and Colonel Brandt, Chief of Staff to the Chief of Operations, General Heusinger. Heusinger was speaking in a droning voice. Stauffenberg looked around. He had hoped the conference would take place in the underground rooms, where the effect of his intended explosion in the confined space would be greater; this room had ten windows and they were all open to catch a bit of air. Still, it was his hope that the conspirators had constructed a bomb with sufficient potency to overcome the lack of confinement.

He glanced surreptitiously at his wristwatch. Four minutes had elapsed since he had broken the glass vial. There were six minutes remaining. He wet his lips and wondered what would happen if for some reason he were stopped from leaving the room before the bomb went off, for there was no preventing its exploding now. And then he consoled himself with the thought that if he went up with the bomb, at least others would go with him, which would be worth it. Others including Keitel, the loud-mouth, as well as the target, the Fuehrer, sitting two seats down.

He listened a moment longer, and then while General Heusinger was in the midst of a long report on the breakthrough on the Russian front, Stauffenberg murmured something unintelligible in the form of an excuse to his unlistening neighbor, and came to his feet. Everyone was paying attention to Heusinger. Stauffenberg was out of the room in seconds.

Keitel, frowning blackly, looked around for the colonel; after all, Stauffenberg's report, sponsored by Keitel, was next on the agenda, and while Heusinger was long-winded, he wouldn't talk forever. Wondering where the colonel could have gotten to, Keitel slipped from the room and looked around. Stauffenberg was nowhere to be seen. The sergeant at the telephone switchboard said the colonel had just hurried from the building. Keitel fumed. He swore to himself he would have the colonel's shoulder patches for this bit of work! What was it now, for God's sake? If it was a matter of weak kidneys, there was a toilet in the conference-room area! He turned back to the conference room as Heusinger continued his report.

"The Russian is driving with strong forces west of the Duna toward the north. His spearheads are already southwest of Dunaburg. If our army group around Lake Peipus is not immediately withdrawn, a catastrophe—"

And the bomb went off.

July 20 passed as every other day had passed since von Schraeder's arrival at Buchenwald; the radio in the command barrack was tuned, as always, to the Berlin station that furnished classical music. Von Schraeder found himself staring at the speaker of the radio, willing it to interrupt the Brahms they were playing, and get on with the dire announcement. But the radio remained true to its classical commitments. At five-thirty in the afternoon, the last to leave, he turned the set off and walked down to his car, frowning. Valkyrie had been postponed, that much was evident. Or, very possibly, it had come off and the authorities were keeping it quiet until they could figure out what to do. That, of course, was a distinct possibility, and one that made him feel better. On the other hand, Gehrmann could have gotten the date wrong, which would not be surprising. He would call Gehrmann at the War Ministry in the morning and see what information he could obtain. It would have to be done with a certain amount of circumspection, and Gehrmann would be nervous as the devil, but this did not bother von Schraeder. He had to know, one way or the other.

He dined alone, read for a brief period, and then went up to bed. But sleep would not come; it was too close to the time he had to make his decision. At last he sat up, took out a book, and put the radio on, tuning it to some martial music being played, and prepared to read himself into sleepiness. And then, suddenly, he sat up, every nerve tingling. The music had been abruptly cut off, in mid-note it seemed, and in the silence that fell a hysterical voice suddenly broke.

Von Schraeder permitted himself a broad smile. They had done it. *They had actually done it.* It didn't automatically mean amnesty, or that he would not need his own plan, but at least now there was a chance! He bent closer to the radio, not wishing to raise the volume, and listened for the first time to the actual words. And then he felt the blood drain from his face. The voice was too, too familiar.

"*. . . if I speak to you today it is in order that you should hear my voice and should know that I am unhurt and well, and secondly you should know of a crime unparalleled in German history.*

"*A very small clique of ambitious, irresponsible, and, at the same time, senseless and stupid officers have concocted a plot to eliminate me, and with me, the staff of the High Command of the Wehrmacht.*

"*The bomb planted by Colonel Count Stauffenberg exploded two meters to the right of me. It seriously wounded a number of my true and loyal collaborators, one of whom has died. I, myself, am entirely unhurt, aside from some very minor scratches, bruises, and burns. I regard this as a confirmation of the task imposed upon me by Providence . . .*"

Von Schraeder stared at the floor, barely hearing the strident voice. So the plot to assassinate Hitler had failed, but then he had never had any great hopes for its success. Besides, even had the plan been successful, he doubted the Allies would have agreed to amnesty. It was the reason he had developed his own plan. The voice on the radio was continuing.

"*. . . the circle of these usurpers is very small and has nothing in common with the spirit of the German Wehrmacht and, above all, none with the German people. It is a gang of criminal elements which will be destroyed without mercy . . .*"

Von Schraeder leaned over and switched the radio off. For a long time he stared at the floor; then he came to his feet and padded over to his dispatch case. He unlocked it and took out a sealed envelope that had been prepared over a month before. He opened it, checked the contents carefully, and then reached for the telephone. It took several minutes before the operator at the camp switchboard answered; von Schraeder could only assume they were listening to the radio. He cleared his throat.

"Dr. Schlossberg in Ward Forty-six," he said into the telephone, and waited. When the ringing was finally answered, he said to the orderly at the other end, "This is Colonel von Schraeder. Tell Dr.

Schlossberg I'm sorry to wake him, but I'm afraid I'm coming down with something."

They sat in the small, sterile office of Dr. Schlossberg in Ward Forty-six, the colonel neat as always in his dapper uniform, the doctor with a laboratory coat over his pajamas."

". . . headache, vomiting. It's typhus, without a doubt," von Schraeder said, looking the picture of health. He waited for the doctor to speak, but the thin baldheaded man sat silent, watching the colonel with no expression at all on his face. Von Schraeder smiled; the shock he had felt on hearing Hitler's voice when he was supposedly dead was now completely gone. Valkyrie had always been problematical at best; now it was time to put his own plan into effect. It was why he had perfected it, gone to such troubles with it, made such complicated arrangements over it. He watched the doctor's face. "I expect this attack will be fatal."

"I'm sure," said the doctor, again with no expression. "And after you are dead?"

"I expect to be cremated together with my uniform and any effects I brought with me to the ward. I expect to be put into a burial sack and placed into the crematorium without any autopsy, since they seldom do autopsies on typhus victims—"

"Not seldom," Schlossberg said. "Never. It's the one disease we all respect around here."

"I meant never," von Schraeder said. "You may be sure I was quite informed on that point."

"I'm sure." The doctor closed his eyes a moment, as if resting them against the bright glare of the lights reflected from the tile walls, and then reopened them. "Of course, after Colonel von Schraeder is dead and cremated, someone will be born in his place."

"Exactly. It's the law of life."

"And who, exactly, will be born in the place of Colonel von Schraeder?"

Von Schraeder leaned forward, his eyes intent on the doctor's face.

"His name will be Benjamin Grossman. His papers are all here." He tapped the envelope he had brought with him. "Grossman is in Ward Forty-six for experimental work, under your jurisdiction. When your experiments on him are complete—that is, when your plastic surgery is completely healed—then Benjamin Grossman is to be transferred to Natzweiler Camp in the Vosges. And your part in the matter will be forgotten."

"Grossman?" The doctor stared. "You intend to take the identity of a *Jew?*"

"That is correct." Von Schraeder smiled.

"And be transferred to a camp as an *inmate?*"

"Exactly."

"Do you know what you are doing? You've seen how—" The doctor seemed to realize he had been on the verge of criticizing the SS treatment of prisoners. He changed his argument. "It will mean being circumcised, which can be extremely painful for an adult. And most of the prisoners—the Jews—speak Yiddish, and you don't. And —"

"I know everything it will mean," Von Schraeder said calmly. "Believe me, I've studied this plan for many months. I know it will mean being circumcised, and I know it is painful. It also means extensive work on my face, and I'm not looking forward to that. Or having my head shaved, or any of the rest of it. Although," he added, smiling, "after some of the barbers I've encountered in the camps, having my head shaved should be no great sacrifice—"

"Anyone who comes into Ward Forty-six as a patient has his head shaved in any event. It's a precaution against typhus."

"I suppose so." Von Schraeder shrugged. "And I shall have to starve myself, which is a pity, although I never allowed myself to get fat as a pig, like Mittendorf. And I shall either have to stop smoking, or discover how prisoners manage to get cigarettes, which I know they do, even without money."

"And what of your not speaking Yiddish? Have you considered that?"

"I believe," von Schraeder said evenly, "that I have considered every possible problem. In the part of Germany where I come from, the Jews never spoke Yiddish. They considered it—one of the few things they considered rightly—to be a bastard language fit for the Russians and the Poles, but far beneath the dignity of a German. And that's the kind of Jew Benjamin Grossman is. An upper-class German Jew." He swung his chair around to face the doctor squarely. "Well? What do you think?"

"Of the scheme?"

"No, Of my face."

Dr. Schlossberg nodded. Contrary to the colonel's idea, the doctor was really not surprised at all. He had long since come to the conclusion that it was his ability as a plastic surgeon that had accounted for his transfer to Buchenwald under von Schraeder's sponsorship. "Yes," he said slowly. "It is very possible. With no intent to insult you, Colonel, but merely speaking as a professional man, I may say that your face is remarkably without distinction. The features are small and quite regular. A slight change to the nose, the raising of an eyebrow, a small scar—nothing disturbing," he added quickly before von Schraeder could object, "merely character-indicating."

"What about the cheekbones?" von Schraeder asked curiously. They might have been discussing the proper selection of a uniform for a formal party.

"I do not believe it vital. Starvation alters a man's face in a remarkable fashion. Before you leave here, your cheekbones will naturally be far more prominent."

"Except, Doctor, I do not expect to continue starving forever," von Schraeder said dryly, "but I do expect to remain disguised forever."

"True. Odd that I should have overlooked that," the doctor said apologetically. "Still, I haven't done any serious plastic work for some time. However, it should be no problem." In an equally apologetic tone of voice he went on. "And what if, under the anesthetic, my knife should happen to slip? I mention this because I'm sure you've considered the possibility. You seem to have considered everything else," he added bitterly.

"Of course I considered it. Either Benjamin Grossman leaves Ward Forty-six to be transferred to Natzweiler, or sealed papers being held somewhere, by someone, will automatically be opened. Tell me," he went on in the same amused tone, "have you listened to your radio this evening?"

"No." The doctor was mystified by the question.

"Ah, well, you'll hear of it in the morning, if not sooner. There was a serious attempt on Hitler's life this afternoon; a bomb exploded at a conference. He wasn't scratched—can you imagine?—but all those involved will be rounded up. The purge of '34 will be a tea party in comparison. They will strangle colonels with picture wire;

they will drown generals in their own excrement. You should never have gotten involved . . ."

The doctor's face had gone white. Von Schraeder smiled and reached over, patting Schlossberg on the shoulder.

"But there is no need to discuss unpleasant alternatives, especially those that need never arise. What other questions do you have?"

The doctor stared down at the hands in his lap a few moments and spoke without looking up. "What of the nurses I will need to work with me in the surgery?"

"You will use orderlies and they will be prisoners. Who, I'm afraid, will not survive. That will also be your responsibility."

"I see." Now the doctor looked up. His expression was more curious than anything else. "And what assurance do I have, when the surgery is complete and the stitches have finally been taken out, that I, myself, will survive?"

Von Schraeder looked honestly surprised at the question.

"The best. My word. Besides, I will need you to arrange my transfer to Natzweiler, to the experimental work there. The papers are all complete; as an ex-*Sonderkommando* and as a volunteer—in quotes—at Ward Forty-six at Buchenwald, I shall go there as an orderly, and the papers will be signed by you. And at that stage, being a prisoner, I would scarcely be in any position to harm you." He sounded slightly hurt by the question. "Besides, what kind of a man do you think I am? If you help save my life, do you think I am so lacking in gratitude that I would allow you to be killed? That's a monstrous accusation."

The sheer inconsistency of the man almost took the doctor's breath away; he mentally shook his head. He means it, he thought; how very odd, but von Schraeder actually means it!

"As a matter of fact," the colonel went on, "among those papers are an introduction to a Major Gehrmann, who will introduce you to a group dedicated to saving people like you, if the necessity should arise. There is also a check made out to cash on a special Swiss account, a bank in Zurich, and signed with a signature they will recognize electronically. You will be well paid for your work, Doctor." And if Gehrmann is picked up and executed for his part in Valkyrie, can I help that? Although the check is honest enough.

Dr. Schlossberg shook his head. "You're a strange man, Colonel."

"Benjamin," von Schraeder said gently with a smile. "Benjamin

Grossman. A product of our times, is all, Doctor. Shall we get started?"

The death of Colonel Helmut von Schraeder caused small stir in the camp; he had not been there long enough to make friends, nor had he appeared to be the sort to make many friends in any event. In Berlin the news was also received with small concern, even by people who, like Willi Gehrmann, had known him for some time. There was too much to worry about at the moment, with the thorough investigation being conducted into the bombing plot, to be greatly concerned about a colonel who died of typhus in a camp hospital. Too many others of equal name and higher rank were being taken prisoner by the Gestapo and the SS and died in far more terrible fashion.

And five days later, when a bandaged Benjamin Grossman lay in pain in his moldy bed in Ward Forty-six, slowly starving on a liquid diet that consisted of a thin tasteless soup and nothing else, desperately wanting a cigarette and wondering, for the first time, if possibly his plan had been unnecessary and that he might have done better taking his chances with the Strasbourg Group, Dr. Schlossberg came by and sat down beside his bed.

"Maidanek fell to the Russians yesterday," he said softly. "You were right; the camp was captured almost intact." He wondered even as he spoke whatever had happened to the girl Sarah; had he known, he may or may not have been concerned. She had been stoned to death by the inmates of Field V the day she appeared there after von Schraeder's leaving. "The gas chambers and the ovens hadn't been touched; the burial pits were as they were. Oh, someone tried to burn the ovens and managed to destroy the wooden shed over them, but that was about all. Most of the prisoners were still there, and even six SS guards, and they were hung by the Russians on the spot. Mittendorf got away, of course, but six of the lesser men were caught."

There was a strange sound from the bandaged face on the stained pillow. Benjamin Grossman was chuckling.

Chapter 5

The boxcar stank with the combined smells of manure, human excrement, vomit, urine, and the sweat of the eighty-four men packed into it. By dint of his greater energy and strength, Grossman had managed a spot on the floor near the door, so that he could press his nose against the crack and get an occasional breath of the hot September air, although more often it was a choking blast of smoke from the engine ahead. How the others managed to survive in the depths of the car he neither knew nor cared; he had long felt that any concentration camp inmate truly dedicated to survival would survive; only the weak, he was convinced, actually perished.

He swayed with the jostling of the car, scarcely aware of the pressure of knees on his back, slightly lightheaded from hunger and the heat, and thought back on the moment he had first seen his new face in a mirror. Schlossberg had unwrapped the bandages carefully and then stood back, unable to hide his pleasure in his work. The shaven-headed man in the striped prisoner's pajama uniform that stared back at Grossman from the glass looked fearful, as if dreading the sight, and then slowly relaxed. It seemed unbelievable that he was looking at himself; Schlossberg had produced a miracle! True, he had always been fond of his old face; it had pleased women and that was important, still, his present face was not ugly except in the sense that all Jews were ugly. Schlossberg had given him a rather interesting nose, nothing at all like the huge hooked nose so characteristic of the cartoon Jew in the national press. And it was amazing the difference created by the changed eyebrow alignment, and the small insertion in his cheeks. And the scar was truly a work of genius, covering as it did most of the tiny stitches along the jaw. The only worry was his penis; he had heard that circumcision greatly reduced the pleasures of sex. He could only hope this was merely a rumor.

He shoved his head closer to the crack of the door, trying to get more air, scratching automatically at the bed sores he had developed in Ward Forty-six, and calculated they should be nearly halfway to the Natzweiler camp by now. And that was another brilliant part of his plan, the selection of Natzweiler. To begin with, it was neither a labor camp nor an extermination camp; it was a detention camp where a good deal of experimental work went on under Professor Hirt; and with his papers he was assured a safe and soft job as an orderly. For in addition to the strong letter in his folder signed with the authority of none other than the late Colonel Helmut von Schraeder, Dr. Schlossberg had spoken to Hirt on the phone, hinting at monetary reward from the prisoner Grossman, once the unpleasantness of the war was concluded.

But equally important with his treatment at the hands of Natzweiler personnel was the fact that he calculated the Allies should liberate Natzweiler in a month at the most, if not in mere weeks. And there he would be, with his new identity, an object of pity to the Allied troops, and with almost assured co-operation for a rapid visit to Switzerland and his money there. One thing was sure; now that Hitler had escaped the assassination plot, the war would go on for a long, long time. But Natzweiler—and Benjamin Grossman—would be out of it in short order.

There was a sudden jolt as the train began slowing down; then it crept awhile, its engine heaving, and finally braked to a stop. There was a rattle as the door was being opened, but after being released for a mere several inches, a bar was jammed behind it, limiting its aperture. But at least air could flow in a bit, and those inside who had been silent began to revive.

"Where are we?"

Grossman tried to get his bearings. "Frankfurt, I think."

A head pressed into the welcome air above him.

"Yes, it's Frankfurt. I used to live in Keisterbach; it's a suburb. We're in the freight yard." The man tried to twist his head to see better. "They're unhooking the engine."

"What! Why, for God's sake!"

"We'll worry about that later," another voice said, a deep voice, and with it a large, knotted hand gripped Ben's shoulder tightly, dragging him away from the opening with small effort. "Here! Let someone else get some air."

The man who had spoken, rather than taking the place he had cleared, pushed a small boy into the opening, holding him firmly by the arm to prevent his collapsing. In the shaft of early-morning daylight that slotted into the car, growing in intensity, Ben took one look at the face of the man who had pulled him from the door, and decided against objecting. This one, definitely, was a survivor! How had a man like this ever permitted the door crack to be usurped the night before when they had left Weimar? He looked at the pale face of the boy, breathing deeply, and then up to the face above him.

"Your son?"

"No. Does it make any difference?"

"Of course not."

"That's right," the man said flatly. The boy seemed to be reviving; the man dragged Grossman back by the shoulder a few more inches to give the boy room to sit on the floor next to the opening. As he bent over the boy his face came close to Ben's. It was a battered face, like that of a boxer, with fine hairline cracks and scars throughout. The sharp gray eyes studied the scar along Ben's jaw, then moved to look Ben in the eye.

"Ward Forty-six?"

For a second a chill ran through Ben Grossman; then he realized the tone had been sympathetic, and he knew he had been foolish to fear this man.

"Yes," he said simply. "Were you?"

There was a raucous laugh from someone in the rear.

"Brodsky? If Max Brodsky had been in Ward Forty-six, in two weeks he would have called it a health spa and charged admission!"

"That's the reason they transferred him," another voice said at Ben's side. "One more month in Buchenwald and Brodsky would have owned the camp. He was getting ready to charge the SS rent when they shipped him out."

Ben looked at the speaker. He was a small man with extraordinarily large luminous eyes that seemed to take up a major portion of his thin expressive face. His oversized pajama uniform hung on his emaciated frame in a manner almost humorous, like the garb of a clown or a stage comic. Little spikes of hair jutted from the top of his small head; he was smiling as he spoke, showing gaps where teeth had rotted out, making his clown-like appearance more evident.

"Wolf, shut up," Brodsky said without rancor. He checked the boy carefully and then looked down at Ben Grossman. Ward Forty-six, eh? He felt a sudden kinship with this blue-eyed, scarred man. In Ward Forty-six Brodsky had lost his best friend in the camp, and he somehow felt the man beside him might possibly have been sent him as a replacement. "Are you all right? Do you want to get back to the door?"

"No, I'm all right."

Brodsky nodded and raised his deep voice. "Let's have someone here from the rear!" His hand rested on Grossman's shoulder; somehow there was something companionable about the slight pressure. "All right! Let him through!"

There was a rough shifting of bodies and an old man was thrust to the front. Brodsky pulled the boy slightly to one side, still allowing him breathing space, and tucked the old man's head near the opening. The old man gasped in thankful relief and nestled on the floor, sniffing the fresh air like a dog at a rat hole. There was a restless shifting of bodies. Someone said querulously, "How much longer are we going to be kept here?"

As if in answer to his question, there was the sound of boots crunching on cinders and two SS officers appeared in the slot of light. Brodsky held up his hand for silence but few could see him. He raised his voice in a bellow.

"Shut up! Shut up!" And when his roar was met by startled silence he added more quietly, "Let's hear what they're saying."

The two officers on the track made no attempt to lower their voices, nor did they even glance at the column of anxious eyes staring at them from the narrow slit.

". . . evacuated," one was saying.

"What!"

"Natzweiler, I said. Evacuated."

"I heard what you said! When?"

"Two days ago." The speaker sounded bitter. "You'd think they would know these things before they send out a string of cars, wouldn't you? You would think at least they might check. Good God! Nancy was cleared out a week ago, they knew that, didn't they?" He stared at the line of boxcars as if they represented a personal affront to him and the papers in his hand. "Cars from six camps, some of them three days on the road, over eight hundred men, and what do we do with them?"

Inside the boxcar voices were breaking out in the darkness.

"What's going on? Who are you listening to? What are they saying? Anything about where we're going? Tell them to open the door more, we need air in here for God's sake—!"

They were answered by a variety of languages from those near the slot.

"Shut up! Keep quiet!" Ears replaced eyes at the slot to catch the words more clearly.

". . . good question. What *do* we do with this lot? Shoot them?"

"Without orders? I can imagine the result." The officer sounded disgusted.

The second officer shrugged. "Why not send them back where they came from?"

"Six camps in six different places? Still, that's what we ought to do." The bitterness had returned to the officer's voice. "Serve them right for not checking before they ship them out. They're the ones at fault, but they'd be sure to manage to blame us." There was a rustling of paper as the man consulted a list. "Here. We'll shift them to Celle. To the Bergen-Belsen camp. I'll get in touch with them and say those were the orders. They won't know the difference, things are so fouled up these days." The two men started to walk back down the track.

Grossman peered up at the shadowy figure of Brodsky between him and the door. "What was it? What did they say?"

Brodsky raised his voice so everyone in the car could hear.

"Two SS, apparently discussing where we're going. It seems we were headed for a place called Natzweiler, but Natzweiler was evacuated a few days ago. I guess the Allies are getting too close for our friends' comfort." There was a weak attempt at a cheer from someone, instantly put down by the man's neighbors.

Grossman felt as if he had been kicked in the stomach. This was certainly no part of his precious scheme! Why hadn't he considered the possibility that the camp might be evacuated before he reached there? Still, it didn't neccessarily mean that all was lost—

"What else did they say?"

"Something about a camp called Bergen-Belsen, near Celle."

Brodsky raised his voice. "Who knows anything about a camp called Bergen-Belsen?"

No one answered. Crouched in his little niche, Grossman felt himself getting physically ill. Bergen-Belsen! A *Krankenlager*—a sick camp! A camp where they send people to die. No gas chambers and the ovens are a joke. They bury their dead in huge pits and why not? There are no gas burns on them, no gunshot wounds, except for those the guards shoot for entertainment. The vast majority die of natural causes, like typhus or dysentery or starvation. Nothing for the SS to be ashamed of should the Allies uncover the pits. Bergen-Belsen! A hellhole of the worst sort, and I've sentenced myself to that! Idiot! Imbecile! Fool! Better the Strasbourg Group. Better even the chances of a war-crimes trial! Better *anything* than Belsenlager!

There was a sudden jar as a new engine was coupled onto the string of cars. There was a harsh rasp as the bar that had been allowing the slot to furnish at least a little air was suddenly withdrawn. The door slammed shut; then there was the sound of a spike being hammered into the hasp, locking them in. The cars began to move, gradually picking up speed until once more they were bumping and jostling about, and the stifling heat began to build up, together with the overpowering stench. Men began to faint, taking others down with them; those above took advantage of the additional room to sit on the fallen, crushing them with their weight. Grossman sensed rather than saw the large body of Max Brodsky braced against the side of the car, forming a shelter for him, the boy, and the old man against the pressure of the others in the car. He heard Brodsky's voice.

"We've come through other camps, we'll come through this one, too." There was grim promise in the deep voice. "Next year in Jerusalem . . ."

More likely next year in hell, Grossman thought. He closed his eyes and listened to the clack of the wheels over the rail joints. Bergen, they said. Ber-gen, Bel-sen, ber-gen, bel-sen, bergen, belsen, bergen belsen, bergen belsen, bergenbelsen, bergenbelsen, bergenbelsen bergenbelsenbergenbelsenbergenbelsen . . .

God!

They arrived in Celle in midafternoon. There was a hammering on the door, the same deafening clangor they had heard before, a muffled cry of *Zuruckbehalten! Zuruckbehalten!* from outside. The door was quickly run back. Those inside near the door fought to keep their balance, gulping the sweet air, staring blindly outside, made sightless by the sudden light, fighting the pressure from behind. The old man, dead many hours, tilted forward slowly into the door opening and toppled to the tracks. The chatter of a machine gun responded instantly, making the scrawny body jerk in almost life-like imitation. The guard who had fired the gun swept the muzzle upward, fanning it across the opening threateningly. An officer walked quickly down the line, calling out:

"*Heraus kommen! Heraus kommen! Langsam!* Slowly! Get down! Fall in line!"

They climbed down stiffly, those who were still alive, and lined up in ragged formation alongside the track, looking down the line and seeing other men climb down from similar cars. The last ones to reach the door of their particular car were ordered to go back and drag the dead bodies to the opening, where other prisoners were assigned to handle them. The bodies were directed to be taken across several tracks and piled up beside a fence that separated the freight yard from the town of Celle. From Grossman's car eighteen bodies were taken in addition to the old man; the boy, he saw, was among them. In the night someone had pushed the youngster to the rear to try for air at the small crack. Through the mesh of the fence several women and children stared at them expressionlessly; they might have been watching the unloading of a cattle car, or a circus.

The guards were walking up and down the line, their machine pistols at the ready, herding the men into files of two. Grossman was pushed up against Brodsky; he looked at him, seeing the man for the first time in proper light. Brodsky was tall, several inches taller than he was, and unlike most of the other prisoners he stood erect and did not stoop. His battered face was thinner than it had first appeared, and although Grossman guessed that the man was no more than thirty years old, the stubble of his beard was streaked with gray. His clothes hung on his shoulders as from a coat hanger, and the huge fists, when seen relaxed and hanging at his side, were large in size but that was all; they looked like bags of bones dangling from his wrists. But it was the eyes, now staring at the boy's body being added to the pile by the fence, that were most impressive. They were gray, set deep in the sunken squarish skull, seldom blinking, steady on whatever they were studying. At the moment they were filled with sadness.

A young lieutenant appeared at the door of the guard's van at the end of the train. He leaned over a short railing, raising a bullhorn to his mouth. His voice cracked as he began to speak, but firmed as he went along.

"You will be marched to the camp! Any outbreak will be instantly punished! You will march four abreast! Stragglers will be shot! Is it understood!" He made it a statement, not a question. "You will be marched to the camp! Any outbreak will be instantly punished! You will march four—"

His voice was suddenly drowned out in the deep baying of an air-raid siren, repeated over and over again in almost hysterical shrieks, as if the person operating it knew the warning was late and was trying to make up for its tardiness in volume. The prisoners stared at each other in alarm, and then cringed as the first bombs were dropped a mile or so away. The trackage there lifted itself in the air as if in slow motion, hesitated a moment, and then crumpled to earth, torn and twisted. The planes were approaching rapidly, low-flying fighters rigged with a few sticks of bombs each, coming in under the radar screen, taking the town by surprise. Their wings waggled as they dove, releasing the bombs. The guards swung their machine guns up and around, firing as rapidly as they could, and then ran for cover as the planes passed over with a deafening roar. The men in line wavered and then broke in panic, scattering, seeking the protection of the boxcars, some rolling frantically under them, others trying to scramble back inside. The guards in equal panic raked the running men with machine-gun fire, and then dove for protection themselves, clutching their guns to their chests, flinching at each explosion as the planes banked to return for a second strike. The air was filled with the *cruummmpppp! cruummmpppp! cruummmppp!* of the explosions. Boxcars lurched and then disintegrated, boards flying through the air, steel tortured, ripped; trucks were twisted from the tracks, upended, wheels spinning. A car with fuel went up with a loud *whooosh*, searing the men under it to coals. Bodies were tossed through the air. They looked like dolls thrown about by a spiteful child.

At the first explosion Grossman felt himself being propelled, half-pushed, half-dragged toward the far fence and the pile of corpses there. Brodsky was bent over, urging him on; a closer explosion half-threw the two men onto the pile. They rolled over the dead, wedging themselves between the bodies and the fence, half-stunned, looking at the continuing scene of destruction in horrored disbelief. Grossman found himself swept with fury, screaming curses. Didn't the airmen see the striped pajama uniforms? Didn't they know who they were bombing? Or didn't they care? Schlossberg was right; the Allies would bomb even their own if there were a few Germans there!

As suddenly as it had started the bombing ended and the planes were merely small specks in the afternoon sky. Behind them they left the twisted rails, the tortured earth, the burning cars, and the endless dead in every posture of ultimate surrender. The young officer appeared from beneath the guard's van, which miraculously had not been hit. He brushed off his knees and raised his bullhorn. Those guards not killed also appeared, their machine guns once more at the ready, their fingers trembling on the triggers. Despite the officer's attempted look of control, his voice was tinged with hysteria, amplified by the bullhorn.

"In line! In line! The first one who attempts to take advantage will be shot! Instantly! In line! In line! *Schnell! Schnell! Schnell! Schnell!*"

The survivors slowly brought themselves together, climbing over the shattered corpses, avoiding in dazed fashion the burning planks of the boxcars scattered about the yard, coming to stand dully beside the ripped track. Grossman looked about, shuddering. There were only about a hundred left of what had seemed to be almost a thousand when they had climbed down from the cars only moments before; the rest were lying where they had fallen, in every imaginable grotesque violation of bodily dignity. The officer walked nervously down the ragged line of men and then walked back to the head of the line. The guards stood well back, their guns trained on the line.

The bullhorn came up.

"March!"

It was evening and a pale listless moon was visible in the darkening sky when they arrived, trembling with fatigue. Camp One of the Bergen-Belsen complex looked like most of the other camps: wired-off compounds, each with its large compliment of wooden shacks scattered between pine trees, the ground flat and muddy, the watchtowers shoddy but well armed, the latrines represented by the open ditches back from the wire in each area. The marching men came into the compound under the plain sign "Bergen Lager" and came to a halt, catching their breath. Fourteen men had died on the march either from exhaustion or from being shot when pleading for a moment's rest.

Across the road from where the men stood, behind a separate wired-in area, a naked woman came from her shack, squatted obscenely over a ditch, relieved herself, wiped herself with her fingers, and then wiped her fingers in the mud, and walked back inside, making no attempt to cover herself. Grossman shuddered. He had never thought the day would come when he would have absolutely no sexual feeling at sight of a naked woman; but then, he told himself, these aren't women. These are animals and so they behave like animals.

The officer who had accompanied them from Celle, the young lieutenant, came from the command barrack with an SS major. The two stood talking, the major looking irritated by their discussion.

"We have no papers on them," the lieutenant said apologetically. "Everything was lost in the bombing."

The major shrugged, trying to sound philosophic about it.

"We'll sort them out in the morning," he said, although he felt more prisoners were an imposition on him. "In the meantime we'll put a few in each of the first thirty barracks in Area Three in Camp One. Those are the barracks with the highest mortality; there's plenty of room."

He called over an adjutant, spoke to him authoritatively for a few moments, and then disappeared into the command barrack, where he had been interrupted in the midst of an important card game. The adjutant barked orders; guards led the file of prisoners away, stopping at each barracks to shove three or four men inside.

In the gloom of the windowless room, Grossman could make out the curious eyes of the inmates lying on their tiered bunks, staring at the newcomers. Like cats in the dark, he thought, or rats—and suddenly received a vicious jab in the ribs. He turned in anger to face a Kapo, a prisoner who kept other prisoners in line and earned special privileges for doing so. A whip was curled threateningly in the Kapo's hand, the butt held ready for another jab. The Kapo was smiling coldly, his small eyes alive with delight that this prisoner apparently was one who could be provoked into asking for the business end of the lash, or even to being sent out to be shot.

"Climb, you Jew bastard! Up, you Jew turd! What do you want? An elevator to your suite? Top tier, Jew pig! Up! Up!"

Another vicious jab with the whip butt and Grossman felt a blinding fury sweep him. This was too much! To be pushed and insulted by another prisoner, a brute from some eastern country, a Russian, or a Pole, or a Lithuanian, to touch him like this? *Him?* There was a sudden painful grip of Brodsky's fingers biting through the thin uniform sleeve on one side. On the other, little Wolf was hissing at him through clenched teeth.

"Climb, dummy! Is this your first camp?"

Brodsky's grip tightened, almost paralyzing him with agony, bringing him back to his senses. He climbed, and Wolf and Brodsky followed. Below they left a disappointed Kapo.

At one time there had been straw mats on the hard planks; now there were only a few wisps of moldy straw, covered with a fine film of delousing powder. The previous inmate had vomited in his place and had not bothered, or had been too weak, to clean it up; it had hardened into a scaly lump that Grossman could feel as he lay down. He tried to roll as far from it as he could, but a sudden shove from the inmate on that side told him in the darkness that space was limited and not to be lightly infringed upon.

The total unfairness of it struck him. What was he doing here along with these stinking animals, lying on hardened vomit, faint with hunger, shaking from weariness? He was still a Junker, still an SS officer! This was ridiculous! In the morning he would go to the camp command and explain the situation. Schlossberg would back up his story, if it needed any backing up.

That was it! He would go to the command barrack in the morning, and there he would tell the whole story. If the guard or the Kapo wanted to know the reason for the visit to the command post, he would say there was a troublemaker in the barrack. That always got attention. And when he finally faced the proper authority he would tell his story. They might laugh behind his back, but they would never laugh to his face. Not to a colonel of the SS! And whether they laughed or not, the horrible nightmare would be over. He would take his chances of eventually getting to Switzerland without the Strasbourg Group if he had to. He'd even take his chances of being picked up and tried as a war criminal. He would take *any* chance! But he could no longer tolerate the monstrous life a concentration camp dealt out. Life in a camp was meant for animals, not for him. First thing in the morning . . .

It was a comforting thought, one that made him a trifle less wretched on the hard bed and eventually allowed him to drift off into a restless sleep.

He woke in the dark, just as the first strands of dawn were beginning to break through the air vents above the top tier, and he knew at once that the night before he had merely been deluding himself. Idiot! Go to the command post barrack and say he was an SS officer who had changed his identity? Who would believe a story as outlandish as that? And even if Schlossberg were so foolish as to back up the story, all that would happen would be they would both be in trouble. And if they believed him—an SS officer who avoided his duty by changing his appearance? And to that of a *Jew?* Let us not even think of the penalty for that!

Or—suddenly—far worse thought!

Suppose they really did pay enough attention to his story to check back? And they then discovered he had gone to Schlossberg *right after it was known there had been an attempt on Hitler's life?* A quick trip to the strangling post, wire cutting through his fingers as he tried to interpose them, but to no avail. A horrible death! No. He had doomed himself. There was no escape.

He rolled over to find Max Brodsky studying him with those deepset gray eyes. On the other side of Brodsky, Wolf snored peacefully. Max smiled at him.

"What's your name?"

My God, Grossman thought, hadn't he told the large man his name? In all those seeming weeks they had known each other, in all those seeming months since yesterday?

"Grossman," he said quietly. "Benjamin Grossman."

"From where?"

"Buchenwald." He suddenly understood. "Oh. Hamburg, originally. Hohelft, to be exact."

The deep voice was sympathetic. "Did you have anyone there—?"

He meant the bombing, of course, that had leveled Hamburg.

"An aunt. The others—" He had been about to say his father had died at Dachau and his mother at Ravensbrook, but he bit back the words. Why invent something he might not remember? Silence would give as good an answer. Actually, it was stupid to have mentioned his aunt, though it was true. How many Jewish women could still have been alive in Hamburg at the time of the bombing in August of 1943? He would have to be careful. "We called her aunt," he added quickly. "She wasn't a Jew."

Brodsky nodded. "I suppose in a way I was lucky—"

"Lucky?"

"If you want to call it luck. My people all died peacefully before the war."

"Where are you from?" To his surprise, Grossman found himself honestly curious.

"Originally? Lublin. A suburb of Lublin, actually. Maidanek. Do you know it?" A chill ran through Grossman but Brodsky did not notice. "I suppose not. It's a small place. I wonder what it's like now?"

"You didn't see it?"

"No. I went to Palestine before the war, to a kibbutz. Then, later, I joined the Mossad. It's an illegal group to bring Jews to Palestine. I was just back in Poland—in Kielce, actually, on my way to Lublin—when I was picked up. He shrugged and smiled. "Don't worry. I've been in the camps for five years. We'll survive." He jerked a thumb over his shoulder. "Look at him."

"Who's he?"

"His name is Wolf, Morris Wolf. He's from outside of Munich. He's been in the camps since 1936—eight years—and he's still alive. We'll survive, don't worry."

"I wonder . . ."

"Don't wonder." It almost sounded like an order. "We have to survive."

"Why?" His very asking was an indication of his misery.

"Because Palestine needs us, for one thing—"

"Palestine?"

Brodsky looked at him in the growing light. "Palestine! Someday we'll have our own nation there, our own country, and you and me and Wolf and all the rest have a lot of work to make that dream come true."

Palestine! Grossman thought. You, possibly, but certainly not me!

If either one of us survives this hellhole, that is. He became aware that Brodsky was speaking again.

"And there's another reason we have to survive."

"Why?"

"To make sure people never forget," Brodsky said flatly, and started to climb down as the shrill camp whistle blew to rouse them for the day.

Chapter 6

An Esthonian named Soli Yaganzys was the Kapo—the prisoner overseer—of Barracks Thirty-eight in Area Three of Camp One at Bergen-Belsen. The Germans had saved him from a terrible death at the hands of the Russians, for whom he had helped betray Esthonia. He might still have been working for them had he not been caught also working for the Germans.

With the Nazis in the early days of his tenure there, Yaganzys had done quite well, until his habit of killing the women he raped forced his employers to recommend a concentration camp for a correctional interlude. Dachau saw him as a prisoner, as did Sachsenhausen, but by the time he had experienced Gross-Rosen and Ohrdruf he had graduated to becoming a Kapo. And as a Kapo he was too valuable to be released.

Yaganzys hated Jews as much if not more than the SS. No one ever did know exactly why, unless it was because his ability to handle Jews in his early days as a Kapo—in the days when there were still more than a handful of Jews alive in the camps—had earned him his continued existence as a prisoner himself. But of all the Jews Yaganzys had encountered in all the camps he had frequented, he hated Morris Wolf the most. Wolf, Yaganzys learned, had been in the camps since 1936, and for a Jew to survive more than a year at the most struck Yaganzys as being criminal. Yet Wolf had survived almost eight years and continued to survive, and every day the little Jew lived was a personal affront to Soli Yaganzys.

The amazing thing about Morris Wolf was that he did not appear to be a survivor. He had never been particularly strong even before his experience in the camps; yet Morris Wolf continued to survive. True, he had wasted almost to a skeleton, but he continued to survive. Yaganzys made sure the worst tasks were assigned to Wolf, as well as those best calculated to sap the little strength the small man had; yet Wolf continued to survive. He survived because he had learned early in his camp experience that in order to survive one had to accept, and Wolf accepted. Or, rather, Wolf had always accepted, but even acceptance has its limits.

In November, when they had been in Barracks Thirty-eight under the control of Yaganzys approximately two months, Wolf revolted. He pretended not to hear an order from Yaganzys. He knew his refusal was suicidal, but after eight years Morris Wolf had decided he had been wasting his time in surviving. Death, after all, could scarcely be worse than survival under Yaganzys. And so he refused an order by pretending not to hear it.

It was, of course, the excuse the Kapo needed and he did not hesitate to use it. Making sure everyone in the barracks was paying close attention, he dragged Wolf from his bunk and stood him in the middle of the room. His whip was curled in his hand. The other prisoners stood back, watching fearfully. Yaganzys smiled at Wolf.

"Jew turd! I told you to bring the soup tonight. If you had done it when I first told you to, you would have had help. Now you will do it alone." He looked around. "You will eat when this Jew shit brings your soup, not before." He looked back at Wolf, his hand stroking the leather of the curled strap sensuously. "You will do it now!"

Wolf looked back at him, looked through him, did not hear or see him.

"Possibly this will help you to pay attention," Yaganzys said, and stepped back, allowing the whip to uncurl itself on the floor behind him like an obedient snake. Then, with all his force and with the skill that had come from much practice, he brought the lash over his head and sent it flying at Wolf. The knout wrapped itself around Wolf's head; blood spurted as the lash curled across the cheek, cutting the flesh to the bone, crushing the nose, the final tip of the strap flicking out one of Wolf's eyes as one might flip a seed from a grape. Yaganzys made a practice motion with his thick wrist; the whip obediently unwrapped itself. Wolf still stood, the blood pouring from his face, his cheek flapping down, the blood choking him as it ran past his rigid lips into his throat; but he did not fall. Yaganzys brought the whip back for a second strike, determined to kill the little Jew, now and once and for all. And then Brodsky was upon him, tearing the whip from his hand, wrapping the thin rawhide about Yaganzys' throat, pulling it taut with all his strength.

The prisoners stood and stared. Yaganzys bellowed and brought his hands up to free himself. Brodsky panted in his effort to maintain his grip, to strangle this monster, but Soli Yaganzys was far stronger. And then Ben Grossman came to Brodsky's aid, fed by his hatred for the Kapo; and then the other prisoners came in a pack and that was the end of Soli Yaganzys. In moments he lay stretched on the floor, his tongue protruding blackly from his mouth, the whip strap buried deep in his throat like the coils of an attacking snake, his dead eyes staring up at them in profound surprise.

The prisoners fell back, appalled by the action they had taken, staring wildly at Grossman and Brodsky, their eyes demanding the two get them out of the terrible dilemma in which the two had thrust them. In the excitement they had forgotten Wolf, but he still stood, his one eye staring down at the corpse of his enemy. Then he fell.

There was a man named Pincus in the barrack, a Jew from Posnan who had been a pharmacist in life before the war. He knelt beside Wolf, tearing off his shirt, pushing the torn cheek into an approximation of its proper position and wrapping it as tightly and as best he could with the shirt. He looked up.

"He has to go to the hospital," Brodsky said briefly, taking command. "Tell them he fell from his bunk. His head hit the water bucket." He looked down at the corpse on the floor as Pincus and another man lifted the unconscious Wolf and carried him out. "Under the floor boards with this one."

Under the floor boards was the locker room of the inmates. It was here they hid things they stole and often lost sleep worrying that the things would be re-stolen. It was here that prisoners fortunate enough to have friends were hidden when it was known their next assignment was the gas chamber. It was here dead rats killed during the night were flung by those too lazy to carry them outside. They lifted the floor boards and dug a grave for Yaganzys, scattering the dirt made excess by his bulk as far as they could fling it under the floor; and they buried his whip beside him.

That night, after midnight, Brodsky was wakened by a sound. Someone had lifted the floor boards again, and in the darkness he could see a ring of bodies around the opening. And then came the other sounds and he knew they had regretted their wastefulness and had dug Yaganzys up again and were sharing his flesh. He shuddered and put his head down again, hoping at least they would bury the remains and put the floor boards properly back in place.

The following day they were told their Kapo had apparently escaped, which did not seem to bother the officials of the camp. A new man was assigned who was little different than Yaganzys.

At Bergen-Belsen the sick died quickly; those who were well enough to do a day's work at the Herman Goering Werke factory in Braunsweig, or to work in Celle, died more slowly. To Benjamin Grossman the camp was all the hell he had known it would be. Each day seemed to bring him closer and closer to the end of his endurance.

He lay on his straw mat as winter came, clutching his thin blanket to him, and tried not to think of the next day. But the routine of each squalid ghastly day had burned itself into his mind too deeply not to repeat itself endlessly in his thoughts. Up at six. A half-hour to straighten the mat, fold the blanket, help carry those who died in the night outside. The burial *Sonderkommandos* would take them to the pits later. Then time to relieve himself at the ditch, shivering uncontrollably as he crouched with the others. Clean oneself as best one could, using snow rather than stand in line at the one faucet. Dry oneself on a jacket sleeve. Then eat a breakfast of one slice of bread and a half-pint of so-called coffee. Then march off to roll call. If the guards were in a playful mood, push-ups in the freezing mud and filth. Then the dash to the labor-assignment area to be crammed with others into the trucks. And off to the steel mill in Braunsweig for a hard day's work.

The mill, at least, was warm, but not the freezing cold of the roll-call area at night. Standing for hours, bumping one foot against the other to keep the circulation going while the names were droned out. And more hours if someone had been so inconsiderate as to die somewhere without advising the authorities. It was almost beyond endurance! Maintaining life on one slice of bread and another cup of thin soup at night. Fortunately, Max Brodsky, with his wits and experience, sometimes managed to scrounge extra rations. He did sewing work for some of the SS guards, or fashioned souvenirs for them from odds and ends in exchange for food. Brodsky always shared with his friends, but principally with Ben. Otherwise he would never have made it.

On those nights when he could pry his mind from the horror of his daily existence, Ben Grossman would feel his ribs, knowing they were getting more prominent. He would run his finger along the curve of his nose, sure it was becoming more and more hooked as the flesh fell away from the bone. He thought of all the food he had wasted in his life. Juicy steaks and rare, half-eaten. Bread broken and even buttered before being abandoned. Thick puddings left untouched, salads overlooked, rich desserts barely tasted. Cigarettes no longer interested him; he wondered at his previous addiction. Anything that could not be chewed, savored, and swallowed was beyond the range of his imagination. He seldom thought of women, or if he did he pictured them only as serving wenches, bringing piles of steaming potatoes to the table, flushed with gravy, or fragrant schnitzels with glistening eggs on top. At times like this he was certain he would not live long. A person could starve just so long and then he had to die. It made no difference how determined a person was to survive. It was ridiculous to suppose otherwise.

Spring came suddenly to Celle and the *Belsenlager*. The snow simply disappeared one day, swept away by the chill rain that came to take its place. The camp was a mire; the rain came in sheets, flooding the ditches, floating the winter's collection of excrement in odorous layers deposited throughout the camp. Men walked barefoot, tucking their thin sandals into their blouses, catching the rain water in cans for drinking; and often coughing their lungs away as they lay in their soaked clothes in their tiers at night. The bread turned moldy; the morning coffee and the nightly soup tasted of the dirty water from which they were brewed.

Rumors flooded the camp, tinged with enough truth to be devastatingly frightening: the Allies had suffered a major defeat the November past at a place called the Bulge and were withdrawing from France as quickly as possible without suffering a total rout; the Russians had been stalled along the Vistula and outside the gates of Warsaw, and now that winter had finally passed, the Panzer divisions were regrouped and prepared to drive the Asiatic hordes to Stalingrad again and beyond. It was a period when Max Brodsky, a bean pole of a man now, needed all his faith not to lose hope. For Ben Grossman it was the depths of despair.

He looked little more than a skeleton now. Even his small ears, once so neatly laid against his head, now seemed to stand away from his tiny skull, almost useless appendages, since he seldom heard or paid attention to what was said to him. He no longer walked erect, but stooped like an old man, and his teeth hurt when he bit into his morning slice of bread, so that he would mouth it, soaking it in saliva, and painfully swallow the mush that resulted. For weeks he had been without a labor assignment. He was totally useless at the mill. His hands shook constantly, and at times he would pause in his shuffle through the accumulated filth of the yard and stop to talk to the corpses laid out awaiting the burial detail. He would mumble to them of his precious plan and how it would have worked had he not been cursed somewhere in life; and then he would listen for an answer from his lifeless audience.

One day Max Brodsky was reassigned from the labor pool, this time to a small factory in Celle that manufactured kitchenware—pots and pans—from unused shell casings. He worked there a week, sawing the bases off the shells and feeding them into presses, before he suddenly realized the opportunity that had presented itself to him. In earlier days Max Brodsky would have seen that opportunity at once.

He had guessed early on that the factory was probably owned in large part by the top SS in the camp, if not by most of the SS there on shares, but it was only after a week that he realized how illegal the use of needed shell casings must be. For several days he pondered his information, wondering exactly how best to take advantage of it; then, knowing no other means and also aware of the risk he was taking, he approached a guard for whom he had done sewing.

"I work in Celle," he began.

The guard regarded him with a thoughtful frown. "I know."

"Where I work, in Celle, we make pots and pans . . ."

"I know."

"From shell casings . . ."

"So?"

"From new shell casings. Not used."

"So?" The guard's frown became dangerous. "What are you getting at?"

Max Brodsky knew he had to take the chance.

"There must be someone in this camp," he said quickly, before he lost his nerve, "some officer, some official, who doesn't know about this. Someone in authority, who knows shell casings are needed for the war—" He saw the look in the guard's eye and added quickly, "When the war is over, there will be inquiries, responsibility for the killing of prisoners, or for torture . . ."

The guard considered him for a long, long time, and then tried to smile.

"Has anyone tried to murder you, Brodsky? You look healthy enough to me. Have I ever tortured you? Or tried to kill you? All I ever did was to give you a few tins of food from time to time. And— like an idiot—get you reassigned to Celle. Was that bad?"

"No."

"Then, what do you want?"

Victory! "I want to be assigned to the Labor-Assignment Office," Max said quickly. "Is that so much?"

The guard shook his head almost admiringly.

"Brodsky, how have you lived so long? Although," he added, "knowing you, that's a stupid question. You're the living proof that what the Fuehrer said of you Jews was the truth. You'd have the teeth from a chicken!"

"Well?"

"I'll have to go through channels . . ."

Five days later Max Brodsky received his new assignment, and the very following day Benjamin Grossman, scarcely aware of what was happening to him or where Brodsky was taking him, was put to the task of stirring the soup in one of the cookhouses in Camp One. It was no great position, and the prisoner-cook, out of pity, often had to interrupt his work and come to put his hand over the skinny fingers of his helper and move the large ladle through the thin mixture, but the cookhouse was warm and protected against the rain, and when one had the strength one could also dip into the soup and taste it. There were even the vegetable tops and the bones, after everything seemingly had been boiled out of them, to stow in one's blouse and secretly chew when unobserved. Or even to share, once one began to gain one's strength.

Ben's hands stopped shaking, although he seemed to have been bent into a permanent stoop. His ears even seemed to be approaching his head again, although he would have been the first to acknowledge this as a physiological impossibility; but his teeth remained loose and painful for a long time, and he had to have Max's help to crawl into his bunk at night. But he was once again beginning to believe in eventual survival, which Max felt was a hopeful sign.

It was a short-lived triumph.

A new batch of prisoners arrived one day from a camp called Neuengamme, and of those assigned to Max and Ben's barrack was a certain Anatole Yashinko, a *musselman*—the lowest of the low in the camps—who bragged loudly in poor German of how he had outsmarted the delousing squad.

"That *dreck* is not for me," said Yeshinko, his voice throbbing with admiration for his own brilliance. "For the others, maybe, but not for Anatole Yashinko. That stinking powder? Who knows what the bastards may put into it? And if I'm going to scratch, at least I want to know what I'm scratching for. Not because some idiot pours that stinking powder on me!"

"So sleep outside!"

Willing and eager hands opened the door while other hands shoved the man out into the rain and held the door against his return. For a while he pounded as softly as he could, not wishing to cry out and make any disturbance that would bring the guards and their wrath upon him; then at last the pounding ceased and eventually the inmates of Barrack Thirty-eight returned to their tiers. Moments later there was the sudden chatter of a machine gun, and in the morning the brilliant Anatole Yashinko was found within the forbidden perimeter near the wire, where he had wandered in the dark. Two prisoners were assigned to take the body to the burial pit; they held him carefully by the sleeves, dragging him all the way, shoving him into the pit with their feet, and then wiping their fingers furiously in the mud to clean them.

After a week, however, everyone had forgotten the unfortunate Russian and his distaste for delousing. When, in fact, ten days after Yashinko had died, Ben Grossman, working over a pot of thin soup, suddenly felt a chill and the beginnings of a headache, he assumed it was probably the fumes from the miserable concoction he was preparing, and only hoped he would not be up all night with loose bowels. But when, only minutes later, the chill disappeared to be replaced by a sudden flush of unbearable heat and the beginnings of dizziness, he had a cold premonition that Anatole Yashinko had left his mark. He was sure he had typhus.

The prisoner-cook excused him and he went back to his wooden tier, once again freezing, and tried to draw a bit of warmth from his blanket, only to throw it off and try to get some respite from the heat the next moment. After that he hung his head over the edge of the tier and vomited up the little he had in his stomach, and then tried to bring up all the imaginary foods he had stuffed himself with in his dreams for so long, but a slight trickle of bile was all he could produce. He lay back and laughed. It was really comical when one thought about it. He had died once from typhus in Ward Forty-six and been cremated; now it appeared he was about to die again, again from typhus, only this time they would bury him in one of the large pits. He wondered if he were ever to be reincarnated and come back a third time, so to speak, if he would again die of typhus. That would really be funny; the ultimate joke. Eight long months he had been at Bergen-Belsen, and now he was about to die. Why hadn't he died at once, before the humiliations, the pains, the suffering? Obviously because it wouldn't have been as funny as it was now.

He was still laughing when Max and the others came in from evening roll call and found him.

The wards in the prisoners' hospital were attended to by a few German doctors as well as by prisoners who had had some medical experience in their prior lives. Ben Grossman was assigned a cot whose previous occupant had starved to death; he lay on the filthy sheets and stared at the ceiling, too weary of life even to think. And woke from a fevered sleep to find Max Brodsky sitting next to him, holding a cup out to him. He brought it to his lips and tasted it. It was soup, good, rich, thick delicious soup. He drank it eagerly and immediately gagged; his trembling hands tried to hold the cup steady as he vomited into it, but much of the hot vomit splashed onto the bed. Max dumped the cup into the pail at the foot of the cot and frowned at his own stupidity.

"It's too rich. You must take a sip, just a sip, next time."

He took a dirty sheet from the adjoining bed and began to wipe up the mess. Ben stared at him, his eyes bright with fever.

"What . . . are you doing . . . here?" His throat felt as if a hot hand were pressing on it, making each word a painful rasp, but he felt he had to know. He dropped his voice automatically to the standard camp whisper although the other three beds in the small ward were empty. "And the . . . the soup . . . ?"

Brodsky shrugged elaborately. "I help make the assignments, so for a few days I'll be a hospital orderly. The doctors don't argue, any help they can get, they're happy to take."

"But . . . the . . . soup . . . ?"

"It's from the SS stores. Mendelsohn from our barracks is the new storekeeper there. I got him the assignment yesterday. Wait—I'll get some more."

"A waste . . ." Grossman wet his lips and tried not to think of the lovely taste of the soup for those precious few seconds he had been able to keep it down, before it had come up. "A . . . waste. I'll never . . . leave here. . . ."

"Why not?" Brodsky said cheerfully. "I'll admit it isn't Mount Scopus Hospital, but you'll still get well." He tried to smile encouragingly. "You have to. We need you in Palestine."

Brodsky and his Palestine again. Every day more and more about Zionism and Palestine! But it made no difference anymore. Nothing made any difference anymore. He wasn't going to Palestine; he wasn't even going to Switzerland. He was going to the burial pits, to lay on the dead and have more dead lie on him in turn. Stacks and stacks of dead and he would be somewhere in the middle. . . . He closed his eyes and let the dizziness sweep him.

"Here—"

He felt another cup pressed to his lips, the same delicious aroma in his nostrils, and then the cup was withdrawn after only a sip, but this time he couldn't even swallow. The soup dribbled from the corner of his mouth. He lay there and began to cry.

"Maybe later," Max said with an encouragement he did not feel and then paused. From outside the hospital there was the sound of a distant cry, a swelling sound of many voices, a frightening sound. Max frowned. He put the cup on the floor and went to the window, staring down. Ben's anxious tear-filled eyes followed him.

"What . . . ? What . . . ?"

"I don't know. I don't see anyone." Suddenly Max's eyes widened in disbelief. "I wonder! No . . . !"

A military car was approaching the hospital through the mud from the direction of Camp Two, driving slowly past the lake. In the front seat a soldier in an unfamiliar uniform was bellowing something unintelligible through a bullhorn. The car disappeared around the far side of the hospital, circled the building, and started back toward Camp Two. As it came to their side of the building the clipped words in schoolboy German were suddenly clearly heard, echoing on the air, fading and strengthening as the soldier turned his head.

"Be calm. Be calm. You are liberated. We are the British Army. You are all very ill and infectious. Quarantine will be necessary. Be calm. Be calm. You are liberated. We are the British Army. You are all very ill and infectious. Quarantine will be necessary. Be calm. Be calm. You are—"

The voice echo died in the distance as the car passed the lake and disappeared once again into Camp Two. Max Brodsky turned from the window, tears streaming uncontrollably down his seamed cheeks, a stunned look of hope, of disbelief, of joy begging to believe, sweeping across his young-old worn battered face.

"Did you hear? Did you hear?"

"What . . . ?"

"We're free. It's the British Army! They're here. We're free." He stared about the room as if he could see through the walls to the fields and roads and endless spaces that surrounded the camp, and then back to the bed where his friend lay. "It's over, Ben. We're free. We did it." He suddenly really realized the truth. He raised his eyes. "We're free! We did it! We did it! Oh, God, thank you, we're free!"

Benjamin Grossman felt his heart contract. He closed his eyes, feeling the tears start again under the lids. Then the trembling

began. No! He would not go to the pits! He would live! There would
be proper medicine, proper care.

He would survive!

But then, that had been the object of his plan all along, hadn't it?

Chapter 7

On May 21, 1945, thirty-six days after liberation and twelve days
after the German unconditional surrender that finally put an end to
the war, the British burned the three camps that had constituted the
monstrosity known as Bergen-Belsen. The flamethrowers licked at
the ugly wooden buildings a few moments and then they caught fire,
flaming quickly into ash. The soldiers wielding the tubular torches
expected some greater reaction from those watching—a cheer, perhaps, cries of delight, of vengeance, something, anything—but the
inmates merely stood back and stared dully, still stunned by the
enormity of their terrible experience, and by the deaths that continued to mount in the thirty-two casualty clearing stations established
by the British. It had taken those thirty-six days for the three camps
to be cleared and for the survivors to be housed in the former German Army quarters a mile away; over three hundred men, women,
and children had continued to die each day during that period. Starvation had advanced too far for many; they could not tolerate food,
and so they died. And typhus had continued to take its toll of the
weakened inmates despite the best efforts of the dedicated British
doctors, and so they died. And many had waited just for the day of
liberation, and now they had nothing left to wait for. And so they
died.

Morris Wolf was keeping a list.

Morris Wolf had come back from the hospital and the dead; he had located Brodsky and Grossman in the former German Army headquarters and had moved in with them, being greeted with great enthusiasm by Max Brodsky.

His list began when Hans Frank, the ex-governor general of Poland, appointed to that position by the leaders of the Third Reich, was picked up in a routine sweep that netted the 30th Infantry Division of the American Seventh Army several thousand prisoners at Berchtesgaden. That night Frank, the "Hangman of Poland," brought attention to himself by attempting suicide; otherwise he might well have been released as most of the others were once the war ended a few days later. Wolf, scribbling the name and date at the head of a sheet of paper and posting it on the wall next to his cot, claimed that Hans Frank had been in Poland too long; he had begun to act like a Pole.

His list continued as the days passed: Seyss-Inquart, the Austrian quisling, May 7; Hermann Goering, number two man in Nazi Germany, May 9; Ernst Kaltenbrunner, successor to Heydrich as head of the SD, the Security Service, May 15; Robert Lay, in charge of labor recruitment, May 16; Albert Rosenberg, the so-called theoritician of the Nazi Party, May 19 . . .

The prize, of course, especially to the inmates of the camps, was Heinrich Himmler, the head of the SS. Himmler had shaved off his mustache, adopted a black eye patch, and furnished himself with false papers in the name of one Heinrich Hitzinger, somehow imagining this would constitute a valid disguise. In the crowd of ex-prisoners of war, discharged soldiers, foreign workers, and refugees that pressed across the bridge spanning the Oste River at Meinstadt on May 21, only Himmler stopped at the control point to demonstrate his suspiciously new identity card; most of the others had no papers and simply crossed the bridge unimpeded. Himmler had also made the rather simplistic mistake of forging his new identity as a member of the Secret Military Police, apparently unaware that all members of that organization were being arrested. As Max Brodsky gleefully watched Wolf add the name to his list, he remarked loftily that Himmler had apparently been in Germany too long; he had begun acting like a German. It was, however, a short-lived joke; there was shocked silence the following day when it became known that Himmler had managed to commit suicide and thus escape what all had hoped would be a more fitting justice.

Wolf's list went on: Julius Streicher, Jew-baiter and pornographer,

publisher of the official Nazi newspaper, May 23; Joachim von Rib-
bentrop, Foreign Minister for the Third Reich, June 4; Baldur von
Schirach, head of the Hitler Youth, June 5 . . .

The interrogation waiting room was stuffy; the small fan droning
listlessly in one corner seemed only to shift the hot air from one part
of the small room to another. Benjamin Grossman, patiently waiting
his turn, wondered how much personal history he should invent.
One could never be sure how much information these investigators
might have unearthed in other camps, or how thoroughly they might
correlate the information they gathered. He should have considered
the possibility of being questioned in depth about his background
during the investigation he knew all prisoners were undergoing, but
he was still not fully recovered from his illness and he wasn't thinking as clearly or as quickly as he once had. Not, he admitted to himself sourly, that he had been thinking so clearly when he undertook
the identity of a Jew!

Still, there were no records; they had gone up in smoke when the
train had been bombed at Celle. Besides, the others who had gone
through the interrogation had assured him the investigators were not
interested in the prisoners themselves; they were looking for
witnesses, for facts, for statements, for hard evidence against those of
the SS they intended to try for war crimes, and Benjamin Grossman
knew what he was going to say in this regard.

He was very thin, finally beginning to walk a bit more erect, but
still slouching slightly; and there were lines in his face that had not
been there before and would never go away again. His hair was beginning to grow in again, and he was slowly getting accustomed to
the strange face that stared at him curiously from the mirror each
morning as he shaved. The new clothing issued by the British authorities, either from captured SS supplies or when necessary from their
own QM stocks, felt stiff and uncomfortable in the summer heat,
and for a moment Grossman wished he had worn his soft, ragged
camp pajama uniform, or at least the blouse, but for the interview he
felt it more appropriate to be better clad. And he really did appreciate the new shoes, even though they were heavy.

He heard his name called and rose slowly, shuffling into the next
room, guided by a young corporal. He sat where the soldier indicated
and stared wordlessly across the desk at the thin-lipped colonel who

was returning his look with no expression at all on his slightly horse-like face. A small plaque on the desk identified his interviewer as a Colonel Manley-Jones. The colonel had a hairline mustache which he stroked constantly, sensuously, as he asked his questions. It almost looked like a form of masturbation, Grossman thought, and found himself wondering what happened when the mustache climaxed. The colonel looked down at a paper on his desk and looked up again.

"Benjamin Grossman?"

"Yes." The colonel frowned and waited expectantly. Grossman finally understood. He added evenly, "Sir."

"Yes," the colonel said, and studied the paper, his thumbnail going back and forth rhythmically across the short hairs on his lip. "Your papers were destroyed in the bombing of a prisoner train in Celle last fall, I understand." The colonel's cold eyes stared across the desk; he managed to make it sound as if the prisoners were somehow at fault.

"Yes, sir."

"We are familiar with the incident." And bored with it, his tone seemed to imply. The colonel abandoned his mustache long enough to shuffle some papers; he located the one he wanted and went back to his mustache, no longer considering Grossman but studying this new document instead. "Do you have a family?" He spoke a stilted but correct German.

"No." Enough of "sirs." To hell with the bastard, Grossman thought. And let us hope we won't have to start inventing relatives who died in other camps or in ghettos, because this colonel looks just prick enough to follow up and disprove anything we said. Still, if there wasn't a Grossman in every camp in Europe, he'd be very surprised.

But Colonel Manley-Jones was not at all interested in either Benjamin Grossman or his family; it was a question on his list that had to be asked, but there was nothing in his instructions that specifically said he had to pay any attention to the answers. At first he had listened to all the tragic stories these people managed to invent, but in the end it became quite boring. Before he had come to the camp, the colonel had supposed a bit of sympathy for them might have been in order, but that sympathy had long since dissipated into an almost active dislike for them. Oh, he supposed some of them had suffered a bit in the camps; but when you came right down to it, they were also a pretty scruffy, unattractive bunch. Guarding them could hardly have been a pleasure, and almost certainly was bound to have led to occasional excesses. Any memory of the camp as the colonel had first seen it, with its skeletal inmates gripping the fence wire for support and silently staring at him with anguished eyes, or the piles of corpses covered with flies outside each barrack or lying about haphazardly where they had fallen and died, had faded once the camp itself had disappeared in smoke and flame. The bulldozers that had filled in the huge burial pits and covered them over had buried the colonel's memory with the dead. Now the prisoners—for the colonel still thought of them as prisoners—were properly fed, probably better than they had ever been fed even before the war, and undoubtedly better clothed, as well. All the colonel wanted from this unprepossessing bunch was information he had been detailed to obtain for the coming war-crimes trials. And those trials were another thing—also undoubtedly an exaggeration, the colonel thought. It was true, he supposed, that there may have been a few sour apples among the accused captured Germans—after all, you can't pick and choose your personnel in wartime—but many of them had also been officers in the regular army, the Wehrmacht, dammit! You couldn't convince Colonel Manley-Jones that very many career officers in any army in the world—excepting the Russians, of course—would behave like that. He stared at Grossman, not pleased by what he saw, and got on with the distasteful job.

"Other than Bergen-Belsen, what camps were you in?"

"I was transferred here from Buchenwald—" Grossman waited to hear the colonel say there never had been a prisoner at Buchenwald named Benjamin Grossman, and then decided he was simply overtired. It was evident the colonel was asking his questions by rote.

"Was that the only other camp you were in?"

"No. I was in Maidanek."

"Maidanek?" The colonel moved papers, bringing a new one to the top. "When you were at Maidanek, who was in charge?"

This was what Grossman had been waiting for.

"A Commandant Mittendorf," he said evenly. "A vicious, miserable, perverted son of a bitch. When you catch the bastard—"

"The Russians have a full dossier on Mittendorf, I'm sure," the colonel said, interrupting. "He's their problem if they catch him. I'm

only interested in war criminals now in the Allied areas. For example
—" He consulted his papers. "There was a Colonel von Schraeder of
the SS at Maidanek, who was transferred to Buchenwald. That
makes him our problem. A Colonel Helmut von Schraeder. What
can you tell me about him?"

Grossman picked his words carefully. "Von Schraeder was the as-
sistant commandant at Maidanek, yes, and he was transferred to
Buchenwald after I was. But he's dead. He died at the camp there.
At Buchenwald."

"We've heard that as a rumor, but we want any further data we
can get. We have a feeling," the colonel said with what passed as
humor for him, "that more SS died than there were bodies."

"Von Schraeder died," Grossman said with all the conviction he
could marshal. "I know that for a positive fact. I should; I was the
one who had to sew him into the burial sack and help cart him to
the crematorium. He died of typhus in Ward Forty-six, and I
watched him burn. With pleasure." The conviction in his voice was
not all acting; he had lived with the thought so long it had almost
become truth to him.

"I see." The colonel made a note, muttering under his breath.
"Von Schraeder's death confirmed by prisoner Benjamin Grossman."
He looked up. "How long were you at Maidanek? You're sure you
knew von Schraeder on sight?"

"I knew him! I was at Maidanek three years—"

For once the colonel was surprised. Maidanek might have been
the problem of the Russians, and the question, like many of the
others, may have been asked without conscious thought, but the answer still surprised him. He looked at Grossman almost with respect.

"How did you manage to survive so long? The stories we've been
hearing about that camp—"

It was a question Grossman had given considerable thought to,
and the answer came easily.

"I was strong when I first went into the camp," he said quietly. "I
know I don't look it now, but I was strong. I could do work. They
made me a *Sonderkommando* . . ." He managed to look ashamed at
the admission, knowing it would be expected.

The colonel's look of near respect changed instantly to one of
deep disgust. They would soon be hanging officers, army officers,
while these filth who cleaned out the gas chambers and fed the

ovens would be pampered heroes! It was a strange world. The colonel changed the subject.

"And in Buchenwald?"

"I beg your pardon?"

"What did you do in Buchenwald?"

"I thought I mentioned it. I was an orderly in Ward Forty-six, in the typhus section."

"And what atrocities did you witness in Buchenwald?"

"There were atrocities in all the camps," Grossman said slowly, "but I was in Buchenwald such a short time, and most of the time I was in the typhus section. But in Maidanek, this Commandant Mittendorf—"

The colonel had had enough of this particular inmate, who in any event would be of no use to him. He interrupted brusquely.

"I think that will be all, Grossman. You can leave."

Grossman cleared his throat nervously. "Colonel—?"

The cold eyes came up, contemptuous. "I said, that's all."

"But, Colonel—don't you issue passes from the camp? I mean, your office?"

"Why? You don't need any pass. If you want to leave, just leave." And good riddance, his tone seemed to add.

"I mean, passes to a different zone . . ."

"Why? Where do you want to go?"

"I thought the American Zone. Or the French Zone . . ."

Colonel Manley-Jones frowned. "Where are you from?"

"Originally, Hamburg."

"That's in this zone, the British Zone. You don't require a pass."

"I know, but Hamburg—" Grossman's shrug indicated there wasn't much left either of Hamburg or in Hamburg to entice a person.

The colonel's voice became accusatory.

"You said you had no family. Why would you want to go to the American Zone? Or the French Zone? You have no one there."

"I have no one anywhere," Grossman said in as reasonable a tone as he could muster, "but none of us can stay here forever. It's been two months since the camp was liberated, and a month since the war ended. There's nothing for me in Hamburg. I thought from the American Zone or the French Zone I might eventually be able to get permission to enter Switzerland . . ."

"Switzerland?" The colonel made it sound as if the suggestion was the most ridiculous thing he had ever heard. "You say you have no family anywhere, so obviously you have no one in Switzerland. So how do you expect to get permission to immigrate there? Switzerland isn't exactly waiting with open arms to be filled with"—with a diplomacy rare with him, the colonel bit back the word "trash" and substituted it with—"refugees." He considered Grossman coldly. "Why, then, do you want to go there?"

Ben Grossman had always known this was a question that would have to be answered carefully. He realized he had not ingratiated himself with Manley-Jones, but he suspected no prisoner really could. He tried to sound as sincere as possible.

"Before the war I often visited Switzerland. I came to like it very much. There was a girl I met when I was in Lucerne, a very beautiful girl . . ." He tried to smile but the result was a rather ghastly grimace.

No muscle moved on the colonel's narrow equine face, but inwardly he was outraged. Those *Sonderkommando* hands that still carried the stench and blood of the dead bodies that they handled, to be thought of touching the body of a beautiful girl, undoubtedly a gentile girl, which all the Jews seemed to prefer? Grossman misunderstood the colonel's continuing silence for some form of understanding. He hurried on.

"Also, I'm an engineer, Colonel, a mechanical engineer by profession. I—I studied in Switzerland. I can easily get work there. I would never be a burden on the state."

The colonel regarded him expressionlessly, and then shrugged.

"I can't imagine where you got the idea such passes are in my department. All passes from the British Zone to any other zone are issued through the office of the military governor. The liaison between that office and this camp is provided by Major Wilson."

He immediately bent over his papers, his thumbnail stroking his mustache almost fiercely. It was an obvious termination of the interview. Grossman stared at the bent head a moment, then slowly came to his feet and shuffled from the room. The colonel looked up to be sure the man had left, then reached for the telephone and asked the operator to connect him with Major Wilson's office.

Switzerland, indeed! Not if Colonel Manley-Jones had anything to do with it! The Russian Zone, perhaps, but no pass to either the

American or the French Zone, if he could help it. From there it would be only a step across the border, and the Yanks and the Frogs would probably close their eyes. They were too soft-hearted, that was their trouble. That *Sonderkommando!* It was a bloody wonder the Jew hadn't demanded a chauffeur-driven limousine to carry him in luxury across the bloody border!

Max Brodsky and Morris Wolf were discussing God.

Time passed slowly in the camp and a discussion on any subject was a welcome relief from the boredom, becoming the principal mental exercise the inmates could indulge in. Besides, being Jews, Wolf and Brodsky were prepared to argue either side of any proposition with a passion that was almost the equivalent of honest conviction.

"How can anyone but a fool deny the existence of God?" Brodsky demanded. "Look around you. Where do trees come from? Or flowers? They say that man descended from the monkeys, but what about trees? Another question—where do *you* come from? Why do you have five fingers—"

"Ten."

"—on each hand," Brodsky said, determined not to be put off by Wolf's so-called humor. "It isn't something that happens occasionally; it happens every time a baby is born. Millions of times a year. Every time the same five fingers on each hand, five toes on each foot. Why do you think the sun rises in the east every morning? According to you, it's all an accident, is that it? On a Tuesday you get up expecting light and that day the sun is just going down—"

"You overslept."

"I'm serious! Everything that happens is following some great master plan. Nothing happens by accident. Look around you."

Brodsky was sitting on his cot, picking the threads from the SS shoulder patch on a woolen shirt he had just "organized" from the captured stores. At his elbow a radio softly gave the news. Max's thick fingers, once again approaching their former strength, held the tiny needle with infinite delicacy.

"All right, look around you!" Wolf countered, no longer humorous. "Take a good look! Go take a look at the burial mounds, go look at the electrified fence, take a look at the watchtowers and the *momsers* there with their machine guns! This is all part of your

God's master plan? All those dead people? The chosen people! That's a laugh! Chosen to be killed. This is your God? The one who fried the people like that dumb Yashinko? On the fence?"

"He was shot. And he wasn't a Jew."

"So that makes him healthy again!" Wolf shook his head disbelievingly. "On a Tuesday the sun is going down instead of up, you don't know whether to eat dinner or breakfast—that's your argument for God? I'm impressed. The gas chambers, the ovens, the pits! Those are *my* arguments. And they outvote you six million to one!"

Brodsky shook his head stubbornly, his thick fingers continuing to pick delicately at the stitching of the patch.

"You don't understand," he said sadly. "You don't want to understand. If there's no God, what makes everything work? How do you explain the fact that every winter it gets cold and it snows, every summer it gets hot. Every year with no exceptions. Answer me that! Accidental? Never!"

"I have no idea," Wolf admitted. "I admit I don't understand, I only know this—leaves or trees or no leaves or trees, sun or no sun, snow or no snow, why does your all-powerful God permit a Hitler to kill millions and millions of people? Does your God think we're overpopulated? What kind of a God lets things like that happen? You answer me *that!*"

Brodsky paused in his work, frowning.

"I don't know," he said slowly, "but God has his reasons. We have to believe that . . ."

"*You* have to believe it," Wolf said bitterly. "I don't. Look at me. I'm a gargoyle. I could get a job swinging from that Notre Dame church in Paris. They could hire me to frighten children. Children? Adults! God needed another ugly man? And if he needed one so badly, he couldn't make one from an SS? He needed me?"

"You don't understand," Brodsky said patiently, and then paused as Grossman came into the room. He smiled and gestured toward Wolf's list on the wall. "They picked up Raeder today. The great Admiral of the Navy was simply sitting at home in the Russian sector of Berlin, can you imagine? Officially registered and completely undisturbed. It's—" He noticed the expression on Grossman's face for the first time. He reached over and switched off the radio. "What's the matter?"

Grossman slumped onto his cot. "I didn't handle it very well."

And thought, a few years ago I would have had that miserable colonel shoveling shit in the gas pens, carting the dead to the ovens, and happy to be alive to do it. Now I sat and *apologized* to the bastard! The time here at Belsen has done more to me than I would have supposed!

"Who did you have?"

"Some colonel. Manley-something."

"Manley-Jones," Wolf said and bobbed his small head. "I had him. He's a prick. There has to be one in every outfit, I guess, including the British. Or maybe especially the British."

Max had stopped his needlework. "So what happened?"

Grossman shrugged. "I should have stopped after I answered his questions and he told me to go. But I thought he was the one who handed out passes to a different zone." He stared down at his new shoes. "Now the son of a bitch is undoubtedly getting in touch with some office and making damned sure I don't go anywhere. Especially Switzerland."

Brodsky snorted and went back to his blouse. "Switzerland, Switzerland! It's all you talk about. You'd think you had a fortune in a numbered account there!"

"If I thought so," Wolf said, "I'd get you into Switzerland if I had to carry you across the border. And don't break our hearts about that girl you say you met there before the war," he added. "You think she's still waiting for Grossman to appear after six years?" He put a hand up to his scarred face, moved his fingers to touch the eyepatch over his empty socket. "For somebody handsome like me, maybe they'd wait—but for you?"

"Forget Switzerland," Brodsky said definitely. "Come to Palestine with us, instead. We've got prettier girls." My Deborah, for instance, he added to himself, and wondered if his Deborah would still be waiting after all the years. He had written to her immediately after liberation, and still had heard no word.

Grossman shook his head. It was an old argument. "If you two want to go to Palestine, go. Nobody's stopping you."

Wolf smiled. "Only the British."

"That's your problem. I'm going to Switzerland, and the British aren't going to stop me. Certainly no British named Manley-Jones!"

Brodsky went back to his needlework, speaking over his shoulder.

"So at least come with us until you're somewhere near the Swiss border. You can say good-bye there just as easy as here. We'll be leaving here in a month or so—"

"A *month* or so?"

"That's right."

"When was all this decided?"

"Today, while you were at your interview. The Mossad man was here, you knew he was coming today. Davi Ben-Levi. You didn't want to see him, remember?"

"I didn't have anything to see him about."

"Well," Brodsky said, disregarding Grossman's comment, "the Mossad are setting up places we can stay until we reach a port in Italy. They have to buy a ship, or ships." He shrugged. "It all takes time."

"And you're going to stay here until they're ready?"

"Why not?" Wolf said. "What's wrong with here? All the comforts of home—" He gestured toward the radio. "Entertainment, good food, good company—"

"We'll stay here a month or possibly more," Brodsky said. "By that time you can put on your camp uniform, the striped shirt and cap, and walk across any zone without any pass at all. You'll see. Besides," he added quietly, "most of the men are in no condition to travel, as yet. You, for example."

"There's nothing wrong with me. Once I get to Switzerland—"

"There's nothing wrong with you," Wolf said, "except if you want to walk, you have to take off your shoes. They're too heavy for you." He shrugged. "I see you now, shuffling across the border, one mile an hour, with the border guards in hot pursuit. Sitting on turtles. *That's* how fine you are."

Grossman didn't argue. Brodsky nodded.

"We're also going to have to organize some warm clothes—"

"In July or August?"

"We'll leave here in July or August, that's true. But we won't be taking the Rome Express, first-class, with meals," Brodsky said dryly. "Sometimes we'll have to walk, sometimes maybe we can hitch a ride, or the Mossad can arrange transportation, but we can't depend on it. Once we cross into Austria without proper papers we may have to hide out a lot, travel by night, hide by day. And once we cross the Italian border it will be worse. The British practically control Italy now, especially the north, and they don't intend to let any Jews leave for Palestine if they can help it. So we don't know when we'll get to a port, or when a ship will be ready." He pointed to the shirt he had stolen from supplies. "So we'll need clothes, warm clothes."

Grossman leaned back on his bed and thought about it. It was true he was still far from his full strength, but he was sure he was strong enough to cross a border. He didn't intend to fight his way across; he meant to use his brain. Still, it was also true that at the moment he was sure Colonel Manley-Jones would do his best to see there would be no travel pass for him to any zone adjacent to the Swiss border; but in a month or so, it was highly possible that Manley-Jones would be out of here. The interrogation process was already nearing an end, with the war-crimes trials already announced by the Russians to begin in Berlin, and the trials in Nuremberg would follow soon after. Max was probably right that in a month or so passes would be a mere formality, and anyone in a camp-striped shirt would be able to go where he wanted without any problem.

He looked up.

"From here you plan to go directly to Italy? Or try?"

"No; from here we'll be going to Munich, to an Allied refugee camp there in Felsdorf."

"And how long will you stay there?"

Brodsky shrugged. "Until the Mossad tells us to leave."

Grossman thought that over. It was true that there would be no harm in going as far as Felsdorf with Brodsky and the others. It was also true that it might be helpful to travel in the company of others. There was safety in numbers; some of the ex-prisoners who had left the camp and returned for a visit had said the world outside was a jungle. Gangs of discharged soldiers, ragged and hungry, often attacked anyone who looked as if he had anything worth taking. Besides, he actually was in no great hurry; since the camp's liberation and his recovery from typhus, he had gone back to considering his old plan as being fully operational. He was no longer a suspected war criminal, and he would soon be in Switzerland; and that had been the original idea, hadn't it? The time lost at Bergen-Belsen had been an unfortunate hiatus, a distressful detour, but now he was back on the track. He looked at Brodsky.

"How do you plan to get to Felsdorf?"

"Hike into Celle and get rides on trucks from there. Hitchhiking."

"And from Felsdorf, how do you plan to go? Where do you intend to cross the Austrian border? Anywhere near Switzerland?"

Brodsky was busy folding the shirt into his knapsack. He slid the knapsack into the small locker beside his cot, locked the locker, and put away the key.

"That's up to the Mossad," he said. "They may take us down to Lindau on the Bodensee, then through Austria to the Italian border, then down to some port on the west coast, like La Spezia or Livorno. Or from Munich they may go down through Innsbruck and then over to some port on the Adriatic, like Chioggia."

"Ask the British where they won't have gunboats to follow us and sink us," Wolf said dryly. "That's probably where the Mossad will take us."

Brodsky suddenly looked at Grossman, sensing that the question meant a surrender of sorts on the part of his friend.

"You mean you'll go with us?"

"As far as Felsdorf," Grossman said. He made it sound a concession.

Brodsky smiled inwardly. Long before Munich or Felsdorf he would have converted Benjamin Grossman to Zionism. Palestine needed people like Grossman: an engineer, a good friend. A survivor.

Switzerland, indeed!

Chapter 8

Karl Neuenrade was not only the only waiter at the Gemustert-Essen-Keller in Celle, he was also the proprietor; his wife was the cook, and his daughter sat at the cash register, her rotting teeth and straggly mustache protection against the most salacious or sex-starved customer.

Life had been good to Karl Neuenrade. Early in his restaurant career he had established excellent relations with the farmers in the Celle area, so that the rationing that had been austere during the war, and which became even more draconian following the war, did not greatly affect him or his fancy food. There was, however, one cloud on Karl Neuenrade's horizon, and it was one that grew in size each day that passed following the liberation of Bergen-Belsen. It was the fact that during the war, while his wife and daughter had run the restaurant and run it quite profitably, Karl had served as the SS sergeant in charge of the prisoner food program at the *Belsenlager*, and as such was known to many of the prisoners, especially those who had worked in the cookhouses. As soon as the camp had been liberated and turned over to the British by Joseph Kramer, the commandant, Karl Neuenrade had hurried home and removed the sign pointing down the steps to his restaurant, informing all customers that it was out being repainted. Nor did the sign go back up again in a hurry, and while its absence undoubtedly caused the loss of some customers, it was better than having the place inundated with ex-prisoners. The ploy seemed to have been successful; while every other restaurant in Celle had been forced to serve God knows how many free meals to the men in the striped blouses as they made their way through Celle on their way home, the Gemustert-Essen-Keller saw none.

June passed, and July and August, and in September, when apparently all the prisoners at Bergen-Belsen had either left the camp or had settled into the former German Army quarters for a long, long stay, Karl Neuenrade congratulated himself on his foresight as far as the sign was concerned, and mounted it once more on the wrought-iron frame that swung over the cellar steps.

He moved a mere few minutes too quickly, for no sooner had he come back downstairs from hanging the sign, dusting his fingers and feeling pleased with himself, than a group of shadows on the steps indicated a clutch of customers, and three men descended. Karl came forward with a smile to greet them—they were early for lunch, but the Gemustert-Essen-Keller was always prepared—and then saw to his consternation they all wore striped shirts and the striped caps he had feared.

They seated themselves at a table in the middle of the room, and smiled at him. Karl stared at them resentfully. He worked hard for his money, while these—these—these *loafers* still expected to sponge meals simply because they had the hard luck of being in a concentration camp. The war was over! It was time to forget the war and the camps and get back to normalcy! Still, when Karl considered the very size of the huge one of the trio, sitting there with the patience of a hungry bear, not to mention the icy look in the slate-blue eyes of the second one—familiar, those eyes; from one of the cookhouses, Karl thought—plus the ugly sneer on the face of the one-eyed one, he realized a free meal would not only be charitable but could be the lesser of two evils. If the three decided to tear his place apart, could he expect any relief from the police? Not a hope! Most of the police were too afraid of being denounced as former SS themselves to take any action against the men in the striped shirts and caps.

Wolf seemed to resent the look in Karl's eye; the delay also did not sit well with him. He tipped up the patch over his eye socket in the manner of a person politely tipping his hat.

"May we order now?" Karl Neuenrade moved hastily back from the revolting sight, and covered his confusion by bringing up his order pad and wetting his pencil with his tongue. "Good!" Wolf said approvingly, and studied the blackboard on the wall. "I'll start with some schnapps—something drinkable—then beer with lunch, which will be the schnitzel with potatoes. And some salad, of course . . ."

Karl Neuenrade's face burned as he filled the orders and watched his good food being devoured, his best liquors consumed. They should have all been killed, these people, these Jew animals; and decent folks like himself would not have to suffer, now!

They finished their meal, belched politely to indicate their appreciation of the cuisine, and marched up the steps in file without—as Karl had so bitterly known—making the slightest effort to dig into their pockets. Still, digging into their pockets would have been pointless; all they would have encountered would have been their fingers.

"Bastard," Wolf said genially. "Did you see the look on his face? We're lucky he didn't try to poison us."

"He tried for the past year at Belsen," Grossman said sourly. "He was in charge of the prisoner food there."

"And he didn't do badly," Brodsky conceded, and led the way toward the edge of town and the autobahn leading south.

For some reason difficult for them to understand, that day all traffic seemed destined for Bremen or Hamburg to the north. All that came along in their direction was an occasional mule-drawn cart, or an even more occasional official-looking limousine passing at high speed, with the British officers inside looking glum and paying no attention to the three waving their arms at the side of the road. Afternoon shadows were beginning to lengthen and they were still less than fifteen miles from the camp. They looked at each other.

"Well?" Wolf said. "Do we go back? That ought to be easy; everything seems to be heading that way. Start out tomorrow again, earlier? Or stop in Celle and take lessons in hitching a ride?"

"We don't go back," Brodsky said with finality, and started hiking down the road. The others hurried to catch up. The afternoon sun burned; it was hot and the packs with their spare clothing and a few tins of food seemed to gain weight with every step. Still, they were finally out of the camp and moving, and that was the important thing. They had walked for over an hour when Brodsky suddenly called out, "Sing!" and Grossman unconsciously started singing. His steps matched the rhythm, his weary mind back in his earliest days in a uniform, marching along, singing as he swung in step with the others:

"Deutschland, Deutschland, Über Alles—"

He suddenly realized that nobody else was singing and looked up from the road to find both Wolf and Brodsky staring at him curiously. He forced a smile and began again:

"Deutschland, Deutschland, Alles Über—"

Brodsky laughed. The three swung down the road, singing, but Grossman inwardly was cringing. And what if he had unconsciously started to sing the "Horst Wessel" song instead?

The farmhouse was set far back from the road, as if ashamed to have its disrepair noted by passers-by, a low sprawling building almost of another age, badly in need of paint. Behind it and a short distance away was a sagging barn with roof shingles missing, and which seemed to be held together mainly by the fading posters that had been plastered on its sides many years before. At first glance the house seemed deserted, but then they noticed the thin wisp of smoke that was curling from the chimney. The three men looked at one another.

"I think we've walked as far as can be expected of hitchhikers for one day," Wolf said.

"I'm hungry," Grossman said. "Do you suppose there's any food inside?"

"We can only hope and pray," Wolf said piously.

"And we could all use a good night's rest," Brodsky added, making the vote unanimous.

They walked down the weed-choked lane leading to the house, aware of the good smell of burning wood as they approached. Brodsky stepped up to the side door of the house and rapped upon it authoritatively. There was no immediate response, and Brodsky raised his large fist to repeat the knock when the door suddenly opened and a woman stood there, a shotgun in her hands. Brodsky brought his hand down and in the same motion simply picked the gun from the woman's hand. He broke it open, removed the shells, and tucked the gun under his arm. The woman was staring at them in momentary shock at having lost her weapon; her eyes were wide with fear. She was a middle-aged woman with straggling hair already touched with gray, wearing torn slippers over bare feet, with a man's shirt that was too small for her ample bust, and a wrinkled skirt that was strained by her wide hips. She started to back away, to try to close the door, but Brodsky's hand prevented it.

"We're not here to hurt you or rob you," he said with as much assurance as he could get into his harsh voice. "We only want something to eat."

"And a place to sleep," Grossman added.

"Which can be in the barn," Wolf added. He tapped his striped shirt. "Fortunately, we've been well trained not to be fussy."

The woman hesitated.

"We'll cut some firewood for you," Brodsky said, as if that settled the matter, and walked into the house, bringing the gun with him. He leaned it against the wall and looked around. The room was furnished in typical German farmland style, with a massive sofa and heavy chairs upholstered in worn, faded velour. Old-fashioned photographs studied the intruders from the papered walls, interspersed with crocheted mottos in cheap frames; there was a foot-pedal-operated organ against one wall. "Pretty," he said approvingly, and walked through to the kitchen, where he nodded in satisfaction. There was a wood fire in the firebox of the oven, bread on the table, several thick sausages hung from the roof beams, and an open tin of some sort of meat lay on the counter. There was also an ax in one

corner. He picked up the ax and went out through the back kitchen
door to the rear of the house. The sound of wood being chopped
came to them.

"If you want, I can cook," Wolf said, and smiled. The woman
shrank back before the horrible grimace. "I used to be a professional
cook, once," he said to Grossman. "You didn't know that, did you?
Now I just scare people . . ."

But the woman was already in the kitchen, hurriedly putting three
plates on the table.

Moonlight slotted the darkness of the barn, angling through the
missing shingles, playing across Brodsky's strong face, touching the
permanent sneer on Wolf's lips and softening it. Grossman turned
restlessly, unable to sleep, and then came slowly and silently to his
feet. He looked down at the other two and then stepped softly over
them and walked quietly out of the barn and toward the house.

There was a light in the kitchen. He stood at a window, peering
in. The woman, her side to him, was standing at an ironing board,
ironing clothes. Her thick arms moved back and forth, pausing only
to move the blouse she was working on, or to exchange one iron for
another, placing the cool one on a gas ring, touching her wetted
finger against the fresh one to test its heat. She had partially unbut-
toned her restraining shirt and her heavy breasts swung slightly with
the rhythm of her ironing stroke.

God! Grossman thought, feeling the stirring in his loins. A woman
like this, old, fat, barefoot, plain! And to be reduced to rape! But it
had been over a year since he had had a woman, and for the first
time since he had entered Belsen he was feeling the insistent necessity for sex. He wet his lips and moved stealthily to the door, turning
the handle as quietly as he could. The door opened with a creak of
unoiled hinges; the woman swung around instantly, the hot iron
coming up protectively before her full bosom. She stared at him.

"What do you want?"

"A—a drink of water, if you please . . ."

She tilted her head abruptly toward the pump handle at one end
of the sink; he walked past her slowly, wanting desperately to brush
one arm suggestively against her heavy breasts but fearing to have
the hot iron thrust into his face. A failure, even with this monster,
he thought bitterly, and found himself at the sink, actually pumping

water, bringing up the dipper and drinking deeply, his hand trembling.

The woman was standing still, watching him, a strange look on her face. The iron had been set on the gas ring. "What's your name?" she asked softly.

"Gross—" He had to stop and clear his throat; it had tightened up on him. "Grossman. Benjamin Grossman. What's yours?"

"Ilsa. Ilsa Pohl."

She stood staring at him, her face revealing nothing. Slowly he put down the dipper and came to face her. She looked into his eyes steadily for several moments, and then reached for his hand, bringing it up, placing it inside her shirt. He felt the soft fullness of her breast, the turgid hardness of the nipple, slightly damp with perspiration; and then she was leading him urgently to the next room. She closed the door to the kitchen and in the darkness pulled him down to the sofa, raising her skirt, fumbling at his belt, breathing harshly. He felt her callused hand on him, caressing him fiercely. They coupled savagely, with the woman whispering *"Bitte, bitte, bitte, bitte, bitte"* endlessly as they pounded at each other, until he climaxed with a sweetness and a fulfillment he could not recall before, forgiving her the drabness of her appearance, forgiving her everything. Beneath him the woman lay, panting quietly, pulsing internally against his slowly reducing organ. He started to raise himself but she drew him to her, holding him tightly. "Later," she whispered. "Don't go out, yet. Don't go out. It's been such a long time . . ."

And when at last he had shrunk so as to withdraw involuntarily, she still held him to her, rubbing her large breasts against him, until at last she realized it was over. She swung her feet to the floor and started to button her shirt. Her voice was low.

"Was it good?"

"It was very good," he said honestly. "And for you?" He was surprised to hear himself ask; he had never asked before.

"It was wonderful. Very wonderful." She reached for his hand and held it tightly, rubbing her breasts with it. "Must you really go tomorrow?"

"Yes."

"This used to be a good farm before the war," she said slowly, and then hesitated as if comparing in her mind the way the farm was then and the way it looked now. "When Hans was alive, and our son. It could be a good farm again. It needs a man." She moved his hand to her crotch, over her skirt, pressing it into her, moving it slowly up and down. "I need a man, too. Stay."

"I'm sorry—"

"For a few days, at least. To see how it goes, how you like it."

"I can't. I'm sorry," Grossman said, and for a moment he really was sorry. It had been exceptionally exciting sex. Who would have thought, with an older woman, with fat hips and a plain face, with heavy legs and straggling hair and callused hands? And the circumcision had certainly not reduced pleasure, which was good to know. But to be in this place? Him, on a farm, with this woman? It was ridiculous. "I have to go," he said quietly. "I have to go to Switzerland, on business. Maybe after that, I may come back."

"You won't," the woman said expressionlessly, and released his hand. She straightened her skirt and smiled in the darkness, a resigned smile. "But it was good," she said softly, promising herself the memory for a long time, to enjoy in the manless nights until someone else came, if they ever did. "It was very good . . ."

And when he got back to the barn and lay down, he found Brodsky's eyes open and staring at him curiously. He lay down and rolled over, and then rolled back.

"A drink of water," he said shortly, and rolled back again, settling his head on his arm, unaware of the woman smell that filled the air, and fell asleep instantly.

They had walked less than a mile the following day before a British truck stopped for them, taking them as far as Würzburg, the soldiers sharing their rations with them, letting them sleep in the truck outside the British depot that night, and even bringing them some blankets to soften the hard floor boards of the truck. And the following morning they had barely reached the outskirts of the town when an American truck convoy came through, the stars and stripes painted on the brown hoods, and the lead truck stopped for water at a gas station that had only water to offer.

A husky sergeant dropped from the cab of the truck and looked the three of them over while the driver, a corporal, filled the radiator. The convoy rolled past, churning up dust. The sergeant nodded and spoke around the stub of an unlit cigar in one corner of his mouth. "Campies, huh?"

"Yes, sir. Bergen-Belsen."

It was Brodsky who answered. His English was poor, but better than the other two, who spoke no English at all. Brodsky had picked some of it up in Palestine from the British there, and the rest at Buchenwald from an inmate from Latvia who had mastered the tongue during a two-week visit to London before the war.

"Where you characters goin'?"

"Munich."

"That's American. You guys got passes to cross into our zone?"

Brodsky didn't know what to say. Wolf was the only one with a legitimate pass to cross into the American Zone; his home had been in Tutzing on the Starnbergersee, and he considered himself a citizen of Munich. All Brodsky and Grossman carried was a bit of paper saying they had been inmates of Bergen-Belsen. The sergeant looked tough and authoritative, precisely the type to turn them in. But for what crime? They were well within the British Zone, and the American sergeant couldn't really do anything to them for telling the truth.

"One of us," Brodsky said hesitatingly.

"Only one, huh?" The sergeant removed the unlit cigar stub long enough to spit, and then tucked it back in the corner of his mouth. "You guys got anything to wear except them zebra shirts and them beanies? Any other duds in them packs?"

Brodsky thought he understood, but it left him more confused than ever. He hesitated. Until now their striped blouses and caps had served them well. The sergeant didn't look as if he were going to wait all day for an answer; the convoy was rolling past. But since Brodsky could see no sense in the question, he could see no danger in an honest answer.

"We have British fatigue blouses—"

"Well," said the sergeant, "then take off them Dodger uniforms and get into whatever else you got. And shove them Sing-Sing hats into your pockets. No sense lettin' the fuckin' MPs have no field day goin' across the line. Cocksuckers hold you up for hours like they got Brownie points, the pricks!"

Ninety-five per cent of this made no sense to Brodsky, but he did get the idea that the burly sergeant, for some unfathomable reason of his own, wanted them to take off their caps and change shirts. Maybe he didn't like people from the camps; a lot of people didn't. Well, they could always change back once the sergeant had taken his truck and gone his way. Brodsky explained the strange situation to the other two, and all three removed their shirts and caps, dug the British blouses from their knapsacks, and slipped them on. And then stood back from the truck as the bulky sergeant climbed in. He leaned out of the window, staring at them incredulously.

"Well, what the fuck you guys waitin' for? A hand-carved invitation? Hop in!"

It was the abrupt gesture of his thumb toward the back of the truck that did it, certainly not the confusing language. The three eagerly tossed their packs in back and tumbled in after them as the corporal took off. The last thing they heard before the roar of the engine drowned out all other sounds was the sergeant snarling at the corporal.

"They payin' you by the hour, Johnson? Step on the fuckin' gas, for crissake! We're supposed to be leadin' this fuckin' convoy, not eatin' their fuckin' dust!"

Felsdorf was too much like the camps they had been liberated from for most of the refugees there to be truly comfortable. The bare wood buildings set on the flat uninspiring plain were terrifyingly familiar. True, the food was good and plentiful, there was adequate water, clean water, not only for drinking but for bathing as well, and the latrines were both housed and clean, and kept clean by ex-SS from nearby Dachau who hoped their newly acquired devotion to cleanliness would earn them a modicum of forgiveness, or at least protection. The medical care was excellent, and there was dental care as well. The authorities were both thoughtful and helpful when they could be; there were no locks on either the barracks doors or on the gate, which was largely ornamental in any event. But it was the sense of returning to a camp, any camp, added to the chilling feeling for many that they were here because they had no other place to go, and would have to stay in the concentration-camp replica for months if not for years. It made for disquiet among those refugees who were not Jews; the few Jews there had the hope of a future in Palestine ahead of them, at least. As tenuous as that hope was, it was better than the despair of endless camp life.

The second day at Felsdorf, Benjamin Grossman, accompanied by Morris Wolf, decided to go into Munich, leaving Brodsky to get acquainted with the camp, as well as to keep an eye on their belongings. Pilfering was not unknown in the refugee camps; concentration-camp habits died hard. And besides, Brodsky had never known Munich and had no particular interest in seeing it.

The two men hitched a ride to the St. Paul Platz across the Bavarian Ring from the Theresienwiese, coming down from the outskirts of the city through the Nymphenberger Park, appalled at the destruction about them. They walked slowly up the Landwehr Strasse, through the rubble that marked the narrow winding streets that constituted the Old City. At St. Peter's Platz they paused and looked about them. There was debris everywhere, the ruins of a once beautiful city. The Peterskirche had been heavily bombed; its thick walls gaped at the open sky with jagged stone teeth. The Neue Veste, lying between Max Josef Platz and the Hofgarten, had been leveled; the former Residenz looked like a huge park with stone shards doing for grass.

They took the one tram line that had been put back into service and rode to the end of the line at the Ostbahnhof on Orleans Strasse, aware of the side glances their striped shirts and caps earned them, but not caring much. Besides, wearing them meant not having to pay fares with money they did not possess. On each side as the tram swayed along the crooked curving tracks, the hard evidence of the destruction of war and the Allied bombing was clearly visible. The four-story houses along the Wiener Strasse, once elegant homes shaded by tall elm and linden, were now split and sliding into the street. Furniture could be seen clinging precariously to the upper, sloping floors, the rooms exposed to view, all modesty gone.

They climbed down from the tram at Steins-dorf Strasse and walked along the Isar, stunned by the destruction, the wreckage, the utter waste. The river was clogged with wreckage: a half-sunk barge had its cargo of grain of some sort dribbling from a gaping wound in one side. Small children were scooping up the smelly mess in tins while rats watched them jealously from the sloping deck.

At Kohl Strasse, Wolf paused and pointed.

"I had a friend who lived there." His finger indicated a cleared lot; there was nothing to show there had ever been a building at the site. In the center of the bare lot an old man fed bits of rubbish onto a fire, although the day was warm. There were tears in Wolf's one good eye; he wiped them away fiercely. "My first job was just around the corner. I washed the floors of a small cafe. I was eleven. It was a good job. It was a good cafe. They fed me."

He sighed; they moved on. At Blumen Strasse an old woman rummaged in a garbage pile, a stick in one hand to protect her against two gaunt children awaiting the opportunity to replace her in her search.

"I don't know whether to cheer or to curse," Wolf said sadly.

They returned to the camp resolved not to return to the city until they were ready to move on, and even then to avoid it if they could. It was too depressing.

Since the formation of the Felsdorf camp, a Mossad Aliyah Bet man had passed through as frequently as his limited time would allow. Together with the Jewish Agency and other groups, he had helped the authorities to organize such activities as theater, concerts either by the refugees themselves or by visiting artists, and discussion groups, activities to occupy the minds of all, but for the Jews a means of passing the time until the Mossad was ready to help them reach Italy and eventually—hopefully—Palestine. There were occasional travel lectures on Palestine and its wonders, complete with lantern slides, always of the most beautiful views, the loveliest beaches, the widest boulevards, the greenest kibbutz, the richest orchards. Even the few slides taken of the Dead Sea area were photographed from angles that made the surrounding hills appear majestic rather than starkly barren; the Negev and the Wilderness of Zin became challenging rather than hopelessly desolate. It was a needless ploy on the part of the Mossad; the Jews at Felsdorf were merely awaiting the word to go.

All but a Jew named Benjamin Grossman.

By the end of the second week the others from Bergen-Belsen had arrived, those who were to be in the first contingent from that group to leave for Italy. There was a meeting of them, for the decision had been made to severely limit the size of the groups traveling together and gather them again in Italy near the ship the Mossad was readying for their trip. Twenty-six had come from Bergen-Belsen in the first group; twenty of them Polish Jews, five Lithuanians, and Wolf the only German. The meeting was held in the mess hall after supper, and Grossman refused to attend. To begin with, he was anxious to get to Switzerland, and the Jews, with their endless meetings and their ceaseless discussions, did not seem to him to be of much help. Then, too, the meetings were conducted in Yiddish, which was, after all, the lingua franca of the Jews in the camps, and while Grossman had picked up considerable Yiddish in his year at Belsen—since it was only a bastardization of German in the first place—the language still grated on his ears. It was still Jew language, and now that the war was over and he was no longer in a concentration camp—and also now that he was near his money in Switzerland and freedom— he felt about the language as he had always felt about it. It was an inferior means of communication between inferior peoples.

The night of the meeting, when Brodsky and Wolf had returned to the room they shared with Grossman, he put the question to them squarely:

"All right! We've been here two weeks; your people are finally all here. When do we leave this place?"

Both Wolf and Brodsky looked at him in surprise. There had been a touch of arrogance in his voice, of command, they had never heard before. Wolf shrugged and went to his cot; Brodsky, in typical fashion, overlooked the tone of voice, putting it down to nerves.

"When the Mossad says so," he said patiently.

"And just when will that be? Next year? The year after? Never?"

"Soon, I hope."

"Soon, you hope! You don't even know what route you'll be taking! I'm only a hundred miles from Konstanz right now, and from there all you have to do is cross a street and you're in Kreutzingler, in Switzerland. What am I doing sitting here, waiting for you people? I must be mad!"

"I'm on your side," Wolf said agreeably. "You must be mad."

"A hundred miles is a hundred miles," Brodsky said quietly. "If we go through Lindau, when we reach Austria you'll be within walking distance of the frontier."

"If!"

"Let's go back to your being mad," Wolf said affably. He was sitting on his bed cross-legged, an ugly gnome with an eye patch, spiky black hair, and a twisted cheek and curled lip. "At Konstanz they'll have more guards than we had at Belsen."

Grossman looked from one to the other, his irritation growing, slowly becoming anger and then fury. Who were they to tell him what to do? Then, with an impulse he would have utterly rejected in his earlier life as a careful planner, he swung open his locker and dragged his pack from it. He opened it and took out the British army blouse, laid it on a chair beside his cot, and tossed the pack with its rations and other clothing onto Brodsky's bed. He took off his striped shirt and added it to the pile, retaining only the striped cap, which he jammed into a pocket. It was, after all, free transportation, that cap. Which was another thing: the Germans wouldn't be letting people travel free much longer, ex-camp inmates or not. Time was running out for him in every sense.

"I won't be needing any of that," he said evenly, pointing. "I'll be off in the morning."

Brodsky looked irritated.

"Ben, don't be a fool! You're making a snap decision because you're angry, God knows why. Think a bit. Hasn't anything I've said to you about Palestine these past weeks—these past months—meant anything at all to you?"

Grossman looked at him. "Hasn't anything I've said to you about Switzerland meant anything at all to you?"

Brodsky stared in frustration at the things on his bed.

"So, if you have to go, at least take some of the tinned goods and some of the clothes. It's almost October. It gets cold in Switzerland."

"I don't expect—" He had been on the verge of saying he didn't expect to be there long, but he caught the words in time. It will be a good thing when I get away from this bunch, he thought. One of these days I'd be blurting out something that would get me in trouble. "—to freeze. I'm not going mountain climbing or skiing. And the less I carry, the faster I travel."

"Grossman, I agree," Wolf said genially from across the room. "Besides, why waste good rations and clothing? If you're going to try and cross at Konstanz, they'd only end up in the Bodensee and get wet."

Brodsky threw up his hands in disgust. For a moment Grossman forgot the other man was a Jew. His anger left him; they *had* been friends after a fashion.

"I'm not doing this blindly, Max," he said quietly.

"Grossman," Wolf said, not argumentatively but merely stating a fact, "you're doing this blindly."

Grossman ignored him, addressing himself to Brodsky.

"There's a regular military bus that leaves the Maximilian Platz in Munich, going to Stuttgart. I'll drop off it at the Ulm road, south. They tell me there's plenty of traffic on that road, coming down from Regensburg and even from Nuremberg, heading for France. I'm sure I'll have no trouble getting a ride as far as Tuttlingen. Maybe even Singen. From there, worse comes to worse, I can walk to Konstanz."

"A twenty-mile stroll," Wolf observed. "Just the thing to work up an appetite before dinner."

"I don't have to get there early," Grossman went on, continuing to address Brodsky, ignoring Wolf. "In fact, I don't want to get there until very late. By morning I'll be well inside Switzerland, far from the border."

"Be sure and get there after the guards knock off for the night," Wolf suggested. "They work only twenty-four hours a day."

Brodsky shook his head hopelessly. "Do you have any money?"

"Who has money?"

"I do," Brodsky said simply, and dug into his pocket. "It's from the Mossad, for our group. You'll need some."

"Don't give him paper money," Wolf advised. "It'll only get wet when they throw him into the lake."

Brodsky paid no attention. He peeled off several notes and thrust them at Grossman. They were American ten-dollar bills, money accepted in any country in those confused times. Grossman didn't refuse; he folded them into a small wad and slipped them into his watch pocket. He had suspected the Mossad might have given Brodsky some cash for the intended trip; it was like the Jew not to mention it before.

"Thanks," he said dryly.

Brodsky looked at him, puzzled by the tone. Wolf raised his eyebrows, his one good eye glancing up at the ceiling in supplication and then down again. "Better get some sleep, all of us," Brodsky said. "What time are you leaving in the morning?"

"As soon as it's light," Grossman said, and started to strip off his trousers. Max flipped off the light and started to undress in the dark. He slid into bed and glanced across the darkened room.

"Good night, Ben."

"Good night."

But Wolf had the last word.

"Good night, all," he said, "and Grossman, I hope you know how to swim!"

Dawn had just started to lighten the eastern sky when Grossman rolled over, considered the now visible windowpane, and then silently swung his feet to the floor. He winced slightly at the dampness of the bare wood and quickly pulled on his socks. His trousers followed, then the British fatigue blouse, then the heavy shoes "organized" at Belsen, and finally the little striped cap. He came to his feet, staring down at the sleeping men. They were Jews it was true, but actually not as bad as most Jews. He had spent a full year with them; Brodsky had been helpful during that time. In a way he would miss seeing him each day; in a way he would even miss Wolf's sardonic humor, biting as it could be at times. But they were now as much of the past as Maidanek and Mittendorf, or Buchenwald and Schlossberg, or Bergen-Belsen and the dead Kapo, Soli Yaganzys. The future was ahead, when he was inside Switzerland. It was time to go.

He walked as quietly as he could to the door, opening it silently, and tiptoed down the steps to the ground floor. There was a faint click as the outside door of the barracks closed behind him. Across the room Max Brodsky sat up and climbed silently from his bed. In the half-light Wolf pushed himself up on one elbow.

"What are you getting up for?"

Brodsky looked sheepish. "I can't let him go alone . . ."

Wolf stared in disbelief. "You're going to *Switzerland?*"

"No, no! I'll be back. It's just—well, he may need help in getting across the border . . ."

Wolf snorted.

"For this he'll need more than the great Max Brodsky. He'll need the American Seventh Army, plus a declaration of war against the Swiss. You think they really need people like Grossman? The man's a nut. He's a menace. Let him go. Let the Swiss worry about him."

"He's my friend," Brodsky said quietly. "He's also neither as strong as he thinks he is, nor as self-sufficient. He didn't think this out; he made up his mind at the spur of the moment. He'll need help." He shrugged. "What's it cost to help a friend?"

"Let's hope it doesn't cost you getting to Palestine," Wolf said somberly. "Or your life." He didn't sound like the usual sardonic Wolf; he was deadly serious. "Max, let him go. I mean it. Grossman's a strange person. I don't think I like him."

"You don't understand him."

"I don't understand alligators, either, but I don't chase them. I think maybe I do understand Grossman and you don't," Wolf said. "He's the German kind of German Jew."

Max was pulling on his trousers, buttoning them.

"Now I don't understand you. What kind of a German Jew are you?"

"A different kind," Wolf said quietly. "Grossman's a German first, then—maybe—a Jew."

Brodsky smiled. "I thought Hitler removed that distinction."

Wolf shook his head; he was deadly serious.

"Max, you don't understand. Some of the German Jews, I'm ashamed to say, mostly from the north, from Hamburg, from Berlin, from Prussia—they always wanted to prove they were more German than the Kaiser. Yiddish was a language they deplored; Russian Jews were all Litvaks even if they came from Odessa; Zionism was a dirty word. It meant there was a country somewhere, a certain place on earth, that had a greater claim on the Jews than Germany did, and those flag-waving patriots couldn't explain that. And since they couldn't explain it, they obviously couldn't accept it." He shrugged. "I've known more than one German Jew who bragged about his saber cut from Heidelberg, can you imagine?"

"In Poland," Max said, putting on his blouse and buttoning it, "we thought all German Jews were like that."

"No," Wolf said seriously, "not all. Oh, there were Jews in Germany who had no real objection to Hitler when he first came along. They even thought he was going to be good for Germany—until he started to kill them personally, of course. He had told them exactly what he planned to do in *Mein Kampf*, when it was first published back in 1925, but I guess they thought he was just using poetic license. Even after *Kristallnacht* in November of '38, when the synagogues went up in flames, when all the Jewish shops were demolished and twenty thousand Jews were dragged from their beds and beaten in the streets and then put in prison—even then these Jews, these superpatriots, these extra-German Germans, claimed that it wasn't Hitler's fault. It was the fault of his subordinates. Or, even if Hitler knew about it and condoned it, it was a temporary aberration on his part that would pass. With castor oil, maybe, it would pass." His voice was bitter. "After all, how could Germany exist without its Jews? Its liberated, educated Jews? Its scientific, cultured Jews? Its rich and comfortable—and German—Jews?"

Max suddenly thought he understood.

"You were a Communist . . ."

"That was the charge when they beat me up and threw me into Dachau back in 1936," Wolf said quietly. "I was one of the founding fathers of that camp, they owe me a medal. Was I a Communist? No. What I was, was the secretary of our union. What I wasn't was a rich, influential Jew. I was a cook in a cheap restaurant in a working-class neighborhood in Munich. Not that it helped the rich, influential Jews very much; the ones who stuck around waiting for Hitler to change, ended up going up a chimney, someplace. Me, I'm still alive at least. And if I can't get a job as a cook in Palestine, I can always get a job in a side show of a circus with my face."

"In Palestine you can cook, farm, do what you want." Max was tying his shoe laces.

"Max," Wolf said in desperation, trying to continue the conversation in order to delay Brodsky's departure, "before the camps, before Dachau and Buchenwald and Bergen-Belsen, I don't suppose I was much of a Jew. I don't know how much of a Jew I am today, certainly not a religious Jew, if believing in your kind of God is necessary. But I know that Germany is not for any Jew. I know that Germany is not for me. But Grossman—Germany is for him." He looked at Brodsky in despair as the large man walked to the door. "Max, don't go. Believe me, Grossman isn't worth it."

Brodsky paused and looked back.

"Every Jew is worth it," he said quietly. "There aren't all that many of us left."

Chapter 9

There was no military bus waiting at the Maximilian Platz, nor any sign of Benjamin Grossman. There was, however, a wrecking crew piling rubbish onto a truck from what had been an office building, from the looks of the debris. The military bus? Of the Americans? Oh, that had pulled out a few minutes ago; it had made room for their truck, as a matter of fact. Another bus? The next day, they thought; or possibly not. They had no idea. Possibly he could get the information at the Hauptbahnhof; the American Military Police had a desk there to help their soldiers traveling by train. It was right where you went into the station from the Bayer Strasse.

The MPs were unable to help him. Whatever military bus was in the habit of either starting or stopping in the Maximilian Platz had nothing to do with their department. To get to Konstanz? There were, of course, trains—but Max had left his prisoner garb at the camp, and without his striped shirt or cap, he would have to pay. And the money he was carrying was not meant for chasing foolish Jews halfway across Germany in order to help them get into Switzerland; it was meant for the far more important job of getting desperate people into Palestine to find safety.

Max Brodsky stood and stared at the jagged holes in what had been the curved glass roof of the railroad station, thinking. He carefully reviewed all of Morris Wolf's arguments, considered the monetary aspects of his chase in all their ramifications, carefully meditated on the chances of finding Grossman, and then discarded all his conclusions and walked into the information room and up to a clerk. There was a train in several hours that went to the Bodensee, yes; not to Konstanz, but to the Bodensee. It was the Alpine express, newly back in service, and it went through Friedrichshafen on its way to Lindau, Chur, and eventually Italy. By getting off at Friedrichshafen, he could catch a bus—whose schedule was admittedly arbitrary—and with luck get into Meersburg by early evening. It would be a long trip, the clerk admitted, but there was no doubt he would arrive. The ferry from Meersburg to Konstanz, the information clerk thought, had never ceased to function, but he was not sure. The ferry, after all, the clerk explained, did not run on rails and was therefore no responsibility of his.

Brodsky thanked him, added up all the disadvantages of his pursuit once again—and then went out and bought a ticket. As he waited for the train to arrive, he promised himself that when at last he caught up with Benjamin Grossman, he would pound on his friend's thick German skull until it rang like the glockenspiel at a Polish wedding.

The clerk had not exaggerated; it was, indeed, a long journey. In compensation for having wasted Mossad money on the transportation, Max forwent both lunch and dinner, and as the ancient bus lumbered north along the clear waters of the Bodensee, with the Swiss Alps clearly visible in the transparent afternoon air, he wondered for the hundredth time exactly what he thought he was accomplishing by the trip. The chances that he could encounter Grossman had to be astronomical. After all, Konstanz was not exactly a crossroads village; and besides, he had never been there before. He would not only be searching for a needle in a haystack, but it would be a foreign haystack, at that. Besides, for all he knew Grossman could be planning on making his attempt in a hundred towns other than Konstanz; the man was not above being devious, and the fact that he had mentioned Konstanz might well mean it was the one place he would *not* try to cross the frontier. How could he hope to locate the man under those conditions? And even if he found him, how could he possibly help him? What did he know about crossing borders? He was an idiot; that was the answer. He was a fool; that was what he knew about crossing borders.

The day wore on, seemingly endless. Max intermittently napped and tried to think of other things besides the meals he had missed. It had been many months now since Belsen had been liberated, and he had become accustomed in that time to regular meals. The bus lurched on and on.

At seven o'clock the tired vehicle finally made it into Meersburg, dropping him off at a newsstand that served the small village as bus station. It was a short block to the ferry slip, and Max just managed to catch the ferry as the landing plate was being dragged aboard by the two-man crew. By now, of course, Max was merely completing an assignment simply because it had been started; it was obvious he was wasting his time, but he could scarcely turn about and go home at this point. That would have been even more foolish than his having started out in the first place, and God knew how stupid that had been!

Under other circumstances, Max might have enjoyed the brief twenty-minute ferry ride across the blue waters of the Bodensee from Meersburg to Staad, the docking area for the Konstanz ferry. The sun was setting now over the huge mountains to the west; the snow-capped peaks rose majestically from the sloping plains that bordered the lake. The growing shadows made the narrow valleys that slotted their way between the ranges a deep blue, matching the dark waters of the lake. There was a freshness in the air, a promise that here in this part of the world which had been spared the devastation of war, one might find peace. Here one could forget the bombings; here one might even learn to forget the horrors of the concentration camps.

How different, he thought, from the land I worked so hard on as a boy, working for the farmer Kolchak, while my parents slaved over their hot irons in the tailor shop in town that was permitted to make clothes just for Jews—who had no money to pay. How different this paradise from the barren soil of Palestine on the kibbutz, growing everything the hard way! Maybe Grossman was right. What was wrong with wanting to enjoy this peace, this beauty? What was wrong with preferring to live here among these great quiet peaks, in the wide green valleys, rather than struggling with the heat and the discomfort of the Palestinian deserts? What was wrong with wanting to live in peace with your neighbors rather than struggling against an inhospitable land in constant war with both British and Arab?

Then his mind cleared and he smiled. Those struggles, he said to himself, made me strong enough to live through the camps—and to bring others through with me, Grossman included. And besides, Grossman was wrong. For any Jew one square meter of Palestinian soil, owned and brought to fruition by his own hand, his own sweat, had to be worth the whole of any country on earth.

The ferry pulled into Staad and docked with a great rush of water into the slip, bouncing jarringly against the straining planks, and settling down only when lashed into growling obedience by the dockside davits. And as Max Brodsky swung along the short road leading to Konstanz itself, he tried to seriously analyze exactly why he was undertaking this obviously useless trip. He decided it had to be because he had too much time and effort invested in bringing Benjamin Grossman through Bergen-Belsen to lose him now. He also decided he had changed his mind as to what he would do when and if he found his friend. Rather than pound on that thick German skull, he would strangle the man with his bare hands, and then toss his dead body across the border into Switzerland, if that was where Benjamin Grossman wanted to go so badly.

It was a comforting thought and kept his mind from food as he marched along.

The seventy-odd miles from Munich's Maximilian Platz to Leipheim on the Ulm road had been covered in a scant two and a half hours, a tribute to the bus driver's utter lack of caution or good sense on the unrepaired road. As Grossman climbed down and watched the bus tear off again, he wished he had waited at least until after breakfast before taking off on his journey. Or had not been so stubborn about accepting a few cans of food before taking off; even a lunch of Spam would have tasted good at the moment. The little money Max had given him—which would have been more if Max had not been so Jew-stingy—he had to save for more desperate times. He crossed the road and started to wave down the trucks that were passing in a steady stream, churning up dust.

As he stood there he felt a fine sense of freedom, simply for being alone. He had always been a loner, and that had been difficult if not impossible in either the camps or at Felsdorf. He was also pleased he had made the decision to leave, certain it had been the right one, even if arrived at on the spur of the moment.

A truck pulled up, interrupting his thoughts, and the driver motioned him to join him in the cab. He climbed in, slammed the door behind him, shoved the striped cap into his pocket, and leaned back, completely at peace with the world. And Brodsky and Wolf had thought there would be some trouble in getting to Konstanz! Here he was, well on the way to his goal, and it was only eleven in the morning! Maybe he could get the driver to buy him some lunch at a roadside inn; or maybe the driver had rations with him. All these Americans seemed to be loaded with chocolate bars, as if they grew them in their back yards.

His thoughts were interrupted and it was a moment before he realized he was being addressed in Yiddish. In surprise, he looked over at the driver, actually seeing him for the first time. It was an American soldier with two stripes on his arm, a corporal, a smallish man far older than one would expect for that lowly rank. He wore thick glasses and his uniform seemed too big for him. He kept wetting his lips as he spoke.

"Where are you going?"

"I'm trying to get to Konstanz, on the Bodensee," he said, speaking pure German. There were enough rides to be had on this road without having to cater to the language tastes of some Jew corporal, probably from New York. Wasn't that where all American Jews lived?

"Konstanz. On the Bodensee," said the corporal, frowning, and then understood. "Oh," he said in English. "Constance. On Lake Constance." He glanced over at Grossman and then brought his attention back to the road, changing to halting German. "I thought— I guess we all have the idea that all camp inmates were Jews. And you look . . ." He let it fade away. Grossman made no attempt to enlighten the man. "What camps were you in?" the corporal asked, trying to pass over the brief silence.

"Maidanek, Buchenwald, and Belsen."

The corporal's eyebrows raised. "Good Lord! You're lucky to be alive!"

"I suppose."

"What was it like in the camps?"

The nosy Jew bastard!

"It was like something I don't feel like talking about."

"Oh." The corporal's face turned fiery red. "I'm sorry. I'm really sorry. I should have realized . . . I didn't mean . . ." As if in compensation for the faux pas, he said slowly, "Constance . . . I'm on my way to Freiburg with medical supplies. I'm a medic, you see— well, a dental technician, actually, but they were short of drivers and I said I'd go. I think I go near there, though . . ."

He pulled from the road, set the brake, and drew a map from the glove compartment, studying it, constantly pushing his glasses into position as they slid down his nose.

"I go through a place called Tuttlingen. Constance is off the road quite a bit, but I guess I could take you at least partway to Constance from Tuttlingen . . ."

"There's a good road from Tuttlingen to Singen," Grossman said.

"Singen . . . yes . . ." said the corporal. He put the map away and got the truck back on the road, after which he concentrated on his driving, saying nothing.

A typical Jew, Grossman thought with disgust. All nosy and pushing as long as you let them; all fawning and toadying once you put them in their place. Although it was true that Brodsky wasn't that way, and to call Wolf fawning was ridiculous. Well, there were exceptions to every rule, and Brodsky and Wolf merely proved it. This little Jew was as standard as they came; he would not only take him where he wanted to go, but he would buy all the meals en route, as well. Grossman would have bet on it.

At Singen the border was only three miles away, at a small village called Thayngen, but Grossman knew the border there would be loaded with guards. According to the stories he had heard at Felsdorf, they constituted half the population of the small town, and the huge dogs they had constituted most of the remaining half. No, Thayngen was not the place to cross any more than Konstanz itself was. Let Wolf and Brodsky think that was his goal; let them think what they would. Grossman knew where he was going to cross and had since he had made up his mind so quickly to make his attempt at last. It made him wonder why he had waited so long.

They had lunch at Ehringen, dinner at Stochach—both meals paid for by the diffident corporal almost as if it were a compulsion—and then under Grossman's direction they took a winding dirt road down to Radolfzell on the Zellersee, only twelve miles from Konstanz. Here Grossman had the Jew corporal turn south; he was giving orders now, no longer asking. They passed through Allenbach, less than four miles from Konstanz, and on the far side of the small town he had the corporal stop the truck and drop him off. He started to give perfunctory thanks and then remembered something. It never hurt to be sure of things. He got back up on the running board and leaned in the window.

"Do you have a tool kit?"

"A tool kit?"

"Yes," Grossman said impatiently. "Tools. To fix things. To change a tire if you have to."

"Oh. I—why, yes. Under the seat. Why?"

"Let me see it."

"I really don't think—" the corporal started to say, and then sighed. He climbed down, brought out the tool kit, and opened it. Grossman leaned over, studying the tools, and then selected the largest screwdriver in the set as being best suited to his needs. He tucked it into his belt, jumped down, and waved.

"Thanks." He backed into the darkness, watching the truck make a difficult turn in the narrow road and flee back toward Radolfzell as if pursued by the hounds of hell. Grossman laughed. Typical! I could have taken the truck from him, he thought; I could have told him to drive me over the border somewhere along the line, and the poor fool would undoubtedly have tried it! We were wrong to try and wipe the Jews from the earth; we should have used them for slaves. They would have made excellent slaves.

It was a dark night, with a sliver of a moon trying halfheartedly to peer through the banks of curdled clouds. He realized this was pure luck; when he had made his impulsive decision to try for the border he had not even considered the phase of the moon. Maybe it augured well for his mission; it was time things went right for him. Still, while he had not considered the phase of the moon, the place of his crossing had occurred to him almost instantly. He had spent many a weekend with girls of various standards of morals here on the Zellersee when he had been at the university in Munich. He remembered well the small rowboats that had been rented out to lovers at the dock below Allenbach, boats one could use to row to Reichenau Island in the lake and there enjoy all the privacy a lover could desire. It was a long row, but certainly within his power to make, for he would not only have to reach the island, but would have to row around the tip to the edge facing the Swiss shore.

He calculated it would take three hours to bring him into the proper position on Reichenau. Then possibly another hour of rowing, but after that it meant a swim, since he could not risk the noise of oarlocks near the shore. But he would still have the boat for support. An hour out of Reichenau he would strip, place his clothing in the boat, and paddle behind the boat to Switzerland. It would be a long job, but it would be the sure safe way to get there; the shore from Steckborn to Gottlieben had to be as deserted as any section of the border. Of course he could row down from Allenbach to Stomeyersdorf in the swamp area above Konstanz and cross there; that was only a few hundred yards wide—but that portion of the border would be heavily patrolled.

No; his way was best. The water would be chilly, and his bad arm would be a problem on the long row, but it was the proper method of getting into the country. Then, once inland, over the low hills to Pfyn and on to Frauenfeld. It was an area he knew well, and he was sure he could get by. There were many out-of-the-way farms in the district, and from them he could get less identifiable clothing, and even—with his money—a ride to Zurich by some farmer pleased to be earning ten American dollars. And in Zurich, once the banks opened, everything would be resolved.

He cautioned himself not to dwell on the future so much, but to concentrate on the immediate requirements of the plan. The small dock with the rowboats had been about a mile east of the town; he was sure they would still be there. This part of Germany and the world had been untouched by the war, people still came here for vacations. The boats might be chained, of course, which is why he had required the screwdriver, but no chain was going to stop him at this point. He hitched the screwdriver into a more comfortable position in his belt and started down the road.

Deiter Kessler had never enjoyed the war, even in those heady days when the armies of the Third Reich were sweeping all opposition easily before them. Deiter Kessler was by nature a peaceful man, as many large powerful men are peaceful, and while he had been forced at times to kill, he had never done it with the obvious pleasure of some of his companions. And as the war continued, Deiter Kessler enjoyed it less and less. But when the war was over, he found that peace had dealt him worse blows than the war ever had. For when he returned to Konstanz, whence he had been called to arms, it was to find that his wife had gone off with another man, taking not only their children but the furniture as well. The factory where he had been employed was no longer in existence, a fire having reduced it to hot bricks and a hole in the ground while he had been away. It never occurred to Deiter Kessler to leave the area; it was his home and the only solid recognizable thing in a world rapidly shifting beneath his feet. In order to live, therefore, Kessler was reduced to taking a job guarding the small boat dock near Allenbach.

It was not too bad a job. It required almost no labor and allowed much time for thinking, although few of Deiter Kessler's thoughts were pleasant. It also paid very little; on his salary it was difficult to find a boardinghouse he could afford. And, of course, the distance from Konstanz made it impossible to pay for daily transportation back and forth. But there was a small boathouse on the dock where oars were normally kept at night, and here Deiter, therefore, had arranged a cot where he could sleep on cool nights. On pleasant evenings, though, he preferred to sleep in one of the boats, lost in its shadows, stretched out on the duckboards with his arm for a pillow, lulled by the pleasing motion of the water. There was an additional advantage of sleeping among the boats; it made it unnecessary to unship and store the oars each night, as well as not having to bring them out again each morning.

The boat in which Deiter Kessler chose to sleep this particular night was chosen because it was the dryest and would remain dry throughout the night, which could not always be said of all the others. As he lay down, Deiter was looking forward to dreaming a dream he often had, of coming home from the war to find his buxom wife there to greet him, kissing him passionately with promise in the kiss, with his son and daughter there, the house all bright and shining, the odor of his wife's excellent cooking even edging into his dream to make him hungry. It was a nice dream, a good dream, and even though when he woke it was always to feel more depressed than ever, he still looked forward to his recurring dream. For that brief period, at least, he was happy.

This night, though, there was an inexplicable variation in the dream. When he came home from the war it was to find the door of his house locked, and to discover he had no key. He started to shake the door, using his great strength, and the lock sprang open, but there was a chain inside, holding the door closed, and he realized his wife must be home to have put up the chain. She not only was home but he could see her inside, talking to some strange man, laughing, paying no attention to her husband. It made him furious. He started to shove the door against the chain, making it rattle, but to no avail.

When at last he stood back to consider some other means of entrance, for some unknown reason the chain continued to rattle.

He shifted slightly on the hard duckboards of the boat and came awake, momentarily relieved it had only been a dream, and that the security of his normal fantasy had not been breached. But some of the fury was still in him. And then he became aware that he was still hearing a chain rattle, softly but insistently. He raised his head slightly, peering over the shadow of the gunwale. Someone was trying to pry the ring loose that held the chain coupling the boats; someone was trying to steal the boats! My God, hadn't he enough trouble in his life? He couldn't even have a decent dream without someone interrupting! Now that someone was trying to get him into more trouble by stealing the boats in his charge!

Deiter came to his feet silently, balancing his large frame with practiced ease against the dipping of the boat. He silently unshipped an oar and raised it over his head, determined to give this one a lesson! He started to step to the dock, but the movement threw his boat against the others, making them all bump the dock, and the man turned, startled. In the little light there was, Deiter saw the glint of steel in the man's hand, and any compunction he might have felt for merely challenging the thief disappeared. With a lunge he brought the oar down as hard as he could.

The man did his best to avoid the blow, but the heavy oar caught him on his shoulder and threw him from the dock. The tool in his hand went flying, disappearing with a slight splash in the lake. There was an almost audible snap as his leg crashed against the edge of one of the boats, and then he was in the water, floundering.

In an instant the anger Deiter Kessler had been feeling changed to compassion. What had he done? The man had been trying to steal the boats, it was true, but was that any reason to try to kill him? Was the crime of theft now to be punished by death? Had he become an animal? The water at the dock was shallow, little more than the draft the boats required; he stepped down into the water and raised the man in his arms.

"Are you all right?"

"My leg—" There was tight pain in the voice.

"Let's get some light."

Deiter carried the thin figure in his arms easily, bringing him to the shack, squelching along the dock in his sodden boots. He put the

man down as gently as he could, and went inside. He brought out a
kerosene lantern and lit it, studying the man on the dock with curiosity. Grossman's eyes were shut, his breathing ragged. He opened
his eyes and then shut them tightly against the glare of the lantern.

"My leg—it's broken . . ."

It was evident he was telling the truth; the leg poked out at an
odd angle, not disguised by the soaking trouser leg. Deiter tried to
think what to do. He had no ability to set the leg himself, and he
knew from his wartime training that the man should not be moved
unless there were trained people to do it. But there was no hospital
in Allenbach; there was not even a doctor, or even a nurse as far as
he knew. The closest help was in Konstanz, three or four miles away,
and he had no transportation. There was a barrow nearby he could
borrow, but he could scarcely haul the man three or four miles in a
barrow; he could be dead from shock long before they arrived. And
the lone constable on duty in town only had a bicycle—

But the constable did have a telephone!

Grossman was shivering violently, although the evening was warm.
Deiter took off his jacket and wrapped it about the injured man,
wincing as the other winced, sorry he did not have any schnapps to
ward off the shock that was coming. "Don't move," he said. "I'll go
for help," and he started off at a gallop.

The small sidewalk cafe on Saarland Strasse gave a view down
Konstanz Strasse as well as down Kreutlingen Strasse to the fence
that constituted the German-Swiss border, as well as to the two
guard positions that allowed passage on the two roads between the
countries to be monitored. At that hour of the night there was little
traffic, and the occasional truck that came along was thoroughly
searched and the driver's papers well studied. Brodsky had come to
the cafe after watching the railroad cars along the tracks on Schiller
Strasse undergo a search at the gate he knew would be sufficient to
prevent any passage by that route. If Grossman seriously considered
crossing into Switzerland from the town of Konstanz, he was obviously wasting his time.

As if in answer to the thought, there was a soft voice behind him.

"Forget it. It's impossible—"

Max turned in surprise; it was the waiter who had served him his coffee, his only concession to his growing hunger and to the responsibility he felt for the funds he carried.

"Were you talking to me?"

The waiter chose to answer in another fashion. He was an old man with a stoop and with sad eyes set in a seamed face; his worn shoes had been sliced with a razor blade to give his corns room. His black uniform was shiny with age, but his paper dicky was spotless.

"They come almost every day, lately," the waiter said. "Before the war they came as tourists, for the lake, for the rest, to cross into Switzerland for the scenery. Now they come like you. They sit and have a coffee, or a *Kuchen*, or sometimes a schnapps to build up their courage or to hide their disappointment, I suppose. But mostly they just sit here awhile, staring up the street to the fence; and then they mostly go away and forget it. Like you should go away and forget it. Pardon me if I speak out of turn, but crossing into Switzerland is not easy."

"You say, mostly they go away," Max said, interested. "Do some of them try to cross?"

"Not many, but some." The old man flicked his towel at a fly who merely circled and returned. The old man sighed; the fly seemed to represent the inevitability of his failures. "They try to swim around the end of the fence out in the lake, mostly. Sometimes they drown. Sometimes they get shot. There was one just tonight . . ."

"There was one tonight?" Max sat more erect. "What happened?"

The old man shrugged. "That one was shot . . ."

"*They killed him?*"

The old man looked surprised at this vehemence at a normal event.

"I don't know if they killed him," he said slowly, wanting to be as accurate as possible with this huge and menacing man now on his feet and towering over him. "There were shots down by the lake; they must have seen him in the floodlights. I'm pretty sure they hit him, because they came and took him away in an ambulance. I mean, they brought him back to the Konstanz side," he added, as if to prove that even the ploy of getting shot would not guarantee entrance into the forbidden land.

"Where did they take him?"

"To the Municipal Hospital, I suppose."

"And where is that?"

The old man shuffled to the doorway and pointed.

"On Leiner Strasse. Up Robert Wagner Strasse three blocks, then left. Of course they might have taken him to the Sisters across the river, but—"

He was speaking to empty space. He sighed and picked up the small coin Max had left for the coffee, tucking it into his change purse and laboriously putting the purse into his pocket. They came and they came, and all they got for their trip was getting shot, or going to jail, or just going back where they came from, disappointed.

The dead man was a stranger, but he was as familiar to Max Brodsky as if they had known each other all their lives. The thin body, the army clothes too large, the sucken cheeks, the hair growing back in patches, the tattoo on the arm that signified a period in Auschwitz-Birkenau on his way here to death beside the Bodensee. Max sighed in pity for the poor soul, and shook his head at the morgue attendant. The morgue attendant pulled the sheet back over the dead face and led Max back to the main corridor of the hospital.

Well, at least it hadn't been Ben Grossman. It seemed a cruel thought, a denigration of that man who lay in the morgue and the value of his existence, but that was the way of life. He paused to allow a wheeled litter to pass. It was carrying a pale-faced man whose leg had just been set in plaster of Paris; the leg jutted from a wrinkled trouser leg, still damp, that had been neatly cut with surgical scissors just above the knee. The man's slate-blue eyes flickered open a moment, and then stared in total amazement.

"Max! What are you doing here?"

"I've come to take you back to Felsdorf," Brodsky said softly, and walked along beside the litter as the attendant wheeled it toward the emergency entrance, quite as if they had met by appointment. He frowned as he walked. *Had* they met by appointment? His frown changed to a smile. Coincidence? He didn't think so.

What had Wolf said about God?

Chapter 10

It was early November when the cast finally came off and Benjamin Grossman could take his first tentative steps without the use of crutches. His leg had not healed perfectly; the medical staff at the hospital in Konstanz had done their best, but the long delay in reaching them, plus the several handlings he had suffered before getting to the hospital, had splintered the bone and made the doctors' task more difficult. Benjamin Grossman would have a slight limp for the rest of his life, to add to the disfigurement of what he had once been proud to consider one of the handsome faces of the Third Reich.

It was not a pleasant thing to think about, and his weeks of convalescence gave him ample time to think. True, it was better than being in the group assembled at Nuremberg for the Allied trials scheduled to begin quite shortly, but the truth was that far more of those sought by the authorities had escaped than had been caught. Oh, the Russians had hung quite a few of the SS they had captured, but the Americans would hold their show trials, hang some and free most, and that would be that. Hitler had been a fool to commit suicide; six months after Nuremberg, he could probably walk down the Unterderlinden and American soldiers would give him chewing gum and chocolate bars. It was the way they were.

Ben Grossman would sit at the window of his room, staring out into the compound, and think about Switzerland. He had been so close, and then his damnable luck had deserted him once again! Would he not have been better off with the Strasbourg Group and their ODESSA plan? Here he was, crippled, scarred and with a big Jew nose, sitting in a miserable refugee camp six months after the war had ended, and almost a year after he had planned on getting his money and being on his way. And not a pfennig in his pocket. Brodsky, the cheapskate, had asked for the return of his twenty American dollars and he had no choice but to give it back. It wasn't fair! He was no more guilty of war crimes than Bormann, or Eichmann, or Hirt, or Mittendorf, or the Mauer brothers, or Mengele, or —but he could go on all day. They had all escaped and were undoubtedly living the good life somewhere. And where was he?

When his thoughts became this bitter, he would reprove himself. The original plan had *not* been a bad one. And he wasn't dead yet— which was more than could be said for Himmler or even Hitler, or would shortly be able to be said for some of the defendants in Nuremberg. He would get to Switzerland yet, by God! Maybe from Italy . . .

That was not a bad idea. The Italians were nowhere near as hard-nosed as the Swiss, and they didn't care how many refugees made it into Switzerland. The guards on their side of the border were bound to be less rigorous than the German guards; it was the nature of the people. The border was also longer and less populated. It was, obviously, the answer.

Now that he was ready to travel, he was anxious to get going. The first Mossad group, originally scheduled to be led by Max Brodsky, had left some time before under the leadership of Morris Wolf, Brodsky electing to stay with his friend until he could travel. Grossman suspected that Brodsky had stayed mainly to proselytize him on the matter of Palestine, but if so he was wasting his time. If he, Ben Grossman, never saw Switzerland, he would see Palestine a week after *that!*

According to Brodsky, the Mossad *bricha*—escape—route lay through Innsbruck and the Brenner Pass on the Austrian-Italian border. From there safe-houses led to Verona, then across to Milano and down through Pavia and Tortona to Genoa. A ship called the *Naomi* was being prepared near there at a small port named Nervi, to take a total of two hundred refugees. Brodsky had memorized the safe-house addresses in case the list was lost, or taken from him in any circumstance, and he was as anxious to leave as Grossman, awaiting only the word from the Mossad.

It came in a way he had not contemplated.

The Mossad man appeared at Felsdorf and called a meeting, stood before those in attendance, and gave them the bad news.

"There is no more room on the *Naomi*," he said. "As soon as it is ready, it will sail for Palestine. However, we are dickering for a ship near Riccione on the east coast of Italy, on the Adriatic. We think we can come to arrangements with the present owner in one or two weeks. Until our financial arrangements are complete, we suggest you people remain here. We will inform you when it is time to travel and where to go . . ."

"Not me," Brodsky said positively as soon as he got back to their quarters. "If worse comes to worse, when we get to Genoa, if the *Naomi* is gone we can cross over to Riccione and wait for that boat."

"You can," Grossman said. "Not me. I'll go with you as far as Italy, as far as Milano, but after that I go north. Anyway," he added, "I thought you said the man said the ship was full?"

"Full, schmul!" Brodsky said shortly. The news had put him in a bad mood. "What's one more person they can't squeeze him on?" He frowned at Grossman. "You really going to try for Switzerland again? You still crazy?"

"I'm going to Switzerland. And this time," Grossman said ungraciously, "please don't follow me."

"Don't worry," Brodsky said, irked by this lack of gratitude. "This time I'm going to Nervi as fast as I can get there. You want to come along, fine. You want to stay here, fine."

"I said, I'd go as far as Milano with you."

"I'm sure the Italians will be pleased," Max said sourly, aware that Wolf would have come up with a more cutting remark. That ended the conversation.

They left the following afternoon, catching a ride with a delivery truck into Munich, planning on trying for a railroad boxcar, always easier to get into after dark. The striped shirts and striped caps no longer meant free transportation; Germany and the Germans were getting back to normal.

It was late by the time they arrived at the Haupbahnhof and trudged down the darkened Arnuld Strasse in the direction of the freight yards. It was a black night, bitter cold, with the first wisps of snow brushing their faces as they walked along, their hands stuffed deep into their overcoat pockets, each busy with his dreams. Switzerland, Grossman thought! To be dressed in decent clothes, sitting in front of a blazing fireplace in some alpine hotel-chalet, a tall drink at his elbow, a pretty barmaid glancing at him and seeing beneath the Jew face the real man, the powerful lover, and letting him know it with a subtle blush. Palestine, Brodsky thought! Warmth of the hot sun, the smell of the earth, Deborah meeting him when she was done at the hospital, raising her lovely face to be kissed, holding his hand tightly as they walked along the streets of the old city, stopping at a Yemenite restaurant to eat spicy kebob and sesame bread and drink that wonderful ice-cold Palestine beer.

The fence had been repaired since Brodsky had reconnoitered the area several days earlier. With a muttered curse for the poor timing of the repair crew, he removed his overcoat and laid it across the top strands, and then boosted Grossman up and over. He tossed his knapsack across and managed to wriggle his own way over. He dragged the overcoat down; it snagged and tore on a point of wire.

"Damn!"

He put the coat on and fingered the gash in the darkness, shaking his head disconsolately. The tear went through the lining and let the cold in. Damn, damn, *damn!* He had needle and thread in his knapsack, but there would be little light for mending the rip; maybe when they got settled in a boxcar, if they ever got settled in a boxcar, he could find a pin. But the trip was starting poorly.

They walked along the row of silent cars trying to be as quiet as possible, straining their eyes to read the destination cards in their metal brackets on the sides of the cars, and then gave up. It was too dark and they could not afford to risk a light, and there was no evidence that the destination cards would mean anything, anyway. On his previous trip to the freight yards Brodsky had been informed by a worker that almost all the traffic from that part of the yard went south, and they could only hope the man was correct. It would be a tragedy to go to sleep and wake up in Berlin, or Hamburg, or—worse —Celle.

There was a car with the door slightly open. They crawled in and slid the door shut before they felt they could afford a light. In the flare of a match they saw they had picked an empty car, but one with straw at one end. It smelled as if it had contained animals, and a second match confirmed this in the droppings on the floor. But it was warmer than the outdoors, and the straw promised some small

degree of comfort. They dragged enough straw clear of the droppings, wrapped themselves tightly in their overcoats, and, with their
knapsacks for pillows, fell into an uncomfortable sleep. The last
thing each thought of before dozing off was the last time he had
been in a boxcar, on the trip from Buchenwald to Celle.

Each hoped this trip would have a better conclusion.

They awoke with a jerk; there had been a loud rattling of
couplings and then the car was moving. There was a faint strip of
light along the edge of the door. Grossman got up, yawned, and
hobbled to the door, shivering. He slid the door slightly open and
stared out. Max was watching him.

"Well?"

"It's morning . . ."

"No!" Max was in a bad mood. He had slept poorly, he was irked
about the torn overcoat, and he was still remembering Grossman's ill
manners the day before. "I thought it was always light at night!"

"And it's cold . . ."

"That's strange. I thought it was hot."

"We're heading south," Grossman said. He hadn't heard a word
Brodsky had said. His voice was tinged with satisfaction. "We're
going through Hohenbrunn; it's a suburb of Munich. This track goes
down to Bruchmuel and Rosenheim, toward Austria. We're all
right."

"And about time," Max said sourly, and started to open his knapsack. "Leave the door open a little for light." He drew out his sewing
kit, selected a needle, squintingly threaded it, and began to repair his
coat. "What I wonder, though, is why they're sending empty cars
south?"

"Who cares?" Grossman brought out a tin of beans and was busy
prying it open. He dug in with the blade of his knife, eating with
quiet grunts of pleasure, speaking with his mouth full. "You want
some?"

"Later," Brodsky said, and then caught his balance as the train
suddenly braked and a shudder ran down the line of cars. Grossman
put down his can of beans and went to the door. Brodsky had
stopped sewing and was watching him.

"Well?"

"We're slowing down . . ."

"You noticed! Why are we slowing down?"

"How the devil should I know?" He suddenly slid the door shut. "They're pulling into a siding."

"Great!" Brodsky said bitterly. "That was some long trip. How far have we come? Two whole miles?"

"Shhhhh . . ."

The train had come to a halt with a final bumping of cars and there were voices outside. They were speaking English. Max came to his feet and edged to the door, listening. He shivered and slipped into his overcoat, the needle dangling.

"—how in hell," one of the voices was saying in a deep aggrieved tone of voice, "are we supposed to ship them fu—I mean, them trucks in closed boxcars? How are we supposed to get them *in?* And why ship the fu—I mean, why ship them in the first place? Why in hell not just drive 'em down, Lieutenant?"

"For a variety of reasons, Sergeant," a second voice said wearily. The lieutenant seemed to have heard this argument before, from others. "There's a severe shortage of gasoline in these countries, for one. For another, the roads are in lousy shape, and we could run into ten feet of snow in the mountains, or lose a couple of trucks over the edge of a cliff. And then there's the big reason—"

"What's that, Lieutenant?"

"Our orders are to ship them by these boxcars, that's why. Never argue with the brass."

"Yes, sir, I agree," said the sergeant desperately, "Only will you please tell me how we're goin' to get our trucks through them skinny little doors?"

"You're going to make the doors wider, Sergeant."

"*What!* Them cars is made of *steel,* Lieutenant!"

"I can see they're steel, Sergeant. You have oxy-acetylene equipment, don't you?"

"Well—yes, sir—but I got maybe one guy can use a torch without burnin' his own feet off, and we got us here a string of twenty-five, thirty boxcars. We'll be here a month!"

"Sergeant," the lieutenant said wearily, "we all have our problems." The lieutenant sounded as if the sergeant was one of his major ones. "Yours is to ship those trucks. In those boxcars. Today. I've told you how to handle it. So handle it."

"Yes, sir . . ." There was the sound of the lieutenant's footsteps marching away; then the dispirited tone left the sergeant's voice as he took command. "All right, you guys! Jackson, go get the oxyacetylene crap; bring everything you got or can cadge. Maybe you can teach some of these clowns how to work one of them fuckin' torches. And make sure you got full tanks. I don't want to freeze my ass here all day while you guys go back and forth like union plumbers. Johnson, get them cars open and aired out. Get them cleaned out, too. They tell me they had cows or pigs in them before we got them, so they're probably full of shit. And get any straw out, too. We don't want no fuckin' fires. You—yes, you, Private, whatever the hell your name is—make sure the trucks got enough gas in them to at least drive them outta the boxcars when we get there. Fill 'em up, if you can." Under his breath he muttered direly, "Gasoline shortage, my ass!" His voice went up again. "All right, you guys, move it!"

There was the rattle of boxcar doors being slid back on the double as the men sprang to their jobs. Brodsky shrugged and snapped the thread loose from his coat. One thing was certain; he wouldn't get a chance to repair the coat in the comfort of the boxcar. Maybe back at Felsdorf, because it looked as if that was where they would have to go. He tucked the sewing kit away and waited. The sound of the sliding doors came closer as the men approached. Then their door was pulled back with a bang and a surprised corporal was staring at them.

"Hey, Sarge!"

The sergeant came along the loading dock, a cigar stub jammed in one corner of his mouth. Both Brodsky and Grossman recognized him at once. There was a frown on the rough unshaven face.

"Well, well! What do we have here? Stowaways, huh? Sorry to evict you guys, but like the man says, we all got troubles. We got a prior use for these cars—" He suddenly stared at them closer. "Hey! Ain't I seen you guys before?"

"You lift us up and bring us to Munich," Max said proudly.

"Yeah, that's right. Couple months ago. Where's the third guy, the little guy with the smashed-up mush?" He looked in the car and accepted its emptiness as the answer to his question. "Well, like I said, I'm sorry but I can't help you guys this time. That ninety-day wonder I got riding my ass—" He noticed the corporal listening and gave him a glare. The corporal suddenly found something to do elsewhere. "Like I was saying, that pissant lieutenant of mine is a cock-sucker for the rules."

Max Brodsky had a sudden and wonderful thought.

"Sergeant—"

"No," the sergeant said firmly. "Look, pal, I'm sorry, but like I—"

"No, no!" Brodsky said hurriedly. "I hear what the lieutenant talk to you. My friend here is a wonderful user of the torch—" He turned to Grossman, speaking rapidly in Yiddish. "Ben, do you know what an oxy-something torch is?"

"Oxy-acetylene. A burning torch," Grossman said, mystified.

"Can you use one?"

"I haven't for years."

"But you know how to use one?"

"Yes."

"Thank God!" Brodsky turned back to the sergeant. "My friend can able you to fix down the doors in no time almost." He stepped from the boxcar, taking the sergeant by the arm, walking him a short distance along the loading platform, their breath steaming in the cold air. Grossman stared after him, wondering what was going on, exactly what Brodsky was promoting at the moment.

The sergeant chewed on his unlit cigar stub, his small eyes watching Brodsky carefully. Sergeant Aloyious Chenowicz had met con artists before, and he had a feeling he was in the presence of a master.

"What's on your mind, chum?"

"Could I ask to where you go?"

"Where we're headed for? Italy. Genoa, to be exact."

"*Genoa?*" Ho, ho, Wolf! No God, eh?

"That's right. Only don't ask me why," said the sergeant, speaking for himself, while his busy eye made sure his men were doing their assigned jobs, and doing them properly. "Probably goin' to ship them fuckin' trucks to Amsterdam and down the Rhine back to here. The way everything else is fucked up in this man's army, it wouldn't surprise the hell outta me."

"We'd be no trouble," Max said earnestly. "Sit in one of trucks. Real quiet . . ."

The sergeant started to shake his head, and then stopped. He looked at Max quizzically.

"Your pal really knows how to use a burnin' torch?" Max crossed his heart. "Well, we'll find out quick enough. You poor bastards still got no papers, huh?"

Max shook his head dolefully.

"They really go for papers in these fuckin' countries, don't they? But why the yen to go to Italy?" The sergeant answered his own question. "Why not, I guess. At least it ain't so fuckin' cold there." He bit his lip, thinking. "Well, if your pal can give us a hand with them fuckin' doors, and if you guys should happen to stumble into one of them trucks while I ain't lookin', I don't know nothin' about it. If the lieutenant's around, though, forget it—though the chances of that are about like Cleveland winnin' a pennant. If it's this cold he'll be in the caboose, tellin' the Heinie brakeman how he won the war." He studied Max's broad shoulders appreciatively. "And you can give us a hand, too. We're goin' to have to push them trucks into them boxcars by hand. Let any of them fuckin' clowns drive 'em in and they'd take 'em right through the fuckin' wall—"

A man in a fur-trimmed overcoat and a neat homburg came hurrying up. He spoke a correct but accented English.

"Sir! Sergeant! One of your men is starting to burn the sides of a boxcar down there! That car is the property of the German National Railways!"

"No shit! Well," said the sergeant helpfully, "stick around and watch us burn out the sides of all the fuckin' cars in the train. We just happen to win this war." He turned to Max, speaking loudly for the benefit of the man who remained standing there, outraged. "I hope this clown raises enough hell to get to the general in the caboose. The old general'll have his balls for door knockers."

The man stared at him a moment, furious, and then stomped off, his shoulders hunched in his overcoat.

"You should of swapped overcoats with the Heinie fucker," Sergeant Chenowicz said sympathetically to Max, and then started off down the line to supervise the work. Max stared after him. He should have swapped coats with the man, at that.

It was eleven at night by the time all the doors had been widened, the trucks rolled in and their wheels chocked to prevent movement during the trip. The sergeant came around, his ever-present cigar stub jammed into one corner of his mouth, making a last-minute in-

spection. He walked into the car with their truck and looked up at
Brodsky in the driver's seat. Brodsky rolled down the window.

"No lights," the sergeant said quietly. "We stop at any border, or
anyplace else for that matter, you guys get out of sight. Scrunch
down on the floor. If you guys get caught, you're on your own. I
never heard of you. I got enough fuckin' troubles of my own." He
started to leave and then turned back. "We put the ignition keys in
the glove compartments. Don't want the fuckers to jiggle out and
get lost with the shakin' I expect on this crapped-up railroad line."

He walked out of the car and waved an authoritative arm toward
the engine; the train started up with a shiver that ran its length, as if
it had stiffened with cold during the long wait. The sergeant
watched as the boxcars clanked along, slowly gaining speed, waited
while the passenger car with the troops went by with someone already setting up a board for cards, and then swung aboard the
caboose as it slid past. He would be goin' home after deliverin' the
fuckin' trucks; he wondered where them poor bastards without
papers in that truck were goin' to end up. And he hoped to Christ
they knew what he was talkin' about when he mentioned that
fuckin' ignition key.

It was cold, bitter cold, and the higher the train went, straining at
the long incline that led to the Austrian Alps, the colder it got. They
chugged their way through Rosenheim and then started the long
climb toward Kufstein and the Austrian frontier. The two men in
the truck cab did not speak; each was too intent upon his own
thoughts. Max, wrapped in his torn coat, was thinking how lucky
they were to be getting the ride, and to Genoa itself! If they were
not discovered and thrown off at either of the two frontiers they had
to pass—or at any other station they had to pass—he could be in
Nervi the following day, and maybe catch the *Naomi* before it
sailed. It was an exciting thought. That was, of course, if he didn't
freeze to death before then; the cold was beginning to make him
numb. Grossman, on the other hand, was adding the discomfort he
was feeling to the long list of bitter complaints against Fate he had
been compiling ever since his great scheme had begun to go astray a
year before. He stared across the truck cab at Brodsky, hunched
behind the steering wheel, watching the vaporous breath come from
that large cocoon. How could they avoid being spotted, for God's

sake? They looked like a couple of geysers at one of the German spas, steaming up the place like that! They had to be caught—or were they supposed to hold their breath for twenty or thirty minutes while the border guards inspected the train at the frontier? And where would they get kicked off? On top of some mountain, without a doubt, where they would die quickly of cold. To try and get his mind off the dire possibilities, he addressed Max, trying to prevent his teeth from chattering.

"Do you know where we're going?"

Max grinned at him. "Genoa."

"Genoa! How the devil did you arrange that?"

Max pointed toward the ceiling of the car. "Not me. Him."

"Did He also arrange for the car to go through Milano?"

"He didn't say."

"Next time, ask Him," Grossman said, and fell silent. He tried to remember the map of Italy he had memorized, but he couldn't place Genoa on it. He hadn't been interested in Genoa; he still wasn't interested in Genoa. "What was the sergeant saying back there? Just before the train left?"

Max shrugged, a movement scarcely visible under all his clothes.

"Nothing. He said not to put on any lights, as if we didn't have enough sense to know that. He said to get down on the floor if the train stops anywhere. What did he think, we were going to stand up and cheer for the guards to see? Oh, and he said he takes no responsibility if we are caught. He said he has enough troubles."

"Troubles!" Grossman said bitterly. "I would love to trade him troubles! That's all he said?"

"That's all, I think." Max remembered. "Oh, he said something about a key, some key they put into the glove something, so it wouldn't drop out and get lost on the floor."

"*What!*"

Grossman stared at Brodsky with a look of combined horror and disbelief. How stupid could the dumb Jew be? Or maybe it was because he was a Pole; Wolf was a Jew but he was a German. He would have understood in a second. Grossman fumbled in the glove compartment with stiff fingers, brought out the key, and shoved it in the ignition. He checked to make sure the gears were in neutral, and then put his foot past Brodsky's to stamp heavily on the floor starter.

Brodsky was looking at him with alarm.

"What are you doing? You're making noise—"

"Shut up! If this thing is frozen . . ."

The shrill whine of the starter was lost in the clanking of the box-cars as they rattled over the uneven track, and in the chugging of the engine as it fought the mountain. God! Grossman thought desperately, if we could have started this thing back in Hohenbrunn and can't now because we waited too long, I'll kill the dumb Jew, big as he is! How could he be so damn stupid?

He kept his foot pressed on the starter, praying the battery would last until the motor caught, and then when he was about to admit defeat there was a cough, then another cough, the momentary rumble as the engine fought to maintain itself, and then silence. Three times the motor stalled and three times it managed to revive itself before it finally settled down to a steady beat. Grossman waited a few minutes and then leaned over and switched on the heater. The air was cold at first, with a musty odor; then it gradually warmed. Soon a steady stream of hot air made the loosening of clothing necessary. The steam from their breaths disappeared from the window; the exhaust fumes swirled about the boxcar and then were swept out of the huge gash in the side of the boxcar, together with the flurries of snow that also swirled about the car.

"That's better!" Grossman said with satisfaction, and reached for his knapsack and the food there.

But Brodsky was worried. "Ben—should we be doing this? The sergeant said—"

"The sergeant tried to tell you about the ignition key, but you were too stupid to understand! How can a person live who is that stupid?" God! When the train got anywhere in northern Italy he would be rid of this dumb Jew, and not a minute too soon! "We could have frozen to death! Stupid! Stupid!"

Brodsky stared straight ahead into the pitch-black end of the swaying boxcar. Well, it was true he had not understood what the sergeant meant, so maybe that had been stupid. He didn't know anything about trucks or oxy-whatever torches, but he had gotten them the ride. If Grossman had been handling the sergeant back in Hohenbrunn, they'd be back at Felsdorf right this minute. Now they were riding in comfort. He glanced across at Grossman, eating from a can, his overcoat open. He wants to go to Switzerland, does he? Well, let him!

Grossman finished his tin and dropped it on the floor rather than roll down the window and try to dispose of it through the gap in the car wall; rolling down the window would mean losing precious heat. He closed his eyes and leaned back, comfortable for the first time that day, the heat making him sleepy. That dumb, dumb Jew!

He woke with a start, instantly aware of one thing: the cold again. What had that stupid Jew done now? He glanced at the ignition key and saw it had been turned off. A wave of unreasoning fury swept him. What was the idiotic bastard trying to do, freeze them both to death? Or was he just being contrary? He reached for the key, but Brodsky's huge hand clamped over his, preventing him from touching it, and he then became aware that the train was stopping, and had been slowing down since he had been coming awake. The train shuddered to a halt and he realized the reason for Brodsky's action.

There were lights from swinging lanterns moving alongside the train, the crunch of footsteps on gravel along the track. Brodsky was hunched down as low as he could; the steering wheel prevented him from sliding to the floor. Grossman pushed himself to the floor and waited tensely. There were a few shouts; a flashlight, angled upward, slid across the windows of the truck and passed on. A hand was banged against the side of one of the cars; the train started to move again. They had successfully crossed into Austria without being detected and the train was now struggling up the steady rise toward Innsbruck.

The snow was coming down steadily now, swirling into the open boxcar, coming up to coat the windshield. Through the side windows they could see the roofs of houses glittering under the snow, their chalet tiles gleaming with reflections from streetlamps. An occasional lit window indicated some poor person unable to sleep, or some festive occasion to keep people awake beyond the normal early hours of the area. It was a strange feeling to inspect the normalcy of life in the neat homes beside the track while they shivered in the dark truck, fugitives from normalcy in every way. Grossman waited until they were once again in the country, the train straining mightily past stands of pine tipped with snow, before starting the truck's motor once again. It responded at once, throwing out heat. Brodsky said nothing. He was sitting erect, staring straight ahead. So he stayed awake and saved us from being caught, Grossman thought angrily.

What does he want, a medal? But he knew, as he closed his eyes and went back to sleep, that if Brodsky had also gone to sleep, at this moment they would undoubtedly still be on German soil watching the lights of the train disappear up the track into the snow and the darkness.

The Brenner Pass was reached a few hours later. This time Grossman woke to both cold and darkness, once again realizing Brodsky had remained awake while he had slept. Again the two men crouched down and waited; only this time a pair of footsteps that crunched through the snow beside the cars stopped at their car, and they could hear the sounds of someone laboriously clambering into the car. A flashlight swept the glass of the window, angling downward, revealing the two men. The handle of the door was being turned. Well, Grossman thought, at least we got this far. Maybe the Mossad outfit had a safe-house near here. If we make a dash for it once they have us on the tracks, we may be able to get by the guards and get lost in the dark and the snow. He tensed himself and then heard a familiar deep voice, unaccustomedly low in volume.

"Keep your fuckin' heads down. And don't talk. I'm doing an inspection. Lucky you found the ignition key; it's colder out than an Eskimo cunt's left tit. I was afraid I'd find you guys dead."

The door was closed; they could hear the sergeant climb down, hear him shout something down the line, and then they were moving again. They were in Italy!

The train was descending now, the chugging of the engine actually sounded cheerful, proud to have beaten the huge mountains, relaxed now and gathering speed. Grossman wanted to ask Brodsky what the sergeant had said, but figured it could not have been too important. Still, they had gotten into Italy with remarkably little trouble, and it was foolish to argue at a time of such success. He smiled across the cab.

"We made it."

Brodsky merely shrugged. He turned the ignition key and stepped on the starter. The motor caught at once, heat gushing from the heater. Grossman's smile widened.

"Not bad. We'll teach you how to handle machinery yet." Brodsky continued to stare into the darkness ahead. "What did the sergeant say back there?"

"Nothing."

"He must have said something."

"He said we were lucky to have found the key. He thought he might find us dead."

Grossman was silent for a moment. Then, to his own surprise, he heard himself apologize.

"I'm sorry about what I said back there. If you hadn't stayed awake, we would have been caught."

"I didn't do it for you," Brodsky said shortly. "I'm also on this train."

"I'm still sorry," Grossman said. "You're certainly not stupid."

Brodsky shook his head. "I'm stupid. Oh, not about the key to start the truck engine. That's ignorance, not stupidity. I'm stupid for having wasted a full year trying to talk you into going to Palestine. That's real stupidity!"

Grossman shook his head, smiling slightly.

"That's not stupidity, that's ignorance. I don't want to go to Palestine. It's that simple," he said. "Look, I'm going to drop off at the next place we stop. I don't know if we go through Milano or even near it on the way to Genoa. Let's say good-bye as friends."

"Friends," Brodsky said without expression, and leaned back. "All right, friend, it's my turn to sleep." And he shut his eyes tightly.

The train was red-balling now, cleared by the authority of the American Army, making up for the humiliating experience of having to crawl practically on its knees up the mountains north of the Brenner Pass. Now it swayed around curves, thundered over bridges, sneering at the mountains on either side of the valley, mountains gleaming white with bare rock in the growing light of morning. The snow was gone now; when Grossman cracked the window of the truck the smell of fresh air was a delight.

He tried to picture the land they were racing through, to place it in relation to the maps of northern Italy he had studied so thoroughly at Felsdorf. The train would probably stop at Bolzano since that was the first major town after the Brenner; from there he would make his way west through Sondrio to the Lago Maggiore. Or, if they didn't stop until they reached Trento, he'd make it through Bergamo and then north to the lake. He had ample time to get there from wherever they stopped, and the Italians were friendly people;

even without money he was sure he could get by. Possibly even work a day or two and earn a few lire; he was strong again, and he knew machinery. One thing was certain; careful planning to get across the frontier this time. No spur-of-the-moment decisions!

They were coming into a town, the houses beginning to cluster, lights beginning to flicker on as the inhabitants rose to face the demands of another day. Bolzano, he assumed, and prepared to climb down from the truck and stand at the open door, ready to drop off when the train had slowed sufficiently. He looked over at the sleeping Max Brodsky, snoring gently. Should he wake him? No, they had said their good-byes a long time ago, when they had still been friends. Let it go at that. But even as he put his hand on the handle of the truck door, starting to turn it, the train was clattering over switching points, not slowing at all. He saw the deserted station flee past in the dawn and then the houses were thinning and in minutes they were in the country again, racing past grape arbors with empty vines clinging to them as if for warmth, past mule-driven wagons waiting patiently at a crossover, past small children staring at them solemnly from tilled fields, their passing the only excuse to abandon labor if only for a moment. The train whistled exuberantly and tore on.

At Trento the same thing occurred, a clatter over switches, staring faces from a station platform from people awaiting a local train, washlines being set out to catch the morning sun, factories interspersed with small home gardens, and then the country again, and the tilled fields and the envious children pausing in their work to travel with them vicariously, if only around the next bend. Over them as they raced, the mountains grew taller as they sunk deeper into the valley. Grossman frowned. He leaned over and shook Brodsky. The large man came awake slowly, yawning, scratching at his stubbled cheek.

"What is it?"

"We aren't stopping! We've gone through Bolzano and Trento! We may not stop even at Verona—!"

"So?"

"So we may not stop before Genoa!"

"So?"

"So, damn it, I want to get to Lago Maggiore! And I'd rather not go there from Genoa! It's a long way."

Max looked at him a moment and then pointed to the ceiling of the truck.

"Don't complain to me," he said. "Complain to Him." He closed his eyes, a faint smile on his face, and in seconds was asleep again.

Chapter 11

They dropped from the string of boxcars when the train finally slowed for a stop, coming into a spur track along the Molo Vecchio in Genoa's harbor area. It was just after noon and Grossman was in a foul mood. Three times that morning he had stood balanced at the side of the boxcar, prepared to drop his knapsack and follow it to the grade when he thought the train was decelerating; and three times the engine's whistle had shrieked delightedly and the train had gathered speed, flashing past people waiting at grade crossings, rattling furiously over switch frogs, echoing loudly through tunnels, tearing through cities and back to the country, pleased with itself, its performance, its freedom. From inside the truck, the windows now rolled down and the heater off, Max Brodsky watched, smiling sardonically.

Leaving the rail yards, they walked along the Corso Quadrio, heading south, the steep hills of the old city rising abruptly on their left, the calm waters of the Bacino della Grazie on their right, the vast Mediterranean visible beyond the stone-block breakwater. Their overcoats had been folded and laid across the backpacks since neither was prepared to abandon them as yet, Grossman for the thought of the colder Lago Maggiore and Switzerland, Brodsky out of natural caution.

They stopped at several *bottegas* along the Corso Quadrio before Brodsky located a small leather shop where the proprietor, an old man with a skimpy white beard and deep-set rheumy eyes, spoke Yiddish. The old man consulted a worn street directory a moment or two, and then shook his head sadly.

"The Via Sclopis? It's in Sturla, off the Piazza Sturla. Miles and miles—" He was waving a palsied hand weakly in the general direction of the south. He looked at their heavy knapsacks. "It's also a very steep climb . . ."

Max's shrug indicated they had no choice. "And the Piazza Sturla?"

The hand was waved again, shaking. "Down to the end of the Corso Italia, the very end, to the Boccadesse at the Piazza Nettune. You can't miss it, stay right along the waterfront. At the Nettune you go up the hill on any cross street to the Via Caprera; it runs parallel. Then turn right to the Piazza Sturla." He studied the thin pale faces of the two, so different from the swarthy skin of the Genovese, but was intelligent enough not to ask questions. "If you need fare for an omnibus—"

"No, no! Thank you very much."

They marched along the Corso Guglielmo . Marconi, sweating mightily, with Grossman getting angrier and angrier every step.

"We could have taken bus fare from the old man! A few pennies wouldn't put him in the poorhouse!"

"We didn't need to take his money. He was kind enough to help us out with directions. We can walk."

"Or you could have taken a few pennies from your own money!"

Brodsky looked at him coldly.

"The only money I have is the money you gave back to me. The rest went to Wolf for any expenses he might need when he left Felsdorf with the group. And we don't need to spend money when we can walk."

"I know. God gave us feet," Grossman subsided into a disgruntled silence for a moment and then exploded again. "One night! One night! I stay one night and then I'm heading north!"

"You can head north right now," Brodsky said shortly. He was tired and in no mood for Grossman's temperamental outbursts. "Right now you're going in the wrong direction. North is the other way."

"One night," Grossman said direly, threateningly, and fell silent.

The Corso Italia seemed endless; the climb up the Via Felice

Cavalotti from the Piazza Nettune to the Via Caprera was brutal. They paused at the top, the square they assumed to be the Piazza Sturla visible to their right, their hearts pumping, their leg muscles trembling, and caught their breath. Below them the sea stretched endlessly to a hazy horizon, a stainless-steel sheet under the glaring sun; to the southeast they could see tiny docks in the far distance, and boats of various sizes tied up at them. Nervi was in that direction, Brodsky knew from studying maps at Felsdorf; possibly the *Naomi* was there, might even be one of them. The thought put strength in his legs; he started off again, walking rapidly. God! If he had come this far only to miss the boat by a few hours! Grossman came limping after, cursing under his breath.

The Via Sclopis rose at a steep angle from the Piazza Sturla, the tall stone and stucco houses climbing one above the other as if each were attempting to brace itself against the mountainside and obtain a better view than its lower neighbor. The two men came to the address they wanted, and slipped off their knapsacks gratefully, wiping the sweat from their faces. The street was deserted, its cobbled pavement hot under the afternoon sun that reflected itself from the pastel plaster and the shaded windows of the houses. Possibly everyone was having a siesta, Brodsky thought, and drew back the bell pull set in the center of the heavy door. There was a faint tinkle, muffled by the door's bulk; then a window shade was pulled to one side enough to allow a cautious eye to examine them carefully. A moment later Morris Wolf had opened the door and was pulling them hurriedly inside. He grinned at the two men broadly, the grimace twisting his scarred face into a macabre distortion. He reached up, patting Brodsky on the back, nodding at Grossman.

"You made it!"

"And you're still here," Brodsky said with profound relief. He hadn't realized how tense he had been. "I was afraid I'd get here too late and miss you."

Wolf's grin disappeared abruptly. He shook his head.

"Come upstairs and we'll talk about it."

The three men climbed the narrow steps one at a time to the next floor. A door at the end of a passage opened and the scowling face of an old woman in black, heavily mustached, glared at them a moment before the door was slammed shut. Brodsky looked at Wolf inquiringly.

"Our charming hostess," Wolf said in explanation. "She hates our guts. Not anti-Semitic, I think, or at least not only anti-Semitic. She's just anti-people. But her husband keeps her in line, or at least has so far. He likes money. Fortunately," he added, "the old lady doesn't know where the boat is, just that it's somewhere south of here. Well, so is Naples."

He opened a door and ushered them into a large room with cots and sleeping bags scattered about, although at the moment the only occupant of the room was a husky man sitting at a desk in one corner, writing something. He looked up as the door opened and then came to his feet, smiling broadly, his hand outstretched.

"Max!"

"Davi!" He turned to Grossman. "Davi Ben-Levi of the Mossad. You missed him at Belsen and at Felsdorf. Ben Grossman."

"I've heard of Ben Grossman," Ben-Levi said, and shook hands. "So you've changed your mind?"

"No," Grossman said shortly. "I'll be going to Switzerland tomorrow. I'm just staying for the night."

"However," Brodsky said quickly, "I'll be going to Palestine with you."

Ben-Levi sat down on one of the cots. "If any of us go," he said somberly.

"What do you mean?"

"We've got trouble," Ben-Levi said, and then paused as if trying to calculate exactly where to start. He took a deep breath and began. "To start with, the British have patrols all over this area, foot patrols on shore, patrols out to sea. Anything that looks like a ship capable of heading for, or reaching, Palestine is checked out thoroughly. They also have all the Italian *carabiniere*—the police—checking constantly as well. The *carabiniere* are afraid not to; a lot of them were *fascisti* and the British are capable of putting on some vicious pressure. And they also offer bounties that not only interest the police but people, too. So it isn't easy. If anyone thinks a ship looks the least bit suspicious, they search it. If they find the slightest thing that even smells of an attempt to reach Palestine, the ship is interned and the crew is given a hard time. If they aren't put in jail, they stand a good chance of being put in an internee camp if they aren't Italian. So it's been almost impossible to get Italian captains or crews; we've had to depend on our own people, and they are not experienced sailors."

Brodsky frowned. "It's been that way for some time," he said slowly. "We've always known the British aren't going to let us get to Palestine if they can help it." He had put his knapsack to one side and was sitting opposite Ben-Levi.

"Yes, we've always known that. So this time we got together and figured out a way to fool them. The boat we have was originally a fishing boat, a trawler, so every day we would take it out and fish. Our captain is an Italian Jew dead set on getting to Palestine; he's had a lot of experience in ships. Unfortunately, he's about the only one. We also have two or three others who speak enough Italian to get by if we're ever hailed; I'm one of them. Sometimes we'd take the boat out in the daytime, sometimes at night, whenever the fish are running, which is the way the fishing boats do around here. And while we were trawling, we had men inside working on putting up bunks where people could sleep, building toilets, putting in a small kitchen for cooking, a small dispensary. And after our day's—or night's—fishing, we'd come back to the dock and take ashore our catch—"

"You actually fished?"

"Of course." Ben-Levi smiled briefly. "It's been the mainstay of our food, and we've also sold quite a lot. The old man here handled it for us." His smile faded. "We figured the British would get used to our going out and coming in at all hours, our unloading fish and stretching our nets, and eventually they'd pay no attention to us."

"And it didn't work out?"

"It worked out fine. It worked out just the way we figured. We also thought if we tried to bring all our people from the camp and from the safe-houses at one time—most of them have been at an Allied camp outside of Rapallo like Felsdorf, except the British treated the camp as a concentration camp, not like the Americans at Felsdorf—the British would become suspicious and figure something was up. And search every boat in the area. So over three weeks ago we began bringing our people out, three or four at a time, putting them up here for a day, some in other houses, getting them on board one at a time at night—"

"Three weeks ago?"

Ben-Levi nodded somberly.

"That's right. Some people have been living on that boat for over three weeks . . ."

"But, how—?"

Ben-Levi took a deep breath and went on.

"We picked the strongest, of course, or those with any carpentry ability, because they were the ones who finished the bunks and the kitchen and everything else. They'd take turns coming up on deck when we were out of sight of land, or when we couldn't see any other ship. But when we got back to port they had to stay below, keeping quiet, not showing a light or making a sound . . ."

"*Three weeks?*"

"Yes. Some have been on board that long, some a few days less, some two weeks or more. And lately we've been bringing the women and children aboard. We thought we were ready to sail. The morale is getting low . . ."

Brodsky frowned. "How many people are on board right now?"

"About two hundred . . ."

"And why haven't you sailed?"

"We've been in port two days, all set," Wolf said bitterly, cutting in. "We have trouble with our engine, and our engineer is sick in the hospital. And nobody else knows a damn thing about the engine. Jews! If we needed accountants, we could float the ship to Palestine on balance sheets!"

"And we don't dare bring in an outsider," Ben-Levi said. "We can't get out to sea to air the place out, or to dump our waste, or even to cook a decent meal. We have no electricity—the batteries ran down. We don't even have a fan—it's like an oven in there. It's only a matter of time before the British begin to get suspicious and check out this ship that never sails, or never repairs its engine. Or until they even begin to smell us. Or," he added bitterly, "until we have to bring some of the children out and get them into a hospital!"

"Where's your captain?"

"At the hospital with our engineer right now. He's all right at sea, but he isn't an engineer. He sees to our supplies, which keeps him busy. He comes back to the boat every night."

Brodsky frowned at the floor for several minutes while everyone waited for his opinion. He looked over at Grossman. "Ben, do you know anything about engines? Marine engines?"

Grossman hurriedly held up a hand.

"No! No! I'm not getting involved in this! Tomorrow I'm leaving for Switzerland. You and your boats and your Palestine and Zionism have nothing to do with me!" He looked aggrieved. "I've said that often enough, you know that."

"I know," Brodsky said quietly, "but you can't get to Switzerland without money. You pretend to think you can, but we both know better. There are no free rides in Italy just by wearing a little cap with a few stripes on it. No free meals. No friendly truck drivers. The British are here in force, and you can't speak either Italian or English. How far do you think you'd get? If you could have jumped the train in Bolzano or Trento, you couldn't have made it. Make it from Genoa? Don't make me laugh!"

Grossman felt himself get hot. "I—"

"You won't get a mile out of this town without being picked up by the British or the Italians and deported back to Germany. Or put in a detainee camp. Look at you! Without me, you'd still be in Germany! You can't even beg for food; you don't know the words!"

"A truck driver gives you a lift and asks where you're going," Wolf said, getting into the act. "You think he's offering you something to eat and you say 'Salami.' He takes you to Bologna."

"Ben," Brodsky said with finality, "without money you just can't make it." He slapped his forehead. "Why are you so stubborn?"

"I can get by," Grossman said, but he didn't sound so confident.

" 'By' is right," Wolf said. "You went by Switzerland once, you'll go by it again." He personally considered Grossman a shit to want money to help the Mossad, but he knew this was not the time to mention the fact.

Grossman considered, then looked up. "How much money?"

Brodsky looked at Davi Ben-Levi.

"Fifty American dollars," Ben-Levi said without hesitation. "And a ride out of Genoa on a truck, as far as Tortona. That will get you well on your way. You can catch a train or a bus north with that much money, and have plenty left over."

"What if I can't fix the engine?"

Again Ben-Levi didn't hesitate. "You'll still get the fifty dollars, just for trying."

Wolf looked irked; there was no expression at all on Brodsky's face.

"And the ride to Tortona?"

"And the ride to Tortona."

"What have I got to lose?"

"Nothing," Wolf said bitterly. Only my respect, he added to himself, and you lost that a long time ago!

Grossman and Brodsky changed to outfits Ben-Levi had, similar to the ones he and Wolf were wearing. They were the clothing of fishermen, worn trousers stuffed into the tops of rubber boots, heavy sweaters that itched uncomfortably in the heat, and knitted caps that were greasy and smelled of fish. All the clothes smelled of fish, for that matter. An old man, summoned from the back of the house where he could be heard in altercation with his wife, disappeared with a toothless smile to reappear a few minutes later before the house, at the wheel of an ancient Chevrolet stake-body half-ton truck. The truck also stank of fish. The truck waited while they climbed in, shaking itself from side to side with ague. If this was the truck that was to take him to Tortona, Grossman thought, he would have to rebuild it in all probability to get them out of town.

The old man put it in neutral and let the truck coast down the steep Via Sclopis, gathering speed. It shot across the Piazza Sturla, narrowly missing an omnibus, two trucks, a wagon selling *tortoni Napolitano,* and a group of schoolchildren who scattered screaming before his wheels. He steered the truck into the Via Dei Mille without any visible concern and let it continue to coast at breakneck speed to the bottom and across into the Via Cinque Maggio, swinging the wheel negligently around a slower vehicle here and there, applying the accelerator only when his speed had diminished slightly on the level oceanside road. He turned and grinned at the men in the open stake body, speaking through what had once been an isinglass window of the cab but was now open space.

"Buono, no? Combustible costoso . . ."

It occurred to Grossman that for a few extra dollars the old man might be willing to take him all the way to Lago Maggiore; or he might agree to the trip for a motor tune-up, something the old truck could stand. Things were looking up once more! What was Brodsky always saying about his God? Well, it seemed his God had broken down their engine to help *him,* not the Jews. The thought made him smile and he stared out at the level sea, preferring its view to watching the traffic scatter as the old man bravely wound his way through it as fast as he could, the engine coughing and sputtering. There was no sign that the vehicle had any brakes at all, or at least the old man never applied them.

The truck coasted to a stop a bit off the road at a point where the coastal highway came closest to the cliffs leading precipitously down to the Portoccilio, the small port of Nervi. The old man remained behind to guard his truck against vandals or thieves while the four men climbed down the steep flight of rickety steps that led to the narrow shingle beach and the small pier below. There was only one ship there, which Grossman had to assume was the *Naomi*. He stared in disbelief. Two hundred people on *that?* The ship was no more than sixty or seventy feet long with a beam of less than fifteen feet, an old trawler with the general air of failure, with flaking paint, an ensign drooping in disgrace, and laying so low in the water that it appeared to be sinking in place. Grossman calculated quite correctly that it was not its load that made it so precariously low, but the fact that its bilge pumps were not working, or were not capable of containing the leakage if they were. The ship carried a small deckhouse forward, with a rooftop that may have once served as a flying bridge in better days, but whose railing had long since succumbed to high waves or rolling seas. On either side of the engine well that lay between splintered coamings aft of the deckhouse, davits angled out for securing the trawls. A narrow companionway led below from the confined space between the engine well and the deckhouse. The entire ship smelled of age and disaster.

The odor struck them as they climbed the narrow gangplank and stepped on deck. Any doubts Grossman had had about the capacity of the ship were dispelled; it had to take at least two hundred people to produce that stench. He tried to hold his breath as he walked to the engine well and looked down. The hatch had been removed and now leaned against the ship's rail. He stepped down into the well; here at least the odor of diesel fuel overpowered the smell from below decks.

He bent over the engine, studying it. There was a sudden wail from below decks, brought from an open porthole, instantly muffled. He could imagine the heat below, and the discomfort; but that was no problem of his. Wolf and Brodsky had disappeared below. Above him Davi Ben-Levi waited and watched.

"Well, what do you think?"

"I don't know. Let me look a minute, will you?"

The engine was a four-stroke single-acting cross-head design, going back, he calculated, to the time of the First World War or earlier. Still, someone had given it rather decent care. The engine itself was spotless, the side rods shone, there was no puddle of lubrication oil in the well to expose either poor packing or sloppy consideration for the engine, the bearings holding the eccentrics to the crankshaft were snug and looked as if they had only recently been babbitted. He pressed the eccentrics back and forth, noting the solid feel as they refused to give. He looked up.

"Externally it seems all right. Exactly what seems to be the trouble?"

Ben-Levi shrugged. "It doesn't start."

"I mean—"

"I know what you mean. I'm telling you—you throw the lever over to start it and nothing happens. Mr. Grossman," Ben-Levi said, "if we knew what the trouble was, we'd be halfway to Palestine by now."

Which I doubt in this piece of junk, Grossman thought sourly, and bent back into the engine well again. He found the air line that fed the caps of the cylinders and began to trace it. It disappeared from the well, running under the deck planking in the general direction of the small cabin. He came to his feet and investigated. Inside the deck housing was an air receiver and off to one side an air compressor. The gauge on the receiver read zero. He walked to the bank of storage batteries and read the instruments, shaking his head at the ignorance of this bunch of amateurs who hoped to get to Palestine on this wreck of a ship; in his opinion they should not have been allowed to take a rowboat out on the Nekkar. He walked back to Ben-Levi, shaking his head.

"Without your diesel you can't generate electricity. Without electricity you can't run your air compressor. Without your air compressor, you can't start your diesel. It's that simple. Don't you have any spare air? Who designed such a stupid system?"

Ben-Levi flushed. "Our engineer checked it out. He's sick—"

"You're probably better off without him. Someone drained the air receiver, God knows why—"

"Our what?"

"The tank that stores the compressed air."

"We had to get some air down below. Some of the children were feeling faint. We ran a hose down from the tank—"

"And drained off any chance you had of starting the diesel. And now everyone below has been a lot worse off for the past two days. God, what colossal ignorance!"

"So we were ignorant," Ben-Levi said, his face white. "What can we do now?"

"You can send the old man off for a tank of compressed air. Or a tank of oxygen, if he can't get air. I can hook it up and get the diesel started, if there isn't anything else wrong. With the diesel you can start your generator, and you'll have electrical power, and compressed air, and fans and everything."

"I'll go with him right now!"

"Bring back two tanks," Grossman said, "in case some idiot decides to drain that receiver again."

"Right!" Ben-Levi said, and ran for the steps.

Grossman walked off the boat to wait, going down the beach to avoid that overpowering smell. It was as bad as Belsen. But at Belsen he had been unable to do anything to help; here he should have the problem resolved in a short time. There was satisfaction in that, and not just for the money or the ride the following morning. He was still an engineer; he could still do a job. Why couldn't people understand that? It was the same challenge he had faced at Maidanek with the ovens and the gas chambers; he had only been resolving a problem. But they still would have tried him and hung him had they caught him. People just didn't understand . . .

Brodsky came up in the growing darkness.

"Where's Davi? What about the engine?"

"I think the engine is all right. Some idiot drained the air receiver just to get some air down below. Without air pressure the diesel won't start. Some start on batteries, some by compressed air; this one starts on air. Not that it would make any difference; your batteries have been drained, too, using lights and fans and God knows what without the deisel."

"And Davi?"

"He went to get some compressed-air tanks."

"We'll be all right after that?"

"I think so. Unless you've used all your fuel up for cooking, these past few days."

Brodsky frowned. He hesitated a moment and then spoke slowly.
"Ben—"

"Yes?"

"We need someone to take the engineer's place."

Grossman laughed.

"Max, Max! If I were dying to go to Palestine, which you know
I'm not, and if I were ten times the Zionist you are, which you know
I'm not, you couldn't get me on that boat. In fact, I wouldn't get on
it now if it wasn't tied to the pier." His smile faded. "Max, you're
crazy to attempt a trip like that in that piece of junk."

"How do you know?" Brodsky sounded bitter. "You didn't bother
to even go below. All you saw was the engine."

"I saw the ship lower in the water than it should be. Your bilges
are full, your ship leaks. Oh, the pumps will help some, but the fact
is that ship is not seaworthy. It's suicide to go in it."

Brodsky shrugged. "Then I guess we'll all commit suicide." He
looked up at a shout from the top of the cliff; Davi was trying to
start down the steps with one of the heavy tanks. Max dropped the
conversation and hurried up the steps to help him.

They wrestled the two tanks down the cliff and aboard the ship.
By the time everything was ready for Grossman to begin work it was
dark and he had to do the job by the light of flashlights and the two
kerosene lanterns the ship boasted. By nine o'clock he had made the
necessary connections of the compressed-air tank to the cylinder
heads; he held his breath as he opened the valve. There was a moment's hesitation as the air rushed in, then slowly the diesel pistons
began to move. One stroke and the engine caught, beginning to run.
Grossman hurried to the deckhouse, watching the instruments on
the electrical panel; when he was assured the generator output was
normal, he put the air compressor into operation and watched the
needle on the air receiver slowly begin to climb. He threw another
switch and the ship's lights came on; there was a small sound of relief from below decks, instantly checked. The fans began to circulate
air again; there was the sound of a toilet being flushed as the pumps
went back into action.

Grossman wiped his hands on a bit of waste. "You're all set." As
far as the diesel is concerned, he thought, but as far as this piece of
junk of a ship is concerned, you're in deep trouble. He turned to
Ben-Levi, who had watched every move he had made. "Never let the

air pressure in the receiver go down. If you lose pressure for any reason, be sure and find out why. If it's a broken line, replace it. Then get started again using the spare tank the way I got it started. In fact, you can recharge those air tanks from the receiver, once the pressure is up. It's a simple connection." He looked around at the faces watching him; their expressions demonstrated a combination of pleasure to have the diesel operating again together with doubt that they could keep it that way without technical help. Grossman spoke quickly to forestall any further attempt to draft him for the job of engineer. "You'll be all right. When do you plan to leave?"

"As soon as possible," Ben-Levi said. He took some money from his pocket, peeled off some bills, and handed them to Grossman. "I want to thank you. We all want to thank you. We'll take you back to the house, get our things, and be off. You can stay there tonight— they'll feed you, if the old lady doesn't poison you—and tomorrow the old man will drive you to Tortona. I'll tell him on the way back. And good luck."

"Thanks. And good luck to you."

"I'll say good-bye to you here," Wolf said. "Max will bring my things." He grinned. "I don't want to risk another trip in that truck if I can help it." He held out his hand; Grossman shook it. He was surprised to think he would miss the little man.

"This time I'll tell you what you told me once," Grossman said, smiling. "Wolf—I hope you know how to swim."

Wolf stared at him. "A sense of humor?" He looked around the ship, then sighed. "Well, maybe not."

The darkened car was stationed on the shoulder of the main road, deep in the shadow of a notch cut in the mountainous road to allow room for the passage of trucks. Inside the car the two *carabiniere* spoke in whispers, although there was nobody within the sound of their voices.

"We should have found out where the boat was, and taken them all at the same time. The old lady said she heard them talking; she said there were hundreds of them. The British would have paid—!" He snapped his fingers to indicate how much the British would have paid.

"Except the old lady had no idea where the boat was," the second one said. "All she knew is that it's somewhere south of here. What good is that?"

"Then we should have taken them in the house."

"And have them jumping out all the windows? And we end up with nobody?"

"If we had more men—"

"We would have had to divide the money more ways." The second *carabiniere* frowned at his companion in the darkened car. "This way is better. We know they have to pass here. This way we'll get the leaders; the British will find out from them where the boat is, all hundreds will be picked up, and we'll still get paid for all of them. Relax."

They waited in silence. A car came roaring up the highway from the south; they leaned forward and then back again. Their description of the truck was complete; surely in the Genoa area there couldn't be two 1931 Chevrolet half-ton stake-body trucks painted purple.

One of the *carabiniere* reached for a cigarette; he had it to his lips before it was suddenly plucked from his mouth.

"No smoking! They see a lit cigarette in a parked car without lights—"

"They'll think we're lovers." The first man chuckled and took the cigarette from his partner's hand, putting it back in his mouth. And then froze before he had a chance to light it. The headlights of a small truck had come wavering around the curve ahead of them, one lamp pointing up and the other down. Even at that distance they could hear the clanking of the old engine.

"It's them!"

The driver put the car in motion and drove slowly out into the highway without turning up his lights. His car effectively blocked the road.

The old man saw the shadow move into the road and stood on what was left of his brakes, fighting the wheel, screaming curses. He managed to swing the wheel to one side, running the truck slightly up the hillside to stop it. He flung open the door and got down, fuming.

"*Ignorante! Stupido! Girando un automobile nelle strada senza badare! E senza luce!*"

"*Sta' zitto!*"

The voice roared out of the darkness; lights suddenly flared from the car. The two *carabiniere* got down and advanced in the glare of their headlights, their batons swinging from their belts. The two came to stand beside the truck and motion to the three men in the back.

"All down!"

The three climbed down and stood beside the old man, who was muttering. "This is the work of my old lady! I'll bet! When I get home—"

"Quiet! Your papers!"

The old man wet his lips, putting down his fury, smiling a bit, cringing subserviently.

"Who carries papers just to go for a little ride with friends? Look, sir, we're only poor fishermen. Look at us, sir, you can see. We stopped for a glass of *grappino*—"

"Your papers!"

The old man sighed and dug into his pocket. He brought out a worn wallet, opening it and thrusting it before the policeman nearest him. The man took it and bent it toward the lights from the police car. He looked up, smiling grimly.

"You said you had no papers."

The old man shrugged diffidently. "I'm sorry, sir, I forgot. I thought I had left them home in my other pants. But they're all in order. May we go now?"

"You may not." He shoved the old man's wallet into the breast pocket of his uniform. "We'll attend to you later. You!" He swung around to Ben-Levi. "Let's see your papers."

"Papers. Yes . . ." Ben-Levi reached into his pocket. His fingers fumbled there a moment and then came out with several folded bills. He held them out. "Will these papers do?"

The policeman counted the money and then sneered.

"Two ten-dollar American bills? You must be joking!" He tucked the bills into his pocket and stared at Ben-Levi. "All right, now! Let's see your papers!"

"If you insist," Ben-Levi said, and reached into another pocket. He brought out a folder and snapped it open, holding it at arm's length. The *carabiniere* moved to see it; Ben-Levi brought his other hand up and down in a vicious chop, smashing the man to the ground, unconscious.

"*Run!*"

The second policeman started to blow his whistle and Brodsky tore it from his lips, threw it as far as he could in the darkness, and knocked the man to the ground. The old man snatched his wallet from the pocket of the policeman on the ground, jumped into his truck, reversed it, and disappeared back toward Nervi without waiting for the others. Brodsky and Ben-Levi were running into the darkness along the cliff, beyond the scope of the fixed beams from the police car. Grossman tried to go the other way, back toward Genoa and the safe-house, but the second policeman staggered to his feet, his baton in his hand, swinging it viciously. He brought it up and smashed it across Grossman's head, knocking him unconscious, and in the same motion stepped over his fallen victim to the *carabiniere* on the ground, dragging the whistle loose from around the other's neck, and blowing upon it madly, furiously. If they had taken a regular police car instead of his partner's own car, just so the other could collect expenses, he could be radioing for help now, instead of blowing his head off like a maniac!

Brodsky paused, panting, looking back. In the light of the car headlights he could see Grossman stretched out on the ground, unmoving. With a muttered curse, he turned back. The policeman was blowing the whistle at the top of his lungs, turning his head frantically in the direction of the city, looking for help. Brodsky came out of the darkness and felled the man, clubbing him in the head with all his force. The whistling stopped abruptly as the man collapsed in a heap over his fallen companion. Then Brodsky picked Grossman up in a fireman's hold and was trotting with him as fast as he could back into the darkness.

There was the high thin sound of a siren rising and falling eerily in the distance, its shrill keening approaching. Someone must have telephoned, Brodsky thought, and slid over the edge of the cliff, hoping the slope at this point would be gentle. He tried to feel his way, bent over with Grossman a dead weight on his back; and then he was sliding, and then tumbling, and Grossman had been lost. Brodsky tried to brace himself, skidding, digging in his heels, trying to stop his precipitous descent with his fingers. He struck the bottom with a jar and then started to feel around for his friend, hoping the noise of his fall had not been noticed by anyone. Where was Grossman? He tried to look back up the cliff but the shadow there was complete. Could he have been caught on a bush or a tree? And how long would it be before the car with the siren had arrived and the cliffs would be swarming with men with flashlights? He went back the way he had come and then stumbled over something soft. It was Grossman. He bent over the still figure, putting his ear to the chest, listening for a heartbeat. It was there, strong and steady. He pulled the flaccid body closer to the base of the cliff and waited, sweating in the darkness.

The siren had paused at the site of the car blocking the road; the car was apparently being moved, and then the spotlight of the police car could be seen weaving about in the night, sliding from side to side of the road, searching for the fugitives. Men were now walking along the edge of the cliff, peering down, their strong flashlights bobbing as they walked and stopped and walked on again. Brodsky waited, pressed into the shadow of the cliff, hiding Grossman with his body, trying to control his breathing, positive his panting would be heard from above. The flashlights lit up the cliffside momentarily and then passed on; there was the sound of a car accelerating. The spotlight disappeared in the distance ahead. The foot searchers had apparently gotten back into the car, but Brodsky took no chances. It was a long time before he moved, and Grossman was still unconscious.

With a sigh the big man finally came to his feet and lifted his friend once again. He realized he was not familiar with the shore line and hoped he could reach the cove with the *Naomi* in it without having to climb the cliff again, hoped the beach did not run out into the sea, but continued giving footroom until the cove and the ship.

So close, he thought! He stumbled blindly through the coarse sand, holding Grossman in his arms, a dead weight, struggling through the beach in the deeper shadow at the base of the cliff. So close, and now this! That miserable old lady! Still, they had escaped, which was the main thing; and he was suddenly sure that Davi Ben-Levi had also evaded the search. His knapsack and the other things they had at the house were unimportant; what was important were people, and they were free. He glanced down at the man in his arms, unable to see anything but a bulking shadow in the darkness.

He smiled grimly. If this was God's way of getting them an engineer, then Wolf was probably right. It seemed an awfully haphazard manner of fulfilling the assignment, no matter what!

Chapter 12

He was on a moving object, his head was splitting with pain, and the world was uneasy about him; he felt clammy and cold and he knew in a moment he would have to vomit. He rolled onto his side, slowly opened his eyes, and then felt a surge of relief. It was only a nightmare, and he had had plenty of those before. He was back in Belsen on one of the narrow plank tiers, in the same semidarkness with the same smell of feces and urine and unwashed bodies, only this time Belsen was swaying from side to side. An earthquake, maybe, or possibly the camp was being bombed, although he could not hear the blasts of the explosions nor the roaring of the planes dipping down as they had at Celle. Still, being bombed in silence would not be inconsistent in a dream. But could it really be a dream when the pain and the nausea were so real? He turned his head and felt relief again; it really was a nightmare and he was really back in Belsen in it, for Pincus the pharmacist was sitting beside him, smiling at him. He closed his eyes, willing himself to waken from the terrible dream, wondering what happened when you vomited in a dream.

He discovered quite soon, for the camp and the barrack rolled once more and he found himself with his head hanging over the edge of the bunk, retching uncontrollably, his head pounding. The typhus was back, or the nightmare of it. Pincus was holding a basin for him; his other hand was pressed tightly against Grossman's forehead. Grossman wondered where Pincus had gotten the basin; usually they used an old can if they were lucky enough to have anything at all.

The spasm passed and he lay back weak, breathing raggedly,

fighting the continuing nausea, staring up at the wooden tier over him, listening to the eerie creaking of the ship's timbers, remembering. This was no dream! He was on that damned ship! They had shanghaied him, taken him against his will. Oh, the bastards, the miserable bastards! This was their thanks for his having repaired their engine for them, for getting them started. He should never have done it. Oh, the miserable ungrateful Jew bastards!

The little light from the narrow companionway was blocked, and Brodsky came down the steps and walked over to stand beside his bunk, bracing himself against the rolling of the ship, looking down at him with concern.

"How do you feel?"

Grossman turned his head away. Brodsky turned to Pincus; Pincus shrugged.

"How should he feel? He's seasick, he's got a lump the size of I don't know what back of his ear—like a goose egg—he didn't want to come and here he is. How does he feel? That's how he feels, I imagine." He tipped his head toward the makeshift medicine cabinet he had rigged up on one side of the bunks. "When he can hold them down I'll give him a couple aspirin; it's about all we got for what he's got."

He got up to empty the basin; Brodsky took his place.

"Ben—"

Grossman glared. "Go to hell!"

"I had no choice, Ben. You were lying in the road, unconscious. They would have put you in a camp."

"I'd rather be in a camp! A thousand times!"

"Except they wouldn't put you in a camp right away," Brodsky said quietly. "First they would have beaten you half to death. Here they had four nice prisoners, almost sure to get some lire from the British for them, and a minute later all they have is you, and both of them dumped on their ass and looking foolish. You think they would have given you the keys to the city? They would have beaten the shit out of you, and then handed you over to the British. I had to try to save you."

"You call this saving me?"

"Yes, I call it saving you. The British would have made you tell all you knew about this ship and the people on it."

"I would have told them!"

"I know. And I had to save you from doing that, too." Brodsky reached into a pocket, bringing out a small cardboard folder. "Anyway, at least you have some papers, now. It's a passport. A legitimate Venezuelan passport made out for Benjamin Grossman, citizen of Caracas. They handed them out in Genoa to everyone; Ben-Levi had spares, he just finished yours. They'll want it back once you're settled in Palestine, for others who will want to try and get in, but in the meantime you finally have papers."

"You know what you can do with your shitty papers!"

Brodsky shrugged and got to his feet as Pincus returned.

"He'll live," he said dryly. "Whatever his temperature is, his temper is right back to normal."

It was two o'clock in the afternoon of their third day at sea, forty-two hours since they had hurriedly cast off from the Nervi port and chugged their way out of the small harbor. In that time they had sighted only an occasional fishing vessel similar to their own, but they were all aware there was a good chance the British might eventually notice the failure of the *Naomi* to return to port, in which case word would undoubtedly go out and sea patrols would be looking for them. Although they did not know it, they had much to thank the old lady at the safe-house for; the British had already discounted the *Naomi* as the ship they were searching for. That small fishing trawler could never hold hundreds of people; that they were sure of. If they searched for the *Naomi*, it would be for humanitarian reasons, only.

There was a conference called in the small deckhouse, attended by Wolf, Davi Ben-Levi, Brodsky, and the ship's captain, an Italian Jew named Bernardo Cellotti, who had been interned in Dachau and who was the only one familiar with ships as well as with Italian waters. Cellotti had been studying the charts and listening to the weather reports on the ship's radio. Now he pointed to the chart.

"We're here. We've been lucky so far, staying as far from the shore as we have. Now we have to go in, between Stromboli and the toe of Italy. We also have to put in someplace for fuel and water. Our best bet would be either Reggio or Messina. Or better yet, Catania, farther south."

Brodsky frowned.

"You mean, go through the Messina Straits? I thought the plan originally was to refuel at Palermo and then go around Sicily. I know it's longer, but the straits? They're always rough, aren't they?"

"They're rough," Cellotti admitted. "They're also unpredictable. They're the original Scilla and Charybdis that Homer speaks of in the *Odyssey*. The rock and the whirlpool. And the weather could also be better. But still, going through the straits will save us over four hundred miles. That's forty hours or more in this vessel, almost as much as we've sailed since Nervi. And the straits are only twenty miles of bad water at the most."

"Like the captain said to reassure the old lady in the storm," Wolf said, " 'We're only a half mile from land, lady—straight down!' "

"Will this so-called ship take it?" Brodsky asked.

Cellotti shrugged. "I think so. It's a better vessel than it looks. If it makes anyone feel better, the chances are the British patrols won't be expecting a boat like the *Naomi* to even try the straits, certainly not in bad weather."

There were several minutes of silence. Then Wolf piped up.

"Well? I vote we try the straits. If we can save forty hours, I'm willing to take the chance. Besides, regardless of what Cellotti says, I'm not sure this tub could last an extra forty hours, even in a calm sea."

"We have over two hundred people on board, many of them women and children," Brodsky said slowly. "We'd be risking their lives, too. Maybe we ought to put it to all of them."

"Then we'd be risking a panic," Ben-Levi said firmly. "No. It's our decision."

"And with two hundred Jews, we'd get four hundred opinions," Wolf said positively. "We're supposed to be a committee; let's act like a committee. I vote in favor of trying the straits."

"I also," Cellotti said.

"I think it's worth the risk," Ben-Levi said.

They looked at Brodsky. He shrugged. "I suppose so." He changed the subject. "By the way, how is the engine running?"

Cellotti reached over and rapped on wood. "Thank God, so far so good."

"And how is our temperamental Ben Grossman?"

"He just sits on deck during the day and then goes down to his bunk at night, not talking to anyone. And not offering to help in anything, either. He just sits and stares."

"Well," Wolf said, "I just hope he's seeing the other side of the straits."

They passed between San Vincenzo, on the island of Stromboli, and Tropea, on the mainland, just as the sun was setting, with the faint lights pinpointing the heights of Calabria flickering uncertainly in the growing dusk. Wolf was in the deckhouse with Cellotti, spelling him at the wheel while the Italian studied the charts for the area. On deck, Ben-Levi and Brodsky had organized the men in the party putting up safety lines, carrying everything portable down to the cabin below, which was already crowded almost beyond endurance. The portholes had been left open to the last minute; people tried to crowd as close to them as possible, hoping for a breath of air.

Below Tropea they saw the lights of Nicotera and Rosarno on their left, sharper now as they came closer to the shore and as the darkness increased. A breeze had suddenly sprung up, gaining in strength as they approached the straits; clouds cut off the little moon there was. There was the smell of rain in the increasing wind. Then the lights of Gioia Tauro could be seen farther along the beach, and a final cluster of lights beyond.

"Palmi," Cellotti said, and took the wheel from Wolf, gripping it tightly. "We're almost there. Get everyone below. Anyone on deck in about ten minutes could be lost. Make sure the companionway is battened down, or someone could drown down below. Portholes to be closed and locked; no fires under any condition. The children should be tied in their bunks, if possible."

"And anyone wants to pray, no objection—right?" Wolf said, and went out to carry out the orders.

Ben-Levi came into the deckhouse, looking worried. The entrance to the straits could be seen now, marked by the light on the Punta del Faro, the extreme northern tip of the Sicilian coast. The wind had increased in velocity, rushing through the canyon of the straits, making conversation difficult in the small deckhouse. A light rain had begun to fall, glazing over the windows before the steersman's wheel. Cellotti looked over his shoulder as he handled the wheel.

"Everything all right below?"

"So far. I hope they stay that way."

"We all hope."

"Bernardo—"

Cellotti looked at him. "Yes?"

"Maybe we ought to turn back. At least wait until the weather improves . . ."

"Too late now," Cellotti said, and gripped the wheel with all his strength. Above them the rock of Scilla loomed, even blacker than the night, and then the ship leaped as it struck the whirlpool. The nose dipped and came up, shuddering, streaming water across the deck, sweeping up over the wheelhouse, making visibility impossible. The ship bucked violently, tearing the wheel from Cellotti's grip, spinning wildly. He tried to brake it, reaching for the spokes only to have his arms and hands beaten aside cruelly, battered. There was a sickening pause as the ship foundered, its screw out of the water; then Cellotti had the wheel again and was fighting it back into position. Ben-Levi came to his help; slowly the ship responded to its rudder. Water poured over the bucking ship, trying to press it under the crushing waves, washing down in torrents over the glass of the windows. With a curse Cellotti looked around for a prod and, finding none, reached across the wheel and punched his fist through the glass.

Ben-Levi stared at him as if he had gone mad. *"What are you doing?"*

Cellotti withdrew a bleeding fist, screaming above the shriek of the wind and the crashing of the waters. *"I've got to see something or we'll be on the rocks!"*

The water poured in. Cellotti stood there, his feet braced, soaked to the skin, shutting his eyes tightly whenever he saw the sea sweep over the bow and up to the deckhouse, opening them instantly once the water had drenched him and sucked back, to stare anxiously for some light, some marker, some rearing buoy, anything that would give him some idea of his position in the churning channel. Ben-Levi put his mouth close to Cellotti's ear, shouting.

"We ought to radio for help!"

"No good! No time!"

Behind them, miraculously, the diesel engine maintained its steady growl, sturdily pushing and pulling the pistons, moving the ship's screw, revolving the generator, pumping electricity into the storage batteries, its sound lost in the greater volume of the storm.

Below, all was shambles. The first shattering blow the ship had taken flung everything loose across the crowded cabin, piling debris against the bodies of those who had thought themselves secure. People were torn from stanchions, dragged free from their grips on the fixed tables and chairs. The small room stank with the smell of vomit; the screaming of the wind was matched by the moans and cries of terror of the people in the airless cabin. The hatch covering the companionway had come loose and each lurch of the bucking ship sent a flood of water rushing down the narrow steps; in the bilges the pumps worked valiantly, but each new torrent added water in the cabin, increasing the almost animal fear of those trapped there.

The small unlit stove broke loose from its moorings and skidded across the cabin deck like a battering ram, to crush the tables and benches fixed to the floor planks. Brodsky attempted to grab the stove, but it took him with it as if it had a life of its own, smashing him against the ship's planking, then retreating in a spray of water for another ramming attempt on the ship's side.

In his bunk Grossman held on tightly, knowing his suspicions had more than been fulfilled. The idiots were going to sink the ship! He braced himself as best he could against the tier above him, wedging his pillow and blanket about his head to protect it from being smashed in the constant shaking of the tortured ship. He knew it was pointless; they had to sink. Damn, *damn!* He had warned them about this bastard ship, hadn't he? God, how could this be happening to him? After all his planning, after all his suffering, was this to be the end? Drowning with a bunch of stinking Jews? They, at least, had little to live for; they were lucky to have made it this far. Most of them should have died in the gas chambers, or in the ghettos. And even now, what could they look forward to? A life of backbreaking toil in a wilderness, slaves to their own idiotic ideals, digging their holes and planting their barren crops with a shovel in one hand and a gun in the other! But he had everything to live for! Money! Freedom! Future! The patent unfairness of it all brought tears of frustration to his eyes.

The ship lurched dangerously, corkscrewing in the convoluted waters, digging its nose into the ocean as if seeking to hide under the tormented surface and find some degree of calm and peace at last; only to change its mind and ram itself upward as if in panic, fighting for air. Children were screaming now in total terror, hysterical. Grossman buried his head in his cocoon of blankets, and waited for the rush of water that would end it once and for all, and then felt himself being shaken roughly. He peered out of his nest to find Brodsky, white-faced, yelling over the roar of the sea.

"Ben! Get down! We need help!"

"Help? You brought this on yourself, on all of us!"

"The stove loosened some of the side planking! We need to brace it before it lets go and we all drown! Come on!"

"You're wasting your time," Grossman said, and as he said it he knew that it was so, that they were all really going to drown, and that it really made little difference. One could struggle so long, endure just so much, and then one had to concede. "You know we're all going to drown, don't you?"

But Brodsky was through arguing. He reached in and dragged Grossman bodily from his cocoon, propelling him ruthlessly to the end of the small cabin, gripping his arm painfully. Men had managed to corner the plunging stove and had lashed it into obedience against a stanchion, where it fought its bounds with each pitch of the ship. Other men were trying their best to maintain their balance as they pressed a plank against the side of the ship where water was beginning to trickle from between two fitted planks. Max added his strength to the weight of the others, motioning for Grossman to join in. The ship rolled beneath the straining men; they slid and fell into the water washing around them, and then struggled upward to press on the plank again.

Grossman raised his voice.

"Idiots! That's not the way! All of you together don't weigh as much as the pressure from the sea, for God's sake! You have to use leverage!"

He jerked a flashlight from Brodsky's belt and flashed it over the deck above, fighting for balance as he did so. There! There was a crossbeam he could use. If only he had a jack of some sort, but of course a shit ship like this wouldn't have anything that useful! He found himself grinning as he contemplated the problem. Drown! Not likely! One man using proper leverage could do the work of hundreds, of thousands. Good old Archimedes! Give me a place to stand, he said, and I will move the world. . . .

"Here," Grossman said roughly, "give me that plank! Find me a couple more. And get some blankets."

Men stared at him a moment and then hurried to carry out his orders. Grossman stuffed the blankets against the seeping spot, placed a plank over the blankets, took the second plank offered, and angled it against the upright board, tilting it against the crossbrace. He then took a third timber offered him and wedged it to act as a pry.

"There! One man putting his weight on this will do more good than all you idiots trying to push against the ocean. If you take turns, changing every five or ten minutes, you should be able to contain that leak."

A man had already taken his place at the pry and was leaning against it, forcing the plank and the blankets tightly against the ship's curved side. Grossman went to the leak and studied it. The water had reduced itself to a small, unsteady ooze. If the ship didn't founder from some other reason, Grossman thought, at least it won't from that leak. God, what idiots! Trying to push back the sea! King Canute, were you Jewish by any chance?

He flashed his flashlight about the room. The sea seemed to have abated somewhat, the water running down the companionway was nowhere near the deluge it had been minutes before. The bilge pumps seemed to be winning the battle against the torrents; the water in the cabin had gone down, and with it the whimpering of the frightened people. Grossman raised his voice.

"All right!" he said to the wondering faces staring at him. "The worst is over. We're not going to sink. Let's start cleaning up in here."

The lashing sea had eased and then given way to calm waters almost as if some unseen barrier had passed, or as if in apology for the roughness of their previous passage. They chugged into a night full of moonlight, with both sides of the narrow strait clearly visible. While those below worked to clear up the debris and move the stove back into place, and while Pincus and his first-aid kit worked on the cut and the bruised, there was another meeting in the deckhouse. This time Grossman attended. Ben-Levi took the wheel while Cellotti pointed to his charts. By unspoken consent nobody mentioned the passage through the straits.

"Catania," Cellotti said. "It's probably the only place this side of the island that has a small dry dock where we can fix the ship's planking. We obviously must repair it before we get out into the sea again."

"I don't like it." Ben-Levi was speaking over his shoulder, his eyes fixed on the buoys through the channel. "Maybe the British don't expect a ship like the *Naomi* to attempt these waters, but they still have patrols in this area, as well as informers, I'm sure. Catania is too big to put into without a good chance the British will hear about it. After all, two hundred people, many of them women and children, climbing out of a small fishing boat? They'd know in an instant what we were and where we're heading. We'd all end up behind barbed wire in Cyprus."

Cellotti frowned. "We still have to repair the damage."

"I know," Ben-Levi said unhappily. "I didn't say we shouldn't do it. I just said I don't like it."

Grossman had been looking at the chart. He looked up from it, curious.

"What's the tide around here?"

"It varies with the time of year, of course," Cellotti said. "I've got the tables here." He reached into a drawer, bringing out a thick book, opening it and running through the pages. "It's fairly high, I know, not as high now as in the spring, but high. It's supposed to be the main reason for the whirlpool effect in the straits. Why?"

Grossman pointed to the detailed map of Sicily.

"We could bring the ship in, almost run it aground, at some beach nowhere near a town or village. It looks as if there's a lot of deserted area around here. We could bring it in at high tide, anchor it to shore, and wait for the tide to run out."

"How do you know she'd tip the right way?" Brodsky asked.

"We use the davit pulleys to make sure she tips the way we want. Then we replace the damaged planking and let the tide float her again."

"Cellotti nodded. "It's a good idea if we can do the job between tides . . ."

"We'll have to."

"Then let's do it!"

Oddly enough for Jews, they didn't even take a vote on it.

They repaired the *Naomi* on a Saturday, on a shingle beach in a deserted cove wall beyond Aciriale, under Grossman's direction, despite the objection of the more religious Jews who felt that labor on the Sabbath should be avoided. These even refused to watch, but marched off over the hills to stare out at the rolling countryside and act, unconsciously, as lookouts against unwanted intrusion. And the following day the *Naomi* was refueled in Augusta, the water tanks filled and additional food purchased and stored aboard. And once they sailed, Wolf brought out the guns that had been hidden in the bilges, wrapped in oiled silk, cleaned them until they polished, and mounted them in a makeshift gun rack set on the wall of the wheelhouse, proud of his work.

There was a holiday mood on board once they cleared Augusta harbor and were out of sight of land. They had come almost four hundred miles without being discovered by the British, and while the closer they came to Palestine the greater the danger, there was always the hope that as long as they maintained their appearance as an innocent fishing vessel, they might continue the deception successfully.

As if to compensate for the rough waters in the straits, the sea turned beautifully calm. When no ship was in sight, which was most of the time, since Cellotti took advantage of the charts to avoid popular sea lanes, the passengers took turns on deck, spelling each other every few hours day and night, luxuriating in the warm fresh sea breeze and the restful motion as the ship chugged its way through the small waves. When a ship was sighted only the men dressed as fishermen occupied the deck and the deckhouse; once the danger had passed the children would swarm back on deck, hanging over the bow despite the warning cries of mothers, or draped over the rail, staring down into the depths of the sea as if searching for some meaning to their odyssey in the green-blue dimness there. The trawls had been stowed, since they slowed the speed of the ship, but many of the men fished from the deck using makeshift poles, shouting with delight on the rare occasions when they caught something.

Ben Grossman's position on the ship had changed. From being a pariah, albeit a self-imposed pariah, he had become a person to be considered in the daily functioning of the ship. As they sailed from the Italian waters into the Aegean Sea, he pointed out that it was possible the British might believe the missing *Naomi* had gone to the bottom, and it would not do to be reported five hundred miles from Nervi; the following day, rigged on ship's cradles, he helped change the name to the *Ruth*. In the hot Aegean winds he had shown the men on board how to install simple air scoops made of cardboard, so that the ventilation in the cabin was immeasurably improved. He had rigged up a small air hose to act as a blower on the stove, pushing the fumes up the jerry-rigged chimney and out of the cabin. And every day he checked out the diesel, making sure its efficiency remained high, watched the generator and the air compressor, and made sure the batteries had plenty of water.

Nor did he mind. It was evident to him that he could not leave the ship before they reached Palestine, but he did have a valid passport, albeit a forged one, and once ashore it would only be a matter of time before he would manage to leave the country and get to Switzerland, because if Brodsky or any of the others thought he had forgotten his resolution, they were crazy. He would need more than the fifty dollars he carried, but they said everyone in Palestine was armed, and an armed man could arrange money. And of course they expected him to forfeit his passport once they were on Palestinian soil, but what they expected and what they got were two different things.

It felt good to be planning again, using the time to stare out to sea as they chugged their way east, laying out a plan in all the detail he had always enjoyed. Banks had money; he would locate a bank and study its operation. And leaving the country should be no great problem in a place where the pressure was on people trying to get in. There were undoubtedly ships for commerce, and if worse came to worse he could always try to ship on as a seaman. Or as a ship's engineer; after his experience on the *Ruth*—he should be able to handle such a job with ease. A pity Switzerland didn't have a seaport.

And so they chugged on, all eyes constantly straining to the east, as if they could see their destination across all the hundreds of miles, through the dark and mist and the sea fogs they encountered. Palestine! Each had his own dream, his own picture of the future.

BOOK II

Prologue

The history of Palestine is one of violence. Its land has been won and rewon a hundred times, and the price has always been death. One might think its soil would be fruitful with the constant gift to the earth of the rich protein of human flesh and the valuable minerals of human blood, but a large part of it remains a desert, the few oases torn from its arid soil only by great determination. Sitting as it does across the main trade routes between Africa and Asia, it has been the target for greedy invaders since recorded time. The Israelites ruled it; the Assyrians and the Babylonians ruled it; Alexander of Macedonia ruled it; the Ptolomies ruled it; the Romans ruled it; Islam ruled it; Napoleon tried to rule it and failed; the Ottoman Turks ruled it, and in between many others ruled it, and each left the mark of his hand upon the land and the people.

Now, in 1946, the country is ruled by the British under a League of Nations mandate approved in 1922, a mandate which incorporates within it the Balfour Declaration of November 1917, promising British support for the establishment of a national home for the Jewish people in Palestine. Still, the British white paper of 1939, which restricted Jewish immigration to 15,000 persons per year is, in this year 1946, still the official British policy, despite the toll of the holocaust, despite the desperate plight of the Jews of Europe. But in the interim six years the Jews of Palestine fought with the British Army on many fronts and were an important factor in the struggle against Rommel and the Afrika Korps. Egypt and the other Arab forces behind the Mufti of Jerusalem, Haj Amin el-

PROLOGUE

Husaiani, on the other hand, actively supported Hitler and the Nazis. As a result, the Jews feel they have a right to expect a relaxation in British immigration policy as the minimum they should receive for their sacrifices.

In November of 1945 an Anglo-American Committee of Inquiry is formed to examine the status of Jews in former Axis-occupied countries and to discover how many are impelled by their conditions to migrate. After all, almost a year has passed since liberation of many of the camps in Europe, and many if not most of the survivors are still living in so-called assembly centers—camps in the very communities where they had been made to suffer. The committee recommends that all countries join in offering a new home to the survivors of the holocaust, and that as part of this program, Palestine permit the immediate immigration of 100,000 Jews. Although Britain has been instrumental in the formation of the Anglo-American Committee of Inquiry, she refuses to follow the recommendations of the committee. The British detain thousands of persons attempting to run the British blockade, stopping their ships even on the high seas, returning the ships and their crews to the ports from which they originally sailed, and interning the passengers, men, women, and children, in detention camps both in Cyprus and in Palestine itself, camps which are simply British-style concentration camps, barbed wire and all.

Britain is neither cruel nor inhumane. They need Arab oil, and to assure themselves of it they accede to almost any Arab demand, including the severe restriction of Jewish immigration. The Arabs honestly fear the immigration of Jews, feeling that the intrusion of Jews on any scale represents a threat to their own national aspirations. And the British have promised all things to all people, Jew and Arab alike, and are now in the uncomfortable position of being unwilling or unable—or both—to fulfill their promises to either side.

In their frustration, the British increase their repression, and the answer of the Jews is disregard for the authority of the crown. The Haganah, the defense forces of the Jews in Palestine, together with its elite striking force, the Palmach, as well as the Mossad, the intelligence arm of the Jewish forces who are responsible for helping the illegal immigrants reach Palestine in defiance of British restrictions, turn their full efforts toward overcoming these restrictions. The Irgun Zvai Leumi and the Stern Gang, underground armies dedicated to violent reprisal for each British act of repression, become more active. The Irgun and the

Stern Gang are not particularly popular, nor are their methods approved by many Jews either in Palestine or in the rest of the world, but emotions are high and both underground armies have little trouble recruiting. Buildings are dynamited with large loss of life, Jews are caught and hung, British soldiers are hung in reprisal.

History is repeating itself in Palestine.

Chapter 1

Naval Lieutenant Dudley Arthur Mullins, commander of British Naval Patrol Vessel *Portland-3* stationed in Yafo, was a man of singular emotions: he hated everything. He hated Jews, but he hated Arabs equally. He hated the weather and he loathed the food; he abominated his quarters on land and he execrated the confines of the ship. He hated his superiors and he hated his subordinates; he hated the girls Mustafa Kamal sent him for his pleasure and he destested Mustafa for selecting them. In short, he hated Palestine and his duty there. Not that he wanted to return to England; he hated that as well.

Mullins was a sour-faced, dyspeptic, overweight man of forty years of age and he should never have been a sailor, since he hated the sea. If it could be said that he abhorred one thing less than anything else, it was the fact that his duty allowed him to take people from illegal ships and see to it they went behind barbed wire.

The night of December 4 was foggy—Mullins detested fog—and the *Portland-3* was doing a routine patrol between Yafo and Ashdod. At the radar station of the ship, the new invention that had been developed and perfected during the war and had now been installed on all ships of His Majesty's Navy including minor patrol vessels in the Palestine sector, was Seaman-First John Wilburson. At his dials in the radio-communications room behind the bridge was Chief Petty Officer George Enderly. Seaman-Second Jonathon Martingale stood yawning beside the 40-mm Bofors gun mounted on the prow of the neat ship; the spotlight over his head was turned off in deference to the impenetrability of the fog as well as the fear of advertising their presence in the area. Eight of the other fourteen-man crew were in their bunks; the other six were about their various duties. It was a normal patrol night in every respect, including the dour looks Mullins cast at his crew as he made his final inspection round of the evening before retiring to his quarters to read a new book of pornography given him by Mustafa which Mullins suspected was intended to lower his resistance to the latest batch of girls Mustafa had brought in from Said.

He had no more than gotten himself as comfortable as possible atop his lumpy and uncomfortable bunk, than the intercom buzzed at his elbow. He picked up the handset, glowering at it.

"Well?"

"Sir, we have a blip on the radar—"

Mullins had never believed in the radar.

"Probably a malfunction in the bloody thing," he said sourly. "I'll arrange to have the port engineer take a look at the damn contraption first thing in the morning."

"Sir—" Seaman-First Wilburson knew his duty and was determined to do it, commanding officer or not. "The radar is working perfectly, sir. There's something in the water about two thousand yards east-southeast of us."

"There are probably two thousand things in the water two thousand yards east-southeast of us," Mullins said, pleased with his humor, "including fish and logs and land, as well—"

"No, sir," Wilburson said stubbornly. "It's a ship, sir, a small ship but a ship. It's moving slowly in the direction of the beach."

Mullins frowned. It seemed there was to be no rest with the crew of eager beavers he had inherited with his command, especially given all the new-fangled gear that had been hung all over the bloody ship. Still, he supposed there was a faint possibility that the radar was actually working the way they said it was supposed to work when they installed it, although that was hard to believe. He cleared his throat.

"And how far is the shore?"

"They have about two and a half miles to go, sir. They're definitely within Palestinian waters, sir."

As if that made the slightest difference, Mullins thought, and sighed. "All right," he said, and pushed the button for the radio room. In the communications center, Chief Enderly touched a switch, opening a line.

"Sir?"

"Radar says there's something in the water about a mile east-southeast of us. Thinks it may be a ship. I know none of ours are around. See if you can pick up any radio communication from them."

"You want me to try to contact them, sir?"

"Good God, no!" What kind of idiots did he have on the ship? "Try to listen to them."

"Yes, sir."

There was a short pause; then Mullins barked. "Well?"

"I'm trying, sir. Nothing so far. Just some dance music from Tel Aviv . . ."

"Forget dance music from Tel Aviv!"

"Yes, sir. I'm running down the frequencies. They may be in silent, sir."

"Or they may not be," Mullins said sourly.

"Yes, sir. Sir!"

"Yes?"

"I'm picking something up. It could be from the ship."

"Well! Cut radar in on this call."

"Yes, sir." Buttons were pushed.

"Radar, this is the captain. We have a radio signal, unidentified as yet, which might be coming from that ship of yours. Get me the bearing, will you?"

"Right, sir."

Mullins tossed the pornographic book onto the narrow shelf that ran alongside the bulkhead beside his bunk. There would be no time to dwell on the houris in Mustafa's book, and he was fairly sure they wouldn't have been worth the effort in any event. He suddenly glared at the instrument in his hand.

"Well? Where is everybody?"

"Radar here, sir. Bearing one-forty-one-fourteen."

Chief Enderly in radio said, "They're in 'open,' sir. No code—"

"I know what 'open' means, Chief."

"—only they're speaking a language I don't understand."

"Yiddish."

"No, sir. I recognize Yiddish." As well I should, Enderly thought. He had been living, quite happily, with a Romanian Jewess on shore for the past two years. "It's something else, sir."

"Probably that new language, Hebrew, they're trying to get everyone to use," Mullins said after thinking it over.

"Maybe, sir, but I don't think so . . ."

"Well, damn it, don't we have anyone who speaks these bloody wog languages? What about Wolfson? I heard he does."

"I'll put him on the blower, sir."

"And advertise to the whole eastern Mediterranean where we are? Send someone to find him and get him up to the radio shack!" God, what morons he had to put up with!

"Yes, sir."

There was a prolonged silence as Mullins glared murderously at the handset he was holding. With crews like this it was a bloody wonder they ever kept a bloody ship from discharging a million bloody Jews onto the bloody beach every bloody half-hour! A third voice came over the intercom, a diffident voice, just about the time Lieutenant Mullins was about to explode.

"Sir? This is Wolfson. Seaman-Second—"

"Wolfson! Get on the radio! Tell me what those wogs are speaking."

"Yes, sir." There was a pause. "Sir? They're speaking Iraqi, sir."

"Arabs?" Mullins couldn't believe it. "What in hell are Arabs doing out at sea at this hour?"

"I don't think they're Arabs, sir . . ."

"Who in hell else speaks Iraqi?"

"Jews, sir. One second . . ."

In the radio shack, Wolfson listened carefully. It never occurred to him for a second that he might be doing the slightest harm to his co-religionists. He was, after all, a British naval personnel, whose forebears had been in England for countless generations, and who was pledged to do his best for King and Country. Palestine was just another foreign land, another outpost of empire, full of infidels, which was to say, non-British.

"Sir, they're saying something about landing. They said something about waiting for trucks to pick them up . . ."

"Trucks, eh? Waiting to land, eh? What do you know!" Mullins felt exultant. Maybe the bloody radar did have its uses after all. The loss of Mustafa's book and the erotic effect he had anticipated from it was nothing compared to the warm feeling he knew he would experience when this bunch was rounded up and shipped off to a camp somewhere. "Call the men to quarters! Wait! No bloody bugle calls over the P.A., for God's sake! Send someone to roust them out and get them up on deck. And send Wolfson to me on the bridge."

He put the handset back into its cradle and came out on deck, moving swiftly in the direction of the bridge. The man at the wheel came a bit more erect when his commander entered, but he said nothing, keeping his eyes fixed on the fog ahead. The ship crept forward silently in the thick mist.

On board the *Ruth*, Davi Ben-Levi was at the radio, holding the microphone, waiting. Standing at the wheel, Cellotti held the ship steady as they now inched slowly parallel to the shore. Their position was less than a half mile from the beach, and the trucks to take them inland were inexplicably delayed. On deck the others of the ship's committee waited impatiently, scanning the waters about them for any sign of a hostile patrol boat, trying their best to see through the fog to the shore and the possibility of foot patrols there waiting to capture them. The waiting made them more and more tense each minute that passed. Below decks the apprehension was even more profound; faces crowded the small portholes, jostling for space to stare fearfully into the darkness, seeing nothing, wondering nervously at the delay in abandoning the ship.

There was a crackle as the radio suddenly came to life. Ben-Levi leaned forward eagerly, listening to the low voice speaking to him in Iraqi.

"Davi—sorry we're late. There was a roadblock at Yavneh; we had to go around. We should be there in fifteen, twenty minutes. Wait for us to arrive before disembarking."

"Don't worry. We—"

Ben-Levi stopped speaking abruptly. A dazzling light had suddenly pierced the fog, enveloping the *Ruth*, glaring into the wheelhouse, blinding him. A voice boomed out of the night, distorted by a hand-held speaker, speaking in English.

"You! Whatever ship you are! Stand by to be boarded! This is a British patrol vessel!" There was a brief pause; then a different voice, a younger less-assured voice, was trying to repeat the same message, only this time in halting Iraqi. "You! Whoever ship you were! Stand up to be landed upon! This is a British patrol—" Wolfson struggled with the word for vessel and ended weakly, "—car!"

Those on the *Ruth* could now see the patrol vessel moving slowly out of the bank of fog, a silver ghost, edging closer, maneuvering for position to run alongside the stalled trawler. Movement on the *Ruth* had stopped; the shock of their discovery was too great for immediate reaction. Then Max Brodsky was in the wheelhouse, wrenching the microphone from Davi's hand, looking down at the man at the radio.

"Who were you speaking to?"

"His name is Yakov Mendel. Why?"

"I know him. Thank God it's him!" Brodsky spoke rapidly into the microphone, speaking Polish. "Yakov, this is Max Brodsky. We've been stopped by a patrol boat—"

The other answered in Polish. "Can you outrun them?"

"Not a chance. Wait—!"

Ben Grossman came running into the wheelhouse and snatched a rifle from the gun rack. Grossman had no intention of being interned in a British camp at Cyprus or anywhere else at this stage of the game. He smashed the rifle butt through the new glass in the wheelhouse window, raised the rifle, and fired. At his side Cellotti groaned.

"You missed!"

"I didn't miss," Grossman said grimly as he pumped the bolt action of the ancient weapon. "That was their radar. Now for the light!" He aimed and fired again; over the crack of the rifle came the explosion as the huge vapor-filled bulb disintegrated. Darkness covered them. Even as he heard a curse from the patrol boat's bullhorn, Cellotti was pressing forward on the accelerator; the diesel responded instantly, roaring, the burble of its exhausts roiling the waters. Brodsky went back to the microphone, grinning triumphantly.

"We shot out their spotlight! We're running!"

"They have radar—"

"Not anymore!"

"Good." There was a pause. "Why the Polish?"

"Someone on that patrol boat understands Iraqi. Let's hope they don't speak Polish—"

His voice was interrupted by a loud *boom* as the Bofors 40-mm gun on the prow of the *Portland-3* opened fire in their general direction. On the bridge of the patrol ship, Naval Lieutenant Mullins was fuming; in over two years of duty he had never had to fill out a form asking for as much as having a scratch on his ship repainted, and here some miserable bastard had not only ruined a perfectly good spotlight, but was continuing to shoot in their direction. Well, he would teach those bloody bastards a lesson!

"Fire! Fire! Fire!" he screamed into the handset.

And Jonathon Martingale fired as rapidly as he could, although he had no idea where the ship was he was firing at. If he could have stopped firing for a few seconds he might have been able to get some idea of where his target was by their engine noise, but with the old man with a hair across his arse, he had no intention of being scientific about it. He simply fired blindly.

On the *Ruth*, Ben Grossman had left the wheelhouse; it was too crowded. On deck he was quickly joined by Wolf and the others, all armed with weapons from the gun rack. They knelt at the rail, firing back at the patrol ship, aiming at the flash of the Bofors. They could hear the whistle of the Bofors shells as they passed near the ship to explode harmlessly in the sea. Cellotti swung the wheel hard, heading the ship west, away from the shore. Brodsky crouched in the wheelhouse, speaking into the microphone.

"They're firing at us blind. Maybe we can get away, at that."

"Good. Head for Tel Aviv. Beach her—"

"Tel Aviv?" It seemed like an insane place to head for; Tel Aviv was the center of British activity in central coastal Palestine; they had to have many troops there. It was also a large city; surely some deserted beach would be better? Haifa, of course, was too far away—but Tel Aviv?

"Tel Aviv!" Yakov said coldly. "Don't argue. Run the ship ashore as near the foot of Ben Gurion Boulevard as possible, onto Orange Beach. Do you know it?"

"I know it," Brodsky said desperately, "but in the dark—"

"It won't be dark. It's a big city, for God's sake, and it never sleeps!"

"But if there are people—"

"I said, don't argue! We'll be there. Just *you* be there—"

There was a deafening crash as a shell from the Bofors plowed through the wheelhouse. It killed Davi Ben-Levi instantly before crashing through the deck into the crowded hold below. The shrieks rose in anguished intensity; the men on deck stopped their firing and stared at the hole in the deck apprehensively.

"It didn't explode . . . !"

"They moved back from the hole in the deck fearfully; then Wolf went toward the companionway.

"We have to look," he said simply and started down. Grossman followed. The shell had killed a woman and a young boy, and had then lodged itself in the hull of the ship without detonating. Pincus was bending over the two dead bodies, flashing a flashlight over the shattered corpses, making sure there was nothing to be done. Water was seeping from the edges of the shell, starting to fill the bilges; the bilge pumps sprang into action automatically. The whimpering and screaming increased as Grossman's flashlight studied the leakage.

"We'll drown!"

Grossman swung around savagely. "Shut up! *Shut up!* You're louder than the engine and that's loud enough. The British won't need their radar; they'll be able to hear us miles away with all your screeching! Shut up!"

The noise slowly abated; people shrank back into their bunks as far as they could from the crushed bodies lying on the deck of the cabin. Pincus covered them with blankets, muttering a prayer as he did so. Grossman swung his flashlight from the wedged shell to Wolf's pale face.

Wolf shrugged. "We can't move it, that's for sure. It might explode."

"We couldn't move it anyway; it's a plug. If we took it out, we'd sink."

Wolf shook his head disconsolately and attempted a weak smile.

"This is the last cruise *I* take," he said. "They can advertise all they want."

Grossman smiled. "Not even for the food?"

Wolf smiled back at him, a small sour smile. He swished his foot around in the water that was beginning to overtake the efforts of the bilge pumps, washing in little waves over the cabin deck.

"Not even for the swimming pool," he said, and started back to the deck above.

On the bridge of the *Portland-3*, commander of the ship Lieutenant Mullins was having a fit. He was bellowing into his handset; at the other end of the connection Seaman-First John Wilburson was wishing he had gone into the submarine service where the worst thing that could happen was not to come to the surface. How did ·a vicious blithering maniac like Mullins ever make command when he couldn't understand simple English?

"I said, we have no radar, sir."

"What do you mean, we have no radar?"

"I mean, someone from that ship shot out our scanner, sir. The radar is not in functioning order, sir."

"Or you don't know how to work the bloody thing!" Mullins said angrily. "I knew it was a useless bit of bumph when they installed the bloody thing!" He hung up with a curse and turned to Seaman-Second Wolfson at his side, listening desperately to the conversation being picked up by Enderly in the radio shack and piped to the bridge. "Well? Well? What are they saying?"

"I don't know, sir. They—they're not speaking Iraqi any longer . . ."

"Well, what in bloody hell *are* they speaking?"

"I—I don't know, sir. It sounds eastern European, but I don't know . . ."

"What kind of a bloody linguist are you, anyway? What are you doing on this ship?"

"I—I was majoring in Mid-East languages at London University when I quit to join the navy, sir." Wolfson swallowed. "On this ship I'm—I'm the cook's assistant, sir . . ."

"Good God!" Mullins stared. "Well, go make some coffee, then. Try to bring it back without spilling it if you can."

He shook his head in disgust as Wolfson made his escape, and returned to staring from the bridge into the night. At the prow the Bofors continued to blast the fog, but Mullins had a cold feeling it was all in vain. The intruding ship was lost. Lost! What a black mark on his record! Could he swear the men to silence, pretend they never ran across the ship at all, give them shore leave more frequently as a bribe? Not very likely; his men were probably not as fond of him as they should be; and besides, there was the smashed spotlight to explain, and, if Wilburson was correct, a smashed radar scanner as well.

He sighed, picked up the handset, and instructed Martingale to cease his bloody useless waste of ammunition; he then instructed Chief Enderly to report the incident and advise all beach patrols and other patrol ships in the area of the presence of the intruder. He then advised the man beside him on the bridge to return to Yafo and the base, and tramped back to his cabin. Maybe when they got back Mustafa would have a girl who enjoyed being beaten—or who did not enjoy being beaten. That might even be better. He was just in the mood.

In Tel Aviv the Mossad was putting into effect an audacious scheme they had long since developed for just such a critical situation as faced the *Ruth* at the moment. The ship, Brodsky had informed them, had been badly damaged; Davi Ben-Levi, a woman, and a boy had been killed by a wildly fired shell from the patrol boat. They had escaped, at least for the time being, but water was rising in the cabin and morale was low. They would do their best to reach Tel Aviv and Orange Beach, but that was the absolute maximum distance their captain calculated they could hope to sail in their precarious condition. Yakov recalled the trucks and then put into effect the alternate plan for saving the people on the *Ruth*.

Each member of the Mossad had long since been assigned ten telephone numbers to call in just such an emergency, and each of these ten also had a list of ten numbers, as did the last ten. Thus, even with the limited telephone facilities of Tel Aviv at the time, there would be no duplication of calls, and a minimum of ringing busy numbers; and within thirty minutes over a thousand members of the Haganah were on their way to Orange Beach by tram, by car, by bus, or walking. They came from as near as Arlozoroff Street to as far away as such suburbs as Bat Yam and Petah Tikvah, from Ramat Gan, from Ramat Hasharon and Bnei Berak, from all corners of the sprawling, growing city.

They came in colorful clothes, as if to celebrate, carrying picnic baskets which, though hastily packed, contained boiled eggs and pickles and fruits and cakes; they came with guitars and violins, with mandolins and balalaikas; they came with sticks and other kindling,

with small logs and paper for beach fires. They came equipped for a
beach party on a grand scale. And they also came with surfboards
and small, tightly packed inflatable boats, and swimming suits to
enjoy the water. And some of them also came, under their fruits and
cakes and napkins and their bathing suits in their wicker baskets,
with guns.

The two British soldiers patrolling along Hayarkon Street, shook
their heads, partly in admiration, partly in wonder.

"Crazy people," said one, watching the fires being kindled all
along the beach, watching a group nearest the road start to build
sand castles at regular intervals, watching the baskets being un-
packed, the musical instruments being tuned. "A picnic at this hour.
I wonder what they're celebrating now?"

"These Jew holidays always start at night," said the other out of
his greater knowledge. "Anyway, who cares what they're celebrating?
They're having fun. I envy them."

"At one o'clock in the morning?"

"At any hour," the second said, and shifted his submachine gun to
prevent the strap from biting into his shoulder.

They paused in their patrol to listen to the music rising from the
various groups, watched the girls alternate with the boys as they
began to dance the hora around several of the many fires. The water
of the warm Mediterranean splashed in the distance as young men
paddled out strongly on their surfboards, drifting farther and farther
out, accompanied by laughing men and women hanging onto the
sides of inflatable boats.

"They got it made, them Jews," the first one said enviously, and
the two resumed their march along the edge of the beach area,
sweating in their heavy uniforms.

In approximately the center of the beach, well hidden by the
group around him, Yakov bent over the huge picnic basket that concealed his battery-operated two-way radio. He appeared to be selecting a sandwich.

"How are you doing?"

"Well, we're still on top of the water, although the boat is getting
sluggish," Brodsky said. He was seated on the deck inside the
wheelhouse, staring dully at the blood of Davi Ben-Levi coagulating a
few feet from him. Davi's body had been taken outside to join those

of the woman and boy on the deck, out of the way of any possible action, covered but not forgotten. "We have to be careful. The fog is lifting."

"Where are you?"

"You mean you can't see us? I feel as if every eye in Palestine is trained on us, every shore battery waiting to fire—"

"Max! Where are you?"

"Sorry. I guess I'm tired. We can see Yafo ahead. Cellotti thinks we're maybe two miles out."

"You should be angling in pretty soon. We're not all that far from Yafo, maybe two or three miles at the most. Can't you spot us, yet?"

"We can see the lights of the city, of course—"

"No. I mean our beach fires."

"No. Wait, let me get a glass." There was a pause. "A bunch of fires along the beach?"

"That's us." Yakov winked at the others around the fire. "They see us." He returned to his microphone. "We're having a picnic. Come join us."

"If they're coming to join us, tell them to bring their own food," someone said. "These sandwiches are awful!"

"My husband," a girl said, and laughed.

Yakov switched off the set, tucked the microphone into the basket beside the set, and covered the equipment with a beach blanket. He turned and stared out to sea, a swarthy man in his late twenties, with a muscular, hairy body in brief swimming trunks.

"Pretty soon, now . . ."

He made a motion to the musicians around his particular fire; they stopped what they were playing and broke into a loud, wild Gypsy melody; at the other fires the music stopped slowly as the Gypsy tune was noted, then the other groups also took it up. The men at the sand castles along the edge of the beach beside the road dug in a little deeper, putting their hands on the butts of their guns inside, under the napkins. The boats and the surfboards paddled a few feet farther into the sea and then spread out a bit to cover the greatest area.

From the deck of the trawler approaching the beach under the noise of the music, it seemed the fires there had to illuminate them, to expose them to the view of anyone not totally blind, but on the contrary the fires made it difficult for anyone on shore to see beyond their glow. The ship, in fact, was within a few hundred feet of the shore with the swimmers and the inflatable boats approaching it from every side before one of the patrolling soldiers noted it, and even then he wasn't positive at first. He tapped his companion on the shoulder.

"Do you see what I see?"

"What?"

"Is that a ship . . . ?" Suddenly the entire beach party made sense. He fumbled for his whistle. "It's that ship we had a flash about, the one that got away outside Ashdod. What bloody goddamn nerve, bringing it into Tel Aviv right under our noses!"

He blew on his whistle with all his lung power; his companion joined in. A jeep pulled up in seconds; the soldier leaned in, speaking rapidly, pointing. The officer inside the jeep stared incredulously out to sea, unable to believe at first that these people could have been so foolhardy as to attempt landing an illegal ship in the center of the largest coastal city in Palestine; they never had before. But even as he rationalized the lack of reason on the part of the Jews, he knew what he was seeing, and his hand was reaching swiftly for his radio microphone.

People were swarming from the *Ruth*, dropping over the sides into the inflatable boats, being lowered into the water to grab at one of the many surfboards and clinging to them, four or five to a board, as the Mossad sea scouts guided them toward the shore. Those who could swim plowed through the water, heading for the beach, clambering through the surf when they were close enough, some falling to their knees to kiss the sand before being taken in hand and hustled off in the darkness.

The first army truck pulled up when the ship was almost totally abandoned; soldiers piled down, rifles in hand, and ran for the beach, but the bonfires there had by now been extinguished with sand and water, and the beach was a jumble of unidentified bodies moving about in the dark. The soldiers dashed into the crowd, trying to grab anyone they could, only to have their grip torn loose by more and rougher hands. The men at the sand castles had their guns in their hands but they held their fire, hoping the British would have enough sense to do the same. A second truck roared up, spewing soldiers as it slowed down; they joined the mob on the beach, adding to the confusion. Orders were being screamed through bullhorns by officers; countermanding orders were being shouted back by those bathers who spoke English. It was bedlam, and in that bedlam the illegal passengers of the good ship *Ruth* were being led away by the pic-nickers as hurriedly as possible.

The ship's dinghy had been pressed into service to bring the older and weaker passengers to shore, returning for several trips before removing the final three, the dead bodies of Davi Ben-Levi, the woman, and the boy. Wolf, who had volunteered to maneuver the small boat, added the arms from the gunrack before beginning the final trip to shore; Ben Grossman dropped into the sea beside the dinghy and paddled along with it until they were near the shore. On the beach there was the sudden sound of a single rifle being fired; then a pause as of people startled into momentary silence by the sound. Then an entire fusillade of gunfire broke out. People scat-tered, screaming, streaming from the beach in all directions. Gross-man, wading ashore, reached into the dinghy for a gun and crouched down on the sand, trying to get his bearings, attempting to locate a familiar face or form in the melee, wondering where Brodsky was, or Wolf, who apparently had abandoned the dinghy as soon as it grounded itself, but in the confusion it was impossible to recognize anyone or anything.

Everyone was running in different directions, dashing madly across Hayarkon Street to disappear down Gordon into Yehoash and Rup-pin, into Lasalle, Bernstein, or Zlotapolsky. Soldiers tried in vain to stem the fleeing mob, to take hostages at least if not prisoners. Some of the British troops shrugged philosophically and walked back to their trucks, prepared to concede victory to the illegal ship and its rescuers; others knelt down, took deliberate aim, and cold-bloodedly shot at the running people. Two of the soldiers who knelt down each got off one shot, but no more; they were cut down by gunfire from the sand castles at the edge of the beach. The soldiers near them scat-tered quickly for the shelter of the trucks, or of lampposts, swinging their rifles about to cover the beach with rifle fire. A third truck rolled up; the troops dropped down and hit the beach hard, grabbing everyone they could, knocking in heads, dragging people unmerci-fully toward the trucks.

Ben Grossman, running now with the others, followed two shapes as they dashed along the water's edge, partially in the sea, partially out; the pair he was following seemed to know their way, but suddenly they seemed to disappear. He paused, panting, and saw they had turned sharply into a small park between the sea and the road and were thudding down one of the paths. He started to follow when he was suddenly tackled from behind.

"I got one of the bastards!" a voice said with satisfaction. "Hey! The bugger's got a gun!"

"Good-o!" a second said with equal satisfaction, and dragged Grossman to his feet, locking a set of handcuffs about his wrists. He brought his gun butt up and slammed it against Grossman's head, knocking him to his knees. "A gun, eh? That ought to get the bastard the rope! Let's go, chum!"

They half-pulled and half-dragged a stunned Grossman along between them, with the larger of the two soldiers carrying both his own gun and the one he had taken from Grossman easily under one arm. They brought him to a truck, twisted him around, and slammed him against the tailgate. The officer there was looking at the second gun the soldier was carrying.

"It's his," the soldier said.

The officer nodded and walked over and started to search the bent-over man. He took out a passport, some money, a handkerchief, made sure there was nothing else on the prisoner, and tilted his head toward the body of the truck. The two soldiers lifted Grossman as if he had been a sack of grain and tossed him into the truck. He landed with a thud and then saw that the truck was fairly full of people. They were dressed as if for a picnic and none seemed to be from the ship. They were all standing, impassive, under the steady eye of a soldier with a submachine gun. Grossman came to his feet unsteadily.

"Who speaks German?" he asked hoarsely.

"I do," said a voice.

"What's happening?"

"What's happening is you should have gotten rid of the gun—"

"Why? I thought everyone in Palestine was armed."

"You're from the ship, that's obvious. The things they tell people!" the voice said. "There were two British soldiers killed on the beach tonight; two at least."

"More!" another voice said in Yiddish with a touch of pride.

"Anyway, at least two," the first man said. "You got caught with a gun. You're in trouble."

"What kind of trouble?"

There was a sudden jar as the truck started up.

"Hanging trouble," the voice said sadly, and fell silent.

Chapter 2

"They picked him up," Wolf said quietly. "I saw him. He started to run along the beach after a couple of people who were running that way. Then he stopped and all of a sudden two soldiers came out of nowhere and knocked him down. They handcuffed him, slapped him around, and dragged him away."

"He had a gun," someone else added.

They were at Yakov's house, a mile from the beach, on Remez Street off of Arlozoroff. Yakov had pulled on a pair of old trousers over his swimming trunks and now wore a white shirt open at the throat. He ran his hand through his thick black curly hair in despair and then looked up at Brodsky standing over him.

"They'll hang him, you know. Several soldiers were killed tonight . . ."

"Eight of our people were killed," someone else said.

"And they started it," another voice said.

"I know they started it," Yakov said patiently, "but they're running the country, not us. Soldiers were killed. Anyone caught with a gun—" His shrug completed his sentence more eloquently than words could.

"We can't let that happen," Brodsky said flatly. "If he hadn't shot out that radar scanner and the spotlight, none of us would be here now. We can't let them hang him."

"It's happened before."

Brodsky stared at the floor, thinking. He looked up. "Where will they take him?"

"To the station on Dizengoff for fingerprinting and photographing and questioning, tonight. Then to Acre Fortress tomorrow, probably. That's where they usually hang them."

"What about a trial?"

"He had his trial when he was picked up with a gun." The voice was bitter. It was the same person who had said that eight of their people had died on the beach that night. "He was found guilty and sentenced, all in that one moment."

Brodsky looked at the man who had spoken. It was Lev Mendel, Yakov Mendel's younger brother. Max hadn't seen the boy since he was fourteen; now, at nineteen, he stood almost as tall as Yakov. Max considered him a moment and then turned back to Yakov.

"You mean he won't have a trial at all?"

Lev answered before his brother could.

"Oh, he'll have the formality of coming up before a military court tomorrow afternoon at Acre," he said disdainfully, "and he'll undoubtedly be hanged at dawn the following morning."

"Really efficient, aren't they?" Wolf said sardonically.

"On things like that, yes."

Brodsky's jaw hardened. "Yakov, we have to stop them."

"Max," Yakov said quietly, "what do you suggest we do? Get eight more people killed trying to save just one? You know as well as I do who was responsible for the people who were killed tonight. We asked the Irgun for co-operation as far as the ship and getting the passengers ashore was concerned. We wanted numbers. But we specifically asked that nobody carry arms—"

"You mean we should have sat there like ducks in a shooting gallery?" It was Lev Mendel; he turned to Brodsky. "Max, if you want to help your friend, don't waste your time with Yakov. He'll still be laying the blame for what happened tonight a week after your friend is dead and buried; in fact, in a week he'll have convinced himself it was all your friend's fault. You come with me and maybe we can help him."

Brodsky looked at Yakov questioningly. Yakov shrugged.

"Do what you want, Max. We just can't sacrifice our people that way. This isn't Robin Hood we're playing, going into a castle to rescue the lady. You've been gone four years; things have changed. Except, unfortunately, the Irgun hasn't changed. They still react like angry children—"

"An eye for an eye is reacting like angry children?" Lev said hotly. "A tooth for a tooth—?"

Yakov disregarded him.

"Max, we're going to be a nation someday; someday soon. We have to start acting responsible—"

Lev snorted derisively.

"There's a war on, the British are killing our people, they're about to hang a man whose only crime was trying to reach Palestine, and Yakov says we should start to act responsible! Does Yakov tell the British not to come to the beach with guns? Oh, no! He saves that for Jews." Lev looked as if he wanted to spit. "Max, make up your mind. If you want to help your friend, come with me. If not, let him hang. I certainly don't care; we lived without him until tonight. But I'm on my way."

He walked to the door and looked back.

"Wait!" Max said, and turned to Yakov. "I didn't agree with the Irgun when I was in the Mossad before I went back to Poland, and I doubt I would agree with them today. But one thing I know—Ben Grossman is not going to hang if I can help it."

"A very fine attitude—" Yakov started to say, but Brodsky had already followed his younger brother from the room.

Wolf sighed in disgust.

"For Grossman, of all people—!" he said to no one in particular, and hurried to catch up with Brodsky.

The cells were in a row facing the corridor; there were no outside windows through which articles might be passed. Grossman sat on his hard bunk and tried to comprehend the thing that had happened to him the night before.

The man in the truck who had spoken of hanging obviously didn't know what he was talking about. Who hung men for no reason? Even at Maidanek they had reasons; possibly not reasons that would stand up in court, looking back on it, but reasons, at least. No; that part was nonsense. Nobody was going to hang anyone. But what was not nonsense was the fact that they had impounded his passport and his money and it didn't look as if he would get them back. Certainly not the passport. At his interrogation the officer conducting the questioning had had the interpreter ask him a question in Spanish and when he could not answer the officer laughed and said something in English he did not understand. The translator had told him the officer said you would think at least they would have the intelligence to give a Venezuelan passport to someone who spoke Spanish; and then the officer had tossed the passport into a drawer. That, Grossman was afraid, was the end of that.

He looked up as an unarmed soldier came down the corridor, unlocked the cell door, and motioned him to follow. He frowned; it seemed very early in the morning, not even light, for anything to happen. It was only an hour or so since his interrogation had ended. But then a possible explanation came to him. He stood up, holding out his handcuffed wrists.

"I'm free to go?"

"I haven't the foggiest notion what you're trying to say, chum," the soldier said in English, "but whatever it is, let me say to you may God have mercy on your soul, because the car is here to take you to Acre."

Grossman shrugged and followed the soldier. They passed through the room where he had been interrogated and he looked about to see if possibly the translator might be around to help explain things, but the room was deserted. The soldier led him outside to a cobbled courtyard; drawn up beside the door was an armored car. There was an armed soldier seated next to the driver, and an armed soldier in back. Ben was pushed into the back seat; a second soldier instantly got in the near side of the rear seat, sandwiching their prisoner between them. The car started off, its headlights on bright, passing the gate into Dizengoff Street and accelerating. It crossed Ibn Gvirol into Kaplan with Grossman trying to read the street signs.

It was still dark and the streets were deserted. The car turned into Petah Tikvah Road with a squeal of tires and accelerated further. Grossman turned to the soldier on one side.

"Do you speak German?"

"Shut up, you bloody murderer! One of the lads who bought it last night was a pal of mine!"

"I do not speak English. Does anyone here speak German?"

"Another word out of you and we'll finish you off here and claim you tried to escape!"

The words were unintelligible, but the attitude could not be mistaken. Grossman moved back in his seat, a cold feeling beginning to clutch his stomach. Was it possible the man in the truck the night before had been speaking the truth? Could he possibly be taken out to be hanged? No, that was nonsense! Still, he was still handcuffed and there were three armed soldiers and a driver taking him someplace in an armored car; they certainly didn't treat all illegal immigrants in that fashion. But he had had no trial, and the British were sticklers for proper form. Hanged? It was ridiculous. He turned to the man on the other side of him, tapping him on the knee, pantomiming his query by pointing his handcuffed wrists to himself, then to the car, then to the road ahead, and finally raising his shoulders in a questioning gesture.

The soldier on the near side had been watching. He laughed and tapped Grossman on the shoulder. When Ben turned around, the soldier grinned and drew his hand across his throat, then jerked it upward. The implications were unmistakable. The soldier on the far side looked disgusted.

"Leave the poor sod alone," he said somberly. "They'll be hanging him soon enough."

"Fuck the bloody bugger," said the second viciously, and settled back, smiling grimly.

It was true! They were taking him out to be hanged! Why? *Why?* It was all because he was here in this filthy miserable country. He looked out at the passing landscape. The dawn had broken as they passed the limits of the city and took to the open country and all he could see in every direction was sand and little clumps of brush and an occasional stand of trees. God, what a desolate place! And how had this nightmare come about? He started to go back over his troubles ever since that fateful night when he had heard on the radio of Hitler's escape from the coup, that night he had been so stupid as to go to Schlossberg for plastic surgery—then he gave it up. What difference did it really make? Much better than to dwell on the past would be to try and use the remaining minutes or hours to see if there was any solution to his problem. Was there the slightest chance of escape? He glanced at the soldier beside him and knew there was none. This one would enjoy nothing better than shooting him in the stomach and watching him suffer. What an end to a useful life! What a waste! And the money in Switzerland—it would lie there and rot, even as he would lie someplace in this horrible land and rot!

They came around a bend in the road; ahead of them a truck had stopped half in the road and half off it. Its cargo of Arab laborers, identified by their kaffiyehs, waited at the side of the highway while two of their members struggled over a tire that occupied the other half of the narrow highway. It was not an unusual sight at that early dawn hour.

"Bloody idiots!" the driver, and slowed down, blasting his horn.

"Asking to be rapped in the arse, the lot of them," said the soldier beside him. "Suicidal beggars, them Arabs." He raised his voice, joining it to the horn. "Get off the road, you bloody black bastards!"

The Arabs looked up at all the noise, quite as if they had been totally unaware of the presence of the armored car until that moment. The two men in the road dutifully started to drag the tire back and then left it; there was still not room enough to pass. The driver leaned on his horn again, while the soldiers waved their guns, using them to point to the tire, yelling at the men to get the unspeakable tire out of the way or have it crushed by the armored car. The Arabs crowded around the armored car, jabbering; suddenly the soldiers were each facing a revolver held in a steady hand. Lev Mendel brought a submachine gun from under his robe.

"The guns first," he said, and picked the rifle from the hands of the nearest man. There was the briefest of pauses as if the soldiers were temporarily considering resistance, but it was impossible. The rest handed their guns over and sat silent.

"Down."

They climbed down uncertainly, angrily, and stood together, glaring at their captors, staring around for some witness to this further disregard for British authority, but there was not a car or a truck in sight at that early hour on the deserted road. Ben Grossman, looking in amazement at the robed figures with the swarthy skin and odd headdress, suddenly recognized Wolf among them, and then Brodsky, who was trotting toward the armored car. He jumped down and went to join Wolf while Brodsky raised the hood of the armored car and reached for the rotor.

"Leave it!" Mendel commanded.

"It'll hold them," Brodsky said, surprised.

"This will hold them better," Lev said, and raised his machine gun.

"No!"

"Yes," Lev said, and pulled the trigger. The machine gun stuttered; the four British soldiers were still staring in disbelief, their hands held before them as if to ward off the bullets, when they died. The men in the group moved in instantly, each taking his proper part in the operation as if it had been well rehearsed. The bodies were tossed back into the armored car and a young man moved into the driver's seat, swinging the wheel, bringing the car behind the truck. The rifles and the tire were piled into the truck and the remaining men jumped aboard, pulling the handcuffed Grossman up beside them. Lev Mendel climbed up into the cab beside the driver, and the truck, followed by the armored car, turned from the highway onto a barely discernible track that led into the barren dunes and rock. The entire operation had taken two minutes from start to finish.

They bumped over the rough trail for fifteen miles before they came in sight of their objective, the remains of an old cluster of cement-block buildings built beside what seemed to be an oasis, although when they reached the trees the reason for the desertion was evident; whatever spring had once nurtured the trees had long since dried up and the occupants of those long-since erected buildings had taken their animals and gone off. The armored car was driven beneath the trees and the men from the truck instantly began spreading brush over it. The others removed their robes and kaffiyehs and stored them in one of the buildings, while from another, one of the men backed out an old touring car. Then the entire group got back in the truck, waiting for Lev.

Lev took Brodsky to one side, but before he could speak, Brodsky got in the first word.

"That was murder."

Lev Mendel shrugged. "That was an execution." He studied Max's face and then shook his head sadly. "We're fighting a war; even the Haganah agrees to that. Shooting those men was essential. They had seen us; they could have described us. It was the only thing to do." He went on before Max could say anything. "Do you remember the kibbutz Ein Tsofar, near Matzeda?"

Max nodded, his face set, his eyes cold as he looked at the armored car with its dead set beneath the tree.

"You'd better take your friend there," Lev said. "Take the touring car; someone will bring it back, or you can bring it back yourself. Leave it at my house. Ein Tsofar isn't an Irgun hangout, if that worries you; it's simply a place I think your friend will be safe. The British seldom go that far from their fortresses, and they seldom bother settlements as far out as Ein Tsofar. Anywhere else he could be in danger, because they'll really put out an all-points bulletin on him as the best way to find the rest of us. And he's the only one they can identify." He looked up at the sky as if looking for aircraft. "You have a few hours until they begin missing their armored car and crew. Don't waste time getting there."

He turned and walked to the truck without waiting for a rejoinder, and climbed in. As the truck turned to head back the way it had come, he leaned from the cab, waving an arm, calling out:

"*Shalom!*"

Shalom. Peace. Lev had been right; the execution had been necessary. But it was still an odd word to hear, Brodsky thought, after that morning's work.

Life at Ein Tsofar was everything Benjamin Grossman had feared life at a Palestinian kibbutz would be, and worse. The kibbutz was set at the foot of a towering mesa quite similar to the cliff fortress of Matzeda, or Masada as the English called it, and less than five miles to the south of it. Like Masada it was about a mile from the Dead Sea. The kibbutz contained many buildings, bare white concrete or cement-blocks squares, fences in from any predators and with outposts at the corners of the compound for protection. It looked, in fact, much like a concentration camp, only one that had been established on the landscape of the moon.

Yet Benjamin Grossman served a very useful function at Ein Tsofar, for in addition to the orchards and the date palms and the fig trees and the even rows of melons made possible by the freshwater spring from which the kibbutz earned its name, there were also caves in the mountain behind the farm, ancient caves which had been used by ancient tribes as cisterns for the capture of water when the rains came, and were now converted to small manufacturing areas, well hidden by camouflaged netting, by racks for drying clothes, and in these caves Benjamin Grossman's ability as an engineer came in handy.

But Grossman hated the place with a hatred that grew each day he was forced to stay there. Every morning he woke in his barren room—his cell, as he thought of it—to face the same monotonous view, the same unbearable hot weather, the same dry wind, the same burning sun; and after a poor breakfast, the same primitive machinery in the same damp caves making the same crude land mines and small bombs. Not even his ability at improving the inadequate operation gave him any satisfaction. He was a prisoner as effectively as he had been at Belsen, nor was there any more escape than at the camp. The British-controlled radio still offered its large reward for his capture; the few newspapers brought in by the rare visitors to the settlement still carried his picture together with the pictures of the armored car and its grisly cargo, which had been located almost a week after the killings. Every airport, every seaport, every bus station had his face on posters and engraved upon the minds of its armed guards. To show up at any one of them would have been suicidal. And to the east, had he been able to cross the Dead Sea or go around it, was the same continuing mountainous desert, and hostile desert tribes.

He had always thought of the desert as rolling yellow sands, as in the films, or in the pictures they had been shown of Rommel's victories. But here the desert was far more formidable. It was a prison of inconceivable and unclimbable cliffs, steep wadis with sharp jagged rocks to break the bones and rip the skin of anyone tumbling into one, stones to trip the unwary, gullies and cul-de-sacs to lead one into starvation or death by thirst, with no one within miles to hear a cry for help. It was the deepest pit of hell, and he was locked into it as effectively as if he had been chained to the very mountain behind them, facing vultures in Promethean fashion.

Most of the couples at the kibbutz were married; the few singles were male and for the most part worked in the illegal cave-factory. They all wondered at the habitual silence of this newest member of their group. They recognized the position he found himself in, an innocent fugitive from the British and the hangman, but having found himself in that position they would have supposed he would have welcomed the safe refuge their settlement offered and would have been more appreciative. But he kept very much to himself, never acting as one of the members of the co-operative, never even coming

into the community room in the evening to listen to the radio concerts, or to join in the discussions or the group singing; never attend-
ing their Saturday-night dances. Instead he would sit in his small
airless room—cell—and stare from the window down the darkening
rock-strewn slopes to the slate-gray surface of the sea, feeling as
landlocked as the quiet mineral-laden waters, and wonder how and
when he could escape. But even the formative action of starting to
make a plan would be stopped by the very nature of the wilderness
that surrounded and confined him. First, to get to Switzerland and
freedom he had to get back to civilization, and as long as the British
maintained their rule of Palestine this was going to be difficult. At
least if the crude land mines and the small bombs he helped manufacture led to an end of that rule, he was doing something, however
little, in his own behalf.

He had been at Ein Tsofar for nearly three months when Max
Brodsky came to pay a visit. With him was his fiancée, a girl named
Deborah Assavar. The three sat in the community hall that evening
after dinner, while Max spoke of his new assignment with the
Haganah in Tel Aviv. There was justice for you! Grossman thought;
Max in civilization—such as it was in a Jew country—while he struggled in the desert, and found himself studying the girl whenever he
thought he was unobserved. She was certainly not his idea of the
typical Jewess, although she did have dark hair cut short, and wide
black eyes, smooth olive skin, and with just the faintest curve to her
aquiline nose. But her lips were full and sensuous, her teeth white
and even, her body full-bosomed, and he realized he was comparing
her to Sarah, the last girl he had had at Maidanek. Suddenly he was
picturing Deborah on a bed, unclothed, her lush body his, his hands
upon her, his lips softly brushing her large nipples as he had done
with Sarah, listening to her begin to gasp with pleasure. He became
aware that Max was speaking to him. He looked up, startled,
brought out of his fantasy with a jar.

"What?"

"I said I'd better go in and talk to the manager, Perez, about a
place for us to sleep," Max said, and came to his feet. "Entertain
Deborah while I'm gone, will you, Ben?"

"Of course," Ben said. He watched Max leave and then fell silent,
staring down at the floor.

The girl looked at him curiously.

"You're not at all what I expected," she said quietly.

He looked up, surprised. "No? What did you expect?"

"I don't know." She smiled faintly; he noticed the smile brought out a small dimple on one corner of her mouth. "Max has told me so much about you, I suppose I thought it would be like meeting an old friend. But you're different, that's all." She laughed. "I know it sounds silly, but I had formed a certain picture of you in my mind, and you don't look like that at all."

"And what did I look like in that picture in your mind?"

She became serious, studying him critically.

"Well, to begin with, you were darker, more like Max; your hair and your eyes—"

"You don't like blond hair? Or blue eyes?"

"I like them very much. And you were taller—"

"Taller? I'm six feet tall."

"I know, but—Max has told me all the things you did together, how you met, how life was in the camps, how you came to his aid when that guard slashed Morris Wolf with his whip—"

"I hated that guard," Grossman said quietly, intently, and could almost feel the hate welling up in him again as he said it. "When you hate a man as much as I hated him, you don't have to be tall or short or anything else to do what I did."

His intensity seemed to bother her. "Is hate that important to you?"

Grossman thought about that a moment and then shrugged.

"At times," he said, and looked at her, interested in her thoughts. "Don't you hate anything?"

"I hate killing," she said quietly. "I'm a nurse and I hate killing. I hate to see children hungry, or hurt. I hate to see people suffer. I hate injustice."

"Then hate is important to you." Grossman couldn't think of anything else to say on the subject of hate, and he didn't want the conversation to end. "What else did Max tell you of me?"

"He told me how you turned on the truck heater on the train, when you went from Germany to Italy, or you would have both frozen to death. He told me how you fixed that marine engine on the ship—"

"I didn't fix it; I merely started it. And you also don't need to be tall to start a marine engine. Wolf could have started it if he had known what to do. Besides," he added, suddenly irritated, "I'm not short. Possibly next to Max, but I'm not short." He suddenly found himself on his feet, surprised to hear his own words. "Stand up. Let's see how tall I am next to you."

She stood up and came to face him. Her eyes were even with his chin. He was aware that she was a tall girl; he was also aware that her breasts were almost touching him. She looked at him, laughing; then her laugh disappeared. They looked into each other's eyes for several long moments; then suddenly she looked down.

"You're tall enough," she said quietly, and went to sit down.

He felt foolish as he also sat down. It's been too long, he thought; it's been many years since I was alone with a pretty girl, flirting, making light conversation, looking into her eyes. And this was a girl he could not flirt with, or, as it was turning out, even make conversation with, light or otherwise. Wolf, short and ugly, would have found the right things to say, the light things, the clever things. Still, looking into her eyes had brought back feelings he hadn't experienced since he was a student at Munich. It made him feel young, and the fact was that he wasn't young anymore. He was old, if not with years, with lost dreams and frustrations. Too old for any girl.

Deborah was watching him, her face serious.

"What did you expect when you met me?" she asked, as if she really wanted to know. "What did Max tell you about me?"

"Max never spoke about you," he said without thinking, and then realized how poorly that sounded. He looked apologetic. "He never did, to be honest, but the reason was that he didn't want to share you, even to that extent. You would have to know the camps to understand that. You would have been demeaned, dirtied, by being spoken of in those places."

"Max is like that," she said, and sighed. "He's a lovely man." She suddenly smiled. "Well, if Max didn't tell you about me, then you can't be disappointed."

"I'm not," he said with a fervor that surprised him. "Oh, I'm not." And looked up in profound relief as Max came back into the room. At least he had been saved the embarrassment of saying something he might well have regretted later. Although, he had to admit, it would have been good to say, regardless of the consequences. She was, indeed, a most attractive girl, and he had been alone a long time.

Lucky Max!

On September 4 of that year 1947, a certain Michael Wishnak appeared at Ein Tsofar kibbutz. That evening after work the people of the kibbutz, including Benjamin Grossman by direct request, were called together in the community hall. Wishnak spoke.

"As you are undoubtedly aware from last night's radio," he said, "the United Nations Special Committee on Palestine, UNSCOP, has recommended in a majority report that the British mandate over Palestine be terminated, and that Palestine be partitioned into sovereign Arab and Jewish states. This morning, just before I left Jerusalem, we also learned that President Truman accepts this partition plan—"

He was interrupted by a cheer; he took the opportunity to take a sip of water before raising his hand for quiet. When the room at last fell silent, he went on.

"The UN General Assembly will vote on the UNSCOP recommendation, probably in two or three months. If they vote for partition—and we believe there is a chance that they will—then it will only be a matter of months after that before the British have to leave. The British, as we know, have not been any great protection against attacks on Jews and on Jewish settlements by Arab bands, but they have been helpful to a small degree. Once they are gone the situation will be much worse. The Arab states, all of them and officially, have said they will attack us and try to wipe us out. For once we see no reason to doubt their word; they will try. We have to start now, therefore, to prepare for those attacks."

He bent over his briefcase; this time the silence was intense as he took out a piece of paper, studied it a moment, and then looked up.

"Up until now, the attacks on the settlements have been sporadic. Once the Arab armies begin to invade Palestine, the attacks will be concerted. This is certainly not to say that attacks on the *kibbutzim* and the *moshavim* will not continue while the British are still here; it simply means that we must be prepared for more concentrated and more vicious and better-armed attacks. The settlements are going to have to be prepared to defend themselves to a large extent; the cities are going to have their own problems. Certain settlements, such as Ein Tsofar, must be strengthened to act as bulwarks for the smaller and weaker settlements in their areas. They must be prepared to give these smaller settlements help, or to take in survivors or refugees from these settlements. Ein Tsofar is a natural choice in this part of the Negev; it is protected at its rear by the mountain; it has water, and it is now sufficient in food, or at least can manage to exist on its own food if it has to. And it has caves, and an arms-manufacturing facility of sorts, primitive though it be. Regarding the arms, we must enlarge the facility to provide better and more land mines and bombs, and if possible small arms. As to water, it must be conserved; old cisterns must be cleared and cleaned to store water during the rains. Food will have to be conserved, and additional stores of tinned foods sent here. Within a month we will establish at Ein Tsofar a hospital with a doctor and nurses to implement your small clinic. Our underground bunkers must be enlarged for the children—"

There was an argumentative shout from one of the women. "Why must the children stay?"

"Because, at present, they have no place else to go," Wishnak said patiently. "Our cities may be overrun; it is almost a certainty that they will be bombed. There is going to be street fighting with the local Arab population. And where else can the children go? No country is offering us permission to send our children to them, any more than they offered the Jewish children of Europe any escape during the holocaust. No country is helping us at all, as a matter of fact." He shrugged. "When there is a safer place for the children, they will go there, but at present nobody has anyplace to go, including the children. Only into the sea."

He waited a moment for further argument; there was none. He went back to his paper almost wearily.

"We must strengthen the defenses of the settlements, and particularly Ein Tsofar, which will be a key point in our defense. We have been in touch with the Irgun and the Stern people; we would expect in the case of an attack by the Arab countries they would be willing to submit to a central authority, that of the Haganah, because as the American Ben Franklin said, if we don't hang together, we shall assuredly hang separately. I should like to see the men in charge of the defense, and the person responsible for arms building, together with Joel Perez the manager, as soon as this meeting is over."

Benjamin Grossman sat through the meeting discussing his requirements for additional raw materials and equipment to manufacture greater quantities of mines and bombs and begin to manufacture larger weapons with no expression on his face, and little attention to the discussion. His mind was on far more important things. The man had said that there was a good possibility that the UN might abolish the British mandate, and once the British were out of Palestine, he would be a free man! And once that happened, Ein Tsofar and their awful food and their pitiful little arms factory and their imprisoning desert would be a thing of the past. And this time nobody or nothing was going to stand in his way. He had waited too long as it was. Let the Jews and the Arabs battle to their hearts' content; let them annihilate each other and blessings on both of them. He would be out of it.

The hospital contingent came to Ein Tsofar in mid-October, trucks rumbling along the dirt road that skirted the Dead Sea, churning dust, led by a jeep with armed men, for the Arab attacks on outlying settlements and small traveling convoys had increased greatly, not waiting for any vote on partition in a land thousands of miles from their own. Ben Grossman heard of its arrival but paid little attention; by the time he had finished his day's work and had cleaned up for supper, most of the equipment for the hospital had been unloaded and temporarily stored in the cave that had been selected for the enlarged clinic. Unlike the other members of the kibbutz who had come from their chores to watch and help with the unloading, Grossman had no interest in the activity. Instead he waited for the supper hour sitting in his room, staring as usual at the slopes leading to the waters below and the mountains beyond that completed the walls of his prison.

There was a diffident knock on his door and he looked up in surprise; as a general rule he was left pretty much to himself.

"Come in."

The door opened; he stared as Deborah smiled at him. He came to his feet in confusion.

"Is Max here?"

"No," she said. "I'm alone. Or rather, I came with a doctor and three other nurses, but not with Max. I'm with the hospital."

"But—" He stopped, still surprised to see her.

Deborah smiled at his expression. "Aren't you even going to say hello?"

"I'm sorry. Of course—hello. It's just—well, I'm rather surprised. I didn't expect to see you again. I mean, not alone. I thought by now you and Max would have been married."

Deborah looked at him steadily.

"Max and I are not going to get married. He's a fine man, a strong man, a wonderful man, and I suppose I even love him in a way. But not in the way you should love a man to marry him and spend your life with him."

He didn't know what to say. He had never in his wildest dreams expected to see Deborah appear at Ein Tsofar, with or without Max, even though he had pictured her in his dreams often enough. He looked about his little room, trying to think of some words.

"I—well, I hope you like it here." He seemed to see his room for the first time. "I'm afraid the accommodations aren't very luxurious—"

Deborah smiled. "I was raised on a kibbutz in the north. Ein Tsofar is far better than the one I knew as a child. We started from nothing, bringing water miles. This is heaven by comparison. And as for accommodations—" Her smile broadened. "I imagine the quarters for married couples are a lot better than this." Ben felt his face getting red. Deborah took pity on him. "It's nearly time for supper. Shall we go?"

They made love for the first time one week later. Ben had spent the evening watching Deborah play chess, sitting on the arm of her chair in the community room; in the background the radio played softly, a concert from Jerusalem. For that moment, at least, he felt peace. It was an odd feeling, a rare feeling. It was even a pleasant feeling, but it was also in a way a disturbing feeling. He could not allow this feeling of well-being to take him from his ultimate goal of reaching Switzerland and his money there; not after all the sacrifices he had made to reach that goal. But still, it was a welcome feeling from those of frustration with which his life had been filled before the arrival of Deborah.

When the game ended—and he had not paid enough attention to even know who won, only that Deborah's arm was pressed familiarly against his leg and that her hair smelled clean and fresh—he walked her to her room. She opened the door and then turned to him, pulling him to her, reaching up to brush her lips against his cheek. They kissed; the kiss grew in intensity as he tightened his grip on her; then she pulled away and took his hand, leading him into the room, closing the door behind them, not bothering to put on the light. They lay on the bed in the darkness, just holding each other tightly, and then he slowly started to unbutton her blouse and free her breasts, and felt her fingers opening the buttons of his shirt one by one.

They made love slowly, deliciously, and when at last it was over Ben Grossman realized that it was the first time since he had lost his virginity at the age of fifteen that he had made love without comparing the woman beside him with some previous woman someplace, sometime. He felt sure he was not falling in love, because he had never fallen in love, but he also knew it was important to him to be able to repeat the wonderful experience, to enjoy again those exquisite sensations. Deborah turned to him and stared at him in the dark, her hand softly rubbing his chest. Her voice was low, warm.

"'I'm sure we can get larger quarters together without getting married. I'm sure Joel Perez would understand. Would you like that?"

For a moment his gratitude at her understanding, together with the emotion brought on by being next to her and still feeling the euphoria of love-making, nearly made him say that marriage was what he wanted, but some inner caution held him back.

"Yes," he said softly and held her tightly, kissing her cheek, then her neck, feeling himself begin to get excited all over again. "I would like that very much."

Deborah Assavar was born of Iraqi-Jewish immigrant parents in the small town of Hadera, almost exactly halfway between Tel Aviv and Haifa, on the Mediterranean. When she was two years old, her father decided that the life of a fisherman was not for anyone both accustomed to the land and unaccustomed to seasickness, and the family joined others to form the kibbutz of Ramat Mizrah in the Galilee. Deborah was too young to remember Hadera on the sea, but as she grew up she was sure there had to be a better place than Ramat

Mizrah, or a better life than being hustled into a shelter to avoid Arab raids every week or so, or carrying water miles from the time she was old enough to handle a full bucket. The settlers of Ramat Mizrah had all been farmers at one time or another in their lives, but none had been fully prepared for the hardship that lay in trying to wrest a livelihood from the inhospitable desert, which had been the only land they could afford for their project.

One by one they succumbed, either to the Arabs or to the sun or to the endless toil of working the harsh land without proper tools. Deborah's father had simply laid down his hoe one day, lay down beside it, and ceased to breathe. Her mother had grieved for a short time and had then taken her husband's place in the fields, to die two months later in giving birth to a dead brother for Deborah.

Nursing was a natural career for anyone raised in such circumstances. There were no doctors nor any hospitals nearer than Haifa, and the settlers had to learn to take care of themselves. Those too young for the field took care of those even younger. The application of bandages, or the dosing of the sick, had to be handled by those who did not contribute to the other labors of the kibbutz, or by those with the stomach to face gunshot wounds without fainting. By the time Deborah was thirteen she was dividing her time between teaching the younger children their alphabet as she had been taught, taking care of the small dispensary that had been established, and taking her turn with her rifle at the guard station at night.

Her ambition had been to become a doctor, but this was clearly impossible under the circumstances; her education was lacking in many respects. But when the settlers finally admitted to themselves that not every kibbutz had to become a success story for the visitors from America, when Ramat Mizrah was finally abandoned, Deborah knew that at least she could and would become a nurse.

She did not return to Hadera with the others but went to Haifa to enter a hospital and work for her room and board, doing the most menial jobs while learning her profession. It was a hard life, but she was used to a hard life. It left little time for friendship and none for love, other than the compassionate love she felt for her suffering charges. But it built a strong woman, a woman strong enough to face the fact that the only man who she had ever felt anything for until that time, Max Brodsky, was not for her; but that a man named Benjamin Grossman, a quiet, at times even sullen man, had something for her that she needed. And that she had something for him that he needed, whether he recognized that fact or not.

She looked at the profile of the man sleeping beside her and smiled. No, she had not been wrong in asking for the assignment to Ein Tsofar. She had not been wrong in falling in love with Benjamin Grossman.

Chapter 3

It was two o'clock in the morning of November 30, with nobody at Ein Tsofar even faintly considering sleep. Even the children beyond the age of infancy had been allowed to stay awake—an unheard-of privilege—and were crowded with the adults into the community room. A samovar of hot tea stood on the table together with the usual collection of chipped cups and saucers, a sugar bowl and spoons, but nobody was drinking. They sat restlessly on the hard chairs or wandered about nervously, pausing to read or reread the notices on the bulletin board, all waiting impatiently for the radio to give them some inkling as to their future. For this was the evening of Friday, November 29, in New York and the United Nations General Assembly was preparing to take a vote on the resolution to partition Palestine and end the British mandate.

Benjamin Grossman sat next to Deborah, his arm about her possessively, waiting as well. A favorable vote would mean that in a short while he could leave the confines of Ein Tsofar, for with the end of the mandate and the departure of the British, all criminal charges of the British against Palestinian residents would automatically end; he would be free. On the other hand, a favorable vote would also probably mean an end to his relationship with Deborah, unless she chose to leave Palestine with him and take up life abroad. Would she? It was a difficult question to answer. He was sure she loved him, but there was also no doubt she also loved her native land. It was something he had never come to understand, this fierce love of these people for this miserable, inhospitable desert, but it was there and he knew it.

Still, an unfavorable vote would mean a continuation of his exile at Ein Tsofar, and while it would mean he would continue to have Deborah, to hold her, to sleep with her, to enjoy her in all the multiple ways he had found he was enjoying her, how long could he tolerate existence in this desolation without going insane? And how long would he continue to enjoy Deborah under those conditions? He blanked his mind to the various possibilities, deciding to wait until the vote was complete before attempting to fit the result into his eventual plans.

It seemed forever to those in the crowded room before the sound of a gavel being rapped could be heard from the radio; everyone instantly swung his head in that direction. Someone attempted to tune the radio finer, resulting in a squeal that brought instant and angry denunciation of the meddler; another hand corrected the sound just in time for them all to hear the voice of Assembly President Osvaldo Aranha of Brazil.

". . . now proceed to vote by roll call on the report of the ad hoc committee on the partition resolution. Delegates will respond in one of three ways—for, against, or abstain."

There was the briefest of pauses, then another voice took over.

"Afghanistan."

"Afghanistan votes against."

A general sigh swept the room. The vote had been expected but the disappointment remained. It seemed like a sign of bad luck, a poor omen, to begin with a negative vote. Why couldn't a FOR country have been alphabetically first? The children, recognizing that something extremely serious was preoccupying their parents and knowing this was not the time to fool around, kept very still, staring gravely at the radio. Joel Perez, at the blackboard, put a short mark under the AGAINST there.

"Argentina."

"Argentina abstains."

People bent their heads, work-callused fingers knotted together.

"Australia."

Heads were lifted to attention. Australia was, after all, one of the Commonwealth nations, the first one to vote, and Britain had made clear to all her allies her violent opposition to the partition plan. A vote against would be understood; an abstention would be a victory.

"Australia votes in favor of partition."

A loud cheer broke out involuntarily and was just as quickly hushed so they could continue to listen to the scratchy radio.

"Belgium."

"Belgium votes for partition."

The background swelling of noise from the pro-partition spectators in the great hall in New York came through the radio clearly, giving a feeling of brotherhood to the people in the lonely settlement on the border between the Negev and the Judean deserts. They were part of a community of people around the world, and the sounds from New York reinforced that knowledge. They were not alone; people knew they were there, even in their little corner of the world. It was good to know.

"Bolivia."

"Bolivia votes for partition."

"Brazil."

"Brazil favors partition."

Other than Argentina, there had been hope that the Latin American countries would be united in their support. Argentina had been a disappointment, but Bolivia and Brazil gave hope. Next to come would be a Russian satellite country, and then Canada, another Commonwealth nation; their votes could give a strong indication of where the resolution would eventually end.

"Byelorussia."

"Byelorussia votes for."

"Canada."

"Canada votes for partition."

"Chile."

"Chile abstains."

"China."

"China abstains."

The smiles that had followed the Canadian vote were gone. It had been strongly hoped that China would endorse the resolution.

"Costa Rica."

"Costa Rica votes in favor."

A balance with China, for there had been rumors of an attempted bribe offer to the Costa Rican delegate from one of the Arab countries. Either the rumor had been false, or more likely—as the people in the room thought—it had been offered and had been refused.

"Cuba."

"Cuba votes against partition."

Deep disappointment. Cuba had been counted on for a certain vote in favor of partition. Heads bent again as if awaiting a headman's ax; hands clasped themselves more tightly.

"Czechoslovakia."

"Czechoslovakia votes for partition."

"Denmark for . . ."

"Dominican Republic for . . ."

"Egypt."

There was an angry outburst from the Egyptian delegate; the sharp rap of an admonitory gavel from the chair, then the expected loud vote against. In the room the people shrugged; Perez duly recorded the vote under the proper heading. The vote now stood at ten in favor, three opposed, and with three abstentions.

"Ecuador."

"Ecuador favors partition."

"Ethiopia."

There was another shrug from the people in the room. Ethiopia had always voted with the Arab bloc; their vote could be calculated. At the blackboard Perez put a mark under the AGAINST even before the Ethiopian delegate could speak.

"Ethiopia—abstains . . ."

There was a shout of joy in the community room; they were not, after all, under the discipline of the United Nations and the gavel there demanding respect. Perez rubbed out the mark with his shirt sleeve, putting it in the proper column, grinning like an idiot. There were instant cries for quiet; people were beginning to believe in the possibility of victory for the first time.

"France."

"France votes for."

"Guatamala—for . . ."

"Greece—against . . ."

"Haiti for . . ."

"Honduras abstains . . ."

"Iceland—for . . ."

The vote stood at fifteen for partition, four against, with five abstentions, but nobody now was cheering. A two thirds vote was required for passage and the Arab states were yet to be heard from. The change in the pattern became evident as the voting continued.

"India votes against."

"Iran votes against."

"Iraq votes against! We will never—"

The gavel and then the impersonal voice again.

"Lebanon."

"Lebanon votes against."

They were below their necessary two thirds; it was not encouraging. Dry lips were dampened with tongues; desperate eyes stared at the radio imploringly.

"Liberia—for."

"Luxembourg—for."

"Mexico abstains."

"The Netherlands votes for the resolution."

"New Zealand—for."

"Nicaragua—for."

"Norway for."

"Pakistan votes against partition!"

"Panama favors partition."

"Paraguay votes—for."

"Peru favors partition."

Breaths were held unbelievingly. One more vote in favor of partition and they would have made it.

"The Philipines votes *for* partition!"

A roar went up in the room; nobody paid much attention to the radio after that. They had won! They were to become a nation! At the blackboard Joel Perez put a huge check mark through the FOR column that broke his chalk; he tossed the remaining piece high in the air. People were laughing and crying at the same time, congratulating each other, kissing, pounding each other on the back, shaking hands endlessly. Someone hurried out and began to bring in bottles of wine and brandy, setting them on the table; children hurried to help with the glasses, unsure of what the excitement was about but positive they would never forget the unusual celebration. Amid the noise the radio continued to give the results of the vote.

"Sweden for."

"Turkey *against!*"

"Ukraine for."

"South Africa for."

"The Union of Soviet Socialist Republics favors partition."

The sonorous voice of the secretary: "The United Kingdom of Great Britain."

Joel Perez raised his voice. "Quiet, everyone. Quiet. *Quiet!*" There was a break in the shouting. Through it they could hear the tired, defeated voice of the delegate from Great Britain.

"His Majesty's Government wishes to . . . abstain . . ."

The roar in the room returned. It was the frosting on the cake, the admission of total defeat from their enemy of many years. The man at the radio turned it off with a wink and pushed his way to the table holding the brandy.

Deborah looked to one side at Ben, her eyes filled with tears of happiness, and reached across to grasp his hand and squeeze it. Benjamin Grossman squeezed back, but his mind was already coping with this new development, adjusting his ever-present plan to take into consideration this new factor.

In a few weeks, or months at the most, his exile in this hated desert would be ended; he and Deborah could go from this terrible place. But would she go with him? Would she leave Palestine? He hoped she would, but he knew if she didn't he would go alone. He would miss her—it suddenly occurred to him that he had fallen in love! How had it happened? When had it happened? And—a sad thought—would it ever happen again?

Because he knew that for him, at least, the power of love was only one power. There were others, older drives, older ambitions, older proddings. Deborah or no Deborah, he had to get to Switzerland!

The British announced that they would leave Palestine forever on May 15, 1948, and on May 1 Max Brodsky came to Ein Tsofar. He came in a jeep at night, accompanied by Morris Wolf and a man named Dov Shapiro, also a member of the Palmach and a man who knew the kibbutz and a relatively safe way to get there. They brought with them three submachine guns and as many contraband rifles and ammunition as could be jammed into the small vehicle. It was a dangerous trip, for the route that Dov Shapiro knew was an ancient desert track that appeared on no map of the region no matter how primitive. They came skirting deep wadis, jostling through the graveled beds of dried-up streams, laboring up steep sandy cliffs and sliding on braked wheels down the far slopes, their trip made the more perilous by having to have their headlamps muffled against discovery. Marauding bands of Arabs were increasing their activities against the settlements and also against lone travelers, seeking loot as much as political advantage, ever since the partition vote.

The jeep was heard before it was sighted, its motor growling in the night as it crept toward the kibbutz from the foot of the deep pass some miles to the south; then its weakened lights could be seen swaying from side to side as it approached the wire fence. A rifle came up in the hands of the sentry there; he waited until the jeep had come to a full stop, his aim steady on the shadow that represented the head of the driver. He called out in Hebrew:

"Who are you?"

"Dov Shapiro and two other Palmach."

A searchlight suddenly illuminated the jeep, its brilliance momentarily blinding the three, and then as quickly was extinguished. Max had to admire the added precautions since his last visit. There was a low greeting exchanged between Shapiro and the sentry and then the gate was swung back. The jeep rolled past the wire; the gate was closed at once. The jeep took the curving road to the main compound and came to a stop before the administration building. Brodsky climbed down stiffly; Dov Shapiro took off at once, driving the jeep in the direction of the caves and the storage area for arms. Brodsky waited a moment, savoring the peace and quiet of the night, relaxing after the hard drive, and then walked into the building. He went down the corridor to the room shared by Joel Perez and his wife and raised a hand to knock, but before he could rap the door opened and he was facing Perez, his hand outstretched. In the background he could see Hilda Perez sitting up in bed, her bathrobe about her shoulders. Brodsky stared at Perez in surprise as he shook hands.

"You have signals from your outposts?"

"Your friend Grossman," Perez said as he closed the door and led the way toward his office. "He ran some simple wires, hooked them up to plain flashlight batteries. You push a button there, a bell rings. One ring, a friendly visitor. Two rings—" He shrugged. "We have them all over the place, between the outposts and the buildings, between the buildings, between the outposts. A regular copper mine, this place is now." He looked up at Brodsky. "And did you see the spotlights?"

"Yes."

"He put them up and put mirrors behind them. It looks like downtown Tel Aviv when they're all lit up. He made the generator work automatically, you don't have to keep going down there to start and stop it every five minutes. He's been very helpful, even if he isn't the most friendly person in the world. Although he's certainly improved since Deborah—" He suddenly stopped in embarrassment.

Brodsky stared at him wearily.

"I know all about Ben and Deborah, if that's what's bothering you," he said. "Deborah wrote me all about it. Actually, I think I knew about it even before they did. When I brought Deborah here the first time, when was it, last autumn? On the way home she was a different person." He shrugged. "I hope she's happy."

"She is," Perez said, not knowing if that was really what Brodsky wanted to hear, but determined to tell the truth. "She's teaching Grossman Hebrew, and he's also getting quite proficient in English from one of the men." Perez led the way into his office as he spoke. "He's a bright man, but—" He hesitated.

"But what?"

"I don't know."

He made it sound like an answer. He sat down, motioned Max to a chair, and reached into his desk for some Palestinian brandy and two glasses. He blew into the glasses in case any dust might have settled there, poured the drinks, and raised his glass in a salute.

"L'hayim."

"L'hayim."

The two men drank. Perez pushed the bottle across to Brodsky; Max poured himself another generous portion but instead of drinking it immediately he shoved it around in small circles on the desk, staring into its amber contents as if wondering where to begin. At last he looked up, his face reflecting his weariness. When at last he spoke his voice was flat, emotionless.

"You know, Ben Gurion is going to declare our new state on the fourteenth, the day before the British leave. As soon as the new state is declared and the British are out of here, the Arab nations have promised to attack and toss us all into the sea, and this time I think we can take them at their word. Or at least they'll do their best. Not that there hasn't been a war on here ever since the partition vote."

"Before," Perez said.

"Before," Brodsky said in agreement. "Up to now, though, Ein Tsofar has been spared the attacks that many of the other settlements have suffered, but that situation isn't going to last long."

Perez frowned. He did not doubt the accuracy of Brodsky's forecast; he was aware of the extensive Palmach intelligence operation. Still, he had a cold feeling hearing the dire prediction. He was responsible for the lives of many people, including many children.

"Who is going to attack us?"

"Local Arabs, as Mishmar Hayarden was, as all of the attacks on the settlements have been up to now. The Arab countries are being very circumspect. As long as the British are here they will not attack us directly. They'll only use the local Arabs to attack us, with all the help they can give them. It's a good way to operate if you can; I wish we had someone to do our fighting for us." He yawned and then stretched himself awake. "Ein Tsofar will be attacked by Arabs from the area around Kirbet e-Hashem."

Perez frowned. "Are you sure? I know Kirbet; it's a small place. How many men can they put together?"

"Plenty," Brodsky said evenly. "They're pulling them in from Abda, Yatta, Dura, Idna, even from Hebron itself. They've decided the strongest settlement we have in the Dead Sea area is the one to attack. Wipe out Ein Tsofar and the others will fall by themselves. At least that's their theory." He shrugged. "They may even be right. They probably are."

"They have sufficient arms?"

"When haven't the Arabs had arms?" Brodsky sounded more curious than angry. "The Arabs ship them in like we ship out melons. The British never raid their villages looking for arms; only ours." He suddenly raised his glass, drank, and set the glass on the table, shoving it away from him to indicate his drinking was done for the night.

"When?" Perez asked simply.

"Very soon, that's all I can tell you," Brodsky said, and found himself yawning in the middle of it. He blinked himself awake. "Our informant didn't know the exact date; the Arabs may not know themselves. An Egyptian colonel is rounding them up. Nothing official, of course. When he's ready—" He raised his shoulders expressively to finish the statement.

"Has anyone advised the British? After all," Perez said stubbornly, "they still have the responsibility to stop this sort of thing until they leave."

Brodsky looked at the kibbutz manager almost with amusement.

"Joel, the sun out there is beginning to soften your brain. Our informant is in the British Army; did you think the Arabs told us? Not only do the British know of the supposed attack, but my guess is they're probably pulling their garrison out of Hebron at this moment, sending them to Haifa on rest and recreation right now, just so they won't be able to help us when we ask." He shook his head in disgust, his weariness overcoming his normal tact. "Has anyone advised the British! Good God!"

Perez looked unhappy at both the criticism and the situation.

"So what do we do?"

"We fight, that's what we do," Brodsky said simply. "I brought three submachine guns and as many rifles as we could spare, as well as as much ammunition as we could scrape up. I also brought a couple of men with me, an old friend from the camps named Wolf, and Dov Shapiro, who you know. Dov worked with the British during the war as a sapper and he's been training Wolf. First thing in the morning we're going to start laying some of those mines you make here—"

"Why not still tonight?" Perez asked, anxious to be helpful.

"Because it might be handy to know exactly where they're being set," Max said dryly. "You'd like to be able to go in and out of Ein Tsofar in the future without blowing yourself up, wouldn't you?" He yawned deeply. "Besides, I'm too tired to think, now, let alone plant mines. I'd fall asleep on top of one of them." He came to his feet and stretched mightily, a weary giant. "Lead me to a bed."

As Perez walked him down the corridor and out into the still night toward one of the dormitory buildings, Brodsky stared at the silent blocks of cement and wondered which of them housed Ben and Deborah. And were they sleeping in each other's arms, still warm from love-making? He tried to push the thought away as he walked along beside Perez, tried to concentrate on the coming Arab attack, but his eyes kept returning to the blank windows of the quiet buildings and his mind kept returning to the same disturbing thought.

It was fine being the strong, silent type. Wonderful knowing that he could cope with problems like Arab attacks and the security of settlements. Great being a hero and standing unselfishly aside when Deborah wanted Ben Grossman instead of himself. But just possibly if he had taken Ben Grossman outside and beaten the living shit out of him for daring to even *look* at his girl, things might have been different.

He smiled to himself wryly. You've been seeing too many John Wayne movies, Max Brodsky, he told himself; but the hurt remained and he knew it would remain all his life.

Chapter 4

Morris Wolf and Dov Shapiro, pushing their material and tools ahead of them in a small wheeled cart, had begun their work as soon as the light was sufficient. Max Brodsky had accompanied them and had stayed with them until the first mine had been planted and the earth above it carefully smoothed over. Then he left them to their dangerous job and went to look up Ben Grossman, to accomplish the second stage of his mission to Ein Tsofar.

He paused at the entrance to the cave that served Ben Grossman as his workshop, letting his eyesight become adjusted to the relative dimness of the cave after the brilliance of the desert morning sun, then entered. Grossman looked up from the table where he had been painstakingly assembling a weapon. He leaned back and frowned at the unexpected sight of Max Brodsky. For several moments the two men stared at each other; then Brodsky pulled up a stool and sat down across from Grossman.

"Hello, Ben."

"What do you want?"

"Relax," Brodsky said quietly. "I'm not here to fight; the day I am, you'll know it. I'm not blaming you and I'm not blaming Deborah. These things happen, people fall in love. And falling in love with Deborah isn't hard. I know."

"So what did you come here for?"

"If you'll listen, you'll find out." Brodsky tried to see in the man across from him the thin, pitiful Benjamin Grossman he had practically nursed through Bergen-Belsen, or the broken man he had brought back in his arms from the Bodensee; but that man was gone. In his place was this strong, self-assured man. Maybe that was what Deborah had done for him, Max thought, and wondered if it had been for the best. He put the character analysis aside and got down to business. "You know, of course, the British will be out of Palestine in a few weeks. You'll be free, then, to come and go as you please." He looked into the slate-blue eyes steadily. "Do you still dream of getting to Switzerland?"

"That's my business, don't you think?"

Max smiled faintly.

"Ben, Ben! You're still on the defensive when nobody is attacking. I asked for a very specific reason." He looked around the small cave-shop and then gestured toward the weapon Ben had been working on. "You know a lot about guns, that's obvious. Where did you learn?"

"Why?"

"Because I asked, that's why."

Grossman shrugged. He had had his answer to this question ready for a long time; he was surprised nobody had queried him before on his knowledge of armaments. But having answers ready was the first requisite of the planner. The answer came to his lips so automatically it even sounded like the truth to him.

"My father was in the first war—a private, of course, since even then Jews weren't made officers easily. He became interested in guns. He became a collector and he passed on his interest to me." Enough of it was true to make it sound quite authentic. For a brief moment he wondered what Brodsky's reaction would be if he told the entire truth: that his father had been, indeed, a collector of weapons, one of which he had used upon himself. He also wondered what had brought on that sudden bitter thought, and looked at Max coldly. "Why?"

Max leaned forward, getting down to business.

"Because we need people to buy guns for us, and we want people who know something about what they're buying. We have people right now in the United States and others in Europe, but we need more. There are gun dealers we would want you to contact." He studied Ben's face. "One of the largest dealers in used armaments in the world is in Geneva."

Ben stared a moment and then began to laugh. "Geneva?"

Max frowned. "What's so funny?"

"You want to *send* me to Switzerland? Pay my fare there? All my expenses? After all the times you tried to talk me out of going? You don't think that's funny?"

"Times change," Max said evenly. "Things change. Besides, while we want you to go, we also want you to come back."

"And you're sure I will?" There was a taunting tone in Ben's voice.

Max continued to consider him stonily.

"Deborah will be here."

"Unless she comes with me."

"She won't," Max said evenly. "She can't."

"What do you mean, she can't?" Ben frowned across the cluttered table. "Who's to stop her?"

"Ben," Max said patiently, "Deborah Assavar is a soldier in the Haganah. She is also a nurse. She goes where she is told to go, not where you might want her to go. Deborah will be here—when you come back."

If it pleased Max Brodsky to believe that, let him believe it. The point was not whether Deborah came with him or not; the point was that he was being *sent* to Switzerland! The matter of Deborah would be resolved later, or not resolved, but the matter of Switzerland was being resolved for him. That certain God Max Brodsky was always talking about had to have a sense of humor! Switzerland! Freedom! Money to spend where and when he pleased, money to take him as far from this hellish spot as he could go!

"When would you want me to go?"

"As soon after the British leave as possible. We'll be declaring our new state on the fourteenth of the month, but there won't be time for countries to recognize us and establish diplomatic arrangements. I'll see to it you get a proper passport and documents. You'll be going with a man named Shmuel Ginzberg. He'll handle the financial arrangements. You'll be his technical advisor—"

(So I won't get my hands on your money, eh, Max? But if you should know how little I need it!)

Max was continuing, leaning forward in the damp room of the cave.

"We want you to go to Tel Aviv tonight with a man named Shapiro who knows the way; he brought me here last night. We have a place you can stay in safety in Tel Aviv until the British are gone; they're easing their security considerably now that they're about to leave. Shapiro should be ready to leave sometime this afternoon. I'd like the jeep to be through the mine field before dark."

Grossman frowned. "Mine field?"

"Yes." Max hesitated as if wondering how much to say, then decided to say it all. "Ben, this kibbutz is going to be attacked by the Arabs very soon. In a day or so at the most, we believe. We want you out of here. We can't afford to lose your expertise at this point."

"You want me and Deborah to leave tonight?"

"Not Deborah," Max said patiently. "She stays." He saw the look on Ben's face and shook his head impatiently. "Ben, can't you get anything through that thick Geman skull of yours? There's a war on! Deborah is a nurse, she's a soldier! She stays where she's needed."

"And you stay with her, is that it?"

"No, that's not it," Max said wearily. He was getting tired of the conversation; there were so many things to do to prepare for the attack, and he was wasting time. "I stay because the best thing I can do at the moment is to stay and try to keep the Arabs from overrunning the place. If I were more valuable buying arms in Switzerland or anywhere else, I'd be going back to Tel Aviv with Shapiro tonight and you'd be staying here whether you liked it or not." He looked around the cluttered interior of the cave-factory with a slight touch of distaste. "Turn everything you have in progress to someone before you leave—"

"I'm not going."

"Not going to Switzerland?"

"I'm not going to Tel Aviv tonight," Grossman said. "I'll go when it's time to leave for Switzerland. Not before."

Max Brodsky shook his head, his jaw beginning to tighten.

"Mr. Grossman, let me tell you something—your heroics really don't mean much to us. I'll tell you this one more time, and that's it. There is a war on. People are getting killed. Settlements are being leveled. You will go where you're sent when you're sent."

"Heroics?" Grossman sneered. "Listen! I'm not a member of your so-called army and I'm certainly not subject to your discipline. If you want me to go to Switzerland for you, fine—but until I go—"

He paused abruptly as the shrill bell mounted at the cave entrance suddenly rang twice. Even before he could come to his feet the bell sounded again, a frantic ringing, and then they could both hear the muffled sound of gunfire. The two men ran outside. People were dashing about, crisscrossing their paths, each running to his assigned post. Rifles were hurriedly being handed out; one man was running toward the community building with an old-fashioned machine gun in his hands while a second ran behind him with a cartridge belt looped over his shoulder, the two of them intent upon setting the gun up on the roof as they had done so often before in practice. Women in charge of the children were herding them as rapidly as possible into the underground shelters and then coming back to claim their weapons and take their places at their assigned posts. Despite the dashing in all directions there was a certain order in the chaos.

Ben grabbed a submachine gun from the hands of a pale young man who looked uncertain as to its use; with the gun nestled familiarly under his arm he ran for the perimeter and the wire. Max, a commandeered rifle in his hand, came close behind. Men from the fields were racing for the wire; the last one in turned and slammed the gate behind him and knelt to bring up his gun. It was Wolf. From the outposts the men were firing steadily down the slope at the wave of fanatical Arabs who trotted toward them up the rocky terrain, yelling incessantly, firing as they came. There were several hundred of them, some in traditional robes, others in discarded or donated British uniforms, all with the kaffiyeh cords set for battle. On the road that edged the sea below the trucks that had brought the Arabs were drawn up beside the water, their officers beside them; next to them were several passenger cars and standing on the road beside them were civilians, men and women, watching through field glasses, come to witness the attack as if it were being staged for their amusement. On the slope between them there were several bodies of men who had been caught in the fields and had not made it back in time; among them was the body of Dov Shapiro, a mine still clutched in his outstretched hand as if he were offering it to the enemy.

Wolf was at the closed gate, kneeling with a rifle he had taken from a dead man beside him, firing it through the mesh. Ben pushed him to one side and swung the gate open to give him freedom of fire. He knelt in the opening, bringing up his submachine gun, sweeping the first echelon of approaching attackers, spraying them evenly with gunfire. He found himself grinning madly, filled with an exuberance he had not felt since the early days on the Polish front, those heady, wonderful days of personal killing before the mechanization of Maidanek. This was battle! The gun chattered comfortably in his hands; how like the Russians the Arabs were, coming into that deadly fire in waves, except that the Arabs were screaming while the Russians had advanced suicidally in resigned silence. The foremost Arabs tried to rush the gate, swinging their rifles now as clubs, only to die before the deadly accuracy of the maniac with the submachine gun at the gate. The second wave of attackers hesitated and then broke in a mad rush down the slope. There was a sudden explosion as one of the land mines went off with a roar and a flash of flame, flinging the body of the unfortunate Arab in the air in doll-like fashion. There was a crow of delight from Wolf, followed by a second as another mine exploded. Ben came to his feet, swept by the passion of battle, and started out the gate after the retreating Arabs, only to be tackled violently and brought down by Brodsky. He felt himself being dragged back behind the wire fence and heard the gate being slammed shut. He turned, furious.

"What are you doing?"

"You idiot! There are mines out there!"

Max was staring down at Ben Grossman with a strange look on his face. In all the time he had known the other man, in all the experiences they had shared, he had had no idea that this mild-looking Jew, Benjamin Grossman, had such fury, such love of battle in him. Ben grinned up at him a bit sheepishly, but the pleasure of killing was still evident on his sweaty face.

"I forgot," he said.

Men and women were carrying the wounded into the makeshift hospital that had been set up in the most central and therefore the most protected of the caves, but at the moment Ben had no thought of Deborah inside, working on those wounded. He had rolled over and was staring down the slope; the retreating Arabs were back at their trucks, out of rifle fire, leaving their dead scattered about the plain, and were conferring with their officers. Beyond them a trail of dust indicated where the passenger cars had fled; the spectacle had not been as entertaining as they had supposed.

Silence fell. Guns were reloaded, ammunition brought from the storage areas to be closer to the wire; a young boy came around with coffee and the men drank it eagerly, with one eye always on the slope and the Arabs at the foot. An hour passed in this manner, with each side merely waiting; then a cloud of dust appeared on the far horizon where the passenger cars had disappeared. Perez, standing at the gate, raised field glasses.

"Half-tracks . . ." He squinted into the glasses, hoping against hope that despite Brodsky's pessimistic statement the British were answering the repeated radio calls that were being sent in a stream from the administration offices at the moment.

"Let me see." Ben Grossman came to his feet, reaching for the glasses. There was such authority in his voice that Perez handed them over automatically. Ben studied the moving cloud of dust. "Personnel carriers, unarmed. Full of Arabs. It looks as if they're merely adding numbers. I'd judge an additional hundred men." He turned to Wolf. "How many mines were you able to plant?"

"Only ten," Wolf said, and shrugged. "Then we saw them jumping down from the trucks and we didn't hang around. One of them got Shapiro with a lucky shot."

"Ten mines," Grossman said thoughtfully, "and two are already detonated. Not much of a deterrent."

"No?" Wolf said sarcastically, stung at this debasement of his efforts. "Did you see those two that went off?"

"I mean," Grossman said patiently, "their officers have seen several hundred men go through that mine field and return. Only two of them killed by the mines. They won't hesitate to send their men through it again. And eight mines won't stop them." He frowned at the ground for several minutes, calculating, and then looked up. "How far from the fence to the end of the mines you laid?"

Wolf, mollified, considered. "Maybe three hundred yards. They could come up to the edge of the mine field and be within easy rifle range of us from there, if that's what you mean."

"That's not what I mean." Ben turned, singling out a familiar face among the men standing at the wire staring down at the Arabs. It was a young man who worked with him. "Ari, get our mortar."

Max was surprised. "You have a mortar?"

"We were asked to try and work one up and we have, at least a prototype," Ben said. "It's a rather small job, no rifling, of course, and it was made from the only decent tubing I could get, but I've also built eight charges for it. It's a copy of—" He had been about to say it was a copy of the Russian 60-mm mortar from which the enlarged British Stokes 3-inch mortar had been developed, but he bit back the words in time. He would have trouble explaining his familiarity with a Russian weapon that had been developed when he supposedly had been in a concentration camp. "—a copy of the early American mortars from the First World War," he ended smoothly. "I think it will work."

"You think?" Wolf said, startled. "You haven't tried it out yet?"

"Not yet."

"And what happens if it doesn't work?"

"Let's not think of that." Grossman looked up at the sun, calculating the hours of daylight remaining, then looked down to the dirt road snaking its way beside the sea. The personnel carriers could be seen now with the naked eye, small bugs bristling with smaller bugs, creeping toward the congregation of trucks and troops at the foot of the long slope. He turned to Perez. "How far away are those trucks? The ones parked at the shore. You must have some idea."

"One point three miles," Perez said proudly, pleased to contribute to the discussion. "Almost exactly from the gate, here. We measured it; we were thinking of running a sewage line there once, but we decided not to. We didn't want to pollute the—"

He was interrupted by a harsh voice from somewhere in the crowd who had been listening.

"You can't reach any mile and a third with a sixty-millimeter mortar, even with a proper one! I was with the British; they had a couple of Yank sixty-millimeters. We were lucky to reach a mile."

"I know," Ben said and turned back to Wolf. "You came in a jeep?"

"We had to," Wolf said with his usual breeziness. "The bus didn't stop."

Max Brodsky, listening, watched as Ben Grossman effectively took charge. Perez, as director of the kibbutz, was normally responsible for the defense of the settlement; Max, as senior Palmach man there at the time, might have asked for and received that responsibility. But Grossman was taking it into his own hands and those listening to him seemed to be prepared to let him do so. Max decided to let the matter ride for the moment and see what happened. Grossman was studying Wolf's face.

"Wolf, do you know where those other eight mines are?"

"Of course. They're—"

"Could you drive that jeep through the mine field without hitting one?"

"Of course," Wolf said, his newly acquired professional pride stung, but he could not help but add sardonically, "that's if the Arabs don't mind all the traffic while they're trying to kill us, of course."

"Could you do it at night? Without lights?"

"At night without lights?" Wolf stared. "Grossman, you're crazy!"

"Could you?"

"No. Anyway, what would be the purpose? How many could you get on one jeep? And if you want someone to go down there and surrender, you don't need to wait for night to do that. Those Arabs would be very happy to massacre us all, white flag or no white flag, in broad daylight." He tried to explain. "Look, the mines were laid mainly in the road, to prevent their vehicles from reaching the fence. And if you get three feet off the road you can break an axle on the rocks. This isn't a tank we're talking about!"

"But if you had light you could do it?"

"With light I could try it. I don't say I could do it." Wolf realized he was partially contradicting himself. "I think I could do it, driving carefully. And I mean *carefully!*"

Grossman looked down at the personnel carriers that were just coming to a halt beside the other trucks.

"I have a feeling the Arabs will wait for dark after their last attack," he said. "By that time we should be ready." He looked at Wolf. "I'll see to it you get light. After that all you have to do is to drive. Carefully."

Colonel Manfred Fitzhugh, commander of the Hebron garrison of the British Armed Forces in Palestine, looked up in annoyance at the appearance of the sergeant at the door of his office, requiring his attention. The colonel was in the midst of composing a letter to his wife explaining that although the departure of the British from Palestine had been widely announced to take place on the fifteenth of May, he was being routed home by way of Port Said and Cairo, which unfortunately would delay his arrival home by several additional weeks. "A nuisance, my dear, but you know the army—" Fortunately for the colonel his wife did not. And he still had to write the girl in Cairo as well as the one in Said before the mail went out, because the postal services in those bloody countries was simply ghastly.

"Well?" he said, scowling blackly. "What is it?"

"Sir," said the sergeant, standing at attention very properly and aware the colonel was not pleased about something, "the Arabs are attacking Ein Tsofar, the settlement just south of Masada. They are radioing for help."

"Who? The Arabs?"

"No, sir. The Jews."

"Well, be a little more explicit in the future!"

The colonel knew full well who was attacking and who was radioing for help; the ploy had been made simply to gain a bit more time for thought. Colonel Fitzhugh drummed his fingers angrily on his desk, cursing inwardly. Why did those bloody Arabs have to attack two days ahead of schedule? They would probably later claim they did it because they suspected a leak in his security, but the real reason was probably because the damned wogs couldn't read a calendar! He was supposed to have most of his men off to Jericho on passes to watch a soccer game against the team of the Jericho Garrison when the attack took place, not sitting in barracks, scrubbed and shining and waiting for afternoon tea. What to do! Well, one thing he did not intend to do was to risk the life of one single British sol-

dier just two weeks before they were bloody well scheduled to leave!
He glowered at the sergeant.

"Send Captain Wiley in."

"Sir!"

Captain Wiley was equally irked at the interruption. He had been
trying to trim his mustache, which had been cultivated to an impressive if slightly unwieldy four inches either side of his bulbous nose—
he hoped that people, especially girls, would mistake him for RAF—
and the scissors were dull, the light poor, and the bloody mirror
wavy. He sighed mightily at the colonel's demand for his presence,
but put the scissors away and duly made his appearance.

"Sir?"

"The bloody Arabs are attacking Ein Tsofar settlement!"

"Oh, no, sir, that's the day after tomorrow—"

"Don't argue! They're doing it right now! Right this minute!
Don't ask me why. What are we going to say if headquarters asks
why we didn't do something about the bloody affair?"

"I—I don't know, sir . . ."

The colonel smote his desk irately. "Just once I'd like a constructive answer from one of my staff! I have to do all the thinking
around here! Well, don't just stand there; get your men on the way
there!"

"Sir?"

"Just don't go too fast," the colonel said, his tone moderating.
"Save petrol, if you know what I mean. Have a couple of flat pneu-
matics, or give ample rest periods on the way. Actually, you will
probably have to bivouac for the night somewhere along the road if
you get a slow start, seeing the hour. You might consider that possibility and load up your extended-operation equipment. That should
take a few extra hours."

"I understand, sir," the captain said, smiling broadly.

"I certainly hope for your sake that you do," the colonel said
sourly, in a tone that instantly wiped the smile from the captain's
face, "because if you get yourself or any of your men actually involved in any fighting, you'll go home a corporal!"

He scowled at the retreating captain's back a moment, and then
returned to his correspondence. It wasn't that he particularly wanted
to see Jews killed, but if anyone had to get killed, better Jews than
British soldiers. He had no intention of spending his final days in the

bloody country writing letters to relatives explaining why their Alf or their Herbert had been killed just a bloody few days before they left for blighty!

There were campfires along the edge of a placid Dead Sea where an evening meal was being cooked before the second, and intended final, attack was launched against the kibbutz. The trucks of the Arab attackers, together with the personnel carriers that had brought the supplementary force, were drawn up near them, their headlights lighting the shore. Across the sea the rugged mountains could be seen in faint silhouette, and every now and then the flicker of a kerosene lantern from some shepherd's tent high on the slopes. Sentries were posted at the edge of the area lit by the headlamps and the fires; from a short distance one might have supposed that an evening picnic was in progress. It seemed difficult to realize that the two enemies were within sight of each other, eating supper with one eye on the dark no man's land between them, planning on doing their best to destroy the other in a few minutes' time.

At the gate of the kibbutz Ben Grossman had completed his preparations. The mortar had been bolted to the floor of the jeep where the rear seat had been removed. The eight mortar charges had been set in makeshift pockets made by riveting webbing along the rear of the jeep inside the body. Wolf sat at the wheel of the jeep looking apprehensive; bravery in the camps had been one thing for death there had been welcomed; but Morris Wolf loved life in Palestine and hated to throw it away. He suddenly swung around, confronting Grossman.

"If we're going at all, let's go, for God's sake!"

"In a second." Ben settled on the floor next to the mortar. He checked the charges, nodded, and then looked up. "Set your mileage meter, your odometer, to an even number—"

"You said that before," Wolf said, irritated. "It's set."

"When you've gone *exactly* four tenths of a mile—"

"You said that before, too. When I get *exactly* four tenths of a mile I stop and stand up and they shoot me."

"We'll be beyond any accurate range of rifles."

"Who said they have to be accurate?"

"If you're going to be shot, you'll be shot," Grossman said coldly. "Are you ready?"

"I've been ready for a week, for God's sake!"

"Good." Ben raised his voice; he could not keep the excitement out of it. "Open the gate!" The gate swung back. "Lights!" The floodlights suddenly flared, making day out of night. "Go!"

At the Arab encampment the sudden blaze of light caught everyone by surprise. There was a sudden rush for guns, and then the men hesitated. A single jeep, with what looked like only two men in it, was emerging from the gate. A surrender? The robed troops relaxed but still held their guns tightly, wondering at the strange excursion.

In the jeep, Wolf pressed nervously on the accelerator; the vehicle seemed to leap forward and was suddenly slowed as Wolf quickly braked, slowing down, staring about. The road was clear enough in the strong light of the floodlamps reflected by the mirrors behind them, but in contrast the shadows were sharper, blacker, everything took on a different appearance than during the day. Wolf felt a band of sweat run down his stomach into his crotch and a part of his mind wondered if he had wet himself. God! Was that lump one of the mines they had planted, or was it just a lump? Why had they smoothed the damned things over so well they were impossible to see? What had made him think he could recognize where the blasted mines were laid? But he couldn't go back now, the danger of that was as great if not greater. He crept along, sweating, trying to make out small landmarks that might help him identify the mine locations.

"How far have we come?"

Jesus Christ! He had forgotten to check the odometer, and they had been driving for what seemed like an hour! He looked down and felt a momentary relief.

"Two tenths of a mile, plus a little . . ."

He shut his eyes a second and then instantly opened them, cursing himself, and then he knew that in all that brilliant light and with those elongated blackened shadows and under that pressure, he had no idea where the mines were. He tried to assure himself that he would automatically miss the mines, that that would only be fair since they were, after all, his own mines; he tried to assure himself that there were, after all, only eight of them and he must have passed at least four so far. But he knew he was steering the jeep blindly, weaving for no real reason at all—

"How far now?"

Shit! He had forgotten to look again! This wasn't his bag of tricks;
he was a cook, and now that he was probably going to be dead in a
few minutes it wouldn't hurt to tell the truth, which was that he
wasn't even a very good cook, but he promised if he ever came out of
this he would learn; he would become the best cook in—

"Wolf! I said how far now?"

Oh, God, he had forgotten again! He looked. "Four tenths," he
said, his voice uneven, "plus a little."

"Then stop. Stop!"

He jammed on the brakes and sat there trembling. They had
missed all the mines. How was it possible? If they weren't killed, if
they managed to find their way back one way or another—and he intended to walk back, at least fifty feet from the road—he would even
go to synagogue. Then he smiled wryly. He wouldn't and he knew it.
He glanced back toward the settlement, directly into the glowing
lights, surprised they were so close; and in that moment two things
happened: the lights were suddenly extinguished, leaving him half-
blinded, and there was the soft cough of the mortar as Grossman
fired the first round.

There was a brief pause, then Wolf's vision cleared as the beach
seemed to rise in the air, taking his mind from everything except the
reason they had come on the insane mission in the first place. The
mortar shell had struck one of the beach fires at the extreme edge of
the small enclave; embers flew through the air, making a pyrotechnic
display that brought Wolf back to his childhood but which did little
damage to the Arabs. But the thing worked, Grossman's idiot mortar
really worked! With a grunt Grossman made a small adjustment and
dropped a second charge into the open maw of the tube; another
cough, another pause, and the encampment on the shore of the sea
seemed to explode, scattering bodies. Now Grossman was feeding his
remaining six charges into the mortar as fast as the weapon could
deliver them. Between the crump, crump, crump of the striking
shells they could hear the screams of the wounded men, and in the
light of the blazing trucks they could see the wildly agitated shadows
of men scattering from the range of the mortar. A personnel carrier
started up and was immediately swamped with men trying to climb
aboard; a truck limped from the devastation with a shattered wheel,
covered with men, only to give up the impossible flight as the men

fled to other transports or charged blindly down the dirt road in the dark, seeking escape.

Grossman was out of shells but there was no way for the Arabs to know that. The two men in the jeep watched the grotesque scene, each trembling but for a different reason, Wolf from nerves now that the peril was over, Grossman from the pleasure of victorious battle. Together they watched the few undamaged vehicles gather together the remnants of the attacking force and disappear into the night, fleeing for home. In a few minutes all Wolf could see where the small encampment had stood were the flickering flames from the dying fires where the mangled trucks were burning themselves out, belching black smoke from the acrid rubber, licking at the edge of the sea. All he could hear were the oddly out-of-place sounds of night birds returning to investigate the torment of sound that had sent them scattering; and the ragged beating of his own heart.

The battle for Ein Tsofar was ended.

The troops of the Hebron British garrison were bivouacked some twelve miles south of Dahiriya, their tent stakes only a few hundred yards from the edge of the road, when the remaining trucks and personnel carriers of the attacking Arab force returned toward Hebron. The command car at the head of the line pulled out of formation and drove toward the encampment while the rest of the battered line pulled over and rested. The Egyptian colonel descended wearily from the command car and identified himself to the sentry; minutes later he was joined by Captain Wiley, who had been wakened from a sound sleep and had only removed his mustache guard and pulled on some trousers before confronting the colonel.

"The Jews have heavy artillery," the Egyptian informed the captain in his faultless but stilted English. "They have heavy guns, mortars, and endless ammunition. The area on all sides of the settlement is thoroughly mined. It is against the mandate to allow the settlements to be armed, as you know. What do the British intend to do about Ein Tsofar?"

"Why," said the captain, pleased by the ease of the solution, at least as far as he was concerned, "I shall have to return to Hebron at once and explain the situation to my colonel."

"And what will he do?"

"I imagine he will inform Jerusalem."

"Who in turn will inform London," the Egyptian said sardonically, "who in turn will inform their representative in the United
Nations, who in turn will eventually inform the General Assembly—
and by that time you will have been out of Palestine a long time."
The Egyptian colonel sighed but it was largely acting, as Captain
Wiley clearly understood. The Egyptian had not really expected any
action on the part of the British; he was merely establishing the cre-
dentials for his failure to take the settlement, which Captain Wiley
was expected to pass along the chain of command until it reached
the ears of the Egyptian's superiors.

The Egyptian shook hands solemnly, saluted briefly, and waved to
his driver to proceed. Behind him he left a happy officer. Captain
Wiley looked at his wristwatch. It was four-thirty in the morning. If
they broke camp now they could be back in Hebron Fortress in time
for a decent breakfast, which would be a vast improvement over the
slop the field cooks dished up. He called over the sentry and gave the
appropriate orders; five minutes later, when the bugler had had time
to soak his head in water to wake up a bit, the bugle went to work
and the camp came to life.

A good campaign, Captain Wiley thought, and began to build it
up in his mind into a proper desert battle à la Lawrence of Arabia,
to intrigue his wife and son when he got home. And the best part of
it was, he knew Colonel Fitzhugh would be pleased, and when the
colonel was pleased life was generally more tolerable throughout the
Hebron garrison.

Eleven members of the Ein Tsofar kibbutz, plus Dov Shapiro,
who had only come to help, had fallen in the fight and were buried
the following day with due ceremony within the borders of the settlement itself. Sixty-four Arab bodies had been recovered along the
slopes and by the shore of the sea, and these were laid to rest in a
shallow mass grave at water's edge where their bodies could easily be
recovered during a truce Perez intended to ask the British to arrange
before they left Palestine for good. Twelve Jews and five Arabs occupied litters in the makeshift hospital, recuperating from their
wounds; the Arabs could be transferred to ambulances during the
truce. The mines in and along the road had been properly located
and every person at Ein Tsofar now had those locations firmly engraved on his or her memory.

Wolf, remembering the position of each mine perfectly in the day-time, could not imagine how he had managed to drive through the field the night before without blowing both Grossman and himself to bits. The hand of Max Brodsky's God? Well, if that was the case he just wished Max Brodsky's God had given some advance notice of His intentions; it would have saved much anxiety. And Wolf had an additional thought: Grossman, the night before, had to notice how nervous he had been, but Grossman had never said a word to the others. A pity he disliked the man, because he had to admit Gross-man had done a fine job the night before. An odd person, Grossman.

When an exhausted Deborah and a very tired Ben Grossman dropped into their common bed that night, they held each other without speaking for a long time. By common silent agreement neither mentioned the battle; it was enough that they had both sur-vived and each had done his best for the common survival. There was no need to discuss it. And they still had each other, which was the most important fact of the moment.

Deborah had her head tucked tightly into Ben's shoulder, her arms about him, pressing him tightly to her. He stroked her head, running his fingers softly over her hair, feeling her breath warm on his bare skin, and then found himself bringing up the one subject he had meant to put off as long as possible.

"There's something I want to tell you—"

"There's something I want to tell you, too." Her voice was muffled by his arm.

He glanced down at her profile, faint in the little light that filtered into the room through the curtain. "What is it?"

"You first."

He smiled at the little-girl ploy. "All right. Max says they want me to go to Switzerland. To buy arms."

"I know."

"You know?"

"I saw Max this morning. He came to the hospital to check on the wounded. He said you had agreed to go."

"Yes." He pulled enough away from her to try to see her eyes; she turned her head and her eyes glinted in the faint light. "I want you to come with me."

"You know I can't, darling. My job is here, or wherever else they send me. I'm not needed in Switzerland—"

"You're needed there by me."

She kissed his cheek and lay back again, smiling contentedly.

"You're not going away forever, darling, just for a trip. You can stand being alone for a while. We've been with each other so much I'd think you would welcome a change." He was staring at her, his face a mask. "Well then," she said lightly, "rush through your job and get back quickly." He didn't answer; she looked at him curiously. "What's the matter?"

"What would you do if I didn't come back?"

"You mean, if something happened to you? I don't know. I'd die, I think." She shook her head angrily. "That's morbid! Nothing is going to happen to you!"

"I don't mean that," he said slowly, wondering why he was talking about it and wondering why he didn't stop. But he could not. "I mean, what if I chose not to come back to Palestine? What if I chose to stay in Switzerland, or go somewhere else from there? Would you leave this place and join me wherever it was?"

She removed her arm from about his body and sat up in bed, completely at ease in her nudity before him. Her breasts, outlined in the light from outside, seemed fuller than usual; even in the shadow he could picture her in his mind in every detail, every curve, every beloved feature. Of late she seemed to be gaining weight, but she was still the most beautiful thing he had ever seen. He reached for her but she put her hand on his chest, not pushing him away, but merely forestalling him until she could speak.

"Darling," she said softly, "I know how you've hated this place. I know you came to Palestine because you were forced to come, and that you came here to the desert for the same reason. I'm glad you did come; if you hadn't I would never have known what it is to be in love as much as I am. It's a wonderful feeling. It's made me feel like a woman, and never as much as right now." She paused a moment, searching for the proper words. "But, darling, we can't abandon reality. We don't live all by ourselves in a vacuum. My country is at war, Ben; we buried twelve of our people this morning. I can help here; I'm needed here. If this were a normal country, or if these were normal times, I would go anywhere with you. You know that; you must know that. But we're at war, and we'll probably be at war for years. Maybe all our lives. It isn't possible, darling. I'm sorry."

She reached up and touched his cheek, running her finger down the scar that lined his jaw, then touching his lips with the tip of her finger as if to keep him silent until she was finished.

"I didn't ask you to marry me because I didn't want to add to your feeling of being under compulsion, of being forced into something against your will. I know it's happened to you many times; I didn't want to make it happen again. I know you felt you were in a prison here at Ein Tsofar, and I wanted you to feel free, at least as far as we were concerned. You're still free, darling. I have no claims on you. If you want to come back to us, to me, when you're through with your work in Europe, you will. I'll still be here. If you don't, you won't. I wouldn't force you if I could; that isn't what love is about. At least not my love."

She withdrew her fingers from his lips, indicating she was through. He stared at the ceiling in silence, his hand continuing to softly stroke her hair. The sad thing was that he would not return from Switzerland; he knew that to be the truth. He would miss Deborah; oh, he would miss her! But he could never return to the misery of this barren land he hated. Just a woman, even as fine a woman as Deborah, was not enough for him to throw away the future.

He leaned over to kiss her, and kissing her, slid down in the bed, pulling her to him. They made love with a passionate fierceness that was unusual with them, a violent coupling that seemed to acknowledge the approaching finality of their parting; and then fell apart, gasping, not speaking. Each turned away from the other as if to avoid the pain of discussion, seeking surcease in sleep.

But Benjamin Grossman could not fall asleep. The excitement of the battle for the settlement, the exhilaration of their tempestuous love-making, the fact that in a short while he could actually be quitted of Ein Tsofar and the hated desert, of Palestine altogether, filled his mind with thoughts that raced. Switzerland! He would actually be there soon, walking down civilized streets, taking an aperitif in some civilized hotel lounge in some civilized town among civilized people. He glanced at Deborah's back, wondering if she were asleep. Maybe when she realized he really was not coming back, maybe then she would join him. Nor would she be sorry. With the money in Zurich they could live where they wanted, how they wanted. France, possibly, or in Portugal. Why hadn't he considered those places before? Or on a Mediterranean island, one of the Ionian islands, possibly. It would be close to Palestine if Deborah ever wanted to come back for a visit.

He closed his eyes, determined to go to sleep, and then suddenly remembered something. He rolled over, speaking softly, hoping Deborah was still awake.

"You said you had something to tell me, too."

She spoke without turning back, her voice wide-awake.

"It was nothing important, darling. Go to sleep."

Chapter 5

Shmuel Ginzberg snored. This is not uncommon among elderly men, of course, but Ginzberg's snores were in a category by themselves. They were not the simple rasping sounds one associates with mouth-breathers, nor were they the half-muttered, grunting, intermittent noises one pictures as possibly accompanying some interesting dream. Ginzberg's snores were loud, earth-shattering, heart-rending, clamorous eruptions that seemed to reveal some inner torment too tragic for expression except through this gasping, snarling, half-neighing racket. He sounded as if he were drowning. Benjamin Grossman had learned to sleep through snores early in his camp experience, since otherwise one received no rest at all, but nothing he had heard before compared to the sounds that emanated from Shmuel Ginzberg.

They had arrived in Geneva after midnight, following a trip that had taken nearly twenty hours from the time they left Lydda Airport outside of Tel Aviv, by way of Cyprus to Athens, then to Naples, on to Rome, a further stop at Milano, and finally Geneva. They had taken the airport bus into the center of the city and from there, with Grossman carrying the luggage, had walked to the small cheap hotel where their reservations had been made in order to save taxi fare. The limited condition of their finances—for money was not meant to be wasted on personal comfort when the need for more important purchases existed—dictated the necessity for sharing a room, and since Shmuel Ginzberg was by far the senior in age, he commandeered the bed without putting the matter to a vote, leaving the lumpy couch for Grossman. After merely removing his elastic-sided shoes, his black hat, and his stiff collar, the old man fell upon the bed, wrapped himself in the single comforter the bare room provided, and almost instantly began to snore.

Grossman's first reaction on hearing the unprecedented racket coming from the bed was to overlook his previous intentions, and instead go through Ginzberg's pockets, extract enough money for the fare to Zurich, and be on his way since it was obvious he was not going to get any sleep. He was, after all, in Switzerland at long last— a fact he found hard to believe, although he knew it would grow upon him once he got a chance to get about in daylight and renew old memories. But while he had known that his visit would eventually end up at his bank in Zurich, he had fully intended to first help Ginzberg in his purchases of arms. To have done anything else would have been to estrange Deborah for all time, and he still had never abandoned the hope of eventually pursuading the girl to join him and share his life somewhere other than in Palestine.

He tried to deafen himself to Ginzberg's snores at first by sheer mental effort, but this was clearly impossible. He next arose, padded in his stocking feet down the dim hallway to the bathroom and stuffed his ears with toilet paper, but this was in the nature of attempting to stop a runaway train with a toothpick. He finally went over and tapped the old man on the arm, but this seemed only to make Ginzberg snore more loudly. In desperation he waited for the neighbor in the next room to finally tire of the disturbance and hammer on the wall next to Ginzberg's ear, but either the neighbor was deaf or the room unoccupied, because no such salvation came. At last he gave up. He got dressed, cast a look of malevolence at the old man, and went down to the lobby for a quiet place to think.

The lobby was deserted at that hour, other than a clerk half asleep behind the counter, and Grossman selected a chair beside a dusty rubber plant, and tried to bring his thoughts and his plans into some order. The clerk, noting that the intruder was a guest who apparently preferred the comfort of the lobby to the discomfort of the room—a condition the clerk could understand—put his head back on his arm and drifted off again.

Grossman pondered, his penchant for planning once again given an opportunity for expression. It was obvious he could not continue to room with Ginzberg, but it was equally obvious he would never get the old man to agree to the expense of separate quarters. Eventually he might become accustomed to the snoring, but until he did, other solutions had to be found. The most obvious one, of course, was to be able to finance the luxury of a room of his own out of his own pocket. It would be hard, it seemed to him, for Ginzberg to object. To do this meant a trip to his bank immediately, at which time he could arrange proper funds, transfer moneys where and how he wished, and in general settle the matter of finances for all time. He would, of course, have to make up some story to satisfy Ginzberg's wonder at sudden affluence right after borrowing the train fare from the man, but a relative in Zurich could serve. A dying and rich uncle, possibly, would be the excuse for the trip as well as the affluence, and they could take up their mission a day late.

Having thought the solution through, Grossman looked about the quiet lobby for some magazine with which to pass the time until Ginzberg's sleep settled into deep-enough narcosis to obviate snoring, or until his own weariness became so acute as to guarantee rest through any disturbance. But other than an old newspaper someone had discarded, the lobby was bare of reading material. With a sigh he retrieved the journal and prepared to bring himself up to date on Swiss events.

The newspaper was from that morning, or, rather, yesterday morning since it was now nearly three o'clock, but at least it was from Lucerne, he was pleased to see, and was therefore in German. He settled back with a yawn, flipping pages, and almost missed the article through lack of interest. But somehow it caught his eye and he went back to it.

His sleepiness vanished instantly; he felt a shock, almost electric.

He bent over the newspaper, gripping it with fingers that ached from the pressure, reading it in total and utter disbelief:

NAZI BANK ACCOUNTS IMPOUNDED

Bern: May 24, by Our Reporter.

By an agreement reached today between the Swiss Government and the Government of the West German Republic, all accounts suspected of having been established in Swiss banks through the deposits of former Nazi agencies, or of governmental funds of the Third Reich by former Nazi personnel, will be impounded until proper ownership can be established. In general, these suspect accounts are those established from Germany or German-occupied territories during the period 1941/1945. Anyone attempting to withdraw funds from such suspect accounts will be called upon to furnish proper identification as well as to give a proper account of the source of such funds. The agreement signed today in Bern will go into effect immediately and will be binding upon all Swiss banking establishments.

The Republic of West Germany feels that this agreement, which has taken over two years of negotiation to formulate, will return to it large sums of money which rightly belong to the government and which can be used for reparation to victims of former Nazi repression. It was felt such moneys were stolen either from victims of persecution or directly from the Reich treasury by dishonest elements in the course of their government service.

The Ministry of Finance, in making this announcement, wishes to advise all concerned that this regulation in no way affects normal confidentiality of normal accounts, for which Swiss banks are so well known.

Benjamin Grossman's stunned eyes went back to read the fateful story for a second time, and then for a third, although by this time the type was blurred before him. Then he looked at the date of the story: Monday, May 24. This morning—or again, rather, yesterday morning. Had they left Palestine—Israel, now, since a week ago Friday—only three days earlier—three days!—he could have cleared his account before the order went into effect. If Ginzberg hadn't been so damned slow in setting up their appointment in Geneva, and then if the old man hadn't refused to take a flight that might have caught him traveling on Friday after sundown but had insisted upon waiting for the Monday flight, they would have been here in time. A fortune lost because one damned Jew was a religious maniac! One more thing the Jews would have to pay for someday!

But it had to be a joke, a practical joke someone was playing on him! It couldn't possibly be true! For three years he had done everything possible to get to Switzerland and for three years everyone and everything had conspired to impede him in every way. And now that he was finally here, actually in Geneva and only miles from Zurich, he was three days late! It simply could not be true. It was a joke set up by Brodsky—no, Wolf!—in fact, he had conspired with the old man upstairs to make those horrible snoring noises, to drive him down to the lobby and the newspaper that had been planted there; one could get them printed at those specialty shops as a joke on friends. And Wolf had probably suspected for a long time he had money in Switzerland, why else had he tried so hard to get there? It was a joke. . . .

But it wasn't a joke, and he knew it. He sat, his head in his hands, wanting to cry but too drained of emotion for even this release. Still, in thinking about it, if Ginzberg's snores had not driven him down to the lobby and the newspaper, he might well have walked into his bank in Zurich the next day and found himself in more trouble than he could handle. He ought to thank the old man for snoring on that basis, but at the moment thankfulness was the farthest thing from his mind.

What to do?

What to do?

Return to Palestine—Israel—at the end of the purchasing mission? No. No. No! That would be the ultimate admission of failure, the final confession that his three years of suffering had truly been wasted. He would stay in Europe, possibly even try to immigrate to the United States; at least in comparison with Israel these were relatively civilized places. His passport had given him no trouble getting into Switzerland, so it must be a good forgery. For one brief moment the thought occurred that he had given Dr. Schlossberg a large check on that Zurich bank; he wondered if the doctor had ever cashed it. Schlossberg had never been caught, and the check had been for a substantial amount. Possibly if he ever ran into the doctor again he might ask for some of it back.

But that thought was also ridiculous, and he knew it. Ah, the mistakes he had made; the many, many mistakes he had made! But at least with the money gone for all time there was no longer any area in which he could make further mistakes, if there was any consolation in that. In time he supposed he would settle somewhere, get some sort of a job, and find another Deborah. He would try to forget the Deborah in Israel, and try to forget the money in the Zurich bank waiting there to rot, and try to forget that if it hadn't been for an old miserable Jew who would not travel on a Friday night he would be a rich man at the moment.

But merely trying to forget—or even forgetting, if it were possible —was no answer to the principal question: *What to do?*

What, indeed, to do . . .

He was still pondering that question without result when Ginzberg came down in the morning, disgustingly refreshed, and led him off to a cheap breakfast before taking him to their appointment, admonishing him all the way that they had very important work to do and he shouldn't sit up all night but should get his rest, it wasn't good for a person.

They spent the next four months traveling from city to city, from arms warehouse to arms warehouse, from fields covered with used battle equipment to other fields equally crowded; for the man in Geneva was only an agent who ran his business by telephone from his luxurious apartment on the Place Bourg-de-Four in Geneva and had never actually seen a weapon in his life. Grossman would inspect the used weaponry, advise Ginzberg as to its utility and relative value, and then listen as Ginzberg tried and usually succeeded in making their limited credits go further. Shipments had to be arranged, proper packaging determined to prevent additional deterioration, freight rates considered, ships' schedules taken into account, and always the desperate word from Israel and the Haganah to hurry, hurry, hurry! And always the problems of money, credits, payments! The work became an end in itself for Benjamin Grossman, a means to take his mind from his bitter disappointment, of drugging himself to the fact of his failure, to the knowledge that his sacrifices had been for nothing and that with his one great dream shattered there were no other dreams, great or small, on his horizon.

One day they went to a warehouse in Vienna, in the inner city, the First District, west of the Danube. Here used rifles, used handguns, used machine guns of many nations and many calibers had been collected and tossed in great piles with no attempt to separate them or properly identify or store them, as if the owner recognized their uselessness. Most were rusting, almost all had parts visibly missing. Ginzberg, who by now considered himself something of an expert on weaponry—even as Grossman was beginning to consider himself something of an expert on bargaining—made a sour face and turned away.

"Pfui!"

Grossman caught his arm. "Wait—"

"For what?" Ginzberg spat, but carefully, to miss his trousers. "This is *dreck*. What I intend to tell that *momser* in Geneva, you can believe! A whole day wasted, not to talk of the fare!"

"Not those guns. Over there." Grossman led the way to some used machine tools lined up against one wall, covered with cosmoline and Pliofilm from old rifle packing. He lifted the film away and studied them. There were lathes, milling machines, planers, drill presses, crank presses, and the other tools needed for any machine shop. Ginzberg watched the inspection, looking at the used equipment suspiciously.

"So what's this? We came here to buy guns, not this *dreck*."

"With these tools you can make your own guns."

"Make? Who's got time to make? There's a war on, you heard? Anyway, we already got factories to make guns, but you notice they send us out to buy more. You think they don't know what they're doing?"

"The war is going to go on for a long time," Grossman said patiently, and felt a twinge as he recalled these were almost the last words he had heard from Deborah. "You can't spend the rest of your life combing Europe for guns; we've seen almost every warehouse there is. Whatever is usable at a decent price is gone. What's left is either too expensive or like that junk there."

Ginzberg tipped back his black hat and studied Grossman. "So?"

"So sooner or later you'll have to either raise enough money to buy new guns, good guns, or manufacture more of your own armaments."

"And what do we make them out of?" Ginzberg asked sarcastically. "Kasha?"

"You make them out of rusty junk like that." Grossman pointed to the piles of rusting weapons. "I rebuilt worse guns with less equipment in a cave at Ein Tsofar. You can probably buy this junk for next to nothing, just to give them floor space, and you can probably pick up the machine tools for not much more. In a short time you can be turning out your own guns.

"Grossman, you're *meshugah*. Look! Triggers missing, firing pins missing . . ."

"So you cannibalize, or make new parts from castings or stampings. Everything necessary is here; it's no great job with proper tools. How do you think those guns were made in the first place?"

There was a few moments' silence as Ginzberg's tiny eyes surveyed Grossman from behind deep-set pouches. He pushed his black homburg even further back on his head, exposing pink skin, and shook his head slowly.

"Grossman, you surprise me. What are you so interested for? You keep saying 'You make them' instead of 'We make them.' Max Brodsky told me you probably wouldn't be going back to Israel after you finish working with me. I'll tell you the God's truth, I'm surprised you're still here. So what are you so interested in we make guns we don't make guns? You going back, or what?"

For a moment Grossman felt anger sweep him. What business was it of anyone what his plans were? He forced the anger back, staring at the old man coldly.

"No, if you want the truth, I'm not going back. It's just that I thought buying the machine tools would be a smart move."

"A smart move . . ." Ginzberg looked around the warehouse, speaking as if to himself. "Well, maybe if we had somebody to put together this factory you're talking about, then maybe you could have an argument . . ."

"You have engineers."

". . . someone who knows what to do with all this junk and also knows something about guns . . ."

Grossman smiled in understanding. "If you mean me, the answer is no."

Ginzberg shrugged elaborately.

"A pity." He looked up at the taller man with true curiosity, changing his tactics. "Tell me something, Ben. What do you have against Israel? You had it so good in Germany before?"

"I merely said, I'm not going back."

"So you were at a kibbutz, Ein Tsofar, I heard about that. So some people like it in the desert and some don't. Myself, I get hives from the heat, I itch you wouldn't believe! But Israel's a big place—" He held up one hand abruptly. "So it's no United States of America, but it's no *shtetl*, either. If it's big enough for all the Jews we hope come, it's got to be big enough for Benjamin Grossman. Anyway, you wouldn't put a factory like you're talking about in the desert in the first place—"

Grossman had to smile. "I said, no."

"And all I said was it's a pity," the old man said and looked at Grossman's set and smiling face. He looked around the warehouse a bit sadly and raised his shoulders. "That's all I said. You heard? Well—let's go, then . . ."

"Then let's go," Grossman said agreeably, and led the way to the large overhead door. Did the old man really think he cared the least bit whether the Jews set up another arms factory or not? He was merely trying to be helpful, trying to fulfill an obligation to a girl named Deborah, not to anyone else. Or did the old man think the thrill, or the patriotism, of working day and night setting up a factory for no pay, or for very little, in a place he hated would bring him back to Israel? What a dream! It was enough to make him smile, but at least he had to admit it was the first smile he had had for a long time.

It was, in the end, a woman who made the difference.

Ginzberg and Grossman had finished their supper in silence, the old man spooning his soup into his mouth with a combination air of aggrieved hurt and a loud *slurping* sound, as if his disappointment in the younger man could not be put into words, and with Grossman efficiently silent. At the end, Ginzberg had wiped his mouth with the back of his hand, the back of his hand with his napkin, and then gone upstairs to their room to try and get a trunk call through to Tel Aviv. For a moment Benjamin Grossman wanted to ask him to speak to Brodsky, to find out if Deborah was still at Ein Tsofar, or how she was, but he knew the old man would only interpret that as a weakening of his resolution about not returning, and at the moment Benjamin Grossman was in no mood for more of the old Jew's sententious homilies about home and country. Further, it was pointless to think about Deborah. Deborah was something of the past. He decided that a long walk was what he needed to get Shmuel Ginzberg, Israel, Deborah Assavar, and everything else out of his mind.

It was a rather chilly September evening with dark clouds beginning to roll down from the hills to the north of the city, and with the threat of showers in the heavy air. He had walked for miles, for hours, without conscious thought of his surroundings, tramping the streets of the old city in the direction of the river without being aware of it. His mind jumped restlessly from one kaleidoscopic picture to another. Vienna—he could remember as if it were yesterday, the day of Anschluss. He had been riding in a car in the convoy that had brought the Fuehrer through the streets of the city, and he wondered now at the intense joy he had felt on the occasion. Ten years gone by. . . . It seemed like centuries. They were still rebuilding the damage done by the idiocy of war. . . .

Stop! Cut . . .

No thoughts of war, or of his own idiocy since those days at Maidanek. Think of other things. Remember that boulder-covered slope running down from Ein Tsofar to the sea. Remember the shower of sparks as the first mortar shell struck. The exhilaration, ah yes! The feeling of power! But so soon gone . . . Think of that slope in earlier days. That hated cell. Remember the sunrise coming over the Jordanian mountains beyond the flat, silvered surface of the water. You had to give the desert credit for spectacular sunsets and sunrises, if for nothing else. But stop thinking of that hated place.

Remember little Morris Wolf snoring away in the common tier at Belsen? Certainly a pitiful exhibit in comparison with the noises generated by Shmuel Ginzberg. Shmuel . . . Once he would have sneered at a name like that. But once he would have sneered at a name like Benjamin Grossman. Now it sounded so natural he could hardly remember any other. Jew names, remember them: Ben-Levi, Pincus, Yakov Mendel, Lev Mendel, who saved his life, Brodsky . . . Remember the first time you met Brodsky? That horrible feeling in the boxcar when he learned they would not be sent to—what camp had he planned on going to from Buchenwald? He could not even remember. But he remembered that night in the boxcar, nearly dying in that stink and heat and the others all crowding over, pressing, pressing. And that other boxcar, from Germany to Italy. Brodsky forgetting to tell him about the ignition key, the idiot! And the American sergeant looking in at the window of the truck. And Brodsky beside him at the battle of Ein Tsofar. That had been exciting. His father would have been proud of him.

No! Stop!

Where had his father come into this, for God's sake? Go back to Brodsky. The first time he came to Ein Tsofar after leaving him there, the time he came with Deborah. A year ago, more or less. Seems like much longer. Deborah. The first time they had made love, the softness of her, the tenderness of her. The *feel* of her! And Deborah the last time he had seen her. In bed, asleep when he got up so quietly and left Ein Tsofar for the last time. Hair all damp with perspiration, matted on her forehead. The womanly smell of her that morning—

NO! STOP!

No more thoughts of Deborah. Think back instead to—what? Go back as far as you can from the present. Remember the faint memories you still retain of the place where you were born? The stables . . . Remember the servant who gave you riding lessons? Remember how those stables looked the last time you saw them? From that horse-drawn carriage, your aunt's arm around you. And then the curve in the road and the trees that blocked your view. Remember moving from that big house to the small one where the gateman had lived. Remember the library, where your father took the gun—

NO! NO!

Why this sudden thing about his father? He hadn't thought of his father for years. At least not consciously. Had he subconsciously thought of him? And why was he dwelling on him now? It was pointless to remember painful things. Stupid. And speaking of fathers, it was the way Ginzberg treated him most of the time. As if Shmuel Ginzberg could possibly be his father. Always with the advice. Unwanted advice. Ginzberg meant well. He wasn't a bad old man, if you overlooked his snoring. But who needed a father? Oh, it would be foolish to deny he had needed one years before when he had been a little boy. But needing one and having one were two different things. You learned to get along without things you couldn't have—

NO! Damn it!

We said no thoughts of fathers. He felt the prickling in his eyes. God, that hadn't happened for years!

He became aware that the rain had started, a little pattering of drops against his bare head, the faintest imagined sound as they fell on the pavement, glistening on the stones, reflected by the street-lamps. There was an increase in the chill of the air sweeping down from the foothills of the distant Alps, heralding an early winter. At least Palestine—Israel—had fairly decent weather. But no thoughts of Israel. Or of Deborah, or of fathers, for God's sake!

And then the woman appeared.

She had been standing in a doorway apparently waiting for the rain to stop and had come to the conclusion it would only get worse as time went on and had therefore decided to abandon her refuge and make her move to cross the street to the protection of the door-ways there, closer to home. She came from the shadows in a rush and caromed off Benjamin Grossman, tried to catch her balance awkwardly, and failed. Grossman instinctively thrust out an arm and caught at her, but the woman was too heavy, her momentum too great, and she fell to the pavement, bringing him down with her. He came to his feet in a temper, prepared to tell the woman to watch where she was going, and then noticed she was having difficulty get-ting to her feet. He also noticed something else; she was quite young, far younger than her heavy appearance would seem to warrant, and she was abashed at having stumbled into him. Her face was flaming with embarrassment, her eyes were the agonized eyes of a cow being led to slaughter, and her stomach bulged.

He put out a hand, ashamed of himself for his anger, and helped her struggle heavily to her feet. Her worn cloth coat was muddy from the roadway, her rough stockings were torn, and the heel had come loose from one of her cheap shoes and dangled from the upper. He wished for a second he could offer her some money to repair the damage but that, of course, was out of the question. She stood, red-faced and uncertain, trying to brush herself off, trying not to look at him.

"Verzeihung . . ."

"An accident," he said. "Are you all right?"

"*Bitte, bitte . . .*"

"Are you sure?"

"Oh, yes, yes! I'm sorry—" She looked down at her stomach in embarrassment, as if laying the blame there. "I'm clumsy . . ."

"It was only an accident, I assure you. Can I help you get somewhere?"

"Oh, no! No! Thank you," she added vaguely, as if uncertain as to what she was thanking him for, and waddled hastily across the street where she paused to remove the broken shoe before limping out of sight down a side street.

Poor girl! Benjamin Grossman found his self-pity of a moment ago transferred in its entirety to the impoverished, unattractive, red-faced girl who had stumbled in the street and had had difficulty getting up. It was an odd feeling for him, a feeling he could not at the moment recall having experienced before, yet it remained. Poor girl, afraid to let him help her home, though God knew what kind of person would covet that grotesque pregnant body! Probably a husband that drank, or beat her, or both; certainly not a man who earned enough to keep a wife properly. You're getting maudlin, he told himself, and then shook his head with a faint smile. No, you're merely making comparisons. What if that sad creature had been Deborah? Yes, if he wanted to think about Deborah, he would. Now—what if that poor girl had been Deborah, out on a rainy night, all alone, afraid, nervous, pregnant—

He stopped so abruptly that a man behind him, head buried in an umbrella, bumped into him, managed to pirouette without damage, and staggered off down the street muttering imprecations.

Pregnant . . .

Deborah's breasts had been uncommonly heavy that last night, but she said that sometimes happened at certain times of the month; besides, he hadn't thought anything of it beyond the fact that he liked her breasts when they were fuller. And it was also evident she had been gaining weight, not that this did anything except make Deborah look more beautiful to him. He walked more slowly, unaware of where his footsteps were taking him, his mind locked on the question suddenly raised. He remembered that last night in its most minute detail.

"*I have something to tell you . . .*"

"*I have something to tell you, too . . .*"

"*What is it?*"

"*You first . . .*"

And he had smiled and told his something; but Deborah's something had never been told. What could she possibly have had to say to him that she decided was better left unsaid—but only after he had more or less told her he would not be coming back to Palestine when he was finished in Europe? He remembered more—

"*If you want to come back to us—me—you will . . .*"

Us!

How could he have been deaf to such blatant hints? Normally he was not stupid. Had his subconscious wanted him not to hear, not to understand? No, that could not be. But if Deborah had been pregnant, wouldn't she have said so, particularly at that moment? Some women, yes; most women, probably—but not Deborah. Never Deborah . . .

Pregnant!

He was going to have a child—no, a son! It had to be a son, but if it were a daughter he'd be the best father a daughter ever had—and the next one would be a son. But this one had to be a son! How could he have been so blind as to not recognize that he was going to be a father? That was something a man should know instinctively. He found himself laughing aloud in pure joy and tried to remember the last time he had laughed with joy. He could not, but it was unimportant, totally unimportant. The only important thing was that he was going to be a father. He had been searching for a future, worrying about a future; what better future could there be than simply being a father? But a proper father, not a deserting father . . .

He stared at the street signs, wondering where he was. He was on the Stephansplatz, near the corner of the Graben, and there was the Karntnerstrasse with all its fancy shops. How had he wandered so far? He didn't even remember crossing the river bridge. But no matter. He started to walk back to the hotel, bubbling with excitement, the rain unnoticed, and then decided that walking was too slow. He started to trot, brought his pace up to a run, and then abruptly dropped back to a sedate walk as a *Polizist* came around the corner, cape gleaming in the drizzle, baton swinging from his belt, and began to rattle the doorknobs of the shops. But as soon as the policeman disappeared into an extended store entrance, Benjamin Grossman was running again.

He burst into the hotel, rang impatiently for the ancient elevator, and then decided the stairs would be quicker. He took them three at a time and pushed open the door of their room, panting, grinning like a maniac. Ginzberg, his tight shoes and stiff collar removed, but not his hat, was sitting on the bed, propped by a pillow, reading a Yiddish newspaper. He frowned at the sight of the disheveled Grossman.

"You're out of breath," he said disapprovingly. "You shouldn't run so soon after a meal, even if it's raining. It's bad for the health. Walk is good but running is bad." He seemed to notice the broad smile for the first time and added suspiciously, "So what's to be so happy, all of a sudden?"

"Have you talked to Tel Aviv yet?"

"Hitler should hang as long as it takes to get a telephone call through from this place," Ginzberg said sourly. "No, I haven't talked, yet. In another fifteen minutes it's supposed to come through, if you can believe these *lignerim*."

"Good!" Grossman pulled up the one chair in the room and sat down facing Ginzberg. "Now, listen! When you're connected, tell them to get in touch with Deborah Assavar—that's Assavar—at Ein Tsofar by radio. She's a nurse there. Tell her I'm coming home as soon as I can get there and I expect to be married the minute I arrive."

Ginzberg frowned. This was a changed man, and God alone knew what could have changed him in such a short time since they had dined together. But God could perform miracles; maybe this was one of them. Anyway, why argue with success?

"Fine! Then you'll build the factory for the guns?"

Grossman looked at the old man with pity for his lack of understanding.

"Build nothing!" he said. "I'm going into the army. I've got a family to protect!"

Chapter 6

Benjamin Grossman and Deborah Assavar were married in the small port town of Ashdod on a Sunday, September 26, in a small synagogue overlooking the blue Mediterranean, with Max Brodsky serving as best man and with everyone with the exception of the bride, the groom, and the rabbi wearing guns strapped across their shoulders quite as if such accessories were normal at weddings— which at that time and in that place, they were. The religious ceremony meant nothing to Grossman, he had witnessed similar ceremonies at Ein Tsofar and they had struck him as no more ridiculous than the rituals in which he had been raised. He paid no attention to the incantations of the rabbi, stepped upon the glass when Deborah squeezed his arm to indicate it was time to do so, took the ring from Max when it was handed to him with a nudge, and slipped it on Deborah's finger. He had a feeling as he did so that another door had been closed in his life, but this time a door he had willingly closed himself, rather than one slammed upon him. And when the ceremony had finally been concluded and the ritual of the *kiddish* completed with its wine and little cakes consumed, Benjamin Grossman kissed his Deborah once again, picked up his gun, waved to his new bride, and went out with his fellows to return to the war. And his pregnant bride went out to her jeep with the two nurses who had accompanied her, to return to their duties at Ein Tsofar.

The war was close to Ashdod, but then in no place in Israel was the war very far away in 1948. The Arab nations had kept their promise and had attacked in force the minute the British left; the first truce of the war had left little changed, and at the time of Ben Grossman's marriage, the second truce of the war was supposedly in effect. That truce had supposedly gone into effect at 7 P.M. on the eighteenth of July, but from the moment of its inception it had been constantly breached. The Arab Legion, under the command of Glubb Pasha, had continued its shelling of the New City in Jerusalem, and had even increased the intensity of the mortar and machine-gun and cannon attacks after the truce had been agreed upon. In mid-August, even though the Latrun pumping station was supposedly under the control of the United Nations, the Arab Legion destroyed it as a means of denying water to the besieged inhabitants of the New City, but the Israeli Army soon had an auxiliary pipe line carrying water up the mountain to the thirsty Jews above. In the south the Egyptians blocked the Hatti-Karatiyya gap in their lines to the passage of Jewish convoys intent upon resupplying their *kibbutzim* and their *moshavim* in the desert; they also repeatedly attacked Israeli outposts. In the north Kaukji's Arab Liberation Army did not even consider the truce as applying to them; convinced that the Israeli Defense Force would be occupied with the Egyptians in the Negev, they attacked settlements, cut off roads, and ambushed reinforcements. Truce or no truce, the war went on.

War covered the country and in every corner of it the Jews fought back, against the Egyptians in the south; the Jordanians and the Iraqis in the east; the Syrians, the Lebanese in the north, all receiving help from the other Arab nations. And from the time of his return from Vienna, Benjamin Grossman was actively involved in the fighting. The fact that he was fighting on the side of the Jews meant nothing to him; he was fighting for Deborah and his unborn son and he was enjoying it. His total fearlessness in battle soon made him a name among soldiers whose dedication to winning the war and saving their land made heroism common. His fierceness, his obvious joy of fighting, began to earn him a reputation both among the troops as well as with the higher echelon of command. At the time of his marriage, Lieutenant Grossman was under the direct command of Major Max Brodsky in the Givati Infantry Brigade—for during the truce months officers had been given rank for the first time in the Israeli Army. The Givati, together with the Negev and the Yiftah brigades, all under the direction of Palmach Commander Yigal Allon, were responsible for the defense of the southern front.

On November 3 a third truce was declared—a "sincere" truce—whose sincerity was demonstrated by being broken as soon as the ink was dry on the paper, broken by both sides. In the weeks that followed it was as if no truce had ever been agreed upon, and as the year ended the fighting grew more fierce with each passing day. And on January 2, 1949, the settlement of Ein Tsofar was once again attacked.

The attack this time did not come from any loosely organized band of Arabs intent upon loot, simply venting their fury on what they considered unwarranted intrusion of their land; the attack this time was a co-ordinated operation between the Egyptian Army and the Jordanian Arab Legion. The Egyptians had come down from El Arish through the edge of the Sinai intending to join up with the Jordanians on the Dead Sea; the Jordanians had come from Ammon through Karak and Safi and had skirted the flat water around the southern tip of the sea between Sdom and the Hakemah Cave. The intent of the operation was to sweep the western Negev and the Judean deserts and then move north to Jericho and join with the Arab Legion fighting in the Jerusalem sector. In the course of the operation all Negev and Judean settlements in the path of the combined armies were to be destroyed, to demonstrate to the world as well as to the Israelis that their hope of settling Jews in the age-old land of the Arabs was doomed to failure, and that when the war was finally over and won, the shifting sands of the region would once again provide terrain for wandering Bedouin tribes, but no permanent enclaves for Jews.

The radio call for help was received by the Givati Brigade at a time when the full effort of the southern command was dedicated to Operation Horev, designed to expel the Egyptians from the area starting at the Egyptian border in the Sinai to just below Ashdod, when every man and machine and effort was desperately needed on the front from Rafa to Yad Mordekhai to Majdal. When Joel Perez's continuing cries for aid increased, a conference was called at Sa'ad.

"We are going to lose settlements," Colonel Wishnak said sadly. Wishnak was in charge of the force assigned to attack Gaza and then move south to cut off aid from Rafa. "It's tragic but there's no way we can hope to save them piecemeal. Normally we send all the help we can, but right now Horev takes precedence. Our best hope to save the settlements that remain is to drive the Egyptians out of the region, to inflict enough damage on them here, where we have them, so they'll sue for peace. And hope our boys in the north, in the Latrun-Jerusalem sector, do the same to Arab Legion. When there is peace, true peace, only then will the settlements really be safe."

Lieutenant Grossman, listening passively, knew better than to raise the argument that his pregnant wife was at Ein Tsofar; many if not most in the room had someone in one settlement or another, and many a kibbutz or moshav had been overrun and destroyed with everyone killed. Lieutenant Grossman was also aware that an army cannot operate successfully without discipline, but he knew regardless of all other arguments that he, personally, would be at Ein Tsofar as soon as he could get there after this idiotic conference was over. The others may put Israel first, but he did not; he was fighting for his family and nothing else. He had no idea of what he would do when he got to Ein Tsofar, but he felt he would have time to plan that on the way there.

Max Brodsky, watching Grossman and knowing of Deborah's presence at the Ein Tsofar clinic, could almost read the lieutenant's mind. He broke into the discussion.

"I know we can't hope to split our forces and try to save each individual kibbutz or moshav one at a time," he said quietly, "but Ein Tsofar represents more than just any other settlement. In fact, most of the other settlements in the area have been abandoned and their people concentrated at Ein Tsofar, since it always had the best chance of survival by itself. So by saving Ein Tsofar we would, in effect, be saving many settlements at one time—or at least their people, which is the important thing. Also, this attack is not by some roaming band of Arabs. This is a joint Egyptian-Jordanian army operation. If the Egyptians can open and maintain a line behind our front, and get tanks and troops to the Jerusalem sector without leaving one settlement standing that we can use as a base later to stop them . . ." He left the balance unsaid.

Colonel Wishnak frowned. "What are you suggesting? That we change our objectives? We can't do that, you know."

"I know. And I know how important Operation Horev is; it's vitally important. But I believe we can afford to give at least three or four tanks and a company of infantry to help Ein Tsofar." He went on quickly before anyone could interrupt him. "I suggest Lieutenant Grossman lead the force; he's familiar with the area." He shrugged.

"Those of us who stay will just have to fight that much harder to compensate for the men who are gone."

There was silence for a moment or two; then Colonel Wishnak sighed.

"We'll have to take it up with headquarters . . ."

"Headquarters has enough problems of its own," Grossman said harshly. He knew what headquarters would say about weakening the striking force at that moment; it would have been the same thing he would have said under other conditions. He stared coldly into Wishnak's eyes. "The object of Operation Horev is to wipe out the Egyptians in the Negev. Well, the brigade attacking Ein Tsofar is Egyptian and they're in the Negev. We're wasting time." He swung around, pointing. "I'll take you—and you—and you. Three tanks is all. And Company B in personnel carriers. Four carriers is all." He glanced at his wristwatch. The total authority of his voice as well as his mien made opposition difficult. "I'll meet with the commanders outside."

He turned and walked from the room without looking back. The three selected tank commanders as well as the commander of Company B looked at Wishnak's expressionless face a moment, and then followed Grossman. In the area outside the command post, the commander of the infantry company brought up a point while the tank commanders waited.

"With only four carriers, Lieutenant, we're going to be crowded."

"You'll be even more crowded," Grossman said succinctly. "I want each tank and each troop carrier to bring along as large a log as they can carry either inside or on top, plus about fifty feet of chain, each."

The commanders all grinned. It had been a tactic that had often been discussed but had not been used as yet.

"Right!" they said in a chorus, and went to make the necessary arrangements.

In the command post there was dead silence when the five men had left. Those remaining looked at Colonel Wishnak, wondering if he was going to counter the orders of the brash lieutenant. Colonel Wishnak studied the curious faces about him for a moment, and then cleared his throat.

"Back to business, gentlemen. Now, about the attack on Gaza."

The three tanks and the four crowded troop carriers traveled almost due east at first, moving at top speed along the Israeli-controlled roads until they reached a point just north of Beer Sheba, where Israeli territorial control ended. Night had fallen before they reached the Arab-controlled area, and from there on they traveled without lights, weaving slowly between the rolling dunes, moving onto the old track on which Dov Shapiro had guided Wolf and Brodsky with the arms for Ein Tsofar so many months before, and on which Grossman had left the settlement after the battle for the kibbutz. Grossman, standing in the hatchway of the lead tank with the tank commander beside him, judged their direction from the stars; moonlight furnished the little illumination they needed to avoid the shadowed wadis. Although Grossman was desperately concerned as to the situation at the settlement, he forbade all radio communication either with the kibbutz or even between tanks. If the enemy forces were as great as Perez had indicated in his radio calls for help, his real weapon would not be his small group, but surprise, and he could not be sure that the Egyptians did not have radio-direction finders.

At three in the morning they came inching their way down the steep pass in the cliffs some six miles south of the settlement, around a sweep in the mountain range, and came to rest near the shore of the sea. Grossman could only hope that the attacking Egyptian and Jordanian forces were resting, putting off their next strike against Ein Tsofar until daylight, because there was nothing he could do before then. Daylight was essential to his plan. The tanks and the carriers waited, black shadows against the blacker shadow of the mountain, total silence imposed, smoking forbidden. Dawn seemed to take forever to break. At five the order was given to drop the logs behind the vehicles and chain them to the tow rings. In the growing light the marks made by the passing Egyptian tanks moving through to join the Arab Legion forces could be plainly seen on the shore of the sea.

Now at last radio silence was broken with a vengeance. Each tank and troop carrier began a bombardment of the air with a series of short orders, barked out in staccato style:

"*Tank Force B, spread out for the attack!*"

"*Commander of Force E, get your tanks in line!*"

"*Six tanks in each column! Ammunition loaders at your posts!*"

"*Carriers A through G to the left echelon, mortars in position!*"

"*Move! Move! Move!*"

With the radio operators constantly barking orders to imaginary forces into their radios, the small force moved out, fanning to cover the area between the sheer mountains and the sea as completely as their limited numbers could manage, plowing across the plain and around the curve in the mountain range into view of the settlement. In the distance across the sandy terrain they could see the faint outlines of the settlement, see the ring of tanks like dogs around a treed animal, barking with the spitting of shellfire, see the flash of answering guns from the roofs of some of the buildings. The commander of the lead tank put his mouth to Grossman's ear, screaming to be heard.

"They're still holding out!"

The logs behind the tanks and the carriers prevented the vehicles from obtaining any great degree of speed, but speed was not what Grossman wanted. He wanted dust, and the bouncing, leaping, twisting logs battered the sandy plain, splintering and rocketing, raising a cloud of dust that rose in a huge curtain, spreading from the cliffs to the shore of the sea and beyond, rolling behind the lumbering vehicles, towering over them. From the kibbutz it must have appeared as if the entire 8th Armored Brigade was coming to the rescue. Grossman only hoped the Egyptians would have the same impression, for he knew if the enemy decided to stand and make a fight of it, his small force would be decimated in minutes. But the Egyptian commander apparently came to the conclusion that one settlement, even one as important as Ein Tsofar, was not worth jeopardizing his main objective of reaching Jerusalem; he ordered his forces to withdraw. Soldiers ran for their carriers, tanks wheeled and lurched away to the north, raising their own dust screen as they pulled out. Ein Tsofar had been rescued without a shot having been fired by its rescuers.

Grossman's small force drew up beside a tank trap that had not been there when he had last seen the settlement. The trap had served its purpose; two Arab tanks were upended in it, burning. They had apparently ventured into the trap in the dark, and their failure had prompted the wait for daylight that had played such a large part in the rescue. There was a brief cheer from the settlement's remaining defenders as the Israeli tanks drew up and stopped; Grossman and the others jumped down and ran for the fence. The wire had been breached in many places and he could see that most of the buildings had gaping holes in them from the intense shelling. Bodies were scattered around the perimeter of the wire; dead men were draped from the small windows of the outposts. Joel Perez lay near the shattered gate, his stomach ripped open by a bayonet; his wife lay nearby, nearly decapitated by the sweep of some Arab blade.

Arab and Israeli bodies covered the area before the administration building; the fighting there had been hand-to-hand and fierce. The generator for the Ein Tsofar lighting system had been blasted from its base and was tilted to one side, half buried in the sand; the fuel that had serviced it was soaking into the sand from a ruptured tank. The flag that had been flown from the roof of the administration building was torn in shreds and lay on the ground in the blood of the Arab who had pulled it down. Grossman and several others ran for the cave that had been the hospital; the opening to the cave had been barricaded completely with beds, litters, and bedding. He raised his voice even as he started to tear at the barricade.

"Is anyone in there? This is Ben Grossman of the Givati Brigade! Can you hear? Is anyone in there?"

There was silence. With a curse and a terrible fear in his heart he started to rip at the barricade and then suddenly stopped, motioning the others to stop also; a bullet could well greet the first to remove that cover and be exposed. He raised his voice again, this time in a bellow.

"Is anyone in there? This is Ben Grossman of the Givati Brigade! We're here to help you . . ."

There was a muffled scream of joy from inside and hands began to tear at the barrier from both sides; the barricade came down in minutes and the men entered. The cave was in darkness except for the slanting bar of sunlight that came from outside. The wounded were lying on the floor, the cots and bedding having been used to block the entrance. Ben stared into the blackness and then grabbed the first nurse he saw.

"Deborah Assavar—Grossman—where is she?"

"Ben! Ben!"

He turned, searching. Deborah was lying on the floor of the cave at the rear, wrapped in a sheet. She was laughing and crying at the same time and he realized it was the first time he had heard tears in Deborah's voice. He hurried to her and knelt beside her, his eyes slowly adjusting to the darkness, searching visibly for the wound.

Then he saw that she was trying to sit up while still trying to protect a small bundle in her arms.

"Your son . . . I couldn't deliver . . . this big cow body of mine and I couldn't deliver . . . I thought I was going to disappoint you . . . I thought I was going to lose the baby, he was so big and he wouldn't come out . . . and . . . and then the shelling started and a shell hit just over the cave entrance and I thought we were all dead and . . . and the baby . . . just seemed to pop out . . ." She looked down at the small red-faced creature in her arms and then looked up at Ben, smiling tremulously. "Our son, Ben . . . your son you wanted so badly . . ."

"Shhhh!" he said gently, and looked down in wonder at his son.

Chapter 7

The war with Egypt ended five days after the relief of Ein Tsofar and six days after the birth of Herzl Daniel Grossman, on January 7, with a cease-fire agreement that led a week later to the start of serious armistice talks, which in turn led on the twenty-fourth of February to a completed Armistice Agreement with Egypt. Operation Horev had been an outstanding success.

With Egypt effectively out of the war, the action against the balance of Israel's enemies became largely diplomatic, and Benjamin Grossman—Captain Benjamin Grossman, now—was not in his proper element as a diplomat. Fighting was his specialty, his love, but at least he now knew what his career would be. He would remain in the army. Someone had to, and he was as qualified as any. He was also convinced, as were most, that the war would go on for a long time. After all, there had been no peace settlements to end hostilities, only armistices until peace would someday come, and that day was nowhere in sight.

The final Armistice Agreement was signed with Jordan on March 4 after a month's negotiation; with Lebanon on March 23; and the final agreement was concluded with Syria on July 20.

The Preamble of the Armistice Agreements stated ". . . that the Agreements were concluded in order to facilitate the transition from the present truce to permanent peace." Article 1 stated that ". . . no aggressive actions by the armed forces—land, sea, or air—of either party shall be undertaken, planned, or threatened against the people or armed forces of the other." Article 2 stated that ". . . no warlike act or hostility shall be conducted from territory controlled by one of the Parties against the other Party."

Everyone knew as the agreements were being signed that the war would go on. The armistices were meant to give time to regroup, rearm, replan. And Benjamin Grossman intended to be part of that replanning. After all, he now had to plan, not just for himself, but for his family.

Herzl Daniel Grossman was everything a father could have hoped for. He was handsome, bright, and healthy. At times Benjamin Grossman regretted that his son could not have been raised with the advantages he had enjoyed on the sweeping estates in Angermünde, of being trained in the Junker tradition to sustain him through life. But he had to admit that in those many absences of his occasioned by his increasingly important position in the Israeli Army, Deborah was doing an exceptional job of raising their child, even though she maintained her job as head nurse at the Magen David Adom. True, she was raising him to a full appreciation of his responsibilities as a dedicated Sabra, but this no longer meant very much to Benjamin Grossman. The important thing was that Herzl was growing up a happy child; thinking back, Benjamin Grossman could not recall having been very happy as a child, even with the estates and the stables and even with the Junker tradition.

In appearance, the boy was remarkably as Ben had been as a child. He had slate-blue eyes, a wide forehead beneath unruly sandy hair, an almost perfectly chiseled profile. He had a quick mind, and from his mother he had inherited a certain steadiness, a dedication to the integrity of his own convictions. A few of his teachers in school called it stubbornness, but it was actually more a refusal to concede when he felt he was right. He was, in short, everything Grossman was sure he would have been himself had he had a father to appreciate him, love him, raise him and direct him as Herzl had been appreciated, loved, raised and directed. It compensated to a large extent for the fact that Deborah could not have any more children; the difficult delivery in the darkened Ein Tsofar cave had seen to that.

Although there were increasingly constant demands upon Colonel Grossman's time by his increasingly important position in the armed forces, he still made special efforts to get home to Tel Aviv as often as possible. And when he was home he spent almost all of his time with his son. Herzl, growing up, was a very popular boy, but he also took time from his own activities whenever his father was available to spend with a parent he respected and adored. Herzl was a lucky boy, and unlike many lucky boys, was wise enough to know it.

When Ben Grossman was home, and occasionally when he was not, Max Brodsky would drop over to have a drink, to share dinner, or simply to pass the time. Following the war, Brodsky had also decided to remain in the defense establishment, returning to Mossad, which handled intelligence and security matters, and in the years since had risen to the position of colonel. He was now assistant to the head of section, and it was predicted in the army that in time he was sure to head the section.

Max Brodsky had never married—a subject often brought up by Deborah in their many meetings, since Deborah had come to believe in the necessity of marriage for happiness—and being alone Max was free to enjoy his friendships where he found them, and the Grossman family were very close to him in many ways.

None of them lived luxuriously; the State of Israel had little money to waste on extravagant salaries either for its soldiers or for its security or intelligence personnel. Still, Max Brodsky and the Grossman family lived comfortably enough in apartments only several blocks apart in the Tel Aviv suburb of Ramat Gan, a little farther from the beaches Herzl liked so much than he would have preferred, but otherwise they were all quite happy there. But money, Grossman often thought on reflection, was certainly not vital to happiness. They lived contentedly; he enjoyed his work and loved his family, and the same was true of Deborah. Life before he had come to Israel —actually, before he had been forced against his will to come to Palestine, as he often smilingly admitted in Brodsky's presence—had faded from his mind completely. He wondered to himself many times why he had set such a high value on that money in Switzerland. With it, where would he be? Wherever it might have been, it would have been without his family, without Herzl, and without Deborah, which would have been unthinkable.

He and Brodsky would often sit on the small porch of the apartment, enjoying the breeze, sipping brandy, watching the neighborhood children shouting and screaming in the street below, and speak of many things. They spoke of the vital necessity to improve the army, to organize the reserves more efficiently, to develop more sophisticated weaponry both offensive and defensive; and little Herzl, forgoing the games in the street, would sit and listen, excited to be in the presence of two men whose influence upon his country's future—his mother continually assured him—was so important. He was proud to be the son of one and the good friend, the adopted nephew so to speak, of the other.

But the times spent with his father and his Uncle Max were not always confined to serious discussion. The two men would take Herzl with them when they went to Morris Wolf's restaurant in the southern sector of Tel Aviv not far from Yafo, and sit for hours, with Wolf telling them of the odd and humorous things that can happen in the life of a German-refugee restaurateur in a Yemenite neighborhood; or they would go on picnics at the beach, and Brodsky would point out the exact spot where the *Ruth* had landed them, and tell Herzl how his father had saved them all that night by shooting out the radar scope and the floodlight on the British gunboat, and go on to tell him how his father had been picked up that night with a gun in his hands and had been sentenced to death by the British, only to be rescued and sent to Ein Tsofar, where he had met Herzl's mother.

Ben Grossman would laugh.

"You make it sound very romantic, very heroic. I was simply stupid, that's all. I spoke no Hebrew then, nor English, and I had no idea of what was happening or what anyone was talking about. My biggest concern when the British took me in that night, believe it or not, was that they were taking my passport away from me and I knew I would never get it back. It was a forged passport, of course, supposedly a Venezuelan one—and I couldn't speak Spanish, ei-

ther." He would laugh at the memory. "How's that for being heroic?"

Or Herzl would take the opportunity at times when his Uncle
Max was around—for he knew his Uncle Max's presence would elicit
reminiscences from his father when nothing else could—to ask his
father about stories of the war of 1948, or the Sinai campaign of
1956 that had ended a few years before. Major Benjamin Grossman
had been one of those responsible for the planning of that campaign,
which had turned out so brilliantly from a military standpoint, and
so disastrously from a diplomatic one. But on the subject of war,
Grossman would put the boy off with a smile.

"War is just a job," he would say to the eleven-year-old Herzl.
"Just another job. It's neither particularly noble nor particularly
demeaning. It's just something that, unfortunately, has to be done
from time to time if you and I and your mother are to survive. And
survival is what is important, not war."

"It's just a job," Brodsky would say, "except you do the job exceptionally well. And you also seem to enjoy the job."

Grossman would shrug deprecatingly.

"One should always do a job he enjoys, or at least try to enjoy
whatever job he has to do. As for doing it well, with enough practice
one has to improve." He would smile at his son and put his hand on
the boy's head affectionately. "When you're a famous surgeon,
Herzl, you won't need as much practice saving lives as I have, sadly,
taking them."

Then there was the time both Brodsky and Grossman decided
they needed more exercise; they were middle-aged men now and
spent too much time sitting at desks. They decided that tennis was
the best sport suited to their age, and that it would also be a good
sport for thirteen-year-old Herzl to learn. One day Herzl sat on the
side lines while his father and Uncle Max played. When the two
men were finished and came to sit beside the boy, wiping the sweat
from their faces, Herzl frowned at his father.

"Dad, were you ever wounded in the war?"

"Wounded in the war? No, why?"

"I don't know. It's just—well, when you serve the ball you serve it
sort of underhand, like a girl. I know something's wrong with your
arm, you never lift it up high, like Uncle Max or me. That's why I
wondered if you were wounded in the war."

Grossman laughed delightedly.

"Herzl, Herzl! You and your Uncle Max insist on making your father out to be a big hero. The truth is, I fell out of a tree when I was a little boy, about six or seven, a tree I 'shouldn't have been up in in the first place. I broke my arm—my shoulder, actually—and the doctor who set it didn't do a very good job." He ruffled the boy's hair and then leaned over to kiss him on the forehead. "And that's why your heroic father can't raise his arm too high."

When Herzl Grossman was fifteen years old, he was seduced by a friend of the family, a widow of thirty-eight named Rifkah Zimmerman. Rifkah Zimmerman's husband had been killed in the Sinai, and as the years went by she found herself more and more missing the passionate nights they had enjoyed. Mrs. Zimmerman began noticing the son of her old friend, Deborah Grossman. As she watched Herzl grow older and larger she often found herself, at first unwillingly, and then purposely, erotically picturing the sexual education of the boy and her own enjoyment at providing it. She would tell herself she was ridiculous, a sick woman; but that did not stop the fantasizing. She could not, however, think of a proper excuse to get Herzl alone at her home, and so she filed the desire, along with all the many other unfulfilled wishes, and went about her life.

But then Herzl began delivering groceries for the neighborhood store, and Mrs. Zimmerman always ordered her groceries from this store by telephone. Rifkah worked and had little time for shopping, preferring to use her one day off doing housework or resting. This particular afternoon, when the bell rang, she had just finished her bath and was dressed in a dressing gown. She went to answer the door and then felt a sudden flush as she saw Herzl there. She swung the door wide to allow him passage with the large carton he carried, leaning forward a bit as she held it open so that his arm brushed one of her full breasts.

"Herzl! Come in. When did you start delivering?"

"Just this week," Herzl said, and turned to leave, his arm tingling from the unexpected and exciting softness it had encountered. He had also pictured being alone with Mrs. Zimmerman; he was at an age when his thoughts were predominantly on being alone with many women and girls. But like Rifkah Zimmerman, he knew it was an impossible dream. He also knew he was too nervous with girls to do anything about any of his dreams.

"Wait," she said hurriedly, trying to form a scenario on short notice, not wishing to lose a rare opportunity. "Have a cold glass of tea, or a soda. Sit, sit. You don't have to run, do you?" She thought for a moment of inquiring about his parents, but then felt it would be a mistake to bring in her contemporaries at this point.

"No," Herzl said, surprised at the invitation, but still convinced it had to only be friendly hospitality, because what else could it be? Anything else could only be another dream to add to his frustrations at night in bed, when he knew he would recall the incident and embellish it in his imagination. "No, this is my last delivery."

"Good! Then sit, sit. Tea? Or soda?"

Herzl sat and thought considering the choice, but his mind was not on it. He tried not to stare at the bulge where Rifkah's fine breasts strained against the smooth cloth of the dressing gown, aware of his growing erection, and also aware that the dressing gown allowed a glimpse of a dimpled knee as it gaped every now and then. Rifkah looked at him coyly, gaining confidence.

"It's such a hard choice, tea or soda? Your mind is on something else? What is it? Your girl friend?"

Herzl blushed. "I—I don't have a girl friend . . ."

Rifkah stared at him in pretended disbelief. "What? No girl friend? A handsome, good-looking, big boy like you?" She shook her head, the movement dislodging the dressing gown a trifle more. "You must be joking! I bet the girls are all over you. I bet they can't keep their hands off you."

"No, really," Herzl said, confused by the discussion. "I never even—" He stopped, his face flaming with embarrassment, forcibly raising his eyes from the now partially visible cleavage.

Rifkah Zimmerman felt a wave of heat suffuse her body. She knew now that she was on a path that could end only in bed, or in a rejection that would shatter her. Should the boy tell his parents—! She forced the thought away. She could not stop now.

"No girl friend?" Her voice sounded odd, even to herself, but the words almost formed themselves. "And what haven't you ever? Don't tell me you've never seen a woman without her clothes? A naked woman?"

Herzl stared at her, speechless. He couldn't believe what was

happening. Or was it happening? Maybe she was merely being curious, making a friendly query, as an aunt might make. Or, rather, an
uncle. He wet his lips.

"No, ma'am . . ." His voice was low and hoarse.

"Would you like to?" Rifkah's voice had also dropped, as if they
were two conspirators deciding on a terrible but needful act.

Herzl could only nod, his throat dry. Rifkah opened her dressing
gown and then watched his face anxiously, as if fearing his rejection.
Herzl's eyes were wide, his face pale. She dropped the gown entirely,
watching him.

"Well? Am I ugly? Say something."

"No . . . No . . . You're beautiful . . ."

"Good. Come." She felt the flush of success and took his hand,
pressing it to her breast, leading him toward the bedroom. "Come
. . ."

Their affair lasted two years.

Once, one evening when they had finished making love, Herzl
pulled Rifkah to him tightly.

"I love you . . ."

For the first time Rifkah's voice was sharp with him.

"Never say that! When you fall in love, you'll know it. Don't
make a mistake about that. You're just a boy; I'm an old woman.
We give each other pleasure; that's enough."

And when, after those two years, Rifkah Zimmerman remarried
and moved to Haifa, Herzl felt betrayed. He had not even known
she was seeing anyone else. But after a short time the ache went and
he found himself realizing how much he owed her. She had taken
him through some very difficult growing-up years, and while he knew
now he had never loved her, he also knew he would always feel a
profound sense of gratitude to her for all she had done for him. He
wondered how he would feel if he ever saw her again, but he never
did.

Colonel Benjamin Grossman's stature in the Israeli Defense
Forces grew as time went on and as his usefulness in assignments
other than fighting became more and more evident. Old Shmuel
Ginzberg was still alive but he was a very old man now, who lived
with a daughter on a kibbutz in the Galilee, and who was no longer

active in any capacity. In his place, Colonel Grossman was often called upon to travel to foreign countries, to make purchases of everything from armaments—which were still needed despite the growing Israeli industry—to supplies of every nature. His technical skills came in handy, as well as what Morris Wolf claimed was his natural Jewish ability to bargain, despite Grossman's evident antireligious attitude. And on several occasions of his trips abroad, Colonel Grossman took his son along, for he felt the boy needed broadening before facing the demands and sacrifices almost built in to the study for a medical career. So Herzl grew up a well-rounded boy in a happy home with a happy future ahead of him—which was exactly as Benjamin Grossman had planned it.

It was very shortly after the 1967 war that Brigadier General Benjamin Grossman was one day asked, rather formally to his surprise, if he might drop into the office of Chief of Security Max Brodsky. The request almost amounted to a demand, and it was therefore with a bit of surprise that he presented himself in the outer office and was told by an extremely efficient-looking secretary that he was expected and could go right in.

Max was sitting behind his huge desk, which, as usual, was entirely clear of papers and supported only two telephones and a note pad. He smiled at Ben and waved him to a chair. Ben took the one directly across the desk from Brodsky, and frowned.

"You wanted to see me, Max?"

Brodsky swung his swivel chair to stare from the window a moment, and then swung back. He tented his fingers and stared at Grossman across them, thoughtfully.

"Ben," he said slowly, "you spent a lot of time at Ein Tsofar . . ."

"Too much," Grossman said, wondering at the statement. "Nearly a year, in fact. Why?"

"Your shop, where you worked, was in a cave, as was the hospital. And there were other caves, as well, where arms were stored, and there were also the old cisterns, I believe, going back to biblical days . . ."

"That's right. Why?"

"What did you think of the caves?"

"In what way?"

"Were you ever afraid the roof might collapse and bury you?"

"Those caves?" Grossman shook his head, becoming more and more puzzled by the direction the conversation was taking. "As you said, they were there from biblical times without falling in; they'll be there forever. They're solid as rock. Why?"

"All of them solid?"

"All of them." Grossman leaned across the desk. "Now tell me why the questions."

"I know you're not a geologist," Brodsky said, totally disregarding Ben's request, "but you are a fine engineer. I don't want to bring in any geologists on this; in fact, I don't want to bring in anyone I don't definitely need. Let me ask you this. If we were to take all of the caves, plus the old cistern excavations, and make one big room out of them or out of some of them, by cutting away the walls, would the mountain simply collapse and fill them in?"

Grossman leaned back, considering the question on its merits.

"I don't believe so, not if you took proper precautions. You would have to shore up the present cave roofs before you started to cut away the walls and eventually, of course, you might want to concrete the entire roof area, but it could be done. Why?"

"How big a room could be built inside that mountain?"

Grossman shrugged. "As big as you want, I suppose. Acres, if you wanted. I understand they have bomb shelters in the United States built under mountains in the west, there, the size of villages. Why? What are you thinking of putting there? Not a bomb shelter, I'm sure, a hundred miles away from people."

Brodsky swiveled his chair and stared from the window a moment before swiveling back.

"I suppose you'll have to know . . ."

Grossman frowned. "You suppose?"

Brodsky laughed. "I've been in security too long, I guess. I mean, of course you must know. I'll need your help. We have a big job to do."

The war of 1967 also had a profound effect on Herzl Grossman. When the war was over and Herzl emerged from it unscathed at the age of eighteen, he strongly suspected that surgery was not the profession he would have chosen without his father's influence. As an infantryman in the attacks on the Old City of Jerusalem, and at Ramallah, Nablus, and later the storming of the Golan Heights by

way of Tel Azaziyat at the northernmost end of the Syrian fortifica-
tions, he had seen enough blood in that short week to last him a life-
time. He recognized that there would undoubtedly be other wars in
the future in which he would be called upon to serve, and he also
knew there would be bloodshed in those. But that was blood that
could not be avoided, while the blood of the operating room could
be. It was a weak argument and he recognized it as such, and so he
dutifully entered the university in the fall of that year, prepared to
continue his pre-medical studies at least until he found some other
profession more to his liking.

Three additional years of university did not make him more ame-
nable to the ideas of spending his life either cutting someone open
or sewing them back together again. They were years that formed a
sort of hiatus in his life, years passed through in a state of inertia
rather than of progress, pointless years. He spent only as much time
with books as was necessary to pass his subjects; otherwise he often
found himself restlessly walking the streets or sitting on the beach staring out to sea, searching for he knew not what. At times he would sit
with his friends at one of the sidewalk cafes on Ben Yehuda Street,
halfheartedly arguing with his more impassioned companions such
youthful subjects as sex, or politics, or religion—for nowhere is
religion argued more vehemently than in the all-Jewish country of Israel. Girl friends he had none; he felt he wanted to settle down to a
meaning, a significance in life before encumbering himself with girls.
On occasion he would visit one of the houses at the upper end of
Hayarkon Street, but he always came away feeling cheated by the
falseness of their affection as compared to the warmth and passion of
Rifkah.

As the years passed Herzl began to feel a sense of panic, as if he
were being drawn into medicine as a future against his will. But he
needed an anchor to hold him from being swept into the operating
room with its sutures and its scalpels and its blood and death, and in
the middle of his final year of pre-medical studies, he found it.

One evening a friend of his, studying Communication at the university, invited him to a club the friend had recently joined, a film
club, and in the course of the three hours spent at the meeting,
Herzl Grossman felt as if a curtain had been raised before his eyes,
revealing his future so clearly as to make him wonder why he had
not found the miracle answer before.

He sat on the floor with the others who could not find seats, and watched a jumpy, amateurishly made picture, filmed with a hand-held camera in black and white, covering a trip the cameraman had made to the Dead Sea caves, and the uncovering of some of the early discoveries of the archaeologists exploring there. The cameraman, admittedly a beginner but a definite enthusiast, kept up a running commentary—for the film, of course, had no sound—describing what was being done, how he and another member of the club had climbed together with the archaeologists to the caves high in the cliffs, how they had managed lights from battery packs or used light reflected from tilted stainless-steel mirrors for some of their interior shots of the caves. He apologized for much of the camerawork, explaining that he had a very limited collection of lenses, and pointed out certain shots he would have improved had he owned better equipment.

When the showing was over and tea and cake served, Herzl listened enthralled as the members criticized the picture, not in any fashion meant to denigrate, but rather with an eye to learning themselves, to fathom the means of improvement. The evening opened an entire new vista for Herzl, and as he walked home that night he pictured the endless things that could be brought to the screen through the magic of the camera. Until that night he had gone to the cinema as most of his friends did, to enjoy whatever was unfolded on the screen for his entertainment, without the slightest thought as to the techniques and combined efforts behind the finished product.

The following week the film club was privileged to have for showing a professionally produced documentary, produced by a small but active company for the Israeli Government's Department of Highways. The film dealt with the construction of the first all-weather road from Ein Bokek at the juncture of the Arad Road and the Dead Sea, down through the Negev Desert to Eilat on the Red Sea Gulf. The film was in color and accompanied by proper sound, and Herzl lost himself in it. It was an area of the country he knew; with his father he had returned several times to Ein Tsofar to see where he was born, and to listen again to the tales of those tense days. Several times on these trips they had taken their jeep down into the desert south of Sdom, once as far as Ein Yahav, nearly halfway to the gulf, bouncing along the barely defined trails, noting the signs that indicated there were mines still scattered about the inhospitable terrain, seeing the depth markers for the water that could suddenly flood, even in that arid region, from a cloudburst over the sharp wadis.

He found himself studying the film from a completely different angle than he had ever watched a film before, trying to picture where the cameraman had set up his equipment for various shots, how they must have waited for a certain position of the sun—for it certainly wasn't luck—to get the reflection just right off the steep cliffs behind the mounds of potash at the Dead Sea Works, or how they arranged the sharp shadows of the broken country surrounding Hatzeva Ir Ovot. As he walked home that night, rerunning the film through his mind, he knew how very little he knew, and how very, very much he would have to learn.

But the university, he was convinced, was not the place to learn. As one couldn't study war properly at the university despite the training one received in the reserves, so one couldn't study film-making there despite the courses taught. During the week he had gone over the curriculum of the communications courses and the little they had to teach in film techniques and the related subjects was certainly not enough to justify the time. He had wasted over three years already; he could not afford to waste more. The field was where one learned, as it was in war. With experience one learned, not with theory. So he went out and got a job.

But he wondered how his father would react.

At the moment his father was in bed, reading a newspaper—he had little time during the day. At his side, Deborah was knitting—she also had little time during the day. She put aside her knitting and turned to him.

"Ben—"

"Yes?"

"I'd like to talk to you."

"Of course." Grossman put down the newspaper he wasn't particularly interested in reading in the first place, since it represented the political opposition, and looked at Deborah with a smile. Married twenty-two years and she still excited him. "What is it?"

"It's about Herzl."

"What about him?"

"He's been talking to me lately. He wants to leave the university—"

Grossman frowned. "A girl?"

"No, no. He doesn't want to be a doctor. He wants to make movies—"

"*Movies?*"

"Ben, listen. Please. He's become totally involved. He told me all about it, about how it's not just pointing a camera and you take a picture, but how it's writing and planning and balancing—whatever he meant by that—and knowing about sets and locations and lenses and angles and lights and shadows—"

"Deborah—"

"And he said there's research, too, because if a film doesn't have authenticity, the people can tell in a second. And he said there's a lot to the business angle, too, the question of financing, which he says is sometimes the hardest part of a project. He went out and got a job with a company named Zion Films—"

"Deborah!"

"—they're a small company making documentaries, but that's what he wants to make," Deborah went on quickly, not looking at Ben, "and he got a job in the research department, which is starting at the bottom, but they're planning a film that will take him to Munich, there's a library there for research—"

"Deborah!" Ben put his hand over her mouth and then removed it when she finally stopped talking. He looked at her, smiling, and then became serious. "You're obviously in favor."

Deborah nodded slowly.

"I wasn't, at first. But Herzl wants it, he wants it very much. And he's a man, now. It's hard to believe, but he's a man. And he sounds very sure of himself. He—he's a bit nervous about telling you."

"Am I such an ogre?"

"You're no ogre at all—no, Ben! You have to get some rest; you have a long trip tomorrow—"

"I'll rest on the plane," Ben said, and drew her close. "How many times have you made love to an ogre?"

Ben Grossman was in the bedroom, packing for his trip, when Herzl came in. He was carefully folding clothing into a suitcase when Herzl cleared his throat.

"Dad—"

Grossman carefully considered the arrangement of his clothing in the suitcase; proper packing for a trip required proper planning, as everything did.

"Yes?"

"Dad, I'd like to talk to you for a minute—"

"Of course—" The suits beneath, folded with tissue paper between, that way they wrinkled less. The shirts on top, spread out for balance, the socks and the underwear and the handkerchiefs along the edge, filling in the irregular spaces. The general tucked them in and stood back, contemplating the result.

"Dad—" Herzl took a deep breath. "I want to quit school—"

"So?" The neckties now, folded over the little bar on the divider. A smart gadget; he wondered who had thought of it.

"Dad, did you hear me? I said I want to drop out of the university. I want to learn how to make films—"

Benjamin Grossman finally looked up from his task. "I know. You went out and got a job with Zion Films. Your mother told me. Did you think she wouldn't? We talked about it half the night."

"I—" Herzl didn't know what to say. "What do you think?"

"Me? More important, what do *you* think?"

"I think it's what I want to do. I mean, I know it's what I want to do. I know I don't want to be a doctor; I've known that for a long time. But I didn't know what else I wanted to be. Now I know."

Benjamin Grossman shoved his suitcase out of the way and sat down on the bed, looking up at his son.

"If you know what you want to do, you're lucky. And do it." He shrugged. "Look at me. I graduated an engineer; now I'm a soldier. Actually, I'm only a soldier when there's a war on; in between I'm a combination peddler and bargain hunter." He tilted his head toward his suitcase. "Now I'm off to trade electronic equipment from Israel for meat from Argentina. Who knows what a person is going to do in this life? If you find something you like, then do it. I wanted you to become a doctor. Why? I have no idea. I've tried to raise you— your mother and I, we've tried to raise you—to make your own decisions. You've made one. If it works out, fine. If it doesn't work out, you'll try something else." He considered his son curiously. "Your mother said your job was in research. What kind of research?"

"For a new documentary they're planning. In the film business, research is important, but it's also about the bottom of the ladder, next to the man who carries the equipment on his back, but I'd have taken the job if it meant painting sets. Eventually I want to work in all the departments. I want to learn it all."

"And I'm sure you will. Your mother said something about a trip?"

"To Munich. There's a library there, a historical research library."

"It sounds interesting. You'll like Munich, I think." Grossman smiled. "The traveling Grossmans," he said and came to his feet, putting his arm around his son's shoulders. "Just one thing—"

"Yes, Dad?"

"Whatever you do, do it well," Grossman said seriously. "Plan it well, plan it fully, and do it well. Look at me; anything I have is because of planning—" He paused a moment and then smiled, a smile Herzl did not understand. "Oddly enough," he went on slowly, his smile fading, "it's the truth. . . ."

And it was the truth. And Benjamin Grossman never felt happier than at that moment, in realizing it.

BOOK III

Prologue

Germany . . .

A beautiful country, from the clean efficient factories in the north widely spaced around such cities rebuilt from the war as Dusseldorf with its famed exhibition hall and its *Konigsallee* all chrome and glass surrounding the lovely canal; and Koln with its impressive cathedral and its pleasant parks and fine restaurants and newly cobbled squares; all along the lovely Rhine with its neatly painted barges plowing their way downstream to Amsterdam and the Waddensee, past the Lorelei and the citadel-topped rocky crags and the quaint chalet-type houses at riverside; Heidelberg with its towering castle ruins on one side and its Philosopher's Walk halfway up the hill on the other and the wide gleaming Neckar in between and the little shops and tiny bierstubes scattered about the University; and Munich with its wide avenues and stately buildings and the Englandischer Garten and the Bogenhausen with the swift Isar cutting through between; and to the south of the country, along the Austrian border, the wooded mountain slopes abundant with pine and beech and spruce; and all throughout the country the lakes and streams scattered about, sewing the rich land together with glistening blue threads.

A truly beautiful country . . .

And a people who are united though they deny it. They are united despite the wide variety of country and city, of sectional interests, of political differences, of diverse scenery or regional accent or intellectual level or financial achievement; united by a past they cannot escape. It is a unity beyond the work ethic for which they are so justly famous; it is the unity of guilt. It is a feeling of guilt so strong as to demonstrate itself at times in terror; a guilt so violently denied as to prove the truth of its existence. But it is not, as many believe, the guilt for the excesses of the Third Reich. It is the guilt of having lost a war and a winnable war at that.

Few Jews can enter Germany without feeling uncomfortable by the national aura of blameless guilt; they are the destroyed victor embarrassed before the guilt of the rich and powerful vanquished. But the lovely flowers in the beautiful gardens cannot overcome the stench of the death camps thirty years after; the newly laid mortar cannot hide the crumbling souls who still stare out with frightened eyes through the electrified fences that were torn down so long ago.

It is a great burden not feeling guilty in Germany.

Chapter 1

The Institute and Library for Cultural Research was financed by Jews, manned and operated by Jews, but was open to any scholar of any religion interested in researching the holocaust. The institute was located in the Burgunder Strasse, in a row of three-story buildings that had once been private homes, and Herzl, ringing the doorbell and looking about him as he waited, had to admit that since his arrival in Munich the German people with whom he had come in contact had been extremely polite to him in every way. At the Riem Airport he had been ushered through customs without the slightest problem; the taxi driver had been informative, pointing out the various interesting sights on the way to the hotel; the room clerk at the Haus Bavaria in the Gollierstrasse had been both polite and helpful, having a room cleaned for him so he could check in before the normal hour. But Herzl still felt very strange. Accustomed to being surrounded by Jews, it was strange to be in a country where they were conspicuous by their absence. In a way he would have preferred to have been treated badly, so as to permit him to exercise his prejudices; then he smiled. If you are going to do proper research, he told himself sternly but with a smile, try not to make your mind up about things until you know something about them. Although he doubted his research on the subject of Zion Films' project—or his innate feeling of strangeness to be in Germany—would alter his opinion very much.

The door was opened at last; a short, stocky gray-haired woman stood there looking at him with the suspicion reserved for door-to-door salesmen or other interlopers.

"Yes?"

"I'm—" He suddenly remembered and brought out his letter of introduction, handing it over.

She put on a pair of steel-rimmed glasses that appeared magically in her hand—for a moment it looked as if they had been secreted in the beehive of her towering bun of hair—and studied it carefully. At last she nodded.

"Ah, yes. Mr. Grossman. We had a letter saying you would be coming." She ushered him into the hall, gave him back his letter, and pointed. "Up the stairs to the second floor, the door right before you. Miss Kleiman will be happy to help you."

"Thank you." He nodded and mounted the steps, pleased to be started on his mission at last. It was the first step in a process that would eventually result in a finished documentary on the screen, and he was involved. It was a good feeling. He took a breath and opened the door before him.

The room was large, running the length of the building, and was lined with bookshelves to the high ceiling, leaving almost no room for the narrow table set in the center. In one corner, half hidden behind file cabinets, was a small desk covered with magazines, books, and newspaper clippings; a girl Herzl judged to be his own age, or slightly less, was sitting there, studying a manuscript. She looked up as he closed the door behind him.

"Yes?"

Herzl patiently handed over his letter of introduction, wondering how many more guardians of the gate he would have to pass before he could get his hands on some of the books that seemed to bulge the walls of the room. The girl nodded, indicating a chair; Herzl sat down. She handed him back his letter of introduction.

"You come here to research the holocaust." It was a statement, not a question.

"In a way; and then again, not in a way—" Herzl was about to try and put it as accurately as possible, when the girl interrupted him, speaking in English.

"You are speaking English?"

For a moment Herzl wondered if his German was so bad as not to be understandable; then he understood. "You mean, do I speak English? Yes. Why?"

"We speak, then, English. I am forced to improve. You are saying?"

"I said, in a way it is about the holocaust, but in a larger sense it is not. You see, Zion Films does documentaries. We're planning one now on the so-called monsters of the concentration camps. We are *not*—I want you to be clear on that—we are *not* planning a film about the camps and their horrors. That's been done many times. What we are planning is a film covering people like Koch and his wife, and Dr. Mengele, and Eichmann, and von Schraeder, and Kramer, and Sergeant Moll, who was at Auschwitz what von Schraeder was at Maidanek—people like that. In the film we want to study their motives, to try and understand what brought them to the point where they could perform the hideous acts they did, without being bothered by them in the least. We want to select some of these people and trace their background, see where they came from, what type home they were raised in, what influence their environment had on them, or their schooling, or their religious upbringing, or their jobs if they had any before they went into the SS. In short, we want to see what made them what they ended up being. They certainly weren't born monsters."

"I am wondering." Miss Kleiman looked around the room, her face sober. "Here in the institute is one of the few libraries in the world dedicated to just the one subject—the holocaust. In London is another, the Wiener. When you are living with these books and the films and photographs we are having downstairs, then you are wondering." Herzl was intrigued by her constant use of the present tense. She went on. "Are you reading the testimony of the war-crimes trials in Nuremberg?"

"Am I reading it? Oh, you mean have I read it." Herzl shook his head. "I've read most of it, but that's not what we want. We don't want the testimony of people who were in the concentration camps. They are too prejudiced."

Miss Kleiman drew in her breath with a hiss. "Prejudiced?"

"I didn't mean it the way it sounded," Herzl said patiently. "What I mean is that the survivors of the camps cannot picture these men as human beings. But they once were human beings, who changed. We want to know why; that's the whole purpose of the film. My father was in three camps, and many of our close friends, as well. I didn't even ask him or them about this. That isn't what we're looking for. We don't want this to be an emotional film. We want this to be—well, a sort of study in psychology. Or psychiatry, possibly."

Miss Kleiman was looking at him strangely. "Not to be an emotional film. Well, possibly you are being able to do it . . ." She came to her feet; Herzl noted that she was tall and extremely well built. Get your mind back on your job, he told himself sternly, and brought his eyes to her face, which merely confirmed his previous estimate that it was very pretty. "All right," Miss Kleiman said. "I am showing you the files and how they work. You are filling out a separate slip for every books and I am getting them for you. The films and the photographs collections are downstairs in the cellar. Incidentally, how many languages you are speaking?"

"English, German, and Hebrew."

"It should be enough."

Well, Herzl thought, I should certainly hope so! "How many do you speak?"

"Eight. Much of the holocaust books are in Polish and Russian, some in Lithuanian. But you are speaking enough languages, I think."

"Thank you," Herzl said, slightly deflated. "By the way—what's your first name?"

She looked at him evenly; her eyes, he noted, were hazel, with little flecks of gold in them. "Miriam. Why?"

Herzl felt his face getting red. "I'm sorry. That wasn't what I meant to say at all; it just came out. What I meant to say was, is it possible to see the film clips first?"

"You are interested in only the people. It will be taking a while for Rolf Steiner—he exhibits—exhibits is correct?—the film. I am calling him. In the meantime, you might wish to start."

"Yes," Herzl said, and went to work, picking titles from the files, filling in slips, watching Miss Miriam Kleiman's lovely legs as she mounted the movable ladders to get him his choices, then digging into the books, pulling out a small fact here, another there.

Adolf Eichmann—starting alphabetically—*originally on file as having been born in Sarona, German Templar Colony, in Palestine, later found to have actually been born in Linz, Austria (the*

birthplace of Adolf Hitler), of deeply religious parents—Presbyterian
—whose father was once the guest speaker of honor at the synagogue
in Linz. He was actually christened Karl, not Adolf; the Adolf seems
to have been adopted later in life, probably due to influence of
Hitler's name. He was oddly fluent in Hebrew and Yiddish in addi-
tion to his native German. (Where did he learn those languages,
and why? Investigate . . .) *He was raised with Jews as a child, was*
always friendly with Jews, and had no record of any trouble with
Jews at school or elsewhere, nor any record of any rejection by any
Jewish girl or woman that might have changed him. He—

"Mr. Grossman?"

He looked up and smiled. "Herzl."

"Herzl, then. Rolf Steiner says he has enough films for today."

"Oh? Good!" He came to his feet, surprised at how long he had
been at the books, extracting the information bit by bit. "Where?"

"In the cellar—the basement. Two stories downstairs."

"Will you be joining me?" Alone in a darkened projection room,
one arm draped casually across the back of her chair—

"No, no! Here I must do work."

Herzl felt a tiny stab of disappointment, but put it aside with the
knowledge that once the films were over, he could come back and
have Miss Kleiman all to himself—if the library wasn't crowded
when he got back. But it seemed unlikely; that morning he had been
the only one there. An introduction was required, and only serious
scholars and researchers took advantage of it, and he hoped that no
serious scholar or researcher, other than himself, needed information
that day.

He didn't realize he was staring at her until he saw her cheeks
begin to redden; then she said rather pointedly, "Rolf Steiner will be
waiting for you."

"Oh. Yes, of course. Well," Herzl said bravely, "I'll see you as
soon as I can." And he walked out of the room, wondering if Rolf
Steiner was handsome, and if a man could work at the same place as
a beautiful girl like Miriam Kleiman and not be attracted to her, and
if that attraction was mutual.

He need not have worried. Rolf Steiner was a short, pudgy man of
seventy years of age, with a red face, a fringe of white hair standing
away from his bald head in the manner of Ben Gurion, and with

what seemed like a permanent smile on his face. He was a happy little gnome who spent his working days in the basement with his miles and miles of film. He lived just for his films and spent hours upon hours sorting through them, trying to organize them better, cross-filing their contents, or spending hours repairing the sprocket holes on films that went back to the earliest days of the Nazi Party and which had been shown until they were nearly worn out. He loved nothing better than to show his films, and now he seated Herzl in the small projection room, chattering as he went about threading the first master reel into the projector.

"Don't exactly know what you want, Mr. Grossman—"

"Herzl."

"Herzl, Miriam wasn't too precise, but we have plenty of film, oh, yes, oh, yes, miles and miles on the camps and some of it shows the people who ran them, if you see anything on anyone you'd like in greater detail we may have special film on them, not much on some quite a bit on others, rather decent cross-filing system if I say so myself—" He completed his work and reached for the light switch. ". . . say so myself . . ." he said again rather vaguely, and then the lights went out.

The films began to flicker and Herzl brought his thoughts from Miriam Kleiman to the scenes being unfolded before him. Behind him he could hear the heavy excited breathing of Rolf Steiner, enjoying the film he had seen hundreds of times before as if it were his first viewing. The films were mostly copies of official German SS film, and the scenes for the various camps were remarkably similar; each camp site seemed to have been selected to oppress the prisoners as much with the bleakness of the terrain as with the cruelty of the punishment and the discomfort of the facilities. Hangings were quite common; the first made Herzl slightly ill, but after a while the horror of seeing men stare into the lens of the camera with dulled eyes and then silently, unstrugglingly drop to their death began to lose its effect. It was too terrible to contemplate, too gruesome to credit as having actually happened. There was an almost disbelief to see recorded on the film the seemingly endless lines of naked women, children, and men lined up to be shot at the edge of a burial pit without the slightest attempt to flee; each succeeding one lessened the impact of the next. It had to be a scene from some badly acted, poorly directed film, Herzl thought, and swallowed the bile that had risen in his throat.

Behind him Steiner kept up a running comment.

"Auschwitz . . . that was taken in Poland in the Krepiecki Forest . . . Russian film . . . had to make all new sprocket holes, awful job . . . this was at Mauthausen, terrible place, killed them by pushing them into a quarry . . . Ravensbrook, that was just for women . . . Auschwitz, again . . . only camp that tattooed the inmates, don't know why, they didn't usually live long enough . . . Maidanek just put a card around the neck and used the number over and over . . ."

A British official film was being shown; it indicated SS Captain Josef Kramer surrendering the Bergen-Belsen camp to a British officer. Kramer stood at attention, his staff lined up behind him, all in order. Steiner laughed.

"Didn't even know he had done any wrong! Surrendered as if he were an honorable prisoner of war! Hung him, finally. I've some film of his trial at Leuenburg—British court—if you want to see it later . . ."

"Possibly."

The film rolled on, Steiner maintaining a running commentary.

"This is an old reel, don't know how it got mixed in." He sounded really put out by a mistake in his department. "Anschluss, in Austria. March 1938. Might as well run it, just as fast as trying to jump it . . ." The film rolled on, cars passed the camera, each with a driver sitting stiffly in his place and with a smiling officer beside him. On each side of the road people cheered and threw streamers. The faces rolled on; Herzl stifled a yawn and glanced at his watch. Six-thirty. At the end of this reel he would call it a day. He brought his eyes up and suddenly stared.

"Wait! Hold it!"

Steiner stopped the projector; the figure on the screen froze, the crowd stopped its activity, hands in the air, mouths open. Steiner was looking at him awaiting instruction.

"Can you run it in reverse?"

"Of course. Tell me when to stop."

The projector was reversed; cars went into reverse, comically; people on the street dropped their arms and walked backward; streamers shot back into little rolls in people's hands.

"There! That car, that man. Stop!" The projector was instantly stopped. Herzl frowned at the smiling face on the screen. It was so familiar! How could he fail to remember a face that well known? "Mr. Steiner, who is that, do you know?"

Steiner knew every inch of his film by heart. "Von Schraeder, the colonel in charge of the extermination at Maidanek," he said at once, and added proudly, "We identified almost every officer in the entire parade."

"He looks familiar . . ."

Steiner shrugged doubtfully. "He died of typhus before the end of the war."

"I know. Well, let's go on, shall we?"

"Right," Steiner said, and pressed the proper switch, while Herzl pondered the nagging sensation of having seen that face before.

It was seven o'clock when Herzl slowly mounted the steps from the basement projection room, rubbing the back of his neck wearily. How Rolf Steiner could sit and watch films for hour after hour was beyond him; in any event the fun was going to be in making them, not in watching them. He reached the first floor and glanced up hopefully toward the second floor, but he was really not too surprised to see the door to the library there closed and only darkness visible through the small frosted-glass window in the door. So he would not get to see Miss Miriam Kleiman anymore that day. A pity; it would have been nice to take her out to dinner and get to know her better. Eight languages; his mother would be impressed. And his father would be impressed with the rest of her. He smiled broadly at the thought. Ah, well, there was always tomorrow. . . .

He heard Steiner climbing the stairs breathlessly behind him.

"Everyone's gone many hours, I'll let you out," he said in his chattering way, and extracted a huge bunch of keys from his pocket. "I must respool the film, take out the Anschluss film, don't know how it got in in the first place, don't usually make mistakes, oh, no, mind must have been on something else, getting old, oh, yes!" He looked up at Herzl, his head tilted bird-wise, blinking with his tiny eyes. "Will you want to see more film in the morning, anyone special, I might get it ready still tonight . . . ?"

"I'll let you know in the morning," Herzl said. "You should get some rest tonight. And thank you, Mr. Steiner. Good night."

He walked out into the evening, hearing the door being locked behind him, wondering if Miriam Kleiman had a friend she saw regularly. He also could not help but wonder in the back of his mind who that face in that parade in Vienna in 1938 reminded him of.

The answer to his first question as to Miriam Kleiman and the possibility of her having a steady friend could not readily be ascertained, although it was not possible to think she would not have. But the answer to his second query came that very evening as he was washing his face before going down to a lonely dinner in the hotel dining room. It made him crow with disbelieving laughter.

The face he had seen in the Vienna parade had been his own!

Chapter 2

He came up the steps and into the main libary room the following morning, pleased to see that Miriam Kleiman was already in, and to note she looked as good the second time as she had the first. She looked up at his entrance and smiled.

"Good morning."

"Good morning. How are you this fine morning?"

"All right," she said, slightly surprised by the effusiveness of the greeting. "You are liking how were the pictures yesterday?"

Herzl's cheerfulness diminished but did not disappear completely. "Liking is not the word for those films. Sickening is closer to the mark. Have you seen them?"

"Oh, yes. They are not pleasant."

"No. Well," Herzl said, drawing up a chair, "I have a favor to ask. Have you any pictures of a Colonel Helmut von Schraeder? He was in charge of—"

"I know. Very few, I am afraid. ODESSA—you are hearing of them?"

"I've heard of them, yes."

"They are destroying many of the data of much top war criminals when the war is coming near to a close. We are having very little pictures and none of fingerprints on von Schraeder, for example, or for many others. But for him"—she shrugged—"nobody thinks of, too much, because he is dying in Buchenwald from the typhus before even the war is ended. But I look."

"Thank you," Herzl said, and waited. She was back sooner than he expected, placing a book before him, opened to a picture.

"Here. Look," she said. "It is taken twenty-seven years ago."

It was not a very clear photograph and had been taken from a distance. It revealed a man in an SS uniform striding toward a line of people who were standing outside a building with bundles and suitcases in their hands. They were quite obviously new arrivals at a concentration camp; at one side of the picture the barbed-wire fence could be seen, and in the background, rising above the low barracks-like buildings and foreshorted by the distance, a chimney could be seen belching smoke. Barbed-wire and chimney bricks, Herzl thought, the way to make a fortune in Nazi Germany! And Zyclon-B crystals, of course. Beneath the photo was a caption:

Colonel von Schraeder inspecting new arrivals at Maidanek.

He looked up. "Do you have a magnifying glass?"

"Yes." She reached into her desk, got a glass and handed it over, then said, "I am getting a more better picture from downstairs. From the photograph files. This is from a book, like you are seeing."

She left before Herzl could answer. He sat and studied the figure in the picture a moment and then brought the magnifying glass to bear upon it, but he could see no resemblance. He must have imagined the likeness the night before; after five solid hours of watching film the mind was prepared, narcotized, to imagine anything! He went back to the photograph. There was an arrogance in the strutting figure of the SS officer. The camera had frozen his motion with his head high, his chest out, one booted and polished leg half extended as he marched along, a baton tucked jauntily under one arm. As far as Herzl could see, the only one the photograph reminded him of was the actor Erich von Stroheim in any one of the many war movies he made. Out of curiosity Herzl moved the lens to the line of people; they were mostly women, toil-worn, disheartened, waiting patiently, for what they did not know. I know what you are waiting for, Herzl thought with a pang, recalling the films of yesterday, and put down the glass and the picture, leaning back, waiting for Miriam Kleiman to return.

She came back in a short while, bearing a large manila envelope.

"Here," she said, her voice triumphant, and opened the envelope, sliding a single picture from it. He reached for it; it was a photograph about five inches by seven inches. He picked it up and studied it, feeling a little shock run through him. He had not been mistaken the night before; it was a picture apparently of himself, except he looked a little older, and he was wearing the uniform of the SS, the cap tilted a bit to one side, smiling with his own lips into the camera. The photograph had been touched in color, and the hair was the same blond hair he had combed that morning, and his own slate-blue eyes looked back at him, a trifle sardonically, it seemed. It was a studio picture, and he noted that the photograph had been made in Munich in the year 1942, which was six years before he had been born. Below, in thick ink strokes placed there, apparently, by some librarian, was the name, *Helmut von Schraeder, Colonel SS.* He looked up to see the girl studying the picture over his shoulder in amazement.

"He is you!"

"Let's just say he looks like me," Herzl said, and shook his head in wonderment. "Damn, but he does look like me! Do you have any more?"

She shook her head sadly. "It is the only picture we have, that and the one in the book. The one in the book is taken by a prisoner with a homemade box camera and some in-smuggled film. He is taking the picture when nobody is watching. He takes an awful chance, but at least we have now the picture, and from it we are identifying three of the people in the line. He is a very brave man. The other picture is being salvaged from a pile of photographs supposedly burned in Munich in a studio. The negative is gone. This is a copy. The original is in the Wiener Library in London."

Herzl went back to the picture, shaking his head in admiring disbelief.

"Remarkable! He looks more like me than I do. He looks like I'm dressed for a costume party." He suddenly grinned, a boyish grin. "Wait until I tell my sabra mother and my soldier-in-the-Israeli-Army father that they spawned a duplicate of the Monster of Maidanek!" He looked up at Miriam Kleiman. "Here's the boy I start with; he should prove interesting. Say!" He grinned as another idea struck him. "Do you suppose there's any possibility that von Schraeder had any Jewish blood in him?"

"I doubt," she said seriously. "We are researching most of the top war criminals in great extension. Extension?" She pondered the word a moment and then went on. "Of course some Jews are disguising themselves as gentiles, and some are even joining the Nazi Party to save themselves. But very few are escaping with it." Her face reddened slightly. "The physical difference, for just one thing."

"I know, but von Schraeder obviously wasn't born or raised a Jew; he wouldn't have been circumcised. It could be possible, couldn't it? Somewhere back in the line of his family? Look at how much we look like each other, and I promise you I'm a Jew from both ends." He heard how that sounded and reddened slightly himself. "I mean—"

"I still doubt," she said insistently. "With a prominent Nazi like von Schraeder there are always plenty of enemies both in and out of the Party always who look for anything they are hanging on him. It is how they operate. No, I think not that he has any Jewish blood."

"You mean you hope not," Herzl said with rare insight.

"That also, of course."

"But if he had it would be generations back, maybe. What a story if he did! Just suppose—" He hesitated as he considered the possibilities, and then continued. "Suppose in some way I was related to the man? Distantly, of course, generations back, but just suppose? Look at that resemblance! It's unbelievable."

"Are you looking like your father?"

"No, not at all. Our coloring is the same, but that's all."

"Like your mother?"

"My mother's family originally came from Iraq. She was born in Israel—Palestine then—but the Assavar family, my mother's, are dark. We're alike in many respects, but not in looks." He waved a hand. "But these family characteristics can jump generations at

times! What if there was some Grossman blood, way back, in the
von Schraeder line?" He rubbed the back of his neck in excitement.
"I could end up with a far better story than I started out for. Let me
at those files!"

"Let me go to the files," Miriam said. "I know them better. You
read— I am getting the reference books. As you say, it is interesting,
no?"

*Helmut August Karl Klaus Langer von Schraeder, born April 14,
1917, in the main house on the family estates at Angermünde in
Mecklenburg. Son of General Karl Klaus Sonnendorf von Schraeder
and Ilsa Gerda Boetticher Langer. An only child. His early childhood normal, the life of a young Junker, with a private nurse and a
governess, and private tutors after the age of six. When Helmut was
eight years old his father committed suicide. The general had accumulated huge gambling debts and had borrowed heavily to meet
them, mostly from Jewish financial houses, and the estates were for-
feited to his creditors, at which point the general shot himself. As a
result, Helmut was raised hating Jews, whom he blamed for his father's death. The boy, his mother, and one servant moved to the
gatehouse of the estate where they lived for the following five
months, at which time Helmut's mother died of pneumonia. The
young Helmut also blamed the Jews for his mother's death, because
of their reduced living conditions. On his mother's death young Helmut was taken to Hamburg by an aunt, the sister of his mother, herself a widow, and Helmut was raised there—*

Hamburg? It was where Benjamin Grossman had been born, also
in 1917 although not in April. It was also where Benjamin Grossman
had been raised until he went away to the university. A coincidence?
Possibly not. Possibly this unnamed aunt of von Schraeder or the
mother might be the connection to some Grossman family in the
past. However—

*Helmut's education was in public school, followed by university at
the Technical Institute in Munich, where he graduated second in his
class with a degree in mechanical engineering—*

That *was* a coincidence. Benjamin Grossman had also graduated
as a mechanical engineer, although in Switzerland, not in Munich.
Although it wasn't all that much of a coincidence—there must have

been thousands upon thousands of students around the world who graduated with degrees in mechanical engineering in the year 1938. Let's move on, Herzl thought, and reached for another book.

In Hamburg, while still in public school, Helmut joined the Hitler Youth, and as soon as he registered for admission at the university in Munich, he went to Party headquarters in that city and joined the Nazi Party. Thereafter throughout his university career he was very active in all Nazi Party affairs, being the leader in the harassment of Jewish students and professors until their banishment from the university. When Germany announced Anschluss with Austria in March of 1938, von Schraeder requested and received early graduation so that he could join the troops as a lieutenant in the SS. His young age—he still lacked one month to his twenty-first birthday— for the rating of lieutenant was due, it was felt in many quarters, to the fact that his father had many friends in high positions in the army who used their influence in the SS for Helmut. Thereafter his career was in the army.

Like my father, Herzl thought without knowing he was thinking it, and went on with his work.

The following year, 1939, as a captain, Helmut von Schraeder was in the first line of mechanized infantry in the invasion of Poland, and received his majority on the field in that country from the hands of Hitler himself. He received his colonelcy in Russia six months after the attack on that country in June of 1941, mainly as a result of his fearlessness and fierceness in battle. His troops were said to admire him extremely.

Again like my father, Herzl thought, and opened yet another book.

Throughout his army career his superiors had noted von Schraeder's engineering talents and ingenuity, and when the Final Solution program was put into effect in 1942, von Schraeder was transferred from the Waffen SS to the regular SS and posted to the concentration camp at Maidanek in Poland as assistant to the commandant. Here he was in charge of the operation and efficiency of the gas chamber and the crematoria ovens, where his work won him many commendations. In 1944, shortly before the liberation of Maidanek by Russian troops, Colonel von Schraeder was transferred to Buchenwald, and shortly after his arrival contracted typhus and died. He was cremated in the camp crematorium. It was suspected

that he was one of the officers involved in the plot against Hitler's life
at Wolfschantze in July of 1944, but no proof of this is available.

Herzl leaned back wearily and rubbed the back of his neck, staring
at the mountains of books he had had to go through to garner the
little information he had managed to extract, a sentence here and a
sentence there. Research, it seemed, was not much different from the
job of carrying the equipment, after all; they both involved hard
labor. But at least he had a base from which to launch his investigation. There had been nothing in his findings to indicate von
Schraeder had any Jewish blood in him, but Herzl had not expected
to find that in his study of the man himself. That would come from
going back into the history of both parents, but probably chiefly the
mother's forebears, the Langers and the Boettichers. Some of the information might be available in the Almanach de Gotha, some in
other records, possibly in the town hall in Angermünde, and in the
records of wherever the Langers or the Boettichers had lived before
the marriage to Karl Klaus von Schraeder. All in all he was satisfied
with his day's work.

He glanced at his watch and was surprised to see it was past six
o'clock. The day had gone by without his being aware of it. He was
also suddenly aware that he had missed lunch and was ravenously
hungry. He looked up; Miriam Kleiman was watching him.

"You are finding what you search for?"

"A decent base for further investigation, at least." He thought a
moment. "Do you suppose Rolf Steiner is still here?"

"He is always here. He lives here. He is being like a watchman."

"I wonder if we could ask him to dig out any films he might have
on von Schraeder—"

"But it is quite very late . . ."

"I know. I mean for tomorrow." He waited while she made a telephone call and spoke into the instrument for several minutes. When
she hung up he said, "And I want to thank you for your help."
Something suddenly occurred to him. "You didn't go out for lunch."

"Often I am not going out."

"I don't believe you. You stayed because you didn't want me to be
at loose ends, wanting for books. The least I owe you for that is a decent meal." He hesitated a moment and then suddenly smiled his
boyish smile. "How about tonight?"

She looked at him gravely a moment, then also smiled. "All right."

"Good! When are you through for the day?"

She smiled again. "An hour past. Come, I am locking up."

They ate at a small intimate restaurant near the Olympiapark, and over their food they spoke of many things, of their mutual love of books, of music, of the interest she had had in languages since a child, inherited, she said, from her father, who had spoken even more languages than she did. They spoke of the difference between being raised as a Jew in Germany, as she had, and being raised as a Jew in Israel, as Herzl had. It was hard for either one of them to clearly understand the difference, and they changed the subject to places they had been or hoped to visit.

"I am hoping soon to go to London," she said. "There is there a library much like our institute here. It is called the Wiener, in a street called Devonshire, number four. You should also be going for your work. Tomorrow I write down the address for you."

"When do you plan to go? Maybe we might go together."

She laughed. "If you wait for me, you maybe never go. I have no plans."

"And if it's the same as here, why go?"

"I go to see London. Also to perfect my English." She put the accent on the first syllable and then smiled, a gamin smile. "Perfect. You see?"

And how I would love to help you perfect your English! Herzl thought, but he said, "You really have no definite plans as to when you go?"

"All I know is, someday."

"Have you ever been to Israel?"

"No, but of course I am wanting someday to go there, also. What is it like?"

"It's—" Herzl stopped. What was Israel like? What would it be like to a person who hadn't been born there, or who hadn't come there to find a refuge from a world that wanted to kill him? What would it be like for Miriam? "It's like many countries all in one, even if it isn't very big," he said. "Tel Aviv has wonderful beaches and the streets are wide and clean, and the buildings are neat and well kept and the weather is good, and I think it's a beautiful, wonderful city. Of course we live in a suburb of Tel Aviv and I'm prejudiced." He suddenly smiled. "American visitors come and they say that Tel Aviv is like Miami Beach, and they don't mean that as a compliment, either. But I don't know Miami Beach and they don't live in Tel Aviv. I must admit, though, that our traffic is far worse than Munich's. Probably worse than Miami Beach."

Miriam was watching him, listening in a fascinated manner.

"And Jerusalem?"

"Jerusalem? Jerusalem is—well, Jerusalem. There is no city in the world like it. It's beautiful—it's more than beautiful. It's history. But Jerusalem is also indescribable; you have to see it for yourself. It's hilly, and the buildings are all made of the same kind of stone that our ancestors used thousands of years before, and when you go into a souk—that's a native street—in the Old City, you swear it cannot be real, that it is a movie set. Munich is old, I know; Paris is old. But Jerusalem was a city when all Europe was merely plains. It's impossible to describe Jerusalem properly. I wish I could, but I can't."

"And the country itself?"

"Well, a good part of it is desert, unbelievably severe, wild, rugged, mountainous, and to me also very beautiful, although to be honest a good many people hate the desert. My father for one. Again I may be prejudiced; I was born on a kibbutz in the desert. And what isn't desert or cities in Israel is good farm land, much of it recovered from swamps; wide green valleys, orchards—" He looked at her across the table, aware of a feeling he had never before experienced with a girl. "When are you coming?"

"Oh, I do not know, of course—"

"You must come, you know, and very soon. We also have a very good library in Jerusalem that is dedicated to the holocaust."

"I know, at Yad Vashem. It is very famous. I want very much to be visiting there."

"Then come. Don't go to England, come to Israel. Look—" Herzl reached out impulsively, putting his hand on hers. "My father, if you'll pardon the immodesty of his son, is rather an important person in Israel; he's a brigadier general in the army, and he travels all over the world for the government. He's in Argentina for them now, as a matter of fact. And our best friend is in the Mossad, head of security in the government. I'm sure they would be very happy to help you get a job in Israel, in your own line. Possibly even at Yad Vashem."

She smiled at him and gently disengaged her hand.

"These are dreams, no? Someday I am getting to Israel, I am sure, or at least so I am hoping, but not so soon."

"Why not?"

"Because," she said honestly, "one does not meet a stranger who talks of Israel, and the next day right away drop a job and travel to a strange place."

"Stranger?" Herzl sounded hurt.

"We are meeting only yesterday."

"I know, but people can know each other for years and still be strangers. And other people can meet and in five minutes know they were meant—" He reddened. "I mean, can be friends."

"Possibly." She stared down at her plate a moment and then looked up, quite obviously changing the subject. "About the movie film you are making—"

Herzl sighed. He had not wanted the subject changed.

"What about it?"

She hesitated a moment and then switched to German, looking at him seriously.

"I'm sorry, I know I should use English if I want to improve, but I want you to understand, and my English is not good enough. You think I am changing the subject because I don't want to speak of anything personal, and that is true; but I also want very much to speak to you of this. I have been thinking of it all day. I think the German people will like the film very much."

"I hope so," Herzl said, also speaking German.

"Do you? I did not mean it that way. The Germans want very much to humanize these men you call monsters. You will do it for them. Many are beginning to deny that the holocaust occurred, that there were any atrocities at all. In the library I can show you books, newspaper clippings, magazine articles, all emphatically denying that people were purposely slaughtered in concentration camps, that any figure like six million Jews—not to mention the millions of Russians, Poles, Rumanians, Gypsies, Germans, and others—French, Dutch, Swedish, Danish, Italian—I could go on—are pure fantasy, propaganda of Israel to extract reparations, lies of Jews around the world."

"But that's insane—"

"Is it? Go to one of the beer halls around the university one night, talk to the people there, the students. Half of them will not even speak of the Hitler era, although many of them think poor Adolf was badly maligned. They do not want to believe their parents were the monsters you are speaking of. They've known their parents all their lives, and they've always been good people, nice to children, pleasant with animals—"

"I know," Herzl said, "but to deny the holocaust is ridiculous! There's certainly enough proof, from Third Reich files alone, and libraries like yours—"

"The people who make these statements and who read these statements do not come to our library, they do not go to the files. They do not want the truth. They want to believe they have not descended from monsters. Your film will help them."

"In what way?"

"You still don't see? What are you going to find when you investigate these people in depth?"

"I've already found why von Schraeder hated Jews—"

She brushed this aside impatiently.

"Many people hate Jews; they don't even need reasons. But they don't kill them by the millions. Did von Schraeder hate Russians? Or Poles? He killed them in battle as a soldier, but does a soldier truly hate the man he is killing to the extent that he also kills that man's mother and father and son and daughter in gas ovens?" She shook her head. "I do not believe so. And did you discover why Eichmann hated Jews? If you do you will be the first. Yet he was in charge of the entire extermination program, and once said he would put his own father in the gas chamber if he were ordered to do so— and there is no indication that he hated his father."

"I still don't see—"

"I am trying to tell you. You do not want emotion; you do not want to show the camps or the horrors because that has been done too many times! Instead you just want to discover why these 'normal' people became monsters capable of the crimes they committed. When you have finished with your investigation you will find you are unable to discover any valid reason for the change. And do you know why? Because these people did *not* change. And the Germans will love anyone who demonstrates that fact."

He stared at her. "You're saying that they did what they did because they were German. You're a Jew but you're also German yourself."

"I'm not saying that at all. And as for my being German or not being German, you don't know Germans and you don't know me."

"My father is German—"

"You insist upon misunderstanding. It's also possible you don't know your father. But I am *not* saying they did what they did because they were Germans. The Russians did it, more than once; the Lithuanians did it. The Turks massacred over 600,000 Armenians in 1915, women and children included; the Manchus killed half a million to subdue Oirat in 1758. Chiang Kai-shek tried to outdo them in 1927 against the workers of Shanghai. The Americans did it to their Indians and they are doing it again this very minute in Southeast Asia."

"You're saying that anyone could do it," Herzl said slowly.

"Yes," she said simply. "All history proves it. Do you want your film to show this?"

"You're saying we are all monsters?" He leaned over the table. "What made you come to an idea like that?"

"The books in the library," she said. "The books in many libraries. You saw only a few in our one library. I've seen almost all of them. You saw a few feet of film. I've seen them all. Do you know that the neo-Nazi party in Germany is growing? Do you know there are neo —why do they call them neo? They're as old as history!—Nazi parties in England, in the United States, everywhere? But I am sure I will never convince you. You live in the safety of a Jewish state."

"With our Arabs," Herzl said dryly. "On all sides."

"Who supported Hitler during the war," Miriam said. "But you want to select a few Nazis and discover why they are different." She shrugged and looked at her watch, changing back to English. "But it's late. I must be leaving."

"No. Let's talk some more. Tell me why you're so bitter."

She looked genuinely surprised. "I'm not bitter. I'm simply a realist, a librarian who reads books. But I must leave."

"Just a while longer . . ."

"No."

"Then I'll see you home."

"No, I am preferring not." She came to her feet. "Thank you for a good—I mean, nice—evening."

He wished he could tell if she were sincere or being sardonic. "But

—wait—at least let me put you in a cab." He raised a hand for the waiter's attention.

"No. Please. I do not take taxis. The trolley passes very near my house." There was a finality in her voice that did not permit further discussion.

"But I'll see you tomorrow at the library?"

"Of course."

"And we won't miss lunch tomorrow, we'll take it together. And dinner. Possibly in a beer hall where I can meet students, and some of these neo-Nazis. Or we can eat anywhere you like. After all," Herzl said with a smile, "I'm a stranger in town, and as a native the least you can do is show me proper hospitality. For example, I would never have found this perfect restaurant if it hadn't been for you. I might have starved."

"Tomorrow in the library I am showing you the telephone book," Miriam said with only the faintest of smiles. "It has lines and lines full of restaurants."

She walked from the table, leaving him to look after her with an odd combination of curiosity and admiration, almost longingly. He had never felt like this before; he had never met anyone like her before. Beautiful, intelligent—although he would scarcely subscribe to her theory that all men were monsters—or potential monsters. Next to her he somehow felt callow, unsure, almost uneducated—with two years in the army and over three in pre-medical school. Rifkah Zimmerman suddenly came to mind. He had felt more adult with her. He suddenly smiled. And thank you, Rifkah, he said silently, for showing me what love was not. Maybe now I'm old enough to learn what love is, or could be. It will be interesting to get to know this Miriam Kleiman better, to prove to her that at least one man is no monster. He suddenly knew he was not going to leave Munich until he had had a chance to convince her of that, although he had no idea what argument could be called upon to help in making the judgment. Still, the longer it took, the better.

The thought was so enticing that the waiter had to tap Herzl on the shoulder several times before he looked up.

Chapter 3

The following day was a Wednesday, a rainy morning with a blustery wind that carried its chill through the streets of Munich, distributing it impartially among the souls leaning into it, struggling to reach their destination; but to Herzl Daniel Grossman the sun might have been shining brightly for all the attention he paid the weather. As he stood and rang the doorbell of the library all he could think of was Miriam Kleiman and the fact that he would be seeing her in a matter of minutes. He had counted the time since their dinner the night before in eons, and his great fear was that somehow she might have disappeared during the night, suddenly taken the job in London, packed and gone, or for some reason decided not to appear at work that day. But after being admitted, and after he had mounted the stairs to the second floor two at a time and tried not to burst into the room, there was Miriam Kleiman, as beautiful as ever, calmly studying a book behind her cluttered desk.

Herzl breathed easier. "Good morning!"

"Good morning," she said in an impersonal tone, quite as if they had never had dinner the night before, almost as if they had not met previously at all. Herzl knew he was being foolish but he could not help but feel hurt. He had known, of course, that she would scarcely throw herself into his arms at sight of him, but a bit more warmth might have been expected. After all, they had held hands the night before; or at least he had put his hand on hers for several moments before she pulled her hand away, and that ought to count for something. Could it be she felt so strongly against the film project that she was allowing it to affect their personal relationship? Well, he had the entire day in which to improve that relationship, and many more days should they be needed, and he expected to work hard at it. Miss Kleiman put down her book. "Your films are ready downstairs."

"Can't you join me? It's only film on von Schraeder, and from what you say there shouldn't be much footage on him. It will probably take only a few minutes."

"I'm sorry, but no. I have much work."

"Ah, well . . ." he said dispiritedly, and trudged from the room. Behind him Miss Kleiman smiled for several minutes, looking after him, before returning with a sigh to her book.

Rolf Steiner looked so sad when Herzl entered the small projection room that for a moment he wondered if something had happened to the film he wanted to see, but as soon as Steiner saw him the explanation was forthcoming.

"Almost nothing, a few clips is all, plus the one of the parade which I also put on the reel, just that part of it with von Schraeder on it, ah, yes, ODESSA, you know, they destroyed so much film, even file film, you know, a terrible thing, yes, oh yes . . ." He clicked his tongue.

"Whatever you have," Herzl said, his mind on Miriam Kleiman and really not all that interested in von Schraeder at the moment.

"Not much, not much, a pity, oh, yes . . ." Steiner clicked his tongue again and reached for the lights.

The first clip was the short section of the parade that Herzl had seen before. There was von Schraeder looking out of the car, smiling at the lens. The resemblance this time seemed to be even stronger at that younger age; uncanny! How could he have failed to notice it the day before? For a moment he had the odd feeling that it was him in the car, staring out at the people throwing streamers, and he could almost feel the car lurch as it stopped and started. Remarkable! he thought.

There was a click, a slight stutter, and the scene had changed. Now they were in a field outside a town that could be seen burning in the distance, the smoke being carried in waves across the sky; planes darted in and out of the smoke, but that was in the upper part of the film. In the lower section a group of German officers were standing next to a jeep whose engine hood was being used as a sort of table for maps which were unrolled on it. From both sides of the jeep officers bent over, their fingers tracing routes. Von Schraeder could be seen in the center of the group, pointing; a breeze came up and von Schraeder put his arm down awkwardly to prevent the top map from blowing.

"Poland," Steiner said succinctly. "October 1939. Near Lezsno, as near as we can tell."

The officers on the screen nodded to one another, raised their arms in an abrupt Nazi salute, and marched off. Only von Schraeder remained, rolling up the maps, smiling broadly. The camera came in close, wobbling a bit as if it had been taken from its tripod and was being hand-held for the close-up. Von Schraeder winked first with one eye, then with the other, laughed, and turned away. Herzl frowned. There was something in the way von Schraeder had half saluted, something in the manner in which he rolled up the maps, that teased Herzl's memory. And that winking first with one eye and then with the other . . . But before he could follow up the thought there was a click, the usual slight stutter from the projector, and they were looking at a new scene. His attention moved with the film.

"Maidanek," Steiner said, and added a trifle apologetically, "We have nothing from his time in Russia although he spent almost a year there. The Russians undoubtedly must have some captured film, but—" He shrugged.

The scene was basically like the one in the first book he had seen, the photograph taken by the brave but foolhardy prisoner. In this one, however, no prisoners or civilians could be seen. The film showed an open area with four uniformed officers standing about as if waiting for someone or something, and while the identifying tall chimney seen in the book was not in evidence, the barracks-like buildings were there, and the barbed-wire fence that stretched almost out of sight before bending to disappear behind a tiny watchtower in the distance, clearly identifying the place as a concentration camp. The men spoke idly to one another and then suddenly could be seen coming to attention, drawing themselves in a line. The camera swung; a car was drawing up, coming to a stop in the area. The driver got down and hurried around the long black sedan to open the rear door and instantly spring to rigid attention. The man who got down wore a monocle; he was tall and quite thin, and impeccably uniformed.

"Eichmann," Steiner said a bit breathlessly. "Eichmann," he

repeated softly, excitedly, and fell silent, watching as if he had never seen the clip before.

Eichmann approached the line of men, smiled, and extended his hand, shaking hands cordially with each one in turn. Then he stepped back and one by one the officers facing him stepped forward to be rewarded with medals which Eichmann took from an attendant at his side and pinned to the man's uniform blouse. Von Schraeder was the last to step forward, bend rigidly at the waist for a fraction of an inch, straighten, and stand like a statue while the medal was pinned to his chest. Like the others he then stepped backward one pace and saluted.

That was when the resemblance struck Herzl—

That raised arm—or, rather, that half-raised arm! That movement in rolling up the maps, as if the full extension of the arm to roll them up in one smooth motion was somehow lacking! And that wink, first with the left eye and then with the right! Benjamin Grossman used to amuse his young son with that droll grimace many years before, laughing afterward and tickling his giggling youngster.

He sat, stunned, as the lights went on and Steiner started to respool the film, talking as he did so.

"It's all we have on the man, I'm sorry but that's all, as I say the Russians may have more but . . . A pity so much was destroyed, ah, yes, criminal, criminal! Lucky we even have this . . . oh, yes . . ."

Herzl sat and stared at the blank screen, trying to bring his confused thoughts into some order. It was a coincidence, of course, a monstrous coincidence. Helmut von Schraeder was dead, that had been witnessed and attested to; he had died of typhus at Buchenwald. The Germans were too organized to make a mistake on something like that. And Benjamin Grossman was alive, a hero of Israel, a brigadier general in the army, as well as being a wonderful father. What he, Herzl, had been thinking was not only impossible, but was stupid, vicious, and cruel. Someone had once postulated a theory that everyone in the world had a double somewhere, someone born the instant he was born, who acted in every respect as he acted, who looked in every respect as he looked—except that the one who resembled von Schraeder in that uncanny fashion was not Benjamin Grossman, but his son. But it had to be a coincidence, because anything else was too dreadful to contemplate. And besides, Helmut von Schraeder was dead. . . .

He could not remember getting up, leaving the small projection room without even thanking the voluble Rolf Steiner, or finding the stairs to the first floor and then to the second. He walked through the door into the large library and stared at Miriam Kleiman as if he had never seen her before.

She was shocked by the blankness on his face, by the ashen complexion.

"You are all right? Is the film bothering you?"

"Von Schraeder," he said, and it sounded to him as if the words were coming from some disembodied person at his side. "What do you have on his death? The details?"

She looked puzzled. "But I am showing you everything yesterday. It is all we have except for the testimony on the war trials that you are already reading—"

"I don't remember. Could I see—?"

"Of course."

She hurried to the stacks while Herzl sank down in a chair and stared numbly at the table. When at last she brought the proper volume and slid it before him, opened to the proper page, he stared at the book for several moments before shaking his head violently as if to clear it of cobwebs, and then forced himself to concentrate on the words before him. Miriam Kleiman retreated to her desk slowly, and watched him anxiously, perplexed at what could have effected the profound change in the young man in such a short time. He had seemed such a stable sort, but possibly he was not; as she recalled, the films were certainly not that disturbing.

Testimony of Colonel Reginald Manley-Jones, British Army interrogator at Bergen-Belsen camp after liberation.

Q: . . . von Schraeder?

A: In regard to Colonel Helmut von Schraeder, I interrogated all prisoners who had previously been at Maidanek and Buchenwald, the camps at which von Schraeder functioned in a supervisory post. All prisoners were quite critical—

Q: In reference to his death, please, Colonel.

A: Oh, that? Well, several said they thought they had heard in a roundabout way that von Schraeder had died at Buchenwald, but one prisoner was more definite. He said he

had been working in Ward Forty-six—the typhus ward, I
believe it was—and was actually there when Colonel von
Schraeder died. He stated that there was no possibility of
error. He said he was the one who had to sew von
Schraeder's corpse into the burial sack and help to cart him
to the crematorium. It didn't bother the man a bit. He had
been a *Sonderkommando* at Maidanek, and they were used
to that sort of thing, I suppose. Animals, really, you know—

Q: If you please, Colonel, those remarks are not in keeping
with the purpose of this investigation. To get back to the
inquiry, do you believe the prisoner—I mean, the liberated
inmate—do you believe his testimony was correct? As far
as von Schraeder was concerned?

A: Oh, he was telling the truth, all right, no doubt of that.
Why would he lie? He enjoyed telling me how Colonel von
Schraeder died.

Herzl turned the page, feeling better, ashamed of himself for the
gross and unwarranted suspicions he had entertained. Colonel Helmut von Schraeder was dead, all right.

Q: And what was the name of the liberated inmate being
interrogated?

A: I have it here someplace in my notes. I remember him,
scrawny bastard, all ears and nose—

Q: Please, Colonel, just the name. For the record.

A: Here it is. Benjamin Grossman. Said he was from Hamburg—

Herzl stared at the words in shock, and then slowly closed the
book as if he could also close the information from his mind with
the motion, but the words stood out in large letters in his brain.
Benjamin Grossman.
Benjamin Grossman, the only one to see Helmut von Schraeder
die, the one who had sewed him into the burial sack and saw that he
was cremated. Benjamin Grossman, who the testimony said worked
in Ward Forty-six; but Herzl's Uncle Max had told him once that
his father, Benjamin Grossman, had been in Ward Forty-six as a victim of bestial experimental surgery. Surgery. Scars. Surgery, Herzl

suddenly thought, but *plastic* surgery! Benjamin Grossman, who came from Hamburg where all records were destroyed, most probably born when Helmut von Schraeder died! Benjamin Grossman, graduate in mechanical engineering, fierce and fearless warrior . . .

Herzl became aware that someone was talking, that it was not just an echo in his mind. He looked up and saw it was a girl sitting at a desk.

"Did you say something? Were you speaking to me?"

"I ask if you are all right. You are not looking too very well—"

"I'm—" What had he wanted to ask her? Oh, yes. "Do you have any further information on von Schraeder—any other books you might have missed, anything at all?"

She shook her head. "I'm sorry."

He remembered something else, but at the moment could not recall where he had heard it. "Somebody said something about another library. In London, I believe?"

"I am telling you myself, last night," she said, and now she sounded really worried. "The Wiener Library. It's on Devonshire Street, number four. Why? You go there? When?"

"Tonight," he said vaguely. "This afternoon, if I can." He remembered something else. "Is it possible to get copies of the film clips I saw this morning?"

"Yes. There is a laboratory in town who does this work."

He drew his checkbook from his pocket, scribbled his signature, and tore the check out, handing it over.

"Fill in the amount," he said. "Add postage. Airmail, first-class, to—" He stopped to think a moment, his mind still foggy. "To Zion Films, to my attention. Herzl Grossman." He fumbled in his pocket for his letter of introduction, handing it over. "The address . . ."

She accepted it, looking at him strangely, wondering for a moment if there had been anything she might have said or done to cause this sudden change in him, in his attitude toward her, in his plans. Surely he understood that a girl did not let a man take her home the first date. But that was ridiculous; they were strangers, and he had been so friendly when he first arrived that morning. A pity he was leaving; he was very attractive and she would have liked to have dinner with him again, to get to know him better, and even let him take her home this time. But he obviously had not been serious, he had forgotten already. A pity . . .

"Wait, I write down the Wiener Library address for you," she said, and reached for a slip of paper. "I am also giving you a little note to them," she added, and wrote.

He waited, staring around the room, his mind in a state of shock. He was the son of Helmut von Schraeder! How long before the same tendencies would appear in him, the same ability to kill and kill and kill without conscience? But it could not be; violence disgusted him, blood sickened him—or was this something he had inherited from his mother? What had someone said to him recently? We are all monsters. . . . But the entire thing had to be a mistake, a horrible coincidence but a coincidence just the same. Benjamin Grossman, his father, the same man as Helmut von Schraeder? Ridiculous!

Actually, what was the basis for this vicious canard? The similarity of his looking like the man; the fact that Benjamin Grossman was the only witness to the death of the man, a pure coincidence since obviously someone had to sew him into his shroud and it just happened to be a prisoner named Grossman; the uniqueness of a few similar gestures that a thousand or a million men probably used to entertain their children, winking with alternate eyes! Looked at in this light, or any other rational light, the suspicion was idiotic. . . .

He became aware the girl was handing him something. What—? Oh, yes, of course, the address of the library in London and a note to the personnel there. He tucked it into his jacket pocket without looking at it.

"Thank you," he said without realizing he had said it, and walked blindly from the room.

The people at the Wiener Library in London were as helpful as possible, but the fact was they had nothing to add to what he had learned about Helmut von Schraeder in Munich. Fingerprints? No, there was no record of any for many of the Nazi war criminals; ODESSA had seen to that. Yes, they were quite sure; the Allies had made a search in depth. Photographs? They had the same studio picture as well as the same book photograph, but that was all. The librarian who helped him was a Miss Pizer, an elderly lady, and he remembered with a sharp pang Miriam Kleiman and wondered at his cavalier action in walking out without giving her the courtesy of an explanation. True, he had been stunned, but in retrospect that seemed like a small excuse. He really should call her, try to explain—

but what would he say? I'm almost positive I'm the son of Helmut von Schraeder, the Monster of Maidanek, the man who was responsible for the gassing and burning of over a million people, including Germans like yourself. How would you like to have dinner with me and possibly get to know me well enough even to fall in love?

Or *am* I the son of Helmut von Schraeder? Wouldn't I have felt it before this if I were? Could my mother, Deborah, have fallen as much in love as she obviously is with a murderer like von Schraeder? At least Herzl was responsible enough, now, to order photocopies of the pictures, and the testimony of Colonel Manley-Jones, as well as the other facts from the files before leaving the library, and then he left to trudge the streets of London, unable to resolve the problem.

He sat in his hotel room the following day, staring from the window at a heavy fog, trying to think what to do next. Go home without knowing for sure, *for absolutely sure*, whether Benjamin Grossman was or was not the man he suspected him of being? How could he go through life with that question always unanswered? How could he face his father? Or his mother? How could he live with the uncertainty?

The answer was that he could not. Hamburg—should he go there and attempt to trace Benjamin Grossman, to try and locate someone who might be able to remember a Grossman family who had a son named Benjamin? Born in April of 1917? Except that Hamburg had been utterly destroyed, wiped out, all records gone as well as all the people who lived there. But some had escaped before the fire storm, before Hitler, gone to America. Advertise? For a fact that was now almost thirty years old, just since the death of von Schraeder, and over fifty since the birth of this mythical Grossman? Not likely. What about Angermünde? On a sudden inspiration he picked up the telephone and was connected with the hotel operator.

"East Germany?" she said. "Of course. What city and what number?"

"Angermünde, in Mecklenburg," he said. "I don't have the number, but I would like to speak with someone in the records section of their city hall. Is it possible?"

"Of course. However," she added, "you may be monitored by the police there if you don't mind."

"I don't mind."

"In that case I will ring you when the call comes through."

He hung up the receiver and shook his head sadly. What was he going to ask them when he was finally connected? Helmut von Schraeder had left Angermünde when he was less than nine years old; what could their records show that could possibly identify—or not identify—the man with Benjamin Grossman? But he had to do something; he couldn't just sit and wonder. He came to his feet and started to pace the room, and then made a sudden move for the telephone as it began to ring.

"Yes? Hello—?"

"Your party is on the line." And in a lower tone of voice, "You are being monitored . . ."

He could not have cared less. There were a series of clicks, and eventually the voice of a woman in German, sounding quite efficient. "Records. May I help you?"

Herzl took a deep breath.

"I hope so," he said. "I'm looking for any information I can get about a family named von Schraeder—"

"Von?" said the voice, mystified. "We have not had any 'vons' for—"

"I'm speaking of a family that left Angermünde in 1925 or 1926," Herzl said hurriedly.

"I'm sorry," the voice said, and it seemed to sound relieved at not being able to help. "Our records were completely destroyed during the war. Totally. All of them. Now they begin again after 1946."

"Not even—" Herzl knew he was wasting his time. "Thank you," he said dispiritedly, and hung up.

It appeared as if both von Schraeder and Benjamin Grossman were beyond investigation. No records anywhere. No fingerprints, and photographs that meant little or nothing at all. Why not leave it at that? Forget it. Put the resemblance down as an odd similitude. Why beat a dead horse? But he couldn't drop the matter and he knew it. Another thought suddenly occurred to him and he raised the telephone again quickly, before he could convince himself it was useless. The hotel operator came on the line.

"This may sound insane," Herzl said apologetically, wondering if she would hang up and call the authorities and not blaming her if she did, "but I'm really quite serious. I want to talk to the oldest person at a church in Angermünde. Not a parishioner," he added hastily. "A priest, a minister—" He shook his head helplessly. "I don't know."

He might have been asking for a connection to room service or to another guest in the hotel for all the surprise his request evinced from the operator; he wondered for a moment at the nature of some of the requests she received.

"Which denomination, sir?"

"I don't know," he said, now convinced he must really be insane. "I have no idea of the denomination." He knew it sounded stupid, but there was nothing else he could say. He felt like kicking himself; surely the information as to the von Schraeder family's religion had been available at either library had he had the intelligence to think of it. "What religion is most common in East Germany?"

"They are Communist," the operator said, as if this answered his question.

"But they must have churches—!"

"A few, probably," she said, conceding the possibility. "Lutheran, possibly?"

It was as good as any. "Would you try them please? If there is only one Lutheran church, I suppose we'll have to try other denominations—"

"There won't be many of those, either," the operator said, and repeated, ". . . oldest person . . . not a parishioner," quite as if the request was completely normal. "I'll ring through to you."

This time the wait was interminable. Herzl looked at his watch every minute until he realized this made the time creep even more slowly. After that he picked up the morning newspaper, but the words made no sense at all and he tossed it aside, staring out the window at the fog. What was the weather like in Munich at this hour? It would be ten in the morning there; what would Miriam Kleiman be doing at this minute? Going through the mail? Having a cup of tea? Helping another researcher who would probably ask her out to dinner? The thought rankled. He really ought to write to her and apologize for his behavior the day before, maybe even go back to Munich and explain to her in person. But if he discovered anything in Angermünde he would have to go there and get affidavits, sworn statements. And he would have to advise Zion Films where he was, and why. That might take some doing, although he really wouldn't have to explain until he got back—

The telephone rang.

He reached for it eagerly. "Hello?"

"Your call."

Another operator on the line, another language. Again, "Your call . . ."

He continued to wait, hearing breathing at the end of the line, but nobody spoke. "Hello? Is anyone there?"

Finally, "Yes?"

"Hello? May I ask who I'm speaking to?"

The voice at the other end was instantly suspicious. "Who is asking?"

"My name is Grossman," Herzl said, feeling ridiculous to be identifying himself to some stranger who had no idea who he was or why he was calling. "I'm looking for information, any information, I can get about a family named von Schraeder. They left—"

"Von?"

There it was again!

"They left Angermünde in 1925 or 1926," Herzl said desperately. "An aunt and a boy, after both parents died. The father was General von Schraeder. The mother's name was Langer, her maiden name. I thought possibly there might be some church records. The town records were destroyed—"

"We have no records of anyone of that name." The voice sounded positive, which Herzl thought extremely odd considering that there had been no attempt to verify any of the facts.

"But—"

"Good-bye!" There was a sharp click as the telephone at the other end was hung up abruptly.

The telephone rang again almost instantly.

"I did not lose the connection to Angermünde," the hotel operator said, and for the first time there was a touch of emotion in her voice; it was pride. "I will now ring the second church. It is also the last church as far as we can tell," she added as if to say I told you so, and disconnected.

He sat with the receiver to his ear, listening to the eerie exchange of sounds and languages between unknown parties, and then found himself alone on the line.

"Hello?" he said tentatively.

The answering voice was faint, quavering with age. "Yes?"

"Could I ask who I'm talking to?"

"My name is Father Gruenwald. You wish—?"

Herzl took another deep breath. He had a feeling he was wasting his time but he also knew there was nothing better to do with his time until the riddle was solved.

"I am looking for information about a family named von Schraeder, General von Schraeder," he said, speaking slowly, evenly, and as clearly as possible, and feeling as if he had repeated the statement a hundred times that morning. "They left Angermünde in the year 1925 or 1926—"

"They did not leave," the wavering voice said, sounding petulant at the incorrectness of the statement. "They are buried in our churchyard, both the general and his wife."

Herzl felt an electric shock.

"Helmut von Schraeder—" he began.

"No, no!" said the old voice querulously. "Karl Klaus! General Karl Klaus! We were children together. He always sat in the front pew, on the left. We played chess together every Thursday—"

"But they had a son," Herzl said insistently, his fingers biting into the molded rubber of the receiver.

"—he always took the black, even without choosing, but of course he was the better player. I don't play anymore . . ."

"They had a son," Herzl said, trying to pierce the curtain of the past. "His name was Helmut. Helmut. There must be some records—"

"A son?" Father Gruenwald sounded doubtful. "I do not remember—"

Herzl gritted his teeth. Not now! he thought. Not when we're this close! "A son," he said, as if by mere repetition he could bring the old man's memory back. "His name was Helmut."

There was a pause as Father Gruenwald did his best to remember; then with a sigh he conceded defeat to the years that had gone. "I'm sorry." A thought occurred. "But maybe my housekeeper will remember," he added with a slight brightening in his voice. "She worked at the von Schraeder estates as a—maid?—when she was young. Or was it as the cook . . ." There was a pause as the old voice could he heard raising itself feebly. "Magda!" There was another pause and then Father Gruenwald returned to Herzl apologetically. "I will get her. She doesn't hear too well without her hearing aid, I'm afriad. I will insist she put it on. She hates it, you know . . ."

There was a murmur of voices in the background; then an old woman's voice was on the line. She sounded very suspicious, as if telephone calls to the church were rare, and then only to bring trouble.

"What do you want?"

"I was speaking with Father Gruenwald about the von Schraeder family," Herzl said, trying to sound as diplomatic as possible, as little like an East German police official as possible, "and I was asking about their son—"

"What about him?"

Herzl felt the repeat of the shock at finally having found someone who might be helpful. He tried to maintain the same tone of voice, afraid to break the spell.

"Do you remember him?"

"He's dead," the old lady said. "His name was Helmut. He was a pretty boy—"

Herzl took a deep breath and asked the important question. It was just the sort of thing a person could so easily slip up on, as he might slip up on winking alternately with both eyes at a spellbound child.

"When Helmut was a child," he said slowly, clearly, "did he ever fall out of a tree and break his arm?"

The old lady took the receiver from her ear and stared into it suspiciously as if the person at the other end of the wire had lost his senses. Who called up to ask a ridiculous question like that about a little boy fifty years before? Then she shrugged and adjusted her hearing aid. If someone wanted to waste their time asking idiotic questions, it was no problem of hers.

"No," she said.

Herzl felt his heart jump. "You're sure?"

"Of course I'm sure," she said disdainfully. "You think I don't remember just because I'm old? I should know, I took him to the doctor myself. It wasn't his arm. It was his shoulder."

Chapter 4

To Brigadier General Benjamin Grossman, the city of Buenos
Aires was quite reminiscent of Paris when he had visited the City of
Lights on a long rest-and-recreation holiday from the war shortly
after the fall of that city to the Germans in June of 1940. He had
been young then, only twenty-three years of age, the same age as his
son Herzl was now, and he now had discovered a similar place, a city
that also made a great impression on him. While the yellow, muddy
Plate was no Seine, and while the rather stocky Argentinian women
were not the coquettes of Paris, still Buenos Aires had the same
broad boulevards, the same florally decorated squares and parks, the
same statues of horsemen carrying unfurled banners or of maidens
modestly covering themselves while water spouted from their navels,
and—the general was pleased to find—the same delicious food,
which was not always the case in most Tel Aviv restaurants. His trip
had been quite successful, his mission being accomplished to the satisfaction of both his superiors in Israel and the generals in the Casa
Rosada, and as he sat down to his dinner in the dining room of his
hotel that night before his departure, he was in the best of moods.

He did not remain in the best of moods for long.

As he studied the menu in the noisy restaurant, attempting to determine the most fitting final meal before leaving such a gourmet's
paradise, he was interrupted by the diplomatic clearing of a throat at
his shoulder. He looked up to find a waiter there. The waiter bore a
tray and the tray bore an empty but sparkling balloon glass together
with a bottle as yet unopened of what he recognized as an excellent
Argentinian brandy and one he had enjoyed before during his visit.
He looked at the waiter in some surprise.

"I didn't order this."

"I know, señor. It is from the gentlemen over there."

The waiter tipped his head the merest fraction of an inch in the direction of a nearby table even as he put the tray down and proceeded to expertly remove the cork from the bottle. Benjamin Grossman turned around with a smile. He had wondered a bit at not having been entertained on his last night by the emissaries of the Departmento de Abasticimientos with whom he had dealt in his mission—especially since they had seemed so insistent upon his eating at this particular restaurant—but apparently their hospitality was to be extended in another form. But the two men at the other table were certainly not the men he had dealt with during his trip, and he felt that most probably an unfortunate mistake had been made. He looked up questioningly at the waiter.

"Who are they, do you know? Is there a card?"

"There is no card, señor. I do not know who they are, but they said they were old friends."

The waiter completed his task by neatly pouring the balloon glass to a faint line in the crystal one quarter way up and left, taking the tray but leaving the bottle of brandy. Grossman frowned and turned again. One of the two men had risen and was approaching his table. The man was tall, a bit stooped, and had a full head of hair fashionably curling about his ears and unusually thick and dark for the lines in his face. He smiled as he came up in friendly fashion and held out his hand, speaking in German.

"Benjamin, it's good to see you after all these years!"

Grossman accepted the hand and shook it in puzzled fashion. "I'm afraid you have the advantage—"

"Benjamin Grossman, don't tell me you don't recognize me! Ah, the hair, no doubt. Still, it would be poor form to remove it here, with all these good people eating." The man pulled up a chair and sat down. At the other table the second man simply sat and waited, his face wreathed in the smoke of the thick cigar between his lips. The man at Grossman's table dropped his voice. "It's been a while, of course. Twenty-seven years since I operated on your face—"

Grossman felt a sudden frightening jolt to his stomach.

"*Schlossberg!*"

"Not so loud. Not that it really matters here," Schlossberg said, and tilted his head to one side, examining the features he had created such a long time before. He nodded in satisfaction. "Not bad, if I say so myself. It has stood up quite well. Of course I do surgery no longer. Actually, you were one of my last patients; I'm pleased it turned out so well."

The doctor had gained a little weight, and the hairpiece changed his appearance greatly; in general, age had treated Franz Schlossberg kindly. The greatest difference was in his attitude. He no longer appeared to be the diffident, apprehensive man Grossman had known in the camps, but instead now seemed to exude a confidence that added to Grossman's sense of unreality. The second man, seeing the ice had been broken, now came to his feet and walked to their table. After the shock of Schlossberg, Grossman was really not surprised to see it was Klaus Mittendorf. Mittendorf smiled blandly and sat down on the other side of Grossman.

"Well, well! Hello, Colonel. Or should I say, Brigadier General?"

Grossman looked around the dining room in sudden panic, unable to believe that all eyes were not upon them, all ears tuned to their discussion, but the other diners seemed to be paying no attention at all, and he realized the restaurant chosen by the two for their confrontation was ideal for their purposes. The noise level was high and the food and drink such as to focus the attention of the diners on their plates and glasses. He brought his own attention back to the men on either side of him.

"How—how did you find me?"

"Find you?" Mittendorf said, sounding surprised. "My dear Colonel, we never lost you." Mittendorf was enjoying himself immensely. They had known who and what Benjamin Grossman was for years, and where he was, and for all those years he had wanted to expose the man. And for all those years the ODESSA organization had insisted they would eventually find a use for Grossman and that they were not interested in personal revenge. And in this respect he had to admit the organization had been right. But, now! What pleasure in combining his revenge with the requirements of the organization! "We never lost you, Colonel," he said again, bringing the words past the cigar in his mouth, savoring the words as much as the cigar.

"My dear Helmut," Schlossberg said quietly, "you always insisted that I call you Helmut, remember?—you didn't really believe I would operate on you, change your appearance, and not tell the Party, did you? We have followed the career of Benjamin Grossman

with intense interest all these years, believe me. We were pleased
when you survived Bergen-Belsen—"

"Some people were pleased, some not so pleased," Mittendorf
said, and chuckled. "How was it there, Colonel? Bad, eh? Real bad?"

Schlossberg cut in smoothly with a chiding glance at Mittendorf.

"And with your picture all over every airport and dock when the
British were going to hang you for murder in Palestine, we could
hardly miss that, could we? With our contacts among the Arabs?
And of course since then you've become quite a hero with your name
in the newspapers quite often. How did we find you?" He shrugged.
"As Klaus says, we never lost you."

Grossman suddenly reached out and picked up the glass of brandy,
downing it quickly. It seemed to calm him a bit. He waved aside the
waiter who had approached once the glass had been emptied, and
poured himself a second drink, but did not drink it. He looked at
Schlossberg evenly.

"I introduced you to ODESSA. It saved your life."

"And I appreciate it."

"Do you? I also gave you money—"

"I appreciate that as well. It enabled me to live quite comfortably
until my ranch began to produce. I'm rather a wealthy man now,
and I admit I owe a good bit of it to you."

Mittendorf laughed. "And you couldn't get the rest out! Ah, Colonel, the mistakes you made!" The heavy-set Mittendorf was having
fun. What a pleasure to see the concern, the panic, on the thin Jew-
face of the bastard when Schlossberg had sat down at the table! No
arrogance now; none of that supercilious shit from the bastard now!
No important friends in Berlin to lean on now; no family name
other than one that didn't even exist! What a joy!

"So you know that, too?" Grossman was looking at him, seeing
the same Mittendorf, feeling the same contempt for the man he had
always felt. The very contempt took the panic away; his mind began
to function again. Mittendorf would really never be a danger, but
the new Dr. Schlossberg might well be.

"We know everything there is to know about Brigadier General
Benjamin Grossman," Schlossberg said quietly. "And about his wife,
Deborah, who is head hurse at the Magen David Adom first-aid station, and about his son, Herzl, and about everything else. Just as we
know everything about Mengele and Bormann and the others who

escaped the hangman and who someday we may call upon for their services."

"So ODESSA still exists . . ."

"Of course it still exists," Mittendorf said contemptuously.

"And you two are still a part of it?"

"We *three* are still a part of it," Schlossberg said evenly.

"And what does that mean?"

Schlossberg leaned back comfortably, the introductions over, ready for the business of the evening.

"It means we have a job for you."

"And if I refuse your job?"

"Not my job; *our* job. And why would you refuse?" Schlossberg asked, as if puzzled by the question. "You, a dedicated member of the Party? You took an oath as a gentleman and an officer of the SS. I knew when I operated upon you that you wished to save your life only for and until the day you could once again do your best for the Party, no? So why would you possibly refuse?"

"Besides," Mittendorf added, his tiny eyes dancing with mirth, the smoke fairly exploding from his cigar as he chuckled around it, "who would put you on trial first? Who would have the opportunity to hang the famous Colonel Helmut von Schraeder, the Monster of Maidanek, eh? Poland? The Russians? Or—Israel, as they did Eichmann?" He laughed. "They would spend fortunes outbidding each other for you."

Schlossberg looked at Mittendorf reprovingly.

"There is no need for threats, I am sure. Colonel von Schraeder knows his duty and as a dedicated officer I am sure he is ready to perform it."

Grossman sat quietly, listening to the not very subtle sarcasm, staring into the amber depths of his brandy glass, fingering the delicate crystal gently. At last he sighed and looked up.

"All right. What do you want?"

"That's better—"

Schlossberg pulled his chair a trifle closer to Grossman. It was evident that he was in charge of the operation and that Mittendorf had been permitted to attend only as a concession to his ancient feelings of hatred. Schlossberg spoke quietly and slowly.

"In 1965," he said, "some six years ago, several hundred pounds of enriched uranium were stolen—or borrowed, or lost, or begged, or strayed, it makes little difference—from an enriching plant in the state of Pennsylvania in the United States of America. The factory, incidentally, was owned by a Jew. You know of this missing uranium, of course." Grossman sat silent, watching the other man, his face expressionless.

"Of course you do," Schlossberg said evenly, not permitting the slightest doubt, and went on. "Then just a few years ago, in France, a truck carrying a much larger cargo of uranium—not yellow-cake but again enriched—was hijacked. This time we estimate the amount taken was substantial; many tons. And with this enriched uranium, as I'm sure you know, any decent scientific organization can quite easily produce atomic weapons."

He was watching Grossman closely now, watching for the slightest change on the man's rigid face, any sign that Grossman's reaction would indicate he was striking home.

"Now," Schlossberg went on, "we are convinced that all of this uranium ended up in Israel." He held up his hand. "Before you waste your time denying this, if you intend to, I might mention that we are not alone in this belief. The Federal Bureau of Investigation and the CIA in the United States are equally sure."

Grossman raised an eyebrow. "ODESSA has men in the FBI and the CIA?"

"ODESSA has men everywhere," Mittendorf said, and suddenly smirked. "We even have a brigadier general in the Israeli Army named Benjamin Grossman, don't we?"

Schlossberg waved him to silence, concentrating on Grossman. "Where we have men and where we don't has nothing to do with it. Getting back to this enriched uranium, we are sure not all of it has been processed into weapons; the amount would indicate an inordinate number of weapons beyond any immediate need. Besides, there undoubtedly will be further developments in the field, developments that will also require enriched uranium. So we believe Israel is holding, in its original pellet form, a great deal of this uranium."

He looked around the room, satisfying himself that their conversation was entirely private and that the three of them appeared to be nothing more than three associates discussing business over a brandy. Grossman waited patiently, his face a mask, anticipating the demand soon to be made upon him. Schlossberg nodded.

"You know what we want, of course. Israel has so much enriched uranium they won't even miss the small amount we need. Fifty pounds . . ."

Grossman pursed his lips. "For exactly what purpose?"

Schlossberg looked disappointed, as if his high opinion of the other's intelligence had suddenly been put in doubt.

"For the obvious reason, of course," he said, and leaned closer, his eyes alight with enthusiasm, almost fanatacism. "Can you picture the power of any group—of our group, ODESSA—holding the threat of an atomic weapon in our hands? We could get all the money we needed. We could get anyone out of prison we wanted, even Hess, the poor sod. In comparison with the idiots who hijack airplanes, we could really *demand!*"

"True," Grossman said in agreement, since it obviously was true. "But who would believe you had the bomb unless you detonated it? And if you detonated it, what would you have left for your threat?"

Schlossberg smiled at him, a pitying smile.

"You were the one who always believed in having two strings to your bow. It takes about twenty-two pounds of enriched uranium to make a small bomb; fifty pounds will do us nicely for two bombs. One bomb will be dropped in a suitable place—the Negev or the Sinai, possibly—to prove we are serious. The second will be held in abeyance as the threat. As a very real threat!" He looked at Grossman directly. "And please don't tell us you know nothing of this material or where it is stored in Israel. We would scarcely believe you."

Grossman looked back at the man, his face expressionless. Mittendorf leaned over.

"And if we didn't believe you, we might have to denounce you to the Jews . . ."

Grossman smiled gently. He had been expecting this threat since the two men joined him at his table, and had formulated his response once his initial panic had left him.

"To begin with," he said easily, "would our friend Dr. Schlossberg, who was tried and sentenced to death in absentia in Nuremberg, and you, Mittendorf, who the Poles and Russians are still looking for after all these years—would you two charming gentlemen be in any position to testify at any trial I might be asked to undergo? I rather doubt it." He smiled and continued. "Secondly, even if you were foolhardly enough to present yourselves, who would believe you? It would be your word against mine—two known war criminals against the word of a man who suffered a year in Bergen-Belsen and later became a hero—if you'll forgive the immodesty—in his adopted country's army. And your motive for formulating this lie would be easily determined—to weaken the Israeli Army, undoubtedly at the behest of the Arabs. Thirdly, of course, is a matter of proof. ODESSA was kind enough to eliminate any records of Colonel Helmut von Schraeder, and the Allied bombers over Hamburg were kind enough to totally eliminate any possible records of a fictitious Benjamin Grossman. So, gentlemen—" He spread his hands apologetically. "I should think if there were to be any threats, they would come from my side, not yours."

"Although they would also not get very far," Schlossberg said, "since both Klaus and I have well-established identities other than our original ones in a place you will never know, and not in Argentina, if that is any help to you. You should be flattered; we traveled a long way to meet you tonight." Schlossberg sighed. "I was afraid a brilliant man such as you would see the weakness of our argument," he said regretfully. "Our first argument, that is . . ."

"And your second argument?"

Mittendorf leaned over, his tiny eyes almost buried in the fat of his face. "How would you like to be found in La Boca or floating in the Plate with a knife in your belly?" he said savagely, almost spitting the words past the cigar.

Grossman brushed away the smoke; he seemed to be brushing the threat away with it. After all, he had always known nothing could be done to avoid the possibility of personal violence.

"If you think that will advance your interests—"

"No, no!" Schlossberg said impatiently. "Klaus, be quiet! That certainly is not our second argument—"

"Then—?"

"Your family," Schlossberg said quietly, and watched Grossman closely. "Our information is that you are quite attached to them. Let me see . . ." He seemed to be considering the matter. "A Jew mother and a Jew son. It would not be such a tragic loss at that, I suppose, so possibly that wouldn't really constitute much of a threat, eh?"

Despite his control, Grossman's face had whitened.

"However," Schlossberg went on in a conciliatory tone, "it is pointless to consider such unpleasant things. Colonel von Schraeder, I am sure, will do his duty."

He smiled and leaned back, a thin figure with sharp piercing eyes and a bushy wig, but impressive despite the overdone hair. He was a far different figure from the indecisive, hesitant Dr. Schlossberg who had ridden with von Schraeder from Lublin to Weimar so many years before, rubbing his bald pate incessantly and mumbling all his patriotic nonsense. What a little money and a little power can do! Grossman thought. Schlossberg leaned forward again, sure his message had been received.

"Assuming you are not interested in the technical side of the material we are discussing," he said, "let me tell you something about the enriched uranium you will be delivering. It will not be a large package; the fifty pounds that we require will fit easily into your attaché case. It will undoubtedly be in the form of what are called pellets, that is, compressed granules; and each pellet will be about the size of a soup can. I would suggest that you take some ordinary kitchen bars of paraffin with you to separate the pellets in your attaché case; cadmium would be better but I cannot imagine where you would locate cadmium without raising suspicions and we do not want to make your mission any more difficult than necessary. Actually, I am quite sure the pellets are already coated, but the kitchen paraffin would be an extra precaution. Incidentally, as I'm sure you already know, there is not enough radioactivity in the material in its present state to affect anyone carrying it."

Grossman sat quietly, his face a mask.

"Now," Schlossberg said, getting to the nub of the matter, "we estimate two weeks should be more than sufficient for you to get your hands on fifty pounds of it. How you manage is your problem"—he paused as Mittendorf smirked—"but I should not fail if I were you."

"And when—and if—I have it?"

"You will be instructed."

"How?"

"You will be instructed," Schlossberg repeated and came to his feet, motioning Mittendorf to join him. He bent slightly at the waist with old-world courtesy and indicated with a slight wave of his hand the almost-full bottle of brandy on the table. "It is paid for. And it was good to see you again. *Bon appetit.*"

He nodded, smiled, and walked away confidently, with Mittendorf

hurrying to catch up. Behind them they left an extremely troubled
Benjamin Grossman, for once without a plan.

In the street Klaus Mittendorf threw away his cigar and looked at
his companion.

"Do you think he'll do it?"

"I am quite positive he will do it."

"But how can you be so sure?"

"My dear Klaus," Schlossberg said, wondering as always why the
organization tolerated an idiot like Mittendorf, "why do you think
we planned this meeting so carefully? Why do you think we planned
the entire operation so carefully?"

"I know, but—"

"Weren't you paying the slightest attention to our conversation in
there? I said we shall have two bombs, one to drop and the other to
remain as the real threat."

"I know. I heard that, but I don't see—"

"Brigadier General Benjamin Grossman will see, and that's all
that counts," Schlossberg said grimly, and ended the conversation.

Chapter 5

Benjamin Grossman could not remember a flight that interminable, that endless, but despite the everlasting hours and despite the
fact that his mind raced the entire time, he could not come up with
a solution. All my life a planner, he thought bitterly, and when I
need a plan the most, I cannot find one! Getting the material would
be no problem. He had often inspected the installation at what had
once been the kibbutz of Ein Tsofar, and his access to all portions of
that factory within a mountain was unquestioned. He had made

many suggestions when the caves were being enlarged to provide for an installation undetectable from the air by planes or spy satellites.

No, getting his hands on the material was not the problem. Even the matter of how long it would be before the loss was detected was not the problem; in the United States it had taken years before the discovery was made and with care the same time could elapse in Israel before it was known. No, the problem was whether or not he should hand it over to ODESSA when and if he had it. His reasons for rejecting the organization back in Strasbourg in the first place had never changed; and to give in to blackmailers was merely to dig oneself deeper into a bottomless pit.

But the alternative to giving them the material was unthinkable. He had little doubt that ODESSA could reach into Israel and harm either Deborah or Herzl, although his knowledge of security made him realize that proper precautions could make it very difficult. But, would giving ODESSA the material with which they could destroy Tel Aviv, if they chose, be any protection for those he wished most to protect? Obviously not. Certainly not. That could not be the solution to the problem. It was an endless chase in his head, and the only answer he could see was hardly an answer at all; and that was that he desperately needed help.

He came down the steps from his plane the following day weary from his trip and from not having rested at all, and from having worn himself out in his search for an operative alternative to the step he was about to take. But there was no other way that he could see. He answered the newsmen who clustered about him asking the results of his trip, but he had no idea of what he was saying, and he excused himself with an abruptness unusual with him. He climbed into his car and as they pulled away from the airport he reached over and tapped the sergeant-driver on the shoulder.

"No, not Ramat Gan. Take me to Mossad headquarters."

He leaned back and watched the scenery pass, realizing he had come to feel deeply attached to this country, that its possible destruction at the hands of ODESSA or anyone else was unthinkable, or if not unthinkable at least not in his own best interests. Here he had been happy, if not for the first year, certainly after that. Almost twenty-five years of happiness, and now this! He should have destroyed Schlossberg after the operation, as the two inmates who had assisted had been destroyed! But it was too late to worry about that.

He closed his eyes, but behind the lids there sprang up a picture of Herzl, stretched out lifeless, and he opened them at once, as if by keeping his vision occupied with the orchards they were passing he could blot out that terrifying thought. Yes, he needed help and he needed it badly!

The car pulled up before the headquarters building; he climbed down and leaned in to the driver. "Call the Magen David Adom," he said. "Tell my wife I'm back and where I am. I'll be home in an hour or so." He turned and climbed the steps, trying to formulate the proper words, and then dropped the matter. The words would come, proper or not; what had to be said would be said.

The receptionist outside Max's office smiled at her employer's old friend. She spoke into the intercom and then looked up.

"You're fortunate, General. Colonel Brodsky is free. He'll see you now."

Fortunate! Grossman thought with an inward grimace, and entered the room. Max got to his feet and walked around his desk, coming to him, smiling broadly.

"Ben, this is a nice surprise! I thought you were in Argentina."

"I just got off the plane. I—"

Max frowned. "What's the matter? You look terrible. Here, sit down—"

"No, I'd rather stand. You sit down. I've got a rather long story to tell you."

Max went back and sat behind his desk, mystified, swiveling his chair to keep up with Grossman as Ben paced back and forth, trying in his mind for the right words. At last he took a deep breath and began, not looking at Brodsky, but keeping his eyes on the floor.

"Max, when I was in Argentina, the night before I left—the night before last—I was approached by two men. It took me a little while, but I finally recognized them. They made no attempt to hide their identity, I might mention. One of them was Franz Schlossberg—he was a doctor at both Maidanek and Buchenwald, and in Ward Forty-six. The other was Mittendorf, the commandant at Maidanek. They said they were from ODESSA. I had thought ODESSA had been disbanded years ago, but apparently not."

"We've always known they still existed." Max was listening very closely now.

"In any event, they knew a lot about me and my family. They even knew where Deborah worked. They—they threatened me—"

Brodsky frowned. "Threatened you? In what way?"

"They want me to do something for them. They give me two weeks in which to do it. If not—"

"If not?"

Benjamin Grossman paused in his pacing. He raised his head and looked Max in the eye. His face was pale.

"Then Deborah would be killed. And Herzl."

Max Brodsky's face might have been carved from granite. "What is it they want you to do?"

"I can't tell you that. But I'll tell you this—" He leaned across the desk. "I want full protection for both Deborah and Herzl. Total!"

"You'll get it," Max said. "About what they wanted—"

"I want that protection *now!*"

"Ben, relax! You say you have two weeks. Let's think a minute. What is it they want you to do?"

"Max, there's no use in asking that question because I'm not going to answer. You're wasting time! You spent enough time in the camps to know these men and how they operate! I want full protection for my family now! Not tomorrow, not a week from now, but *now!*"

"Ben," Max said patiently. "I said, relax. You'll get total protection for your family. You still have time. Herzl is in Europe someplace, still, isn't he? Well, get him back if you want me to protect him fully. Or let me know where he is and I'll have a reliable man there as soon as he can get there, and I'll also contact the local authorities wherever he is. And I'll have people at the first-aid station in fifteen minutes." He frowned at his bare desk a moment and then looked up. "Is security involved in whatever it was they asked you to do?"

"No comment. You're still wasting time!"

Brodsky's look changed, becoming very official and very tough.

"You listen to me! If security is involved I mean to know! Your family will be protected, but when a general in the army is threatened, is asked to do something he won't discuss, then we here at Mossad are concerned. Do you have any idea what names those two in Buenos Aires were using?"

"Max, for God's sake—!"

"Just answer."

Grossman sighed helplessly.

"Schlossberg called Mittendorf Klaus, but that was his name, and I have no idea what names they've taken. Or where they live. Schlossberg said he had a ranch, if that helps. He also said they had traveled far to get to Argentina to meet me, but that could be true or not. It's obvious ODESSA has men in the Argentinian Government, or at least informers or sympathizers. It's customary for a visiting dignitary, or negotiator—which I was—to be wined and dined, especially on the last night. My staff was, I later learned, and at a different restaurant. But I was practically sent to this restaurant, the way one forces a card in a trick, so they could talk to me. It was well organized."

He sat down, facing Brodsky, looking at the other man angrily.

"You keep asking questions about those two, as if picking them up would help! Do you think ODESSA would stop, that their threats to Deborah or Herzl would be ended if you picked up Schlossberg and Mittendorf, even if you could? Someone else would take over. While you're sitting there asking a lot of fool questions—"

"Nothing will happen to Deborah or Herzl," Max said calmly. "And if we pick up those two, there will be two less of ODESSA for any future threats to Israeli generals. What did they want you to do?"

Grossman was already sorry he had come. "Max—!"

"At least tell me if you plan on doing it."

"No! Not if you—"

The telephone rang. Max motioned Grossman to remain where he was while he answered. His face whitened as he listened to a hysterical receptionist. He turned his chair to stare wordlessly from the window as the details were given to him, and when he hung up he remained looking from the window blindly for several moments before he swung back. It was difficult to face his old friend, Benjamin Grossman.

"Ben—"

"What?"

If it were to be said it had to be said quickly.

"Deborah," Max said quietly. His hand, clutching the edge of the desk, was white from the pressure. "She's dead—"

"Dead?" It was said as if the word held no meaning to him.

"An explosive in a package delivered to the first-aid station, supposedly of some drugs they were expecting—"

"Dead—?" Grossman stared, unbelieving.

"There would have been no way to prevent it," Max said, fighting to keep his voice even, to believe what he was saying, trying his best not to picture his ever-loved Deborah lying shattered and beyond help in the Magen David Adom station. "Even if we had sent men there the minute you came in. But I'll call Zion Films and find out where Herzl is, and get someone there to protect him—"

"There is no danger to Herzl. Not now," Grossman said, his face blank, not even looking at Brodsky accusingly for the time that had been wasted. "Now you have those two weeks you kept talking about. Deborah was killed to let me know they mean business. Herzl is the threat."

The closed-casket funeral was a small one, restricted to the immediate family, to Max, Morris Wolf, and several close friends of the dead woman. Herzl's plane had arrived in time for the funeral and he stood at graveside, dazed by the sudden and inexplicable death of his mother, and listened to the murmured ceremony without actually accepting that it was happening. He dropped his handful of soil on the casket with the others and walked away, trying to comprehend the tragedy. Someone had purposely killed his mother; it had been no accident. The receptionist had come back from a coffee break to find the package on her desk; they had been expecting a small package with drugs that day and she had automatically supposed that had been it. She had had no way of knowing; God, no! If she had she would have cut off her arm before—

Herzl stared at the men bending down, shoveling earth on top of his beloved mother. Could her death in any way have been connected to his investigation in Munich and London and Angermünde? Who would want to kill his mother? Could someone he had seen, someone he had talked to—? But that was impossible. Still, nothing new had happened in the family except his trip to dig into the pasts of Nazi war criminals. . . .

He found himself standing outside the cemetery fence, shaking hands with Morris Wolf, seeing the sadness on the crippled face, and watching him walk slowly away with the others, leaving him with his father and Max Brodsky. Through the fence he could see the men complete their task of filling in the grave, see the earth left over as if it represented above the ground someone he loved very much beneath the ground. He discovered that his father was speaking to him, and turned.

"Let's go home, son." Benjamin Grossman was shaking his head as if with ague, as if still trying to comprehend the suddenness and totality of his loss. "We have to start to plan how we live from now on."

"Later," Herzl suddenly said, and turned to Brodsky. "Max, I want to talk to you—"

"Yes?"

"No, I mean I want to go with you and talk."

"Today?" Brodsky asked, surprised.

"It's important." How could he go home and look into the face of a father he knew to be one of the leading Nazi war criminals? His revulsion would be apparent in everything he did, everything he said. He could not possibly go home and share sorrow with the man he knew to be his father. He needed to talk to someone first, and the logical person was Max Brodsky. At least, Herzl thought, drawing the small amount of comfort he could derive from the thought, at least Mama never knew of her beloved Benjamin's history. . . .

"If it's really that important," Brodsky said, conceding, and turned to Grossman. "Ben, go home and get some rest. I'll bring Herzl over as soon as we're through talking. We'll sit and discuss things."

"Discuss things," Grossman said, repeating the words as if by rote, and wiped tears from his eyes. He seemed to have aged years in the one day since his wife's death. "Discuss things . . ." he said again, and walked slowly to his car.

Herzl climbed into Max's car and sat beside him as Max swung the wheel as if to go to his apartment.

"No," Herzl said. "Zion Films, on Dizengoff. I have something to show you." Brodsky obediently turned the wheel again. He knew that whatever Herzl had on his mind had to be important to take the boy from his father on a day such as this. Herzl looked across the car. "Max, who sent that bomb? Do you know? Arabs?"

"Not Arabs," Brodsky said quietly, his knuckles white on the steering wheel. "They may have handled the delivery, but we'll probably never prove it. The bomb was sent by an organization called ODESSA."

Herzl felt his stomach contract in sudden panic. Somehow, then, in some inexplicable fashion, his investigation *had* been responsible. But in what way? He felt the blood drain from his face.

"They threatened your father in Argentina," Brodsky went on, not noting the look of horror on Herzl's face change slowly to puzzlement. "Two men, a Dr. Schlossberg and a Klaus Mittendorf. Schlossberg was at both Maidanek and Buchenwald; Mittendorf was the commandant at Maidanek. Both are still wanted for their war crimes. They live somewhere in South America, and they're active in ODESSA, if you know what that is."

"I know." Herzl was now totally confused. "Why did they threaten him?"

"He won't say, and I didn't have time to get it out of him."

"It doesn't really matter," Herzl said. "Whatever it was he must have refused them and they killed my mother. Is that it?"

"He had no time to refuse them or give in to them," Max said bitterly. "They threatened both your mother and you, the two things your father loves above everything else. They killed your mother to demonstrate their power, to prove they're serious." He glanced over at Herzl. "But you'll be totally protected . . ."

Herzl didn't even hear this last statement. His mind was racing, trying to understand this information, to fit it into what he had discovered in Europe.

"Why did they pick Benjamin Grossman to get whatever it was they wanted? Why Benjamin Grossman out of all the Israelis?"

Brodsky shrugged. "I assume they picked someone they thought had enough authority to put his hands on what they wanted; and also someone they thought could be pressured through threats to his family."

"That's the only reason?"

"That's the only one I can figure out."

"I may be able to give you a better one," Herzl said quietly, and felt his hatred for Helmut von Schraeder grow. Because of that Nazi criminal, an innocent, lovely woman—his mother—had been buried that day, and it made little difference if that criminal's loss was as great as his own, or not. Brodsky was looking at him curiously.

"What do you mean?"

"I'll show you when we get to Zion Films," Herzl said, and went on to get some information that had puzzled him during his investi-

gation. "Max, you were transferred from Buchenwald to Bergen-Belsen, weren't you?"

"That's right," Brodsky said, wondering what Herzl had in mind.

"That's odd . . ."

"What's odd?"

"To be transferred from Buchenwald to Bergen-Belsen . . ."

"What's odd about it? Horrible, maybe, but not odd. Actually,"
Brodsky said, his intelligence-service mind insistent upon exactitude
at all times, "we were supposed to be transferred to Natzweiler, where
they also did medical experiments under a Dr. Hirt, but Natzweiler
was on the verge of being liberated by the Allies, and the train was
rerouted to Bergen-Belsen instead." He smiled grimly. "Do I remember that night! We were jammed into these cars like cattle,
worse than cattle. That's where I met your father . . ."

Herzl nodded. It all made sense, now. He had been unable to correlate von Schraeder's actions before, with his being transferred—obviously at his own arrangement—to a horror camp such as Bergen-
Belsen; but if the man's plan was to be sent to a camp soon to be liberated, then it made sense. Brodsky turned into Dizengoff, drove
down it three blocks, and drew the car up before the building that
housed Zion Films. He turned to Herzl as he set the hand brake.

"Exactly what is it you want to show me?"

"Something you'll find hard to believe," Herzl said expressionlessly, "even as I found it hard to believe." Even, he thought, as
I find it almost impossible to believe that Mama is dead. She never
got a chance to meet Miriam Kleiman—he forced the thought away,
wiped his eyes to take away the sting, and climbed down.

The films were in the projection room, untouched as he had
requested in his call from Angermünde, the case locked. He sat
Brodsky down, closed the door to make sure they remained undisturbed, and opened the sealed can, beginning to thread the projector.

"This first bit of film was taken in Vienna in 1938," he said, and
completed the threading task. "It was during Anschluss. Watch." He
switched off the light and pressed the projector switch; the film
began to roll. At the proper time he stopped the machine. Helmut
von Schraeder's handsome smiling face filled the small screen.
Brodsky frowned.

"Who is that?"

"Don't you recognize your favorite nephew? Don't you know me when you see me?" Herzl asked sardonically, waited a moment while an amazed Brodsky stared at the almost identical resemblance. Herzl started the forward action of the film again. "In Vienna in March of 1938, ten years before I was born—I was known as Lieutenant Helmut von Schraeder." The film changed. "This next one," he went on, "was filmed in Poland soon after the invasion in 1939. I was Captain von Schraeder by this time, standing there with those officers. Now they are leaving me with the maps. See how I roll them up, as if there was something wrong with my arm. See me wink, first with the right eye and then with the left, as if I were entertaining a small child—my son, possibly—who loved to see me do it . . ."

He tried his best to keep his voice impartial, the voice of a good commentator, nothing more, but the bitterness of his discoveries during his investigation, added to his wretchedness at his mother's death and funeral, could clearly be heard. Brodsky was sitting, staring at the screen, his face rigid.

"This film was shot at Maidanek, where I was assistant to the commandant, whose name was Klaus Mittendorf. Our chief medical officer was a Dr. Franz Schlossberg. I was a colonel by now. Schlossberg and Mittendorf, two men you mentioned before, who approached Benjamin Grossman in Argentina and tried to blackmail him for what you suspect may be Israeli security secrets. In any event, I was known as the Monster of Maidanek. My job was to see to it the gas chambers and the crematoria ovens functioned at top efficiency. I did a very good job; here you see me being decorated by none other than Eichmann himself for my excellent performance."

The film ran out. Herzl switched on the lights, threaded the film for respooling, and pressed the proper button. There was a whir as the film began running back.

"From Maidanek," Herzl said, his eyes fixed on the running film, not looking at Brodsky at all, "I was transferred to Buchenwald. Here I contracted typhus—strange in a camp where the officers' quarters were kept spotlessly clean, usually by Jehovah's Witnesses prisoners—and I died of it. If I wasn't the only officer to die of typhus at Buchenwald, I was certainly one of the very few. And do you know the strangest part of the entire affair?" Now he turned and looked Brodsky in the eye. "Who do you think attested to my

death? Who was the only man brave enough to take up a body dead
of the dread disease typhus, wrap me in my shroud, jam my uniform
and all my identification into the burial bag with me, and see to it
that I was burned to an unidentifiable crisp in the camp crematorium without a single other soul seeing me? And then swear freely
that he had done so? By the sheerest of coincidences, the only man
who ever saw Helmut von Schraeder dead was a man named Benjamin Grossman—"

"No!"

"Yes," Herzl said quietly. "I have a copy of the testimony taken at
the war-crimes trials."

Brodsky stared at him speechlessly. The film completed its rewind-
ing and flapped helplessly. Herzl turned the machine off and stood
looking down at Brodsky. His face was tortured.

"I don't like saying this, but there is more, much more. Benjamin
Grossman had experimental surgery on his face as a helpless victim
in Ward Forty-six at the same time that von Schraeder was dying
there—except it wasn't experimental surgery and he wasn't a victim.
It was plastic surgery, performed by Dr. Franz Schlossberg, one of
the leading plastic surgeons in Germany before the war. I should not
be greatly surprised if, before his surgery, Benjamin Grossman didn't
look a great deal like his son does now. Add to this the fact that
both Benjamin Grossman and Helmut von Schraeder were both
raised in Hamburg and could answer questions about it, both were
mechanical engineering graduates, both had reputations as fierce soldiers who loved battle. And then add this—do you remember once
when we three were out to play tennis and I asked my father why he
didn't serve overhand like others, and he said he had fallen out of a
tree when he was a small boy and had broken his shoulder and it had
been badly set? You saw the films; now I'll tell you something. When
Helmut von Schraeder was a young man, he also fell from a tree and
broke his shoulder, and it was badly set. And I have an affidavit
from his old nurse to that effect. And thereafter he could not salute
properly, or roll maps properly—or serve a tennis ball properly . . ."

Brodsky was looking stunned. "It's insane—"

"It's true."

"It's impossible—"

"But it's true," Herzl said, and then he broke, his voice trembling.
"Max—Uncle Max—what should I do?"

Brodsky rubbed a heavy, callused hand across his deep-lined face. "Ben Grossman . . . God! It's impossible. Unbelievable . . ." He looked up. "Has anyone else seen these films?"

"They are file films; these are just copies. I saw them first in a library in Munich. I imagine many copies exist and they're available to anyone who wants to see them." He suddenly understood. "Nobody here at Zion has seen them yet, if that's what you mean."

"But nobody anywhere else ever drew the conclusions from them you did."

"Nobody knew Benjamin Grossman as well as I did," Herzl said bitterly.

"There were no fingerprints?"

"I was told there were not. ODESSA destroyed them all." Herzl sat down next to Brodsky. "Max, what do I do?"

"Let me think . . ."

Brodsky forced aside the shock of the revelation and attempted to put his mind to work on a logical consideration of the situation. His brain, trained in the intelligence service, tried to view the matter as it would any other security problem. Proof? There really was no proof that would satisfy a court, certainly not against Brigadier General Benjamin Grossman, Hero of Israel.

Brodsky closed weary eyes. He could see the scene as if it were before him.

Your honors, my client's son looks like a Nazi war criminal; we admit the resemblance and point out he also looks something like a well-known American film star. Will the prosecution next claim that Benjamin Grossman is also the father of that film star? The prosecution claims that both my client and von Schraeder were mechanical engineers. Your honors, you and I—and the prosecutors as well—are all attorneys. Exactly what does that mean? That I am you or you are the prosecutor? They made much of the fact that my client was the unfortunate one who had the piteous task of placing the body of von Schraeder into his shroud. My client never denied this. He could have. He could have easily disassociated himself from that death, but he did not. We ask for fingerprints, which we are quite willing, even anxious, to compare, but the prosecution says that ODESSA destroyed all fingerprints of von Schraeder and others. We know that ODESSA destroyed many records and fingerprints of many war crim-

inals, but Benjamin Grossman, by the prosecution's own story, was a prisoner in a concentration camp in early 1944, over a year before the war ended, and before there was any great need for ODESSA to take the action we know they took at a later date. And then there is the matter of the broken shoulder. We admit our client had a broken shoulder as a child, in fact we were the ones who introduced x rays to demonstrate the fact—but to begin with, he did not receive it falling from a tree as the affidavit—which may or may not have been elicited from an old, senile woman by any number of means— claims happened to von Schraeder. Two people claim Benjamin Grossman said he fell from a tree as a child. Who are these witnesses? A man who has admitted on the stand that he was in love with the general's wife, and a young man whose hysterical testimony you heard, a young man who blames the general for the death of his wife when in fact, as you all know, the general was a victim of a vicious threat by the same group the prosecution claims destroyed the finger-prints of von Schraeder. An odd group, you must admit. Friendly one moment and threatening the next—and more than threatening —killing. And let us talk about that group, your honors. Tell me, your honors, if Benjamin Grossman were Helmut von Schraeder, would he immediately have gone to the authorities and told of that meeting in Argentina? Would he have spent a year in a horror camp such as Bergen-Belsen where even the prosecution admits he came close to death from starvation, depredation, and even typhus? Your honors, because of a few outlandish coincidences, one of our most honored people, one of our bravest and most decorated soldiers, is being pilloried in this courtroom and we are forced to question the motives of those who bring these monstrous charges against him. Who are they serving, these false accusers? What enemy of our beloved Israel is paying to see Benjamin Grossman brought down and thus see the Israeli Defense Forces weakened . . . ?

That would be the scene in the courtroom, but in his soul Max Brodsky knew the charges were, indeed, true. He hated the knowledge, for Benjamin Grossman had been like a brother to him; but the charges were true. Ben Grossman and Helmut von Schraeder were the same person. A hundred little things would come to him in time, he knew, that should have led him to at least suspect the truth long before, things he never noticed in depth because who looked for such guilt in a Jewish prisoner in a concentration camp? Who questioned the small things, the oddities, the uncharacteristic responses from one who was supposedly a Jew, when they came from a person who, despite everything, did help him and many others to reach Israel? The thought came to Brodsky, as it had to Herzl, that he was thankful, at least, that Deborah had never known the truth about her husband. But would anyone ever know the truth? Without more proof than they had, how would they know it?

He pondered the question. Suppose that nobody ever did know the truth? Because among the many truths that were to be known was the additional truth that Benjamin Grossman had truly done great deeds for Israel. Did he therefore deserve redemption? Could a man who had committed the crimes Helmut von Schraeder was known to have committed ever earn forgiveness? Could he ever redeem himself no matter what acts of contrition or contribution he performed? Suppose that nobody ever learned the truth. . . .

But a Dr. Schlossberg and a Klaus Mittendorf somewhere in South America both knew the truth, as well as all of ODESSA, and as long as they knew it, others would have to be given it, for otherwise there could be a threat to Israel's security. A true Benjamin Grossman might put the interests of Israel ahead of even the safety of his loved son, depending upon the degree of security they could give the boy; but a Helmut von Schraeder would have no such compunction . . .

"Max—"

Brodsky looked up.

"Max, am I wrong? Did I make the whole thing up in my head? Am I crazy?"

Brodsky took a deep breath. "No, you're not wrong. You're not crazy."

"What should I do?"

Brodsky sighed and sat more erect. His mind was finally working.

"First, I'll take the film with me. And the affidavit and the copy of the war-crimes-trials testimony, and everything else you have, notes, everything. And then I'll take you home to your father, and you will act as if there was nothing between you two except what there has always been between you, love and respect—"

"I can't!"

"You can and you will!" The sternness left Brodsky's voice. "Herzl, it's essential."

"But, why?"

"Because I want to know what he does, what he says, where he goes, and when . . ."

"And then what will you do?"

Max Brodsky shrugged and came to his feet. "That I don't know," he said heavily. "Yet."

Chapter 6

It had taken a good deal of surveillance by Hans Richter to identify two of the Mossad security men who looked like taxi drivers on a break in the neighborhood of the Grossman apartment, but he had done that as a routine and not because he meant to attempt to reach the general at home. He assumed, quite correctly, that all mail and packages intended for that address would be x-rayed and thoroughly examined prior to delivery, considering the fate of the woman who had opened a package at the first-aid station, and considering that the son was still under threat. He was equally sure that any attempt to give the general his instructions for delivering the uranium by some exotic scheme such as a false milk bottle in the morning would be equally unsuccessful. He correctly calculated, in addition, that the apartment telephone would be tapped and that communication in the general's office would be equally unsuitable for his purpose, since in his experience conversations in and out of high military offices were normally tapped. These multiple precautions, however, did not disturb Richter in the least. He cared not a whit about the telephones the Mossad tapped, because the one *he* had tapped belonged to a certain Sergeant Mordechai Saul.

Sergeant Saul had been the personal driver for General Grossman ever since the general had earned his latest promotion. At the moment Sergeant Saul was on a day-to-day pass, for it was assumed the general would not be going to his office for a decent period following the death of his wife. Still, Saul stayed at home and near the telephone, for he knew the general was not a religious man and would not observe the normal period for mourning. In fact, if Saul knew the general, he would try to ease his pain with work and more work. So Mordechai Saul was not surprised to receive a call from General Grossman some five days after the funeral, advising him that the general expected to be picked up and taken to his office at seven-thirty o'clock the following morning. Saul said, "Sir!" with the proper deference and went back to the television program he had been watching, but his evening was not to remain undisturbed, because less than twenty minutes later there was a knock on the door of his room and he opened it to see a fellow soldier standing there, also a sergeant, he noted.

"Yes?" Saul said, surprised at anyone calling at that late hour.

"General Grossman wishes to be sure the car has ample gasoline when you pick him up tomorrow," the stranger said.

"I filled it yesterday and it's still in the garage downstairs," Saul said, irritated that anyone would think he would overlook such a detail.

"Still, he would like me to check personally," the stranger said apologetically, and shrugged. "You know generals."

Mordechai Saul knew only one general, and he thought it very odd for the general he knew to send someone to check the fuel in his car. Still, generals were permitted to have whatever idiosyncrasies they desired as far as sergeants were concerned, and it was possible that the murder of his wife had made the general supercautious in all matters. With a shrug, Saul flipped off the television and walked down the steps with the stranger behind him. Saul opened the garage door, then opened the front door of the car; he took out the ignition key, leaned over, and inserted it in the lock. He turned it to the right and the fuel-supply needle obediently slid to the extreme edge of the dial.

"See?" Sergeant Saul said disdainfully.

His answer was a sharp blow across the nape of his neck with the hard edge of Hans Richter's hand. Richter bent over the body of the unconscious man, saw that he was still breathing, and instantly closed the garage door. He flipped on the headlights for illumination and disrobed Saul; he then wrapped Saul's army blouse about the handle of the tire jack he located in the car's trunk and proceeded to beat the sergeant to death with the muffled jack handle, the blouse absorbing most of the sound as well as a good part of the blood.

When Richter was quite sure Saul was dead, he smiled and calmly loaded Saul and the jack handle into the trunk of the car, tossed the soiled uniform on top, closed the trunk, and then opened his shirt. From about his waist he removed a thin coil of wire. One end of the wire had been divided into two strands, and each strand held an earplug similar to a doctor's stethoscope; the other end was fitted with a small battery-operated pickup head. With patience Richter went over the car from one end to the other, from top to bottom. Taped inside the rear bumper he located the first of the signal broadcasters; a second was discovered inside the left-front hubcap. There was no third, nor did a thorough search for any possible voice pickup inside the cab reveal any further danger to his security. Richter nodded. Apparently General Grossman had gone to the authorities with some story of danger to his family and whatever had been said had aroused Mossad to the point of putting a bug on the general's car. It really made no difference though, Richter thought as he carefully removed the two bugs and placed them on the garage floor; he would replace them in the morning when he was finished with his night's work. Satisfied that everything was in order, he raised the garage door, backed the car out, got out to close the garage door again, got back in the car, and drove swiftly from the city.

He took the road to the airport, but turned off it after two miles, bumping over rough sand dunes, with only the aid of his parking lights, to end up in a grove of trees he had reconnoitered a few days before in a rented car. Here he switched off the headlights altogether and got out. In the distance the string of lights from cars traveling the main airport road gave sufficient glow for him to do his work. He brushed aside the sand that covered the shovel he had hidden on his previous visit and then opened the trunk and dragged out Saul's flaccid body. Then he dug a grave and twenty feet away he dug a second one. After he had placed Saul's body in one and the bloody uniform in the other, he filled both. Then, a shovelful at a time, he took all excess sand and walked a good distance away before scattering it to blend into the dunes. It was a hard job, but ODESSA did not train men to take the easiest path. The spot Richter had selected for the dual burial was as deserted a one as he had been able to find within a reasonable distance of the city; still, there was no sense in taking a chance simply to avoid a little labor.

When at last he had scattered leaves and a few branches over the sites of the two graves, he took the shovel a fair distance in another direction, buried it under the sand, brushed it over, and then returned to the car. He climbed inside and set his wristwatch alarm to ring and wake him at six. He knew the clock in his head would wake him a minute or two before the wristwatch buzzed, but Hans Richter had not been trained to take chances.

General Benjamin Grossman had spent five days in deep thought. His son Herzl had seemed excessively withdrawn for those five days, but that was only to be expected after the death of the boy's mother. But the boy would recover; it was the way with youth. Benjamin Grossman was not as sure that he, himself, would ever recover from the loss of his Deborah, but he supposed that in time he, too, would be able to look back on her death without that terrible pain and anger he felt at the moment. He would retire from the army as soon as the uranium was delivered; take Herzl with him to another place. Surely the boy would not object to leaving a country that now held such tragic memories for them both. They could build a new life; he could still work as an engineer and Herzl was now so wrapped up in film-making that the greater opportunities offered elsewhere should be an additional incentive. Herzl would marry and give him grandchildren, and he would be as good a grandfather to them as he had been a father to Herzl.

But that was all in the future. The thing now was to get his hands on the uranium; ODESSA wanted it in exchange for the life of Herzl Grossman and they would get it. And if they blew up half of Israel with it, he only hoped the Jew Brodsky would be directly under the fireball. Less than a week ago he had held a kinship with this country, had been happy here; the Jew Brodsky with his interminable delays during their interview had destroyed all that. The Jew Brodsky with his endless questions, stupidly wasting time while someone was delivering a package that would have been instantly stopped by a security man, had one been ordered to the first-aid station at once. Jews had cost him his father and his mother; now they had cost him his beloved Deborah. And what, exactly, did he owe to either the Jews or to Israel? Without him the Jew Brodsky would not even have been able to reach the place, nor would any of the others on the *Ruth*. And since then he had risked his life countless times for Israel in battle. And his thanks? The loss of his Deborah.

He forced the wormwood-bitter thought aside only to have an even more bitter one take its place. He should never have gone to the Jew Brodsky in the first place; only temporary panic, induced by that sleepless night on the plane, had made him do it. He should have gone from the airport directly to the first-aid station and taken Deborah home. Then he should have put his own troops in charge of security, and not the Jew Brodsky. Now, what was the situation? Because of his visit and his talking to the Jew Brodsky, there could be little doubt but that his telephone was tapped, and that he was undoubtedly under constant surveillance. Oh, if he ever discovered who was watching him Brodsky would claim he was mistaken, that it was all for the safety of Herzl, but now Herzl was in no immediate danger. Still, as long as Brodsky had that excuse, they would be watching Benjamin Grossman. And as long as Benjamin Grossman stayed in that apartment, it would be almost impossible for ODESSA to give him instructions for delivery of the material; and as long as he could not deliver the material, Herzl would then really be in danger. He had to get out of the apartment, back into circulation, at least give ODESSA a chance to get in touch with him. And as for any surveillance, once he had his instructions and could move ahead —well, he had no doubts at all that he would be able to handle that when the time came.

It was at that point that Brigadier General Grossman raised the telephone and called Sergeant Mordechai Saul.

"He's left the apartment," Herzl said into the telephone. "He said he was going to work."

"We know," Brodsky said. "We heard him order the car last night."

"Will he be followed?"

"He is being followed."

"But I didn't see another car when his car left," Herzl said. "I was watching from the window."

"Don't worry about it," Brodsky said in a kindly tone, "and stay away from windows."

General Grossman climbed into his car, surprised to find another soldier at the wheel other than Sergeant Saul, but at least the sergeant's replacement held the door open for him and saluted smartly, which was not always the case with Sergeant Saul, who did these things only when he thought of it. The general settled back in his seat as the car left the curb.

"To my office . . ." he began.

"Yes, sir." Richter sat ramrod straight in the driver's seat, handling the car excellently.

"We know," Brodsky said. "We heard him order the car last night."

"Right after you called," Richter said, switching from Hebrew to German, "the sergeant had an unfortunate accident."

Grossman felt a slight shock run through him. So his driver was ODESSA! Whatever else one might think of the organization, in a way one had to admire it for the excellent German planning and execution. Richter had spoken Hebrew; Grossman was positive the man also spoke Yiddish fluently, as Eichmann had. ODESSA did things in a proper fashion, you had to give them credit for that. They were also murdering bastards, but he would handle that problem when the time came.

"Fatal?" he asked, although he was sure he knew the answer.

"Unfortunately," Richter said evenly. He spoke without turning his head, almost without moving his lips, nor did he make the mistake of glancing in the rearview mirror to watch the general as he spoke. To the most observant outsider watching he would have appeared at most to be mumbling to himself. "He will not be found, so that is no problem. However—your instructions, Colonel von Schraeder. Get them right the first time, because after I leave you at your office, you will not see me again until the time of delivery. Are you ready?"

"Yes."

"Good. A week from tomorrow is the fourteenth of May. It is both the Sabbath as well as being the twenty-third anniversary of the founding of Israel. It is a day when security forces are generally more lax, with most people worrying more about celebrating than anything else. You will give your driver the weekend off; it is a time when this can be done without the slightest suspicion. You will drive yourself. We suggest you arrange matters to deliver the materials that night; at midnight to be exact. You can arrange to pick it up whenever you wish; that day or earlier. It is your problem. Is it understood?"

"Yes." The fourteenth of May was a day that Grossman had already considered, although he obviously had been unable to finalize his plans before this meeting. They thought of everything, this ODESSA!—including how to deliver explosive packages to innocent women.

"Good. Now," Richter said, driving expertly through the heavy morning traffic, "are you familiar with Eilat?"

"I've been there."

"You may know, then, that on the road leaving Eilat to the south, you first pass the old and new ports, then the glass-boat pier, and a short distance beyond the pier you come to two hotels on your right, across from the diver's club. A bit further along you come to the undersea observatory. At the observatory you will set your speedometer. Exactly two and three tenths miles past the observatory, you will leave the road and drive on the sand. The sand is firm; there is no problem driving on it. Exactly two miles further, on the sand, you will see a small dock. I shall be there with a speedboat. You will deliver the material to me, I shall verify it, and after that you are free. You can either go with me or stay. If you stay, we may have other work for you; if you leave with me, we can always use a man of your talents. The choice is yours."

His tone of voice changed from the impersonal flatness to one that was more intimate.

"I should imagine your going or staying will depend upon how much exposure you suffer in getting the material, or how much you disclosed when you went to the Mossad after returning from Argentina—"

Grossman frowned. "You know that, too?"

"Not directly. It is something I deduced, you might say, from the fact that there are two bugs—signal generators—in operation on this car at this moment. One is taped inside the rear bumper; the other—"

"Is mounted with a magnet fastener in the left-front-wheel hubcap," Grossman said. "I know."

Richter came close to permitting himself a smile. Colonel von Schraeder had lost none of his intelligence and little of his skills in his years in Israel. It augured well for their mission.

"Very good," he said, and pulled up before the building in which the general had his offices. He got out and opened the door, saluting smartly with his other hand. "Good luck, sir. Your car will be in the battalion garage when you want it."

He closed the door as General Benjamin Grossman slowly mounted the steps of the building, then Richter climbed back into the front seat and drove to the battalion garage, not even now permitting himself the small smile that had almost escaped him before, not even to congratulate himself on a scheme well planned and well executed. Major Hans Richter was a well-trained soldier.

"The general has reached his office, sir," said Brodsky's aide, standing before him, and then in a more personal tone, he added, "We'll see to it he's well protected. Nobody wants anything to happen to the general, sir."

Brodsky had instructed his men that General Grossman was being threatened, that the people who had murdered his wife were still a threat to the general. It was all he had told his men and it was all he needed to tell them.

"Good. Any stops on the way?"

"No, sir. He came directly from his apartment to the office."

"And the signal?"

"It worked perfectly, sir. You could almost tell when the car turned a corner."

"Very good," Brodsky said with satisfaction. "All routine, eh?"

"Yes, sir. Except—"

Brodsky looked up. "Except what?"

"Well, sir, it's probably of no significance, but you said you wanted complete details on the surveillance—"

"Get on with it," Brodsky said impatiently. "Except what?"

"He had a different driver today, sir. Not the usual one."

"What?" Brodsky frowned. "But he telephoned his regular driver last night—" His frown deepened; it seemed to puzzle his aide.

"Sir? Does the general having a different driver have any special significance?"

"Never mind," Brodsky said. "You can go."

As his aide walked from the office, Brodsky swiveled his chair and stared from the window. A new driver . . . He would give odds that this new driver was from ODESSA, and while he would put men at once onto the garage and wherever uniforms could be obtained—which in Israel was almost anywhere—the driver by this time was probably in Jordan or possibly even on his way back to Germany. He would also put men onto Sergeant Mordechai Saul, but he was fairly sure that Sergeant Saul was dead. They would not have left a loose end like that.

He swiveled back and stared down at his bare desk. So whatever instructions were to have been passed, had been passed. Well, in a way it was good. It would bring the business to a conclusion. Now they would have to keep a tighter control on Colonel von Schraeder, that was all. Give him leeway without actually giving him leeway. Let him think he's home free. Let him lead the Mossad to his ODESSA contacts; there were others who could take over from there. But putting their hands on any ODESSA agents was only a small part of the plan. Far more important was the fact that while there might not be sufficient proof to put Colonel Helmut von Schraeder on the gallows where he belonged, catching Benjamin Grossman in an open act of treachery, of betrayal of his country, added to that other proof, should wind up the matter of Helmut von Schraeder quite satisfactorily.

Chapter 7

The feeling of celebration was everywhere that Friday the fourteenth day of May in that year 1971. One saw it in the faces of strangers in the streets, of visitors from abroad, in the singing and dancing almost everywhere, the extra smiles and congratulations, the unusual politeness at the beaches and in the hotels. Twenty-three years of nationhood had been passed, three wars had been fought and won, and there was no indication that there would not be more wars in which many would die and Israel's existence would be threatened. But these were thoughts for yesterday and for tomorrow— today was Independence Day, and nowhere in the world is Independence Day celebrated with as much direct personal memory of the bitter struggle for that independence than in Israel.

It would be more accurate to say the feeling of celebration was almost everywhere. To Colonel Max Brodsky of the Mossad, as well as to those under his command, that Friday was a day like all other days, with work to be done and, in fact, extra precautions to be taken. Brodsky had long considered the strong possibility that Independence Day, particularly when combined with a Sabbath, would be an excellent time for whatever mischief ODESSA had in mind for Benjamin Grossman. But the report his aide gave him was the same as it had been every day that week.

"Sir, General Grossman has arrived at his office. No stops on the way. No contacts with anyone. Same driver, a Sergeant Breil. Thoroughly vetted, sir." The aide had served in the British Army during the war.

"Good—" Except Brodsky was really not sure it was all that good, although he did not know exactly why. He did know, however, that the two weeks were about to pass, and he did not believe that when an organization such as ODESSA said two weeks, that they meant fifteen days.

And later, "Sir, the general has arrived home. He's driving himself. He gave his driver the weekend off for the holiday."

There was nothing unusual in that on Independence Day, but still Brodsky felt that slight chill that came to him when something was about to break. General Benjamin Grossman had also gone home early, again nothing unusual on Independence Day. Still . . .

"Keep an ear on him," Brodsky said, and leaned back, thinking.

To Herzl Grossman that day had an air of unreality about it. It had been increasingly difficult as the days went by to act as if everything between himself and his father was as it had always been, but this Friday when his father had returned from the office early he had paid little attention to his son or anything else, sitting in his study with the shades drawn, his briefcase inexplicably on his desk before him and his hand resting on it as if for comfort, seemingly staring at the wall, thinking. But of what he was thinking, Herzl could not imagine. What did a man think who had put to death almost one million Jews and then falls in love with a Jew? What does he think when the woman he loves is killed because of something in his past? Does he blame himself? Or does he put the blame on someone else? Colonel Helmut von Schraeder would undoubtedly blame someone else. Who did Benjamin Grossman blame?

It was all very confusing. . . .

It was also very confusing as to what game Max Brodsky was playing in giving a criminal like von Schraeder the time he was giving him, the freedom of action he was allowing him. Why had Max Brodsky taken away all the evidence he had amassed in Germany? Why had Max Brodsky not brought Helmut von Schraeder up before the authorities at once? Accused him to his face and had him arrested and brought to justice—and the hangman? Because it would be Helmut von Schraeder they would be hanging, not Benjamin Grossman, his father. Could it be possible that Max Brodsky, who had been closer to him than an uncle could be, almost a father, could be part of some grotesque conspiracy? If his father, Benjamin Grossman, whom he had loved and trusted all his life, could be exposed for the murdering criminal he was, could anyone, including Max Brodsky, be trusted?

And who was really being under surveillance, his father or himself? It was very suspicious being a prisoner in his own apartment, told not to leave when his father came and went whenever he wished and with no indication that he could see that there was any surveillance there at all. And also the business of the telephone being tapped; von Schraeder could stop anywhere he wanted and make as many unrecorded calls as he wanted, but every word Herzl spoke into the instrument was being picked up. Three times in the past week he had picked up the telephone to call Munich and try to reach Miriam Kleiman, and three times he had hung up just as the overseas operator came on the line. Whatever he had to say to Miriam—and he had no idea of what that might be, especially under the circumstances of his parent's past—was certainly not to be said with someone with earphones on in a little room somewhere listening to every word.

Herzl sat in his room, trying to read, and then gave up. He looked at his wristwatch. Eight o'clock. God, how that day had dragged! His father had confirmed Max Brodsky's instructions as to the necessity of his not leaving the apartment, saying it would all be over in a few weeks, but those few weeks were about at an end. And, besides, his father was not to be trusted, and very possibly the same was true of his Uncle Max—

He became aware that he was being scrutinized and he looked up to see his father standing in the doorway of his room, his attaché case in hand. The general had changed to civilian clothes and was smiling at him in a strange manner.

"I have to go out," he said. "I may be gone all night. But I'll be back as soon as I can. It's nothing to worry about," he added.

He came and put one arm around the stiff shoulders of his son, squeezed him once with affectionate camaraderie, and walked from the apartment quickly, closing the door behind him. Herzl stared at the telephone, wondering if he should call. But he knew he would not. Only one person he knew could truly be trusted, and that was himself. Besides, he had started the investigation into the past of von Schraeder-Grossman, and that investigation was not finished. He walked to the window, staring down into the street as the general emerged from the front of the building and walked to where his car was parked in the street.

Then Herzl ran for the basement garage and his own little sports car.

"The general's left in his car. He's driving." The little square box on Brodsky's desk imparted a metallic tone to the speaker's voice.

Brodsky sighed. Whatever was in prospect was at work.

"Trail him," he said, "but not too close. Not even in sight. He may have noticed you during the week." He had given up all pretense of his men protecting the general; at the moment he didn't much care what his aides thought as long as they followed their orders. He just didn't want to lose the man. "The signals are coming in clearly?"

"Like a dream," Michael said. "The radio-direction finder is working perfectly. We could follow him blindfolded."

"Just don't lose him."

"We won't." There were several minutes of silence. Then, "He's on the Lod road. He's leaving town."

In his office Brodsky stared at the map of Israel pulled down on the wall, his pulses quickening. The chase was on; its success or failure could be vital to the security of Israel, to his future, to the life of Herzl and possibly many more people. He studied the map. The Lod road led to the Ben Gurion Airport, but it also led to Jerusalem with a turnoff at Ramla, and it could also lead to Ashdod, cutting west beyond Gedera, or it could even lead to Ashkelon or Gaza on the sea. It could lead to just about anywhere in southern Israel, or Grossman could be simply leading them in the wrong direction as a precaution against being followed before losing his pursuers and turning to the north. All they could do was wait until a further turn might give a better indication of his end destination. And, of course, not lose him.

"He passed Ramla heading in the direction of Gedera," the tinny voice said. "Sir, we might be able to come in closer with all this traffic. I doubt he would notice us—"

"Stay well back out of sight!" Brodsky said irritably. "That's why we hung all that electronic gear on the car!" He wished now he had chosen to go with the pursuit car; sitting in his office and merely waiting for reports was damned irritating.

He swiveled his chair, staring from the window out over the lights that sparkled from the sprawling city. I should be down there celebrating with the others, he thought sourly, instead of trying to find out what my old friend Benjamin Grossman is up to. I only hope it isn't what I think it is, because if anything goes wrong and he gets away with anything, I should be taken out and shot for not having dragged him in in the first place, sufficient proof or not. But we have to catch him with the goods; otherwise he'll continue to be a hero in Israel and continue to have endless chances to harm us. And I'll end up, as his accuser, in jail as an accomplice to our enemies. No, we have to catch him in the act, or with the goods, and we'll never get another chance like this one. Ben was in a panic when he told me of that meeting in Buenos Aires; he had to be to tell me what he did. And he must have hated himself the next day. But he needed protection for his family. . . . Brodsky shook his head in disgust. Protection! That was great protection I gave Deborah. . . . Let's not dwell on that!

Or am I totally wrong? Is it possible that Herzl's information is wrong, or that we are putting the wrong interpretation on it? Could it really be just some monstrous coincidence? After all, I've known Benjamin Grossman for almost thirty years; could he have been von Schraeder all that time and I not note it? The time we spent in the camps, our travels together from Germany to Italy and then to Israel, his saving us all when that gunboat stopped us when we arrived —would I not have known if he were a Nazi? Would I not have felt it? At that time in the Zion Films projection room, it seemed incontrovertible that Grossman was von Schraeder, but here, now, at this moment, it did not seem possible. The Mossad agent I sent to Europe to search for fingerprints or other information about von Schraeder has gotten no further in almost two weeks than Herzl did in a few days. What I should have done, of course, he thought, was simply to confront Ben, face to face, and ask him to give me an explanation. But if he were innocent of the monstrous charge, he would have no explanation, other than to say it had to be a gross coincidence. And if he were guilty? He certainly wouldn't admit it—

"He didn't turn at Gedera, he went straight through—" There was a degree of puzzlement in the metallic voice. "That leads to secondary roads, I think. Wait—" There was a pause as the agent checked his car map. "That's right. The road splits into two secondary roads, short ones. They both end up at the Ashkelon-Latrun road."

In his office Brodsky left his chair and was studying the wall map. The microphone on his desk picked up his voice, relaying it to the men in the pursuit car.

"It's also the shortest road to Kiryat Gat and Beer Sheba," he said, and added to himself, and also to Arad and Ein Tsofar. Let's just hope that's not where he's heading! "We'll be able to tell more when he comes to the Ashkelon-Latrun road. Just be careful when he hits those secondaries. Stay well back. There'll be less traffic there."

"Tonight? Less traffic?" said Michael in the trailing car with disbelief. "Tonight there's traffic everywhere. Why aren't they all home watching television, or in *shul* where they belong? I know, it's Independence Day, don't tell me." He added, suddenly realizing to whom his remarks were being broadcast, "Sir!"

"Just stay back," Brodsky said, unimpressed by the other's evaluation of the traffic problem. "Don't take the slightest chance of being seen."

"No, sir, we won't." There was a pause. Then, "Hey! Take it easy! You want to run up his tailpipe?"

Brodsky stared at the speaker. "What was that supposed to mean?"

"I was talking to Ari, Colonel. He's driving. The general must have stopped, the signal's steady. It was getting louder; we're stopped too, now. Maybe he's got a flat. Maybe something's wrong with the car. Do you want us to get closer and see?"

"And do what? Help him fix it?" Brodsky said sourly. Good God! All the signals for disaster were ringing in Brodsky's head; it accounted for his unusually savage tone. "You stay where you are. You're still receiving?"

"Yes, sir. Steady as a rock. He's stopped up ahead."

"How far from you?"

"I'd say about a mile, sir, from the strength of the signal. Say half a mile from the fork in those secondaries. He's parked, sir."

Brodsky studied the map with a puzzled frown. The place where Grossman had stopped was about halfway between a place called Hatzor Ashdod and a tiny village called Kfar Akim. Brodsky knew positively there was nothing of a security nature anywhere in the vicinity. So what was Grossman doing there? Maybe he really did have a flat tire; or he may simply have stopped to relieve himself. He spoke up for the benefit of the desk microphone.

"How heavy is the traffic?"

"Heavy, sir, even here and even at this hour. I never saw it so heavy. Everybody and his uncle is out tonight. I'm sure we could get a lot closer to him—"

"Stay where you are!" Brodsky was thinking furiously. "If the car doesn't move in the next five minutes, get going again. Pass as if you were part of normal traffic. See if he's inside. And report!"

"Yes, sir. Five—*sir!*"

"What?"

"*The signal stopped!*"

"*What! Both?*"

"Yes, sir." The agent was shocked. "I switched on the auxiliary at once, sir. Both units are out." There was a very brief pause. "Sir, do you want us to try and follow him visually?"

Brodsky stared at the speaker on his desk, his mind running through possible scenarios, even as he silently acknowledged that Grossman had led his pursuers into a spot from which it would be virtually impossible to trail him without electronic aids. They were far too distant to catch him, and there were at least six roads going in different directions he could take from within a mile or so of where he was—or, rather, from where he had been when he had managed to dismantle both of the signal broadcasters. Damn! One would think, or at least hope, that with two distinct and separate electronic systems, the man might not have discovered one!

"No," he said slowly, "you'd be wasting your time. Come back in."

He studied the map and then made up his mind. He had always feared the possibility that the ultimate direction of Grossman's defection might be the material or the secret at Ein Tsofar; he remembered all too well the help that Benjamin Grossman had given in the construction of the facilities at Ein Tsofar. Certainly from the point where Grossman had last been located, a move into the direction of Ein Tsofar was very possible. If that was his destination, the man would still have almost an hour and a half driving time to reach the old kibbutz. If he were wrong and Grossman was heading someplace else—

He clicked his intercom for the night receptionist.

"Notify all checkpoints in the country," he said, his voice expressionless. "They are to report the passage of a brown army sedan, license plate number AR 436 T. They are not to stop or interfere with the car or its driver or to indicate any interest in it; merely to report its passage and the time of its passage to this office. You will then relay any such reports to me at Ein Tsofar. Repeat."

The receptionist dutifully repeated the instructions word for word, reading from her pad.

"Good. Now order my car," Brodsky said, "and call the airport. I want a helicopter waiting on the pad when I get there in half an hour."

He hung up and came to his feet heavily. The problem, of course, was that Grossman might well be taking roads where there were no checkpoints; since the 1967 war checkpoints had been sharply reduced. And a further problem was that not all checkpoints had communication equipment either to receive or to send; they were usually little shacks to which a soldier would be assigned, dropped off in a jeep and picked up in a jeep, and which was merely for the stopping of suspicious-looking cars for illegal arms or contraband—and they would scarcely find an army car driven by an army general to be suspicious.

Benjamin Grossman smiled to himself grimly as he got back in the car and stepped on the accelerator. Did the Jew Brodsky really think he was dealing with children or idiots? He had located the signal producers long before the ODESSA man had come on the scene. Good God! Did they all think they were dealing with children or idiots? All right, he had made a mistake by going to the Jew Brodsky when he first came back from Argentina; he had been exhausted. But his brain had begun to work again in a short while. He had simply put himself in Brodsky's place. Certainly surveillance would have to be placed on a man who had met with ODESSA agents and refused to disclose what their demands had been; and it would obviously have to be the type of surveillance that would cover the condition of a car being driven at night. And that meant a bug. And if that one might be located by a suspicious general named Grossman, obviously the answer was a second bug, better concealed.

He turned into the road for Kiryat Gat, humming lightly to himself, for he was sure there were no voice pickups in the interior of the car. He had searched for them carefully, and he was sure that the man from ODESSA, whatever his name was, had done so as well. His hum faded, replaced by bile in his throat. Whoever the man from ODESSA was, he undoubtedly was the person who had handled the delivery of the explosive that had killed his Deborah. Well, once he was certain that the threat had been removed from Herzl, then he would find this man from ODESSA, whoever and wherever he might be, and he would also find Schlossberg and Mittendorf. The Jew Brodsky wanted to know how to reach these men for his purpose? Well, for once he, Benjamin Grossman, would do the work of the Jew Brodsky, and maybe even take care of the Jew Brodsky, for dessert.

And thinking of the Jew Brodsky, what would he do when his men reported that the signals had stopped, that obviously General Grossman had dismantled them? What he would do would be to instantly contact as many checkpoints as he could reach and tell them to report the passage of a brown army sedan license number AR 436 T. Would the Jew Brodsky tell them to stop that car and hold the driver? Very doubtful; the checkpoints were under the command of the army and such instructions could be overridden by a general, even one in civilian clothing. Besides, the Jew Brodsky would gain little by having the car stopped; no, what he would ask is that the passage and the time of passage be reported, nothing more. Grossman smiled in the dimness of the car, because it really made no difference what instruction the Jew Brodsky handed out; the roads he had selected for the first part of his journey had no checkpoints, he had determined that, and the few after that in the desert had no communication.

He grinned to himself savagely and drove on.

Brodsky's helicopter gave the proper recognition signals, received permission to land, and settled down past the sheer cliffs to touch lightly onto the brilliantly illuminated pad. The lights were extinguished as soon as the helicopter made contact with the concrete; the rotor engines were cut and in the silence that fell the pilot could hear his instructions.

"—into the hangar with the bird, and you too. Stay out of sight," Brodsky said, and set off at a brisk walk for the command post.

The command post was set in the rear of one of the auxiliary caves, and Brodsky could not help but recall the place when it had been a simple kibbutz, with its plain cement-block buildings, when its products were melons and figs, and when the major problem had been water, the lack of it, or Arab attacks; when its boundaries were the old fence where Grossman had so recklessly knelt with the machine gun during that battle so many years before. Now the buildings were all gone, and the people and the melons and the figs were also all gone, and where the old fence had stood was less than a quarter of the way to the new electrified fence and the new watchtowers that were manned day and night by soldiers, not settlers, and the entire area was restricted. Brodsky sighed at the necessities of defense and security, and walked into the command post.

The majority of the personnel of the Ein Tsofar facility were off duty, spared from labor by the Independence Day celebration; they were either home in one of the major cities or in Arad, thirty miles away, enjoying the celebration that was going on in every town and village in the country, no matter how large or small. A captain was on duty, the result of losing a coin toss to see who would be stuck with the duty; with him was the radioman who had accepted the helicopter's recognition signal. He was not there as the result of a lost bet; he was there—like the sentries and the soldiers at checkpoints—because he had been ordered to be there.

The captain and his superior shook hands; the captain reseated himself, indicated a chair for his guest, and reached into a drawer for a bottle of brandy. He had always liked Colonel Brodsky, and a little conversation would be a pleasant break in the evening's dullness, although he was surprised to be hosting the colonel. If he were not a mere captain, he would certainly not be stuck out here in the desert on a night such as this one.

Brodsky checked his watch. If his theory was correct, Grossman still had at least thirty minutes of driving to reach the facility. He sat down, accepted the drink, and sipped from it. He put his glass down.

"Were there any messages for me from my office?"

The captain paused in raising his own glass. "No, sir."

"Ah . . ." Brodsky took another sip of his drink. It was possible to reach Ein Tsofar without passing any checkpoints, or at least any with communications, simply by staying with secondary roads, and Grossman would be aware that the checkpoints would be notified. He looked at the captain. "General Grossman will be coming here tonight, I believe. In half an hour or so, if I'm right. Driving."

The captain looked surprised. "General Grossman is coming here, sir?"

"I think so."

"Again?"

Brodsky froze. "What do you mean, *again?* When was he here last?"

"Just this morning, sir. He arrived by helicopter about nine o'clock. He made a brief inspection by himself, just walked through the facility—briefer than usual, but of course no one is working today—and then he left. You say he's coming back, sir?"

Brodsky's hand flew to the telephone, and then stopped. Who was he going to call? Any message from any checkpoint would be relayed to him, and tying up the line with pointless calls, especially when he had no idea of who to call, was fatuous. Grossman had gone to his office in his usual manner, had undoubtedly simply told his secretary he did not want to be disturbed for either visitors or phone calls for several hours, had then walked into his office and locked the door, gone out the other door, down the back stairs to the street, and taken a cab to the airport. All very simple. And his men were glued to the car in the garage all the while. Great work!

"No," he said. "I was mistaken. I doubt very much the general will be coming back."

He reached for the brandy bottle and refilled his glass. As long as he had to await word from his office, he might as well use the time to get drunk. There was a very good chance he had just seen his future go down the drain, and worse, there was a good chance that the country's security had been compromised. And then Max Brodsky had a second thought, one he wondered had not occurred to him before, and he pushed the brandy bottle away, reaching for the telephone instead, speaking to the captain as he raised the receiver.

"Have my helicopter brought out and kept ready for instant departure."

He brought the receiver to his ear and clicked for the operator. There *was* a call that just might do the trick.

Trailing a car at night, Herzl discovered, was far from an easy job, especially if one was to be careful and keep two or three other cars in between in order not to be identified. It required constant concentration, but even then Herzl had time to wonder that no other car, as far as he could determine, seemed in the least interested in the movements of the man he knew to be Colonel Helmut von Schraeder. Cars between his little sports model and the general's large sedan would pass the general's automobile to disappear into the night, to be replaced by other cars that first passed him and then passed the general's car, for the general seemed to be driving unusually slowly for a man with a temperament of Benjamin Grossman. Well, if nobody was interested in where von Schraeder was going, then he, Herzl, would follow him all night, if necessary. Gasoline was no problem, fortunately; one tankful in his little sports bug could take him from one end of the small country to the other.

He suddenly found himself without an intermediary car and he slowed down precipitously, just as the general's sedan pulled to the shoulder of the road, and he saw his father get down and bend over as if inspecting the front tire. He flashed past, relieved not to have been seen, drove down the highway a bit and pulled off into a narrow trail leading into the dunes. Had something happened to the other car? He backed around with difficulty in the narrow space, cut his headlights and waited, the engine of the small sports car panting as if anxious to take up the chase again. Herzl wondered if perhaps he had been detected or, even if he had not, if the maneuver were merely a move to do precisely what it had done—put a potential pursuer up some trail waiting while the other car turned and went off in another direction. But before he could worry about this possibility very long the brown sedan swept past his hiding place, no longer at such a leisurely pace, and he barely made it back to the highway in time to see the taillights of the other car disappearing in the distance. From then on it took all his attention and driving skills on the narrow, winding road to just keep up with the car ahead.

Traffic thinned considerably as they passed Kiryat Gat on the road to Beer Sheba. Herzl was now positive there was no surveillance at all on the other man, for now there were no other cars in sight for long distances, either ahead of them or behind them. He realized that in time the man in the car ahead would know he was being followed, but other than keeping the car in sight, he knew of no way to discover where the man was going. But even though the man might eventually suspect he was being followed, there would be no way he could determine he was being followed by his son.

An occasional Egged bus, loaded with passengers, would roar past him and he could see it ahead cutting around the brown sedan; otherwise they seemed to be alone on the road. Where could the man possibly be going? There was nothing ahead except desert. And why was von Schraeder being permitted to move about so freely? Herzl was very glad now that he had resisted the temptation to call Max Brodsky; certainly there had to be something very suspicious in the way Brodsky was acting—or, rather, not acting.

At Beer Sheba the streets were bright with streetlamps and he had to drop back, but at least both cars had to move slowly through the people that moved about on the main street, bottles in hand, celebrating. The brown sedan took the road to Dimona, and as they passed that little village, also alive with music and dancing, Herzl knew he could not continue to trail the other man without being discovered, for now, other than an occasional Egged bus no other traffic was to be seen. When the car ahead passed the cutoff to the old road leading down the mountain, Herzl made up his mind. He had to take the chance that the man ahead was going to Eilat; there was nothing on the road before that point. With the extra speed of his small car he could get there first, but it meant taking the old road down what was known as the Scorpion's Ascent, coming into the Eilat road at the small settlement of Hatzeva Ir Ovot. With a shudder at the thought of the road ahead, he swung into the old road, hoping he was not making a terrible mistake. The taillights of the other car disappeared into the night.

For approximately ten miles the road was paved; then he turned into the trail leading to the Scorpion's Ascent, his wheels spurting sand, trying to concentrate on the road immediately before him and not on the torturous decline he would soon meet. He had come here with a group of friends one summer vacation in a jeep, and he remembered the frightful descent at a creeping pace; now he intended to take it as fast as he could without sliding from one of the precipitous cliffs into the jagged chasms that lined the snaking road.

He seemed to be alone in the world, the overhead sky flooded with stars, the sliver of a moon the only things to keep him company in the night, the road a constantly curving ribbon of sand, barely marked; and then he was at the Scorpion and on it, fighting the terrifying, twisting, dropping curves with sweaty hands, wondering what he was doing here. The headlights of his car seemed to bounce off the cliffs beyond the chasms on either side as he braked and swung into each curve only to step on the accelerator momentarily with his other foot on the brake pedal, the wheels skidding obediently to the very edge of the treacherous drop, barely gripping in time. The twisting road that swung before his sweeping headlights seemed to be almost vertical in places, as if he might slide down it rather than drive down it. To Herzl it seemed he was driving in a nightmare, and a small portion of his mind detached itself from the terror of the road and the necessity to calculate each co-ordinated movement of his hands and feet, to wonder if he went over the edge whether he would float down and down with the weightlessness of a dream and then suddenly waken to discover it had all been unreal, for the Scorpion's Ascent was like nothing but a scene from Dante's *Inferno*. And then, when it seemed he had been fighting the frightening road for hours, the lights of the settlement could be seen far below, and he was out of the last curve and onto the straight stretch that dropped down the last of the mountain to the intersection with the Eilat road.

He turned into the Eilat road and found himself back in the world again. No car headlights could be seen in either direction; he could only hope he was ahead of the other car, because if he had gone through the nerve-racking torment of the Scorpion for nothing, if the other car was still ahead of him or—worse thought—if the other car had not been destined for Eilat but had turned north and was now miles away . . . It was not wise to think of such things. He *had* to be ahead and the other car *had* to be going to Eilat. And he was going to get there as fast as he could. He stepped on the accelerator and closed his mind to any thought except to reach his destination. What he would do when he got there, and when the other car got there—for it was pointless to think the other car would not get there—was something he would have to worry about at the time.

It was on the road from Beer Sheba to Dimona that Benjamin Grossman was finally certain he was being followed, and after the two cars had both passed Dimona and faced nothing but desert, he determined to find out exactly who was following him, and to handle the matter. He certainly did not intend to fail at this time. He eased his revolver from the holster set beneath the dashboard and held it in one hand even as he started to pull onto the shoulder; then the headlights that had been trailing him for so long swung off onto the road that led to the tiny settlement of Oron, deep in the Negev. With a humorless smile at his own display of nerves, Grossman completed braking the car and turned off his lights, waiting. If it had merely been a maneuver on the part of the other car, its driver would get a good surprise when he came back and passed this spot, but no car appeared and after a brief wait he put the revolver back in place and pulled back onto the highway, resuming his journey. It had been an idiotic thought in the first place; who could follow a man at night in the desert, where headlights are necessary to avoid disaster, and hope not to be detected? He had better not start imagining things; he was too close to completion of his mission for that. On the other hand, there was no point in taking needless risks.

He came to the intersection of the Dimona road with the Eilat road and paused, glancing at his wristwatch. Ten o'clock and about a hundred miles to go to reach Eilat, with paved road all the way, and the few checkpoints with no means of receiving instructions to watch for General Grossman and his brown army sedan. No problem; plenty of time to meet his appointment and with nothing in his path. He smiled and glanced almost automatically at the attaché case at his side, and then turned onto the deserted highway and stepped on the accelerator. He wondered how long, if ever, it would be before the fifty pounds was missed. It was an interesting question. Even if it should be missed at once—which was doubtful since as far as he could determine there was no reason to institute an inventory —there would be no reason to connect a highly respected general in the army with its disappearance. If and when the discovery was made, the Jew Brodsky might connect it with his conversation after his trip to Argentina, and he might suspect all he wanted. There would be no proof. His trip to Ein Tsofar that morning? He had made many inspection visits to the facility; it was part of his responsibility. This morning he had simply made one more. And could the Jew Brodsky admit he had put signal bugs onto the automobile of the respected General Grossman? He could not. All he could do was to keep quiet about it. No, there was no reason not to return to Tel Aviv, wait a few weeks, and then put in for his retirement, and leave with Herzl. Nor would he miss Israel. Without Deborah he felt about the country as he had felt when he first arrived: a desolate desert, and the scenes lit up by his headlights as he drove was the proof.

But once he was settled someplace else, he would see to it that the ODESSA man he was about to meet would pay for the death of his Deborah, no matter what it took to locate him nor no matter how long it took. Nor will anything happen to our son Herzl; I pledge you this, he said silently to the picture in his head of his dead wife that never left him. Both things I pledge you.

The celebration in Eilat had moved mainly to the hotels, and as Herzl drove into the small town he could see the lights blazing from the group of tourist hotels beyond the Arkia Airport along the beach. He could picture the excitement, the happiness, the singing and dancing and drinking that was going on there, and he only wished he was a part of it. He had been born the same year the nation had been born, and he never had failed to celebrate each Independence Day as if it were his own actual birthday. But his mission tonight was far too important—that was, if he hadn't miscalculated and made the two-hundred-mile drive for nothing.

He pulled into Hatmarim Avenue and parked between the darkened post office and the brightly illuminated bus station, with the Egged buses angled in like behemoths nuzzling the building for sustenance. Any new arrival in Eilat would have to pass his vantage point, and he was suddenly sure that von Schraeder was heading for Eilat. The brown sedan should be appearing soon. The full significance for the long trip to the town had finally come to him. Somehow—possibly through his old friend Max Brodsky, who had also gone from Buchenwald to Belsen instead of Natzweiler, now that he thought of it—Helmut von Schraeder had learned that his past had been discovered, exposed; Eilat was the most logical point from which to flee the country. Much better than from any Mediterranean port. Five minutes in a fast speedboat and he would be outside Israeli territorial waters; fifteen minutes and he could be across the narrow gulf and on friendly soil.

But not if I can help it, Herzl promised himself grimly, and settled down to wait. From his position he could see the road at the end of the airport runway that led to the beach hotels, all lit up and gleaming in the night; in his imagination he could almost hear the music. Every now and then a car, usually a jeep, would come into view from the long stretch of desert and turn into the road toward the hotel; every now and then a car would appear from the south, coming up, possibly, from as far away as Sharm e-Sheikh to join in the festivities. But in general traffic was very light; most people had already arrived for the celebration hours before. Herzl consulted his watch; it was eleven-thirty. He had been here ten minutes. Could he have been wrong? Had the other man stopped somewhere else, or had he turned north when he came to the Eilat road? But why drive through Dimona to reach the Eilat road and then turn north? It made no sense. No, his man was headed for Eilat and an attempted escape across the gulf. Any other conclusion was not to be considered.

He was concentrating so hard on trying to find a flaw in his logic that he almost missed the brown sedan when it passed Hatmarim Avenue; he woke up and pulled into the main road to see the sedan pass the cutoff to the beach hotels and continue in the direction of the old port. He turned on his headlights and followed. The car ahead seemed to be in no hurry; Herzl dropped back and held the same speed. He had no idea how far he would have to go, but he knew that as soon as the car ahead made the slightest attempt to get near a boat, he was going into action.

In the brown sedan, Benjamin Grossman was relaxed. He had made the trip down through the desert with ample time to spare; once the delivery was made he might even consider putting up at one of the beach hotels and joining the celebration there the following day. Possibly even call Herzl and have him come down to join him. He had stopped several times on the long trip to make sure he was not being followed, and now he was certain of it. Nor had he been bothered at all at the several military checkpoints that he had passed, although he was sure that Brodsky would have contacted them if there was any way he had been able; but there were no telephones out there, and the soldiers he had seen at the checkpoints had not even bothered to come out of their shacks as he had passed. Probably all thinking how badly they had been treated to be assigned this lonesome duty on a holiday such as this one.

He passed the Arkia Airport and drove toward the old port. The lights of a car that was now behind·him meant nothing; someone driving to one of the two hotels across from the diver's club, or some poor devil heading down to Sharm e-Sheikh, and if it was the latter he didn't envy the man; he himself had had enough desert driving that day.

At the underwater observatory he slowed down to set his mileage meter, and then went on. It was ten minutes to midnight, giving him plenty of time. He felt a bit proud of his timing; he would arrive almost to the minute. Not bad after over two hundred miles of driving on roads that at best could be said to be paved, but that was about all.

At the proper point he left the main road and started along the sand. As the ODESSA man had said, it was hard and bore the weight of the heavy car, even though he could feel the car drag a bit as the wheels sank in a few inches. Still, he could now understand why he was completing his journey on the beach; the main road cut away from the water's edge at the point he had left it, disappearing behind high cliffs. Two miles to go. He began to accelerate and then reduced his speed again as the wheels began to dig in more at the higher speed. And then suddenly he frowned in alarm. The headlights that had been following him had also swung from the main road at the point he had and were following him on the sand!

Could it be that the ODESSA man had been waiting for him in Eilat and was just now coming to the boat? That didn't sound like the ODESSA man, arranging to leave behind a car to be found. He stepped on the accelerator once again, but the car behind him was apparently lighter and sank into the sand less, because it was also accelerating and was overtaking him. In the distance Grossman could now see the dock and the small speedboat waiting at the point where the beach ran out and the cliffs dropped abruptly into the sea; but then his attention was taken by the car that was now beside him, and now was drawing ahead, as if it were a race. Grossman slowed down, reaching for the revolver under the dash, and then suddenly had to slam on his brakes as the other car slewed in front of him, scattering sand. The two vehicles shuddered to a halt, almost touching, their wheels dug into the sand. It was only then that Benjamin Grossman recognized the car and the young man climbing down and walking in his direction. He got out, staring in total surprise, his briefcase in one hand, the revolver dangling idly from the other.

"Herzl? What are you doing here?"

"Von Schraeder—what are you doing here?"

Grossman felt the shock almost physically; the blood left his face, leaving him momentarily dizzy. "Von—?"

"Don't lie to me. You're Colonel Helmut von Schraeder." Herzl's voice was harsh with tension. "How did you ever become Benjamin Grossman?"

Grossman was still in shock. "I don't understand—"

"What don't you understand? How I discovered who my great father was? How I worked so hard to prove my distinguished hero-father was the Monster of Maidanek? I found out because you changed your face, but you never changed mine. That was your mistake, von Schraeder. You should have had plastic surgery done on me when I was a child." Herzl's voice was trembling now that he was actually pouring it all out to the ashen-faced man before him; all the frustrations of all the days since his discovery were in his bitter voice. He found himself fighting tears. "I found out because you used to wink at me first with one eye and then with the other when I was a child. I found out because you fell out of a tree when you were eight years old. I found out because you couldn't roll up maps properly on the hood of a German army jeep in Poland thirty years ago . . ."

Grossman was slowly getting a grip on himself.

"Herzl, you don't understand—"

"I understand you murdered almost a million people at Maidanek. How could you shove them into gas chambers—?"

"Herzl, Herzl! I was under orders. If you had been there, in my position, you would have done the same—"

"You're a liar!" Now the tears came. Herzl shook his head violently to clear his sight. "It isn't true! It's a lie! You're a liar!"

Grossman sighed. "I hope you never find out . . ." He stared at Herzl and shook his head. "What a pity you had to find out! What a stupid tragedy! I had such hopes. . . . Now I will have to go with the boat. Now I'll never know my grandchildren . . ."

Herzl moved in front of him, his face determined, the tears gone, leaving streaks on his face. "You're going nowhere, von Schraeder. You're going on trial for the murders you committed. You're going to hang, von Schraeder, as Eichmann hung."

"No," Grossman said gently. "I have to go. Please, Herzl, don't try to stop me."

He walked around Herzl, starting for the waiting boat. Herzl turned and tackled him, bringing him down to the sand. Grossman dropped the attaché case and revolver and swung about, breaking Herzl's grip, struggling to his feet. Herzl came to his feet as well; the two men faced each other, both about the same size, Herzl younger and stronger, Grossman still in excellent condition and with far more experience at fighting. The tableau held for only a second and then Herzl was on top of the other man and the two went down, rolling over and over in the sand.

On board the speedboat Hans Richter stared in speechless disbelief. What on earth was the matter with von Schraeder? Richter had
no idea who the other person was or what he was doing there, but
the briefcase held the promise of the material he had been assigned
to pick up, and von Schraeder had a revolver but the idiot was making no attempt to use it! With a muttered curse, Richter picked a revolver from the weapons rack and started to jump from the boat, determined to end the matter once and for all, but at that moment
Grossman rolled over, his hand fumbling in the sand, coming up
with the dropped weapon. He reversed it and brought the butt down
on his son's head with force. He came to his feet, panting, looking
down with pained eyes at the unconscious boy; then he bent down,
kissed Herzl on the head, picked up the briefcase, and ran for the
boat.

His path was suddenly lit by the sharp glare of spotlights from the
sky and the two men at the boat could hear the whir of rotors as the
giant helicopter slowly began settling to the sand near the fallen boy.
Richter dropped the gun he had with a curse, picking a grenade from
the weapons rack instead. Grossman reached the boat at the same
time, jumping over the rail, putting himself in front of Richter. He
was furious.

"What are you doing? That's my son out there!"

"That's a helicopter full of Jews out there, you madman!" Richter
said coldly, and pulled the pin. He brought his arm back in a practiced motion to throw the grenade toward the helicopter and the
men who were pouring from it, when Grossman grabbed his arm,
dragging it down viciously with all his force, pulling it and Richter
into his strong arms. A sudden picture came to him of Buchenwald,
then in the hospital at Belsen; at least he would not die of typhus a
third time. The picture disappeared as quickly as it had come. The
last and final thing that Benjamin Grossman had the pleasure of seeing was the sudden look of animal terror on the face of the man who
had killed his Deborah.

Then the grenade exploded.

"Egged buses," Brodsky said, his tone blaming himself for his stupidity. "I should have thought of them at once. They cover the
country from one end to the other, in all directions and on every
road. Most of them have two-way communication with their dis-

patchers; those few that don't still stop at places where they can be given messages and relay any information they get. They drive faster than almost any car, and to flash their bright lights to pass and check a license plate at night—a license plate of a brown sedan—is the work of a second or two."

Chapter 8

Colonel Max Brodsky gave the eulogy at the funeral of Brigadier General Benjamin Grossman while Herzl sat in the front row staring blindly at the casket that contained what had been collected of his father's body.

"My very dear and close friend, Benjamin Grossman," Brodsky said, "a dear friend and warm comrade to so many of us here today, has been a hero for all the years he lived in Israel. His contributions to the defense of his beloved land need no repeating here. In his rise to the rank of brigadier general he gave constant proof of that heroism time after time; his men loved him as well as respecting him."

He paused and looked down at the casket sadly.

"Now he is dead, and in dying he gave further proof of that heroism. He was investigating an organization of enemies of Israel, the organization that had killed his beloved wife, Deborah. At the time of his death he gave his life to save the lives of others, including my own, and that of his son. But Benjamin Grossman will never really be dead to those of us fortunate enough to know and admire him. He will live in our hearts and memories as long as we live. And he left a fine, strong sabra son to carry on his name."

He looked down at Herzl; Herzl's eyes left the casket to look up at the speaker at the podium.

"For all the time I have known him, Benjamin Grossman was a

fine man, a dedicated husband, a wonderful father, a great Israeli, and he gave his own life to save others. There is little more any man can wish to have said for him when his time comes."

Herzl and Brodsky stood alone after Morris Wolf and the other old friends of Benjamin Grossman had left the cemetery.

"Remember what I said," Brodsky said in a kindly tone. "Forget everything else. For all the time I knew him he was a fine man, a dedicated husband, a wonderful father, a great Israeli, and he gave his life to save yours and mine. Those are the characteristics you've inherited, Herzl. No others. Plus the wonderful ones you have from your mother. Don't think of the past; you are the present, and the future." He hesitated a moment and then said, "We're both alone. Why not come and live with me?"

Herzl shook his head slowly.

"No," he said quietly, "I'm going to Munich. And when I come back I hope not to be alone."